And The Waters Shall Cover The Earth

a tale of the drainage of the Fens

Forbes Bramble is an established author who has already written seven previous novels brought to the public by a leading British publishing house. He has also written plays for stage and television. In addition to his literary activities he is a trained architect and acts as an expert adviser. He is married, with three sons, and lives in East Anglia. His novel, ***And The Waters Shall Cover The Earth***, presents a vivid and poetic description of fenland life in the 1690s, and is an intriguing tale of love and communal conflict, based around the drainage of that part of the country which was eventually to produce the richest soil for fruit and vegetable horticulture in Britain.

By the same author –

Captives

Dead of Winter

Fools

Regent Square

Stone

The Iron Roads

The Strange Case of Deacon Brodie

A Fenland scene

And The Waters Shall Cover The Earth

a tale of the drainage of the Fens

Forbes Bramble

Arena Books

First published in 2008 by Arena Books

Arena Books
6 Southgate Green
Bury St. Edmunds
IP33 2BL

www.arenabooks.co.uk

Distributed in America by Ingram International, One Ingram Blvd., PO Box 3006, La Vergne, TN 37086-1985, USA.

Bramble, Forbes, 1939-
And The Waters Shall Cover The Earth *a tale of the drainage of the Fens*
1. Reclamation of land – England – Fens, The – Fiction
2. Dutch – England – Fens, The – Fiction 3. Fens, The (England) – Social conditions – 17th century - Fiction
I. Title
823.9'14[F]

ISBN 978-1-906791-14-8

BIC categories:- FV, 36D, 1DBKAE, TNFR, RPG, RNF, TNF

Printed & bound by Lightning Source UK

Cover design
by Jon Baxter

Typeset in
Times New Roman

For Anna

"Come, Brethren of the water and let us all assemble

To treat upon this Matter which makes us quake and tremble;
For we shall rue, if it be true that Fens be undertaken,
and where we feed in Fen and Reed, they'll feed both Beef and Bacon.

They'll sow both Beans and Oats where never Man yet thought it;
Where Men did row in Boats, ere Undertakers bought it;
But CERES, thou behold us now, let wild oats be their Venture
Oh let the Frogs and miry Bogs destroy where they do enter.

Behold the great Design, which they do now determine
Will make our Bodies pine, a prey to Crows and Vermin,
For they do mean all Fens to drain, and Water overmaster,
All will be dry and we must die – 'cause Essex calves want pasture."

From ***The Powte's* Complaint***
A song from the Fens
1630 – 1660 approx.

*a 'powte' is a sea-lamprey

Chapter 1

Sarah Warburton had turned her diary so that the candlelight was not obstructed by her hand or the quill. She penned the date then wrote without pause -

5th day of April 1690

Father is delighted today, almost jovial and at dinner he said such a long grace that mother said the food would be cold. We all drank wine, I with water of course. The Partners have received Parliamentary permission for the dyckage, as they call the drainage works. An engineer has been appointed for the enterprise, which father says will be enormous, with a great deal of money invested. It is set to make great changes for the better, he says and will turn our swamps and marshes into the best tillage and grazing in the Eastern counties.

Richard seems to me to take less interest than he should, since father has made him a Partner. He drank a great deal and fell silent. Father did not notice or affected not to – he makes exceptional allowances for Richard.

She stopped to read the entry, nodding slightly to herself and mouthing the words. She smiled at the last sentence, closed the book and put it in the drawer of her desk.

Chapter 2

Jacob de Vries had taken an English ship from Harlingen with his wife and daughter at six in the morning. At that hour the sun had already been strong over the Waddenzee, rising above the sea mist and the grey line of the island of Texel. Now, two hours into the journey the Frisian Islands presented a continuous wall of land that appeared to bar the cutter from the North Sea.

The English master was sure of his course between the islands of Terschelling and Vrieland, sure that a gap would appear, widening to form a safe channel through the sand bars. It was a familiar route for him, back to Lowestoft. Outward he carried linen, broadcloth, sailcloth and herring, inward it was gin, lace, potatoes, roof tiles, spices or any other cargo light or heavy. The small ship had a simple passenger cabin with a bed, table, chairs and candles and because of this the agent at Harlingen had sought him out.

"Captain, I have passengers for you - if you want them. Good pay." Captain Burgess grunted.

"What sort?"

"A man, his wife and daughter".

"Don't like women on board, Cornelius."

Burgess had been a navy man. He was well bearded and what was left of his face was like polished walnut.

Cornelius the agent grinned at Burgess from under his brown felt hat.

"I know, I know. You are a daft man. Don't want money, don't need money!"

"English or Dutch?"

"Dutch"

"Their business?"

"The gentleman is something special. An engineer, a drainer. A well dressed, well educated man. He will pay well I imagine. The women are well dressed. No trouble!"

The agent shrugged, waited.

"What the devil is a drainer?"

" Dykes, sluices, ditches, drain the land."

"All right, have them on board. How much luggage?"

"Six pieces"

"How will they pay?"

"Guilders. In advance"

Burgess nodded.

"We leave in two hours."

*

The single masted ship bore to port, leaning easily in the light wind; the passage between the islands shone in the sun. De Vries emerged from the cabin and took the three steps that brought him on deck.

"A fine day, Captain Burgess"

He spoke good English with a moderate accent.

"Yes. We should make a fair time Mr. de Vries. I could wish for a bit more wind, but we shall be there in under twenty-four hours if this holds."

"The agent said that would be so".

The two men automatically looked up at the mainsail, then watched the two man crew going about their business, one man tightening, checking, one man steering.

"I'm sorry there are only two bunks Mr. de Vries. I hope the ladies are good sailors."

"I will sleep in the chair. No matter. My daughter sails well, my wife, not."

"Are you accustomed to the sea?"

"My job takes me many places by water, and I suppose I spend nearly as much time on water as I do on land. Water is my element, so to speak!"

"The agent told me you are a drainer. A man who controls water?"
De Vries thought of the huge flat polders of Zeeland and the terrifying power of a wall breach, the feeling of helplessness.

"No Captain. You do not control water. You guide it."

"Perhaps you're right. We seamen plough it!"

They both leaned on the rail, listening to the slap of waves, watching the land slip past. The sandy beaches were clearly visible and the clusters of houses at Oost Vlieland and West Terschelling. Chimney smoke put a tang in the air.

"Lookout to bow."

"Aye aye."

The crewman positioned himself carefully.

"The sand bars move all the time. Those barrels mark the safe passage, but even then the freeway goes. The local men put down their own markers – see the long poles. We must stand off them at least fifty feet."

"This is no place for a stranger."

"No." Burgess pointed ahead: "Here come your countrymen from the fishing."

A small fleet of six herring busses were heading towards them, single sails distended. The voices of their crews could be heard, shouting among themselves.

"So where are you going to, to guide this water, Mr. de Vries?"

"To Norfolk. Near the border with Cambridge. What you call Fen country I believe."

"Deep dark fens."

"You call them that?"
Burgess snorted.

"I'm a man of the sea. Men of the sea get worried by mud and reeds. Sailing up creeks is not my game. Full of strange things, strange people."

De Vries laughed.

"It's a Dutch pastime. Strange Dutchmen!"

"You don't seem too strange to me." Said Burgess.

Attracted by the conversation, the two women appeared. They had embarked cloaked but now appeared, gowned and □ated in Dutch fashion, stiff with lace headdresses, ruffs, and linen bibs. Burgess noted that both women were attractive, particularly the daughter, with blonde hair and blue eyes. De Vries beckoned to them.

"They do not speak much English," he explained, "but they can understand. My wife Cristeen, my daughter Katja."

Burgess made a brief bow to each. They reciprocated with a curtsy.

At that moment the Dutch fishing boats swished past. A welter of whistles and calls floated across, one lad blowing kisses and hugging the mast, another holding up something wriggling and yelling suggestions. Neither woman looked, but the girl blushed. The calls and banter quickly receded.

"Fishermen!" said de Vries. "No manners. Impudence! Impudence!" Burgess saw his passenger was upset. He tried to pacify him.

"All the same, everywhere. Just fishermen. Have you been to England before?" he enquired. He saw de Vries regain his composure.

"I have been to see the problem of course, to see my future employer. But the ladies have not. However I do not think it will be so strange to them. The countryside is very like Holland. Some houses are brick and have tiled roofs just like we have. Fishing and farming. It is not so different. There has always been a lot of trade between Holland and that part of England."

De Vries repeated this in Dutch to the two women, who nodded and made polite noises.

Cristeen had understood perfectly well, Katja's English was less sound. Cristeen was feeling queasy. The yells of the fishermen and the sight of the sea had not improved things. She wanted to tell her husband, and ask what she should do. Katja, warm from the obscenities of the fishermen ("look at the tits on that! They'd fill a sail! How about a huge eel darling!") watched the disappearing herring boats. She could still make out the figure of the lad who had caught her eye, the lad with the skimpy beard and the tangle of blond hair. He had waved directly to her and blown extravagant kisses. She had seen her father's reaction.

The adults talked on. To Katja it was all boring trade, boring commerce. Talk to pass the time, a kind of tapestry work with words, as when her mother's friends came round on afternoons. Katja made a pretence at interest in the passing villages, lifting a hand to her eyes and stepping forward to the ship's rail. Such separation from so little distance. She watched the water shushing past and mourned what she had left behind. Her friends, the town, her room, her curtains, the view over a canal to flat fields trimmed on all sides with a bristle of rushes. She mourned the black and white cows, and she told herself that she supposed she mourned Lucas the boy she loved. She dared not look back to the mainland as her eyes filled with tears. Looking into the sun, she could make it the scapegoat. Lucas had held her desperately when they had met to say their goodbyes. She had told her mother she wanted a last walk by the big dyke to see the nesting birds. She half suspected her mother knew what she was really up to, although it was true that Katja knew every species of bird and where they nested. She had walked with Lucas for a while, she pointing them out, he distracted, both of them sick with misery. They had sat on a grass bank, out of sight and Lucas had kissed her, saying she mustn't go, but what he hoped instead she had no idea. Not knowing what to do, she had unbuttoned her dress and had taken his hand, laying it on the naked warmth of her breast. To her surprise, he had let out a cry, withdrawn it as though it were fire, and flung himself face down.

"I'll be back. I haven't gone forever. In a year or two."

Lucas had responded by thumping the ground with his fists.

"Its forever for me. You'll find an English boy!"

She wished he would get up off the ground. His manner dismayed her. All romance gone she had re-buttoned her dress awkwardly and stood up, distancing herself from him. She felt angry.

"I'll have to go."

"Why?"

The word reminded her vividly of a seagull – plaintiff and ugly. She struggled to contain her sudden dislike of this boy.

"I must. Now get up. I have to get up very early tomorrow."

Lucas leapt up. Taking her shoulders, he thrust an angry face into hers. She noted the blond fuzz on his upper lip. She noted the spots on his nose and forehead.

"You don't care, do you?"

There was nothing to say. She turned away miserably and stamped homewards in her clogs. Lucas followed at a distance, failing to make any amends but turning to go his own way with an angry shout.

"Goodbye then. I don't care, you know!"

She had scuttled homewards confused but relieved.

*

The boat was now passing between the islands. The long sides of these faced landward and seaward so that the passage was brief. The houses on the landward side passed out of view, dropping behind outlying arms of sand that were secured against the sea by marram grass. The illusion of solidity created by this vegetation soon gave way to beaches, dunes and sand bars as land slipped into water. Cristeen stared after the receding land. Despite the comfortable weather, they had now encountered the North Sea swells. The boat picked up a rhythmic roll that she found even more uncomfortable. Prospecting gulls took to following them, believing that all boats were fishing boats, falling behind them, overtaking, then falling behind again. To distract herself from her physical discomfort and from her fears of the sea, of the journey, of the whole enterprise, she ran through passages of the scriptures in her head, but the circumstances and the seagulls disrupted her concentration. She took to the Lord's Prayer and from the corner of her eye she scanned Katja. She was troubled by the girl, her blushing, her blooming body. Cristeen had watched her slip away in the evening hours of their departure when the house had been in unaccustomed uproar. Their baggage had been all over the tiled hallway. Outside, the carter was hunched in a heavy coat against the damp April evening. The candle lamps on the wagon were lit already, giving him a sickly yellow complexion. The man must have been seventy if he was a day and hardly looked fit enough to raise his whip. He also had a cough.

"When you're ready, madam". Cough cough cough. "I'll pack when you've finished." Cough cough. "Otherwise I won't know the order to put it in." Cough.

"Are you sure you can manage? Abram will help you."

Abram was their manservant.

"I don't need no Abram, madam!" Cough cough." I never needed no Abram." He muttered something incomprehensible and probably rude. Cristeen removed herself quickly. She saw Katja slip out of the back door, dressed in her best, and had been deeply shocked. She dared not let Jacob know. Fear forced her into complicity.

"What *is* all this clutter in the hall? What's it all for? I suppose this is all our clothes? I need room for my instruments and books and papers. They are the important things not all your fripperies. I have a job to do!"

She tried to soothe him.

"Of course your things take priority. It may look a lot, but Katja and I have only the basic things …"

"Where is that girl when she is needed?"

"She's around. I saw her a moment ago. We'll go through her things."

A quick reply. A truth. Only just a truth.

Jacob must not get even a hint. He would storm out after her and drag her back, or get his Spanish pistol from the big dresser. His sternness often terrified her. But he was by common opinion a good man.

"A good man, a good man," she found herself mouthing at the waves. The shrieking of the gulls had never stopped. It was too much for her.

"I think I'll go back to the cabin," she said to Katja.

The girl nodded. "I had better stay here for a while."

*

"So what does a drainer do, Mr. de Vries?"

"Jacob, Captain."

"Thank you Jacob. Is your daughter going to be all right on deck? Should she join her mother? I think your wife is suffering a bit .... The swell."

"No. The air will do her good. She's a healthy girl .... Give her a fine complexion."

He translated this into Dutch for Katja. She responded with further blushing.

"Red as Edam cheese!" said de Vries.

*

Katja wished she could escape, but knew she must do as he said. Or let him believe she did. There were terrible reasons for this obedience. Her little brother Jan had not done what he had said, and Jacob frequently reminded her of it.

"Honour thy father and mother, that thy days may be long in the land which the Lord thy God giveth thee."

Jan had died in a polder when the ice broke. He should not have been on the ice. He should not have been out on his boxwood skates. Katja should not have been with him. An older sister had the authority, even at fourteen ......

Her efforts to reach him had been useless. With each step the opaque sheet cracked and collapsed. She struggled in the mud and rushes, lacerating her legs on the ice. Jan floundered and yelled, and then began to cry. She had had to make a decision and decided to run for the house. Screaming to Jan, "Hold on, hold on, I'll be back!"

How could he possibly hold on? Had it been the right thing to do? Had Jan even heard? When she returned far behind Jacob, gasping and retching in the frozen air, Jan had already gone. Jacob had flung himself onto the ice, crashing through it towards the broken circle. Up to his chest, he had shouted Jan's name over and over, ducking under the water as though he might see, striking at plates of ice with his fists. The other men arrived with ropes and ladders, taking it in turns to rope up and crawl out, but Jan floated out from beneath an unbroken sheet, still and dead. Katja had watched it all as though it were some terrible nightmare. It had not gone away. The women had wept. The funeral had been and gone. Jacob had been bleak and unrelenting.

"The boy was told not to go. You, Katja, knew he was not to go, you were not to go. You disobeyed me. This is the lesson we are taught by the good Lord."

Katja had not been able to see how death could be considered a lesson. There was nothing to be learned from poor Jan, laid out in the church, cold as the water that froze him, white as the ice.

Jacob refused to shed a tear because it was a lesson.

Cristeen could not give full rein to her grief, because it was a lesson.

Even the minister seemed to think it was a lesson.

*

"So what does a drainer do?" De Vries pondered. "We are engineers by trade but I like to think we fulfil the task of the Lord!"

He waved a hand at the sage-green sea as though it was his to command.

'*And Moses stretched out his hand over the sea and the Lord caused the sea to go back by a strong East wind all that night and made the sea dry land*' "Are you a religious man, Captain?"

Burgess was caught by the unexpected turn of the conversation. He reddened.

"I don't know ... I wouldn't say so, but I consider myself a God-fearing man. Perhaps that is the same thing, perhaps not. I attend church on Sundays and keep the Sabbath. Perhaps I am a pious man, but I wouldn't say religious ..."

"You part the sea yourself, in the course of your trade. Sailors *are* religious men in my experience. They know the strength of the Lord ...."

*

"The ship parts the waves. It is nothing to do with me. It seems to me Mr. de Vries," said Burgess drily, "that if the Lord had provided the Israelites with boats the affair could have been equally well managed."

De Vries stiffened visibly.

"The Lord will have had his reasons."

Burgess shifted his feet. He was aware that de Vries was offended and briefly debated whether to conciliate him or laugh. The man was a prickly devil, but he was his passenger.

"Doubtless," he said. "Just my joke. Anyway I'm weak on the scriptures. Some call us sailors superstitious, and mock us you know. We have no book learning." De Vries, mollified, made a sympathetic face. "You know the things sailors say, it must be the same in Holland. We say 'Friday's sail always fail' and at the table, 'Don't let a loaf lie on its side or a boat will go over,' and all sorts."

De Vries snorted.

"You don't really believe that, do you Captain? I know you can't, you are an educated man. These things are quaint - is that the word - and they are meant to amuse.
They are what you call sayings."

"I don't, but many do," said Burgess. He crossed his fingers behind his back in case his lie found him out.

*

Night time. They were halfway there. A bright half-moon turned the sea to quicksilver and stars were sparks. It was much clearer, much colder. The wind remained moderate and the motion and speed of the boat constant. Burgess had slept for a few hours and risen again with the punctuality born of experience. He found his pipe and tobacco, which he treated himself to only at night. Preparations over, he lit it from a candle holder stuck in the wood of the hull, and went on deck. His mate Thomas nodded to him from the wheel house.

"All well, Thomas?"

"Aye aye Captain, I see your Dutch trio are still awake."

He gestured amidships to the cabin. A yellow light could be seen along the threshold.

"Light's never gone out while I've been here."

"Poor sailors," said Burgess, drawing on his clay. He automatically carried out his checks – the set of the sail, the tightness of ropes here and there, the course, the sound of things. Standing at the rail he stared into the path of moonlight. A man could lose himself in it for hours. The sail shifted slightly, ropes creaked, waves slapped at the hull.

"Have we passed any vessels? Anything to report?"

"Two ill-lit fishing boats out of Harwich," said Thomas. "Bad boys with dark lanterns. Poaching herring on the Dutch side!"

The men chuckled.

"What do you make of our Mr. de Vries, the Dutch drainer?" Burgess kept his voice low. Sound travels on clear nights on the water.

"I've hardly passed the time of day with him. He seems a proper sort of chap, but a bit serious for me. A bit holy."

"I reckon he thinks he's Moses, Thomas. I should like to see him waving his hand in the Fen country. It'll take more than that to drain out that bog sodden country."

Burgess, from the dry Brecklands of Suffolk, viewed the Fens as worthless, neither land nor water, a farmyard midden.

"I feel uneasy with a man who quotes the scriptures. I think we have seen enough of that from our own sort ..."

"Someone stirring, Captain."

A shadow had moved across the strip of light below the door; moved again. The door opened slowly and de Vries emerged carefully. He was now cloaked but still dressed in his day clothes. He shut the door and joined them.

"I thought I heard voices. I hesitated for some time but I cannot sleep, so why sleep? Just look at that moonlight. Man can make a candle, God makes the moon! Are you smoking a pipe Captain?"

The question was put sharply. Burgess was irritated by the Dutchman's tone.

"I am, Mr. de Vries. A thing not unknown to your countrymen. Indeed, they are heavy users of tobacco from my observations."

"Regrettably," snapped de Vries.

Burgess rolled his eyes at Thomas. It was obvious that de Vries intended to intrude on them. The two seamen resented it. Night voyaging is close to sleep. The mind sets a slow course of its own choosing.

"Is your wife well?" said Burgess. He could think of nothing more extending to say.

"She is exhausted, that is all."

*

Cristeen's supposed exhaustion did not prevent her from sitting upright as soon as the cabin door closed behind Jacob. Her starched clothes rustled vigorously. Katja's heart sank. She suspected what might be coming.

"Katja. I know you are awake. Listen to me."

Her mother's voice was low but insistent.

"Not now mother. I'm trying to get some sleep."

"Most certainly now! We must sort things out between us before we get to England. There are things to be said, and things to be explained.

"Please not now! I thought you were seasick."

"There's much worse than seasick, Katja. There is the misery you cause me by being a deceitful daughter! You have no idea what agony you cause me. I know what you were up to. Abram saw you too. You slipped away to see that boy Lucas. How could you do that!"

Katja held her tongue. She had that amount of sense and experience.

"I saw you heading for the polder. What a time to do that, and what sort of behaviour?"

"I only wanted to say goodbye ...."

"Did you now. What if your father had seen you? That boy is nothing but a wastrel. His father is a coarse fellow, and he will go the same way."

"That's not true, mama, Lucas is going to go to University at Leyden..."

"Is he now," Cristeen interrupted. And what is he going to study, and who is going to pay for him?"

"He's going to study to be a doctor."

"So he says. If your father found you were seeing him - seeing any boy at your age, he would be furious. You know that. What were you doing? What were you and he up to?"

"Nothing."

Katja's face burned with embarrassment. She moved away from the candlelight so that her face was in shadow. This was awful.

"You had better behave yourself in future. Your father has an important job to do in England. We want no nonsense, no finger pointing. You've been brought up to be a God-fearing girl - how could you behave so badly?"

Katja remained silent, knowing the path her mother's complaint would run. She felt nothing for Lucas anyway - it was all a waste.

*

Dawn at sea begins with a trembling illusory light, like a fluttering of the eyelid. As it gathers it appears to be a faint pulse, but this may be a trick of the eyes. The Westward course of the ship meant that the feeble light was behind them, while in front the English coastline merged with cloud, forming a mountain landscape of fantastic proportions heaped layer upon layer. With the passage of time and miles the flat dark line of the land could be distinguished.

De Vries had come and gone to the cabin during the night, finally propping himself up on deck with a coil of rope for a seat. He was wrapped in his cloak, appearing to be asleep. Now he stirred and stood up, looking towards the land. Burgess, watching him, felt remorse. He had been short with the Dutchman, making it plain that he preferred solitude but he did not want de Vries to think badly of Englishmen.

"There you are, Mr. de Vries."

He pointed to the coastline.

"Another two hours and you'll be ashore."

"I see it, Captain."

It looked similar to Holland, thought de Vries. He could not distinguish a single salient feature.

"How do you know where we are?"

"By our course. When we get nearer, we'll know by the shape of it, by churches and headlands, woods and bays."

They pursued their course to a position from which they could see a ruined church on the edge of the shore.

"Dunwich," said Burgess. "Once a fine town, Mr. de Vries, but gone under the sea mostly. Once one of the principal ports of England, now ruins on the cliff, ruins in the sand. A sad sight. Perhaps they needed your sort of skills? Too late now ..."

The cutter turned Northward to follow the coastline, past the flint church towers of Walberswick, Southwold, Covehithe, Kessingland. Churches built from the profits from wool. The sun cleared the eastern horizon by half past five. A glittering day. To port the ship passed headlands and woodlands, fields of young green corn, fields white with sheep. The lowing of cows could be heard as they waited to be milked. Early morning woodsmoke drifted out to sea from farms, sweet in the salty air. They passed fishing boats by the dozen about their business, ignoring all other craft, guarding their secrets. They negotiated the sand bars off Lowestoft and headed for the harbour mouth. De Vries left the deck to prepare the two women for imminent arrival. They had evidently anticipated him, for before many minutes they were all on deck to view their approach, the women dressed in style in goffered ruffs and layers of stiff linen.

"I imagine you are being met, Mr. de Vries?" asked Burgess. "What about your baggage? You will need a carrier. Where are you heading from here?"

"We are being met. Mr. Warburton is sending a carriage for us, and his carrier."

"Mr. Warburton?"

"My employer. Of the manor of Oxay. Have your heard of it?"

"I'm afraid not."

"It is near King's Lynn."

"I've heard of King's Lynn."

"On the border of the fens, as you call them, the Bedford Levels. The great drainage works of my countryman Vermuyden ... the Hundred Foot Drain, the Forty Foot Drain, the Nene, the Ouse."

"You are well up on our geography."

"I have, of course, studied Vermuyden's work, and his techniques. I have seen maps of them."

"They don't always take to foreigners in those parts. And believe me, Mr. de Vries, I would be a foreigner in those parts. And what with the late Dutch wars ..."

"I am aware of that Captain. But we are all good Christians, are we not? I will of course be careful and let the good Lord be my guide. I must work with these people, I understand that. You know, Captain, that a considerable amount of the Bedford Level was drained with Dutch labour?"

The two women had moved to the bows, where they held hands and took in the busy scene.

"I didn't know about the labour ...."

"Prisoners, Captain, as well as free men. Five hundred men captured by your Admiral Blake in his engagements with our Admirals Tromp and De Witt and De Ruyter. All at work together. With Flemings and Huguenots and your own countrymen. It will be quite an undertaking. And all the time these Fenmen who oppose it ..... say we are taking away their livelihood! What do they eat? Eels, ducks and pike! Is that a Christian sort of life? Living in swamps!"

Burgess was disconcerted by the passion of the man's outburst.

"In Holland, we call this work the "Engelse Dyckage! We are experienced in this, Captain. We know our business."

"I never for a moment thought otherwise," ventured Burgess.

"I have felt, Captain, that you were not entirely full of sympathy for us. Now that our voyage is nearly concluded, I feel I can say that. I thank you for your courtesy, but I have felt that."

"I'm very sorry if I have given that impression" replied Burgess. "No discourtesy was intended. I am just a seaman with no manners." He was impressed by the man's dignity and bluntness. He had been in danger of underestimating him.

"Well, we part on good terms anyway!" The small ship was entering the harbour at the river mouth. "I see you must go about your business!"

The harbour was crowded with craft of all sizes. To the North, the long shore below the town was covered with beached fishing boats, nets and blackened smoke houses. The smell of fish, smoke and tar was intense. The ship dropped sail as they slid towards the quay. Waiting men moved forwards to lower fenders, seize ropes, and for some time the passengers were ignored for the scuffling and shouting and adjustments of tying up and making fast. Finally Burgess attended to their disembarkation. Thomas deposited their luggage on the quayside and a carrier was called for.

"Where do you go in Lowestoft?"

"The Lion Inn. Where Lion Score meets the High Street. I have stayed there before. A carriage is to await us there."

The carrier was already loading their baggage into a cart and men were gathering to be paid to unload the cargo. They stared openly at the passengers. Burgess would take the evening tide to Yarmouth to take on another cargo. The Lowestoft agent had details and was waiting for him, papers in hand. Waiting for the human cargo to clear the working space. Burgess shook hands with de Vries and made a short bow to each of the women.

"I wish you all the best of luck in your endeavours."

"God be with you, Captain."

De Vries emphasised the first word.

Chapter 3

The April day continued as it had begun, with a pretence of summer. De Vries watched the passing landscape through the small glass panel let into the leather wall on his side. He had a sense of recognition. The bursting hedgerow buds and tender leaf of hawthorn exposed the true season. It was on the edge of being cold and the coach would take twelve hours, with stops at Beccles, Harleston, Diss and Thetford to relieve themselves, eat, change horses.

The journey took them from the coastal strip. Through the good agricultural land of High Suffolk and on to the dry, sandy Fieldings, or Brecklands which form a sand and shingle barrier to the intrusion of sea from the Wash. This open countryside, home of stone curlew, hare, ringed plover and snipe, gradually dips down to sea level and below. Casual dumps from a glacial past form low islands in the immense marsh.

De Vries noted that field ditches became drainage ditches, dry beds became water courses and the road became softer and muddier. The coach ran parallel with water in man-made courses. The level and speed of flow showed that the present sunshine was no indicator of recent weather. The dykes were laden with brown silt and carried reed and drowned grass. Increasingly, they passed half-flooded fields with furrows standing out like ribs. The sun, reflected from so much water, dazzled de Vries, dazzled the coachman and the horses and formed a dancing square on the coach ceiling.

"Look at this Cristeen, Katja," de Vries urged. "The land is like soup. Loose peat and silt. You can see it needs more drainage. Our wheels are almost in the water… "
Katja was relieved when the road rose again and they quit the reeds and sedge for hedgerows and dry land. She had never been fond of the sound of wind in rushes. In Harlingen they said that if you fell asleep amongst them, they would make you mad. They told of a boy who woke up as a creature and ran off on all fours into the depths of them, never to be seen again but sometimes to be heard, at night, howling. She shivered. She was seated beside her father and was able to examine his face in profile. He was leaning forward, his face animated. A good profile, she thought, he must have been handsome in his youth. She tried to imagine him as a young man.

Cristeen, seated opposite, was making an effort against tiredness to take an interest. She nodded more than was necessary as a substitute for words. She liked to see Jacob talk like this for he was seldom animated except in matters of his work, God, or Katja's behaviour. She caught Katja's eye and raised one eyebrow in complicity. Katja suppressed a laugh, enjoying the mood of optimism. The coach began to judder as the wheels struck the flints of a metalled road. The driver halloo'ed at the horses and slapped them with the reins and they quickened pace on the harder ground.

"On the road to Lynn, now!" he called, leaning down from his seat. Katja felt a thrill of excitement. She realised that the shadows of Lucas and Jan had somehow been left behind.

Three men crouched in the hide. It had been constructed on a slight rise so that it combined the advantages of dry ground and a view over the reed beds. These stretched in front of the hide as far as the eye could see, punctuated here and there by alder or willow and cut by watery ditches of all widths. The hide was made of a willow frame thatched with reed. Into the thatch, further upright reeds had been inserted so that the structure resembled a natural mound.

Two of the men wore trousers and jackets of coarse woollen cloth, the third a leather jacket with silver buttons and serge trousers. All wore a broad leather cross-belt from shoulder to waist from which hung a powder horn, shot pouch and charges. They nursed long-barrelled fowling-pieces. The younger of the two men in woollen clothes peered across the marsh from an opening.

"Flight of mallard," he whispered. The other men nodded. They listened silently to the rush of wing beats overhead.

"Don't think they were disturbed, Mr. Turner."

The man in the leather jacket took out a handkerchief and wiped his nose. Despite the sunshine it was cold in the shade. The dampness rising from thc ground was inescapable.

"They're out there somewhere, Peter, give them time. Remember that lot from Eriswell?"

This was addressed to the oldest man. "Tell him, Felix."
Felix Hare grinned toothily. Clouds of whiskers surrounded a saddle-leather face with a hooked nose.

"I remember them all right! Out on the flats. Tied their punt to a tree, and out they went after the geese. Was a good year for geese. We was rightly poisoned with 'em! So they walked right out, daft beggars. We heard them, and we see'd them, and they see'd us and they let fly at us, boom, and we let fly at them, bang, and they came running. In the mud they were, falling down and slithering around like so many old stranded seals!"

The unsavoury man laughed. It sounded like sneezing.

"Anyhow we took their punt and left 'un to learn a lesson. They came in with the tide. Mostly."

"Mostly?" asked the young man.

"Mostly. Except one. One went other way. Went out with the tide!"

He laughed again. Sneeze, sneeze sneeze. The young man looked shocked.

"He drowned?"

"Well they do say he had too much to drink!"

Turner and Felix sniggered like schoolboys, egged each other on to laughter until Felix dared to nudge Turner and Turner slapped his shoulder. Seeing the young man's expression, Turner became defensive.

"What? Fowlers know the score. They fired first. If we had of caught them, they would all be in jail. You don't go setting decoys on Master's land."

"But to let a man die …."

"We didn't let a man die," snapped Turner. "He done that himself. If he couldn't get out of there quick enough, he shouldn't have been there in the first place. Theft is theft, young Peter. '*He that diggeth a pit shall fall into it.*'"

"That's right," said Felix, "truly right." There was an awkward silence. It was obvious that Peter was far from accepting this viewpoint.

"Water level's high." Said Turner. "Noticed it this week. Dutchman's due to arrive today. That should prove interesting. See what he makes of it."

" I don't hold with Dutchmen." Growled Felix. "Supposed to be our friends again. Easy said, not so easy done. All they do is start wars and steal our trade."

A flight of geese could be heard calling to each other. In a scarce tree somewhere a blackbird practiced. Felix straightened himself, grunting, and looked out of a spy-hole in the thatch. The sun was already sinking, yellowing. Numbers of birds were passing over, some in ragged flights, some in well organised "V" formation, heading for feeding grounds at the salt water edge. The old man watched with appreciation.

"Going to be a rare old sunset." He turned back towards Turner, "Well, what do you think? What's he going to do?"
Turner shrugged.

"Says he's going to treble the amount of summer pasture. That's where the money is, that's certain."

"I've heard tell of things going wrong with Dutchmen and drainage." Said Felix. "There's that one that dammed up the River Don so that it flooded half the world, they say! At least, round Doncaster!"

"Well, that's Yorkshire," said Turner slyly, "so that'll be all right then!"

Felix slapped his thighs with appreciation snorting and sneezing. He noted Peter made no response, tugged at Turner's sleeve and pointed to the young man.

"He's a miserable fellow," Felix growled, deliberately audible. "He don't want to worry about that fellow drowning. All before his time. Long ago."

Any response that might have been forthcoming from Peter was stilled by Felix abruptly raising his head.

"I heard a shout," he hissed, "Listen up!"

They held their breaths. At first they could distinguish little from the rustle and squeak of dry sedge. Then came a man's distant voice, calling, echoed by another voice, urging, herding something.

"That's what we're after." Turner sounded grimly satisfied. "Remember lads, we want them in one piece. The Law is to take care of them. No fireworks unless we have to. Into the boat."

The boat in question was a long flat bottomed craft that they had used to get to the hide and it was moored in the adjoining waterway. Peter lifted the rear wall of the hide and the trio emerged. They cautiously seated themselves, guns aloft as the punt rocked to and fro. Felix took the bow, Turner the central seat and Peter, who had paddled them to the hide, took the rear. He handed his gun to Turner, and fishing in the bottom of the boat, produced a wooden paddle. Two dips of the paddle and it was gliding smoothly forward. In this fashion they moved cautiously towards the source of the voices. The course was so narrow in parts that Felix had to part the reeds before the boat, as though dividing curtains, so they could ease their way through. They could hear occasional calls, nearer.
A moorhen, nesting to the side, hopped from its nest, running across the water, making them jump. Peter stopped his work and laid the paddle across the boat. They listened intently for a long minute but there was no sound except the music made by water drops from the paddle. The birds nest bobbed alongside the boat on a raft of reeds, its cargo of eggs lying in a woven depression. Suddenly Turner held up a hand. Faint but clear came the sound of whistling and halloo-ing. Turner motioned Peter to continue.

As they slid forward, Turner reached out with the butt of his gun, with three blows he destroyed the year's work, leaving a mess of yolks and blood. He washed the butt over the side.

"Vermin, vermin."

The waterway abruptly opened at right angles onto an expanse of open river. On the nearside grew deep reed beds. On the far side mudflats stretched to the horizon, flat and black, held together by the roots of samphire and sea aster. On these, back-lit by the sun were the silhouettes of four men, several wooden poles and a long decoy made of net and supported on hoops. The next striking thing was the presence and din of wildfowl. This had not been audible in the reedbeds. Disturbed geese, ducks and waders appeared to be everywhere.

Two of the men were conducting their own unruly ballet within the decoy, waving their arms like windmills and advancing on a trapped tumble of birds. These were being driven to the far end of the decoy into a tunnel of netting that diminished to not much more than a large stocking. Over this a third man stooped with a sack, grabbing a bird by the neck and despatching it with a skilled flick. He stuffed the bird in the sack. The fourth figure was holding on to two supporting poles. The structure appeared to depend on him.

The drivers of birds accompanied their motions with yells, clapping and whistling. All of them were oblivious of the watchers. Turner leaned forward towards Peter.

"Paddle across," he whispered. They won't notice us."

Doing as he was told, the flat bottomed craft reached the other side, sticking in the mud just short of the bank. There was no alternative but to get their feet wet. At that moment they were seen. The pursuit that followed was muddy and confused. The stooping man let out a shout and grabbed his bag, immediately starting to run. The man holding the poles released them, picked up another bag and was off. The two inside the decoy were temporarily trapped in the netting but managed to fight their way out. The netting collapsed on the birds inside. The two paused briefly as though to recover the decoy, then they too ran. Peter could see at that moment that they were boys, possibly about thirteen or fourteen years old. Turner was shouting;

"After them, after them!"

Sliding and sinking, Peter pursued the man who had been stooping by the neck-end of the decoy. The boys had shot off like rabbits and were well ahead of everyone. Turner and Felix wallowed after the fourth figure, Felix falling behind after a few strides. It was impossible for him to run while clutching a fowling piece.

"Halt!" shouted Turner. "Halt!" as though he really believed they would.

Felix, bogged to a standstill, let out a baffled roar, lowered his gun and discharged it in the approximate direction of the fleeing man. It had no effect on him, but the concussion sent every bird into the air within quarter of a mile, creating aerial mayhem. A cloud of grey smoke rose into the swirl of birds. Felix continued to roar.

Peter, young and fit, was gaining on his quarry who was hampered considerably by the sack. The objective of the fowlers had become clear. They too had arrived in a small boat which they had moored some way off. The mud flat on which they all stood was an island at this stage of the tide. Both men were now coated with mud. The problem for both was how to run without losing boots and this dictated a strange high-stepping gait. The firmer ground formed by plant growth gave way to liquid mud, beyond which the small boat was tied to a stake. Peter's target plunged into it, took two cantering steps into the sea and fell flat. Peter followed, jumping on him and grabbing his neck in a lock. The man struggled, then finding this useless, gave up, spluttering and choking. Peter pulled him out of the ooze by neck and armpit. There was little unmuddied of the man except parts of his face. There was a moment of mutual recognition.

"Peter Dade, let me go!"

"Ezra Dunn!"

Nesting terns were dive-bombing at their heads, screeching and snapping with their beaks. Ezra Dunn was of similar age to Peter but much slighter in build. He flinched, cowering from the attacking birds.

"You shouldn't be fowling."

"It's only ducks and eels!"

Both men were still panting from their exertions. Having seen Ezra's distress at the terns, Peter turned his face skywards. Ezra shut his eyes, fearing for his sight.

"It's nesting season, Ezra, see, they ain't happy."

"We've got to eat! Nesting season don't stop us needing to eat. Let me go!"

"But these birds ain't yours to take."

"They don't belong to no-one. They flies here. Who says who owns what flies? I got a wife and children!"

Peter looked about him. He knew the truth of what Ezra said and was seized by fellow-feeling. Felix and Turner were far behind, the sun was low and blinding. He released the man, who immediately ducked his head.

"Shove me and run."

Ezra Dunn gawped at Peter but obliged with vigour. Peter sprawled backwards in the mud watching his getaway, watching the angry terns chasing him. He allowed himself a smile.

Turner and Felix had no idea what had happened. He allowed them to believe he had lost his man – which they were keen to believe as they had lost theirs.

"I got his sack though!" said Peter with triumph. "Got it off him!"

"I know who my man was," said Turner. "I know him well. That was Ecclesiastes Dunn, old poacher, Lord knows what else. Villain!"

"What's in that sack?" asked Felix.

From the distant safety of their boat the escapees yelled derision. No one turned to look.

"Twenty four ducks," said Peter, "and a bag of eels."

"Ah well," said Turner with a grin, "Even if we didn't get 'un we got the decoy and scared 'em good, and there's even ten ducks for the master.

Oxay Hall was surrounded on three sides by a moat filled with water. On the fourth side this had been partially filled in to leave a smooth grassy depression spanned by a three arched bridge. Over this a roadway approached the main façade of the house. The architecture of the building showed it to have been constructed over a number of centuries. The central section was the oldest, consisting of a timbered hall which had been enlarged and added to under a thatched roof. On each side this was flanked by red brick Elizabethan wings, each larger than the hall. Behind this façade were two courtyards and a chapel, leading to an arch. Beyond the arch lay working outbuildings and the farmyard. In the last hundred years or so, the whole arrangement of parts had been equipped with a unifying array of tall brick chimneys vigorously carved and twisted.

The meeting of the Oxay Drainage Partners was convened in the timbered hall. The interior was panelled to half its height and a large log fire burned in the fireplace at one end. The principal item of furniture in the room was a massive trestle table surrounded by equally massive chairs. The Partners were compressed at one end of this table, as far as possible from the heat. Its comfort had become an affliction. John Warburton, who appeared oblivious of this, occupied the head of the table.

On the polished surface lay various maps and books. Candelabra had been lit and dotted about, as, despite the sunlight, the room admitted scant light through small leaded windows. Seven men were present. It was obvious that they were at ease with each other by their postures. Chairs were pulled back, two of the men smoked, and bottles and flagons had been circulated according to taste. The convivial air did not diminish the general attention when Warburton rapped on the table with an ink pot and rose to speak, clutching a bundle of papers. A man of his mid-forties, he had dressed in his best wig, coat and cravat for the occasion, while under the table, high-heeled boots added to his stature as he was quite a short man. He made up for any shortcomings in his physical appearance with a resonant voice and firm delivery.

"Gentlemen, I have prepared for this meeting by writing down much of what I have to say. If I repeat things that some of you already know, it is because others may not. But first, I think we should remember what men we are and give thanks to the Lord. We will say the Lord's Prayer."

The assembled men lowered their heads and Warburton led them through it in rumbling unison.

"The support of the Lord for this venture is what we all seek."

He paused, selected a sheet of paper.

"As I think everyone knows, I applied to Parliament on behalf of our company for permission to carry out the drainage works and dyckage of the marshland and fens that we call Oxay Fen, Oxay levels, Ditchmarsh, Aken

Carr, the Severalls and Grimes Hill. I can now report to you all formally that we have received that permission ..."

He was interrupted by the others clapping approval on the table with their hands. Not a man for smiling, Warburton waited for silence.

"I have managed to put in place the indentures and agreements, discharges and undertakings necessary to secure the land, the access and the waterways necessary to execute our undertaking. I have on your behalf signed the Articles of Agreement, indented, made and concluded upon the 15th Day of April, this year of our Lord 1690."

He passed a long document to the man on his left at the top of the table, John Sylham, neighbouring squire. It circulated to the others, Walter Tyson, Thomas Latimer, both neighbours, then across the table to William Emms, Vicar, Robert Edmonson the estate manager and back to his right hand side and his son Richard, who returned it to him. Each man glanced at the document, checked the seal and signatures.

"It will be left on the table for everyone to read. We are now permitted, in the words of the document, to undertake our best endeavours to ..."

He scanned it, and finding the place, read;

"'drain and lay dry the said drowned and surrounded lands, waste grounds and commons and make the same fit for tillage or pasture by inning and draining, and shall cut dig or make or cause to be made such and so many watercourse, banks, highways, sasses, sluices and other receptacles for water as may be necessary and shall have for himself and his servants and workmen with carts and carriages fit and convenient free ingress and regress for the perfecting and performance of the said inning and draining without the let denial or hindrance of any person and take such quantity and proportions of earth, reed and other things and materials from the said grounds for perfecting the same as shall be thought necessary or useful and shall have the benefit of all channels, watercourses and sluices now already made and to turn change or alter the same as necessary for the perfecting of the work as shall be thought fit.'"

Warburton paused for breath from this recitation. There was a mumble of laughter. Sylham, a large florid man in his fifties, took his chance.

"I hope you know what that all means, John. I fear I don't."

"Have we proper protection in the document?" asked Emms the vicar, in his rather clipped tones.

"Protection? What sort, vicar?" Warburton's tone was dismissive.

"There are many things." The vicar leaned forward, his thin face catching the candlelight. In his hand he held a piece of paper. "I took the trouble to go to Hatfield Chase and Axholme to inspect the works done there, and I talked to all manner of people. I talked to other men of God and in particular the vicar of Sandtoft. I expect you've heard of Sandtoft?"

"Can't say I have," growled Tyson, Sylham shrugged and made an enquiring face at Latimer.

"I've heard of it. There was trouble there," said Edmonson, the estate manager, in his broad Suffolk accent. "Some years back. Riots and the like."

"Only four years ago," Emms continued. "The church of Sandtoft was wholly burnt down by the Commoners."

"Why? "asked Warburton. "And why should you think we'll have the same trouble here?" His tone bordered on rudeness. Sylham and Tyson exchanged glances. The antipathy between Warburton and Emms could always be expected to develop.

"I hear the sort of things they mutter, John. They may not say them in earshot of you, but believe me, they have the same grievances, and the same attitudes to change. You've seen their suspicion of new ways. What I am saying is that we should take account of it. Now."

Warburton was not impressed.

"I think you're overstating it."

"The affair in Axholme isn't even finished. They've had riots, on and off, for over forty years! The case is still running in the Courts. Look at the time and the expense .... It started during the war!"

"All sorts of things happened during the war!" Sylham was as dismissive as Warburton. "Damned Commoners, vicar!"

Emms was not to be deterred. He had been hurt but not surprised that Warburton had usurped his authority by leading the Lord's Prayer. The tension between them was long-established but he was not going to allow his researches or his moral authority to be dismissed.

"I don't agree with that approach. The participants there bought thousands of acres, for drainage and improvement, like us. But the Commoners said it wasn't flooded, or it was only flooded on occasion and that their land was being stolen and they got a lawyer and petitioned Parliament, gentlemen, with their rights of fishing and common grazing and wild fowling and turf cutting and willow cutting and flax retting and everything else they could think of and demanded compensation. And got it! And through all that they destroyed crops and broke the dams and sluices. Damned Commoners as you say John."

This produced an uneasy silence. Latimer coughed purposefully. Grey faced and gaunt, he commanded respect whenever he spoke. He had served as a magistrate locally and was known for his uncompromising line of justice for miscreants. His standing amongst landowners was correspondingly secure. These issues were his concern and they looked his way.

"Thomas?" prompted Warburton.

"Have we a list of the rights of our Commoners and Freeholders?" Latimer asked.

"No, we have not," replied Warburton, "But we all know who does what and how the place runs."

This brought murmurs of assent.

"You see, everyone knows."

"We don't need a list," said Tyson dismissively. "There is nothing more dangerous when dealing with Commoners and Freeholders than setting things down on paper, when they are only understandings and the like. You see, we're already talking of rights! Thomas – you used the word. You started it, vicar, talking about 'ancient rights'! Father tells son that's what he did, and where he did it, and his father did it before him and before long they think they own it, when at best it was a privilege and at worst a trespass!" He paused for a swig from his flagon. "And all you need is some lawyer holding on about their livelihood depending on it and writing it down and hoodwinking the fancy gents in Parliament and before long you have trouble and a Court case and Sheriff's men trampling all over the place! Let well lie, that's what I say."

"That's true," said Sylham. "What ain't already written must be privileges, by common sense, so why write it? Privileges can be given and taken. What are you thinking of, vicar?"

Emms appeared to have expected this sort of reaction. His tone was still measured.

"We all know gentlemen, that when we drain the fens and the marsh, the ponds will drain too, and all the places where they rett flax and fish and fowl. As a consequence they will have less to eat."

The reasonableness of his speech produced a gloomy silence. The fire shot sparks as a log collapsed. Emms mopped his brow and undid a button on his jacket. Tyson stared at the table, Sylham at the ceiling and Latimer into the distance. The silence was broken by Robert Edmonson.

"Excuse me, Mr. Warburton, gentlemen, but there's truth in what the vicar says. I hear a thing or two, as you might imagine, and there has been muttering about the works. They reckon it will bring in lots of foreigners, and they don't like foreigners. They know about the Dutchman, Mr. de Vries, and they reckon back to the Dutch wars. Forgive me for saying this, but whatever we do, they reckon we buy cheap and make much profit. They are ignorant people. I'm sorry, vicar, but they are."

"That's hardly their fault," said Emms. Tyson snorted.

"It don't help!"

Warburton intervened.

"This was supposed to be an occasion for celebration. And the Dutchman arrives this evening. With his family."

"Where are you putting him?" asked Sylham.

"I've had Elm Farm tidied up, to put them there. There's plenty of outbuildings and they'll do for offices and stores. And workmen can put up in the barns."

"It's a good house," said Sylham. "I hope these workmen can be trusted. How do we know what sort of people they are? What sort of trouble they'll make? Drink! And women probably."

"Lots of these people are good Protestants." Emms protested. "Huguenots and Dutchmen! We have more to worry about from our own!"

"If you have people in mind, name names." Said Warburton testily. It was no oversight that he had led the Lord's Prayer. He considered Emms to be a dangerous reformer. Warburton needed no one to interpret the word of the Lord. If it was in the Bible, he held to it word for word.

"Of course I have no one in mind," said Emms.

"Then let's get on with the maps, otherwise de Vries will be here before we've finished."

This broke the ill-tempered mood. The men got to their feet, cleared the table and rolled out the maps, pinioning them with glassware. Richard Warburton, who had said nothing so far, took over from his father, explaining the proposed routes of dykes and drains. His presence as a Partner neither pleased nor displeased anyone. It was recognised and understood amongst them, (though never mentioned in front of Warburton) that his position was simply because he was his father's son and could be provided in this way with a useful occupation. His education appeared to have taught him to understand maps, which was more than could be said of the others.

William Emms brooded and held his tongue. The friction between Warburton and himself was embarrassing. It lay smouldering, likely to ignite on any public or private occasion that they both attended. He knew Warburton to be a devout, God-fearing man, who held prayers in his house three times daily, who attended church unwaveringly whatever weather,

illness or business befell, but his beliefs stood between them. Warburton the creationist, viewed enlightenment as the peddling of falsehoods, brooking no questioning or interpretation of the Old Testament. The certainty of his raw convictions led him to be contemptuous of Emms whom he saw as a meddler with truth.
Emms had a further deep concern. He had invested all he possessed in the project, and he feared for it in Warburton's hands.

A comedy of errors had developed before him as Sylham turned a map this way and that while Tyson tried to pin it down with the palm of his hand.

"Gentlemen, you'll tear it," fussed Warburton. Latimer conceded a rare smile.

"May the Lord help us!" he declared, "if we don't know where the thing is going, I hope the surveyors do!"

"It's all Dutch to me!" exclaimed Sylham in great good humour. His witticism brought disproportionate laughter. Warburton waved a bottle over the tankards to general assent.

Emms, choosing to be remote from this joviality, was offered nothing. He could read the maps better than anyone, and he alone amongst the Partners had walked the route from Oxay Fen to the sea. He glanced down the double blue line marked "New River Cut", noting the familiar names – Dicken-Dyke, Aken Carr, Oxay Level, Eriswell, Black Carr. The map-maker had added his own fanciful decoration of imaginary islands, fishes heads, peering from the water, small serpents (eels?) as if Oxay Fen was some part of the New World. The spot where the Cut ran into the sea was marked by a half-naked Neptune, complete with trident, reclining in curling billows. Emms had the pessimistic thought it had better have been illustrated with "ignorant people" spaced along the way to block it. He hoped the Dutchman had a better grasp of reality than the map-maker.

*

Mrs. Ruth Warburton had prepared all day for the arrival of the de Vries family. It was dark by the time they reached Oxay Hall and she had made sure candles were in the windows. The serving girl and cook had been kept in the kitchen, the dining table had been laid with the best silver and pewter. Both tea and coffee had been purchased in order to show the Dutchman how the English lived.

The welcome was well-managed. Ruth had met de Vries on his previous visit and was expecting him to arrive in a large hat. She was not disappointed, and could barely suppress her smile. She had formed no advance opinion of his wife and daughter and took in the crisply collared woman, her red cheeks, her pretty daughter, thinking they looked surprisingly fresh despite the journey. Tidy people, she thought; decent looking.

Warburton had seized de Vries' hand as soon as he stepped down, then turned to Cristeen and Katja. De Vries advanced on Ruth with a smile of recognition.

"Mrs Warburton, it is good to see you again!" She had forgotten how strong his Dutch accent was. He doffed his broad-brimmed headgear and was uncertain what to do next. Ruth proffered her hand, causing de Vries to replace the hat on his head before he could shake it.

"Welcome to Oxay," she said. "Come in and get warm."

"Meet my wife and daughter ...." De Vries ushered them forward for introductions to Sarah and Richard, before they were taken in and baggage removed upstairs. The two women accompanied it, while Warburton insisted that de Vries join him for a brandy in his study.

Ruth and Sarah occupied themselves by carrying out an unnecessary review of the setting of the dining-room table.

"They are very neatly dressed," said Ruth, "but their style is rather heavy. I would feel captive in all that cloth. And did you see Richard? Offering his arm – and did she blush. She is quite the pretty thing. And well built, and she knows it!"

She looked at Sarah who pulled a face, and they both laughed.

"Lord make us appreciate the good things thou providest," said Warburton. He sat with his eyes closed and his hands palm down on the table. The others followed suit except Richard, who took the opportunity to scrutinize Katja.

"May we eat from your table with proper humility that thou hast provided such bounty to thy unworthy servants. Amen!"

"Amen," they chorused. The maidservant who had been hovering in the doorway, brought in a steaming joint of mutton, served with carrots and potatoes. She stood it beside Warburton. He brandished his wine glass.

"Your good health, Mr. de Vries and to both the ladies!"

"To all the ladies!" protested Ruth, to laughter.

"And to success for the venture!" added de Vries. Cristeen sipped wine hesitantly, unfamiliar with the business of toasts. Katja and Sarah drank wine and water.

"Now tell us, did you have a good journey?" Warburton carved as he talked. The maid took meat round the table. "I have never been to sea myself. More a man of fields and horses."

"It was without incident, which is the best you can expect. Your Mr. Burgess is a competent man."

"And did the ladies like the sail?" He looked to Cristeen.

"We were a little troubled, Mr. Warburton, a little troubled ...."

Richard sat with his chair pushed out. Katja sat opposite, Sarah to his right.

"The sea air is good for the complexion," he observed, smiling at Katja, who blushed furiously despite keeping her eyes fixed on the table.

"You must not pay any attention to him!" said Sarah, coming to her defence. "I'm not sure Miss de Vries understands us very well and you should be considerate."

"I do understand quite well," said Katja, both embarrassed and excited, "but I do not speak so good."

They became engrossed in the formalities and informalities of eating – which for de Vries was none too soon. Sarah, with one eye on Richard, was embarrassed by the intimate attention he focused on the girl and covertly nudged him when she had the opportunity, only to be ignored.

"There is some hostility to our plans which we should be aware of," Warburton was saying, chasing juices round his trencher with a piece of bread. "It is not universally accepted that drainage is for the common good."

"How is that? It creates the very best land ...." de Vries followed Warburton's lead and mopped with his bread. The women did not follow suit.

"It is accepted that the land is good, but there are always ignorant people – people who don't want the land in the first place."

De Vries made a face showing polite surprise.

"There is a long tradition in these parts," Warburton continued, "among those people who live like amphibians." He looked to de Vries to see if he understood. "Creatures that can't make up their minds to walk or swim!"

"Ja, I understand," said de Vries. "We have the same word."

"We breed solitary men here – I suppose I'm one of them myself. Perhaps we watch the rising and the setting of the sun too much in the fens. If we are good men we are alone with God – we're God-fearing people – if we are not, we are alone with other forces. There is a long tradition of fishing and fowling ...."

"It is part of their livelihood," explained Ruth, attempting to lighten the conversation. "The fen is their larder."

"A free larder," said Richard. "They pay nothing for eels or fowl or wood or turf, or anything else they can take from the fen and we wonder why they don't want change!" You'll see them staggering about on their stilts, sloshing around like storks ...!"

"I have heard," said Sarah, distressed by Richard's attitude, "that if they don't have eels and birds, all their food would be salted which can lead to illness or even death."

"Then every sailor would be ill or die!" scoffed Richard, making a face at her.

*

Later when the tea and coffee had been served, conversation stumbled to a halt.

"We must allow these good people to retire!" proclaimed Ruth. "We have put such a burden of talk on you and you have been too polite to protest!" She escorted the family de Vries to their rooms. Sarah, in her room, wrote up her diary entry for the day as was her habit.

*

"The whole day spent preparing for the Dutch family de Vries. Jacob de Vries is to superintend the project for the drainage of the marshes. They arrived very tired by carriage at 7 of the evening. He is quite an average man and wore an enormous hat. Mrs de Vries is well fed but her skin is not smooth. The daughter is called Katja and is younger than me. She is quite a beauty in an obvious way but does not have too much to say for herself. She also eats too fast for good manners. She blushes often when spoken to and has immediately captivated Richard, who has not behaved well in her presence. I think they are going to be dull people. When father said grace Mr. de Vries insisted on saying a prayer, which he did in good English, but it was not necessary. We all drank coffee after eating which I had not tasted before. It is very strong. Tomorrow will go riding."

*

William Emms was pleased to be back in the familiar security of his study. His housekeeper, Mrs Strutt, had left candles lit and placed bread and cheese and a bottle of Rhenish on his desk. He helped himself to these and prowled the room. It was lined with bookshelves and cabinets. His second vocation was easy to see as his collection of books was interspersed with specimens and artefacts of all kinds. There was a conspicuous lack of religious tracts. Fossils, bits of pottery, wood and shells were on display, labelled in his fine copperplate. Going to a mahogany cabinet he pulled out a drawer labelled "Aken Carr" and removed two objects which he laid on his desk. Each object lay upon a piece of card which bore a description. The first read:-

"Dicken-Dyke. Bronze axe-head (??) Found five feet below leather sandals and sword. Aken Carr."

The object was about five inches long, green-grey and axe shaped with a socket at the rear of the head. From the top of the head projected a half-ring of metal. The piece had been cast as one.

The second object consisted of scraps of red-brown rust arranged in a row. These were labelled "Sword". Beside these lay a piece of shrivelled, biscuit-hard leather. Stitches had opened around the edge like worm holes. This was labelled "Sandal (?)"

From the next drawer down he took a rolled map on which Aken Carr and Dicken-Dyke were identified with a cross in red ink. The proposed routes of the new dyke and the straightening of the river were marked upon it in broken red lines. Emms propped open the map, sat down at his desk and took out a leather-bound book, inscribed "Journal". He chose a quill and began to write:-

"Soon will start the excavations across Oxay levels and Aken Carr. In times past this marsh must have resembled islands surrounded by water, rather than the present sea of reed-mace. These islands were doubtless inhabited for all of ancient time until today, as seen by relics uncovered. Our stratagem is to scoop a straight line through the marsh and by affording a truer and deeper course, persuade the water from its habitat to the sea in a shorter time. We are to build sluices at intervals to prevent the ocean taking advantage of what we have made at high tide. I have no doubt that many things will emerge from the silt and peat. Peat is a wonderful preservative of objects capable of corruption, as bone, wood, iron and leather, and of objects of noble metal as gold, silver and bronze.

It is most likely that artefacts will be exposed at different levels during the works and the levels should be studied with the artefacts still in place to gain a proper understanding. It is no use if some careless fellow tumbles them into a ditch. My studies show so far that there is no sign of disturbance above many artefacts. These I call 'ancient' artefacts. This lack of disturbance seems to indicate a very great age for when a burial is uncovered, even of such an age that it must be Roman, the ground above the grave can be seen to lack homogeneity. Where an ancient artefact is several undisturbed feet below one that is already old, it must be supposed to be of a very great age. What are we to say of those things that are so very old? What are we to say of those things made of flints that lie below everything else?"

Emms paused from his writing to pick up the bronze axe-head, which he examined. Laying it down he wrote:-

"John Warburton would have everything ancient to be Roman. All fossils from the Flood." He dusted the page with sand and shut the book.

*

The events of the afternoon, and in particular the loss of the decoy were a blow to the Dunns. It meant a meal from a barrel of salt fish. This made Ecclesiastes Dunn disagreeable.

The meeting in the Dunn cottage had been called covertly. Ezra had moved from door to door of the straggling village in the early evening, making sure he was not seen. Only a local man could do that, and only a local man could find his way home again. Even with a glittering sickle of moon it was a perilous world, between land and water, over slippery wooden bridges, beside drowned fields. While candles and lamps lit gentlemen's houses, the Dunn cottage was lit mainly by firelight. The fire was in the brick pit in the centre of the floor of the single main room. As a reminder of the afternoon four pairs of boots steamed beside it. A major proportion of the smoke rose in a column to find its way out of the hole in the roof. The proportion that did not, made an acrid fog. Furnishings were sparse and makeshift. Four chairs had been supplemented with trestles and planks, a ladder on barrels, a log box, stumps of wood. The room was packed with men, women and children, the majority standing. Rush lights had been placed around the walls. These short-lived lamps were tended with noisy glee by a group of girls.

Ecclesiastes Dunn and his son Ezra stood, their wives sat. The firelight picked out Ecclesiastes' features – a strong hooked nose and boney brows. Mr. Punch. His voice was penetrating.

"The Lord bring blessings on us all! Can you all hear me?" There was a scattered response. Dissatisfied, he repeated the question. His audience, unaccustomed to the discipline of meetings, kept up their conversations. "If you'll be quiet, we can begin!"

He waited, glowering around, until talk dwindled and died.

"Ezra told you why to come. Mynheer the Dutchman arrived this evening, de Vries by name with wife and daughter. He is an engineer, a drainer." He had their attention now. When he paused there was no chatter, no sound except the sparking of the fire. In the darkness men's pipes glowed. Even children were still.

"Do you know what that means? He is staying with Warburton, and Warburton has been recruiting men – workmen from all over – and they're ready to start. The course has been decided and the next thing they'll strip off the turf for their new river cut, as they call it, and start digging. Perhaps you've seen their poles and pegs, marking it out – I have and it's what we thought. It goes straight through everything, our meadows, cuts them in half; our wetlands and fen, you wouldn't believe it, and no bridge from here to the sea."

"Sea's over six miles," said a voice.

"That's about right," said Ecclesiastes. "I make that a long walk with your beasts, six miles there and six miles back to get to pasture!" This produced mutterings. He let them digest the matter.

"Can't they bridge it? Can't we bridge it?"

The speaker was John Lambert, Ezra's brother-in-law, a man with a broad forehead and long nose. His long hair hung down like the ears on a spaniel. John Lambert had sheep on the wastes and water-meadows of the fen. Ezra thought it was time he made a contribution.

"You think they'd do us a favour, John? Can you see these Partners building us a bridge so's we can move our beasts! And pigs might fly! And we can't bridge it, it's to be a forty foot drain, not something we can get over with trees and planks. It's all part of the plan, John, to get our animals off the fen. As Ecclesiastes said, it goes through our meadows, through ten acre meadow, through Oxay Levels, through the fen, through Ditchmarsh and Aken Carr and Severalls and Grimes Hill and everywhere our Oxay Drainage Partners care to put a line on their bits of paper. They don't care if they cut a field in half, and if it's fen, they'll drain it!" He paused.

"It must be worth it for them," said Lambert. "I hear this cut is going to cost a fortune."

Ezra looked to Ecclesiastes to reply.

"You know what it's about. They're going to take our land. Does any of you have a proof of ownership? A bit of paper?" The ensuing silence was the reply he expected.

"They say the land is worthless except our rent, but when it's drained they'll plant cole-seed and cabbage, and we can sing for our grazing and our fowling and eels and the land will be worth ten, twelve, sixteen shillings an acre. To them! And if we want it, we shall have to pay. That's what it's all about. And where shall we get our fish and fowl? What do we eat?"

"From Warburton's as usual!" came a shout from the back to scattered laughter. Ecclesiastes was angered. He was their acknowledged leader. Hadn't he taken the trouble to find out the route of the new cut – information given in confidence when he had caught up with Edmonson and the surveyors in the fen? Edmonson had waved a map in front of Ecclesiastes out of respect, one local man to another.

"Now, you haven't seen that," he said while the surveyors watched with pursed lips.

"This isn't a matter for laughing!" he declared hotly. "It won't be there, don't you see? It'll be Warburton's dry land." He emphasized the word dry. "Warburton's carrots and Warburton's ploughs and horse drills, and Tyson's and Sylham's and Latimer's where we drop a net today. Every bit of wet, think about it, don't laugh, they'll make it dry and when it dries it's theirs!" He turned away to show his exasperation, waving an arm in the air.

"He's right," said an elderly man in slow tones, moving towards the fire to a spot where he could be seen. "You don't see the workings of it because it happens bit by bit. I've seen drainage. It spreads, sucks the juice out of the land. One graff, then forty dykes, then four hundred ditches, then half a county."

"So how do you know all this, Thomas?" demanded Ezra's wife Harriet. "And what shall we do about it?"

Thomas Fox, the elderly man, moved forward slightly.

"I've been told. By Warburton's man, Edmonson. He's a good man. I saw him in the fields. He had two fellows in fancy breeches and they had a machine for looking through. It was stood on legs like a table and made of wood and brass and had this half circle of brass on top, and rods and sights. And the two fellows were turning it this way and that and putting numbers in notebooks. I asked Edmonson what they were doing, and he says 'surveying', and that they can put dimensions on anything, a whole estate in a few days. They set the lines. It goes in those books. And Edmonson said they cut a graff and then the dykes, and he showed me a map, and it was on it like I don't know what, like veins on a leaf."

Harriet Dunn leaned forward to put a log on the fire. It was out of reach.

"You do it gel."

Her daughter Esther, a pretty girl, picked it up and placed it. Sparks rose, died in the air. There was silence, broken by Ecclesiastes who had recovered his poise, demonstrating the aptness of his name.

"Bring damnation to them all, that's what I say. '*He that diggeth a pit shall fall into it and whoso breaketh a hedge, a serpent shall bite him. Whoso removeth stones shall be hurt therewith and he that cleareth wood shall be endangered thereby.'* Mark my words." He could feel the salt fish lying heavy in his belly.

"We shall have to get the bells out!" came a clear sharp voice. It was instantly recognised. The crowd parted, drew back to reveal a woman, who could have been in her forties, her face smoke-blackened (by choice, as those around her knew, - a smith is never without fire and water) her pores engrained. Clara Hare, blacksmith, sister to Felix. Clara Hare, shirt sleeved, arms bare, hard biceps, forearms of ship's cable, fingers fit to grip the tongs and hammers of her trade. Clara Hare that no one went near at night, who lived by herself and had no man. And some would emphasize the word "man" and roll their eyes or even cross themselves. When she worked at night, as she would on occasion, there were those who swore they heard two sets of hammers an the anvil. She was never seen on Sundays, and those that crossed themselves said she changed her form, so completely did she disappear. The new log added to the occasion by bursting into flame.

She moved forward and instinctively people drew back, awed both by her appearance and her reputation. The sudden brightness of the fire revealed that in other clothes and other circumstances she might be a good-looking woman. Clara knew very well what they all made of her and what was whispered about her. Part of her enjoyed it and the power of distance it gave her, inhabiting a life half-in and half-out of the village and its affairs.

"Talk won't stop them, talk's a poor thing." She turned so that her back was to the fire. Whether or not by intent her face was now in partial darkness and her silhouette fringed by light. Her unkempt hair took on the firelight glow.

"A curse on them, we shall have to play the Jack with them, and spook them and set old Grim at their hearts!"

The contrast between Ecclesiastes' sacred and Clara's profane utterances produced an embarrassed silence. Clara held her ground, waiting for some response. Ezra obliged, speaking with the voice of reason.

"We don't want to get into a fight with Warburton, or the others. Next thing we'll have the Sheriff down and we'll all be in trouble. Best thing is that we wait and watch before doing."

This brought a chorus of assent, but Clara was not to be mollified.

"While you do your waiting and watching, they'll be digging. Digging in places that are best left alone. There's places there that no one should touch. You know that, I know that."

"We should be praying to the Lord!" cried a woman from the back of the room. "We need His help, Clara Hare – this is a Christian village."

Many opinions were held of Clara, but it was inescapable that she was part of their lives – as much part of it as the very seasons, the winter frost, the spring floods and summer jostling of the rushes. From that stemmed a cautious tolerance. The fire in the forge was always alight – sometimes no more than a wisp of smoke that needed her bellows to revive it, but it was a certainty for which they were grateful – where they could go for an ember when the fire at home went out. Clara would never comment, but digging in the ash would give them the lost element on a small shovel. And men would call into the forge from winter fowling to stand sheepishly by the fire with extended hands until feeling returned and their teeth stopped chattering and they could leave for home. And Clara was high-priestess of the flames when a fork was needed or chain or hinges or barrel hoops.

She drew herself up and snorted to make her feelings known. Ezra dared to try to lighten the situation by teasing her for her known cupidity.

"Think of the business Clara. They'll come to you for iron for this and mending of that and bolts and nails and all sorts ...."

"I'll make 'em what they wants, but I shall see them off the fen!"

"Take their money first!"

The laughter that followed was short-lived. Clara's technique was to go from one to another of her startled audience and subject them to an individual glare. Following this she stamped out into the night.

"Has anyone anything more level headed to say?" asked Thomas Fox.

No one was in a hurry to follow Clara into the night.

"That woman is damnation!" said Ecclesiastes Dunn, but said it quietly lest too many heard, or even Clara heard by some magic means.

"All the Hares are a damnation!" rejoined Ezra, less cautious.

Ecclesiastes was about to blurt out words about witches but they choked in his throat. On the west wall of Oxay church had been a medieval

"Doom" that had been his education as a boy much more than the endless sermons. The painting had been hacked and whitewashed by soldiers in the name of the Reformed Church, while others cut the heads off the pew ends or shot at angels in the glass. Its outline could still be seen in slanting sunlight, at the right time, in the right season. It had been his introduction to the ever-present nature of sin for in the centre of hell stood a naked female figure amongst the damned and the petal-like flames of hell-fire, round of breast, pink of nipple, revealing a darkness between her thighs that stirred and shamed him. Clara had become inseparable in his mind from that figure.

"Damnation," he repeated forcefully, ashamed of his earlier caution.

"Get on with your job girls, it's getting dark!" commanded Harriet Dunn. The rushlights had been dying. It was a relief that the girls scampered off to obey. People began to talk amongst themselves.

Clara sang to herself in the clear starry night, her voice surprisingly sweet, making up words to tunes she knew, uncaring if the fragments had connection or made sense. The night was a friend to her, giving her the use of a quiet world. The woman passed by the house where Peter Dade lived with his mother.

"There goes the witch," she said. Peter was making her a bowl of milk and sops, holding an iron pan near to the fire, careful not to let it boil. Bent with premature age, his mother sat wrapped in a shawl.

"Where's she been? What's she been up to?"

"There's a meeting tonight at Dunn's house," said Peter, sounding as off-hand as possible.

"What about?" Her query was sharp.

"The drainage. The Dutch engineer has arrived." The fire was low but he could not be bothered to go outside for more wood. He turned the embers with a poker, stood the pot to one side.

"Why didn't you go? You never go to things. I never know what's happening!"

It was a familiar cry. Her husband had died young – of a fever they said. He had only a vague recollection of a man coughing and coughing, of people coming and going. He had been told to sit downstairs in this room, and keep the fire alive, as if somehow this would keep his father alive, but after two days the coughing stopped and people stopped coming and going and he let the fire go out. What he most remembered was hunger. No one fed him or remembered he was there until they discovered him asleep by the cold grate. He had been looking after his mother ever since.

"Nobody's welcome who works for Warburton." He poured the milk into a bowl, deciding he could wait forever for it to get really warm. He handed it to her. Her extended hand was skin and bone. She sipped from the bowl, letting some of the milk run down her chin.

"It's cold," she complained. "Cold cold cold."

"The fire's nearly out. It's the best I can do. I'll help you to bed."

"You don't care," she said. "Don't care I get the death of cold. Nobody cares when your body goes. You'll be old one day, old and crippled."

When she had finished, he half lifted her up the steep stair to her room. With her gone he could light a candle and read what he could of the book that Emms had given him.

*

Sylham was in no hurry to return to the cold husk of a house that contained Arabella and her silences. He had drunk more than he ought and it had taken the combined persuasive powers and lifting abilities of Tyson and Warburton to get him onto his horse and on the road while Ruth prepared for the family de Vries. He narrowly avoided that event had he known it and now found himself at a standstill, smiling at the moon in the half-light. His horse had sensed his master's indifference to direction and decided it was best to halt.

Sylham looked around. There was nothing of note in sight to tell him where he was. Such light as was left seemed to pulse as it does when the sun has set. Sylham's sky was an indigo porcelain bowl clapped down on the world. The horse ground its teeth on the bit and shifted feet. Sylham patted the animal. He loved this time of night. Owl time. Bat time. Time of black trees and distant dogs.

He heard Clara before he saw her. Where the horse stood beneath an oak, shadow piled on shadow, dark on dark so that Clara for all her awareness, saw nothing. Sylham heard the swish of her skirts and the thud of her clogs. She was visible for a moment crossing the lane in front of him. Surprise and indecision kept him in the saddle for some seconds, then he dismounted with all the care he could muster. He tied the reins to a branch and walked carefully to the spot where Clara had disappeared. She had slipped into one of his fields between gatepost and hedge and he could see her figure receding towards the far side. He followed into the field, moving quietly as large men can, but she was moving quickly.

On a still night the fens are almost silent. Wild fowl sleep and the only noises are the rustlings of creatures that live and eat among the stalks and the hunting owls that hope to take them. There are few landmarks by day and none by night – horizon is inseparable from sky. Into this darkness Clara walked with assurance following raised banks made long ago and newer paths made by reed-cutting. Her first destination was a small, drier area of grass and sea aster. On this, just visible in the starlight, stood a white pole, no thicker than a broom handle. She stooped to sight from this, seeing in the distance a similar marker. Taking hold of the pole in both hands she tugged it from the ground and turned round and round, round and round, stamping at the ground in a circular dance until she had obliterated the spot where it had stood. Puffing from the exertion she shouldered the pole and set off for the next.

*

Sylham had lost her. Cut off from advance by a water filled dyke, he retreated to his horse which snorted softly with impatience.

"Whoa boy!" he said, patting its flank. "Where has Clara gone? Do you know? Wouldn't we like to know what she's up to?" His heart was pounding, but whether from exercise or excitement he had no idea.

"Opportunity lost!" he said, not really understanding what he meant or why he said it, but it brought a recognisable feeling of guilt. If he took stock of himself, he inhabited a world of rents and debts, crops and finance, tenant farmers, complaints, harvest and Arabella. Of not living up to expectations and being reminded of it. Of the pressure to improve. Improve the cattle, improve the corn, improve the land, drain the land.

"By God you don't know how lucky you are to be a horse!" he said, pulling himself up in the saddle. "Hay to look forward to, nothing to think back on." He nudged the horse with his knees and they moved on.

"And what was Clara up to?"

Chapter 4

De Vries dreamed that he was alone in a small boat made of silver, except that in the next moment he wasn't alone. There was a shadowy person with him that he knew but couldn't identify. The boat was too heavy, low in the water and filling with successive waves. He tried to right it by leaning as much as he could one way and it steadied. With huge relief he could see the shore. He paddled towards it using one hand but when he got to the shore it was ice and the water tried to freeze around his wrist. He scrambled onto the ice, followed by this person who had become his responsibility. The ice was thin as a wine glass and crackled under his feet. He shouted to be careful, but his companion ignored him, running ahead, until to de Vries' horror, he tripped and crashed through the ice. De Vries struggled towards him but the ice gave way, surrounding his legs, slowing him hopelessly. He reached out a hand to the figure but it was Jan, floating beneath a sheet of ice. He tried to break it with his fist, punching at it vainly. Then he awoke.

He lay exhausted, half asleep, half awake, subduing the remnants of the dream. He felt his heart pounding with panic and held his breath, waiting for it to quieten down. Noises of feet on gravel drifted in the window. That could have been the crackling of ice. He concentrated on the unfamiliar sounds of a strange house awakening. Pale pink light showed round the edge of heavy curtains. Birds were louder here, he thought, and the sound of clogs, clop clop clop in the streets, was missing; otherwise he could imagine himself still in Holland with Cristeen breathing deeply beside him, snoring slightly. He would get up shortly.

He heard horses being led across gravel, then cobbles, and reality abruptly intruded. People were up and about. It must be late and he must have missed Warburton's morning prayers. It was the last thing Warburton had reminded them of as they retired, and now he had overslept. He sat up and took his watch from the bedside table, where he had propped it up. He could not read the time, so got up to open the heavy curtain sufficiently to see it was half past seven. Prayers were at seven, Warburton had said, breakfast at eight. So he had missed prayers – he was determined not to miss breakfast.

"What's the matter Jacob?" Cristeen's voice was drowsy.

"We've missed prayers. You sleep on. I must get up and get out."

"I'm getting up too. We're going to our new house today, to set it up."

"Are you getting help?"

"Mrs Warburton is sending a maid, a man and her housekeeper."

"Good," he grunted, "are we dining here tonight?"

"Yes."

Struggling with his shirt buttons, his thoughts returned to the previous evening.

"Did you see the attention that Katja was receiving? From that young man."

Cristeen's reply was careful.

"I saw nothing special. You're reading things into nothing."

"Hum," said de Vries. He vowed to talk to Katja about her behaviour while in England. He had been heartily embarrassed by the incident of the fishermen on the boat. "Modesty!" he declared. Cristeen said nothing.

He felt down his shirt front to be sure all the buttons were doing the job, and shrugged into his jacket.

"I'll go ahead."

*

De Vries had never encountered such a large breakfast. It was far removed from his customary bread and cheese, but he felt hungry enough after his travels to do it justice.

He had been confronted by a row of covers set over on the dining room sideboard. Each carried a coat of arms which he assumed to be Warburton's, and each was identical. There was no-one in the room and it was evident from half eaten remains and the general disarray of the table that others had already been and gone. He pause a moment to consider the propriety of the situation, shrugged, and lifted each cover in turn to find cold lamb chops, cold beef, ham and shelled hard boiled eggs. This was evidently to be eaten with dense bread and washed down with beer from a large jug.

Helping himself to something of everything, he sat down at an undisturbed table setting and had begun eating, feeling disconcerted by his solitude, when the serving girl tapped on the door and entered. Instinctively he put down the cold chop he had been chewing.

"Sorry to disturb you Mr. De Vries, but Mr. Warburton says that as soon as you've finished, will you please join him. He has a horse waiting for you, ready saddled and hopes you will accompany him to the works."

"Thank you. I will be ready in just a moment." De Vries swallowed the rest of the chop too fast, following it with a boiled egg and bread. He washed it down with a mug of beer, grimacing at the unexpected bitterness. Eat all you can, he thought, you never know where the next meal is coming from.

*

Warburton was in the saddle already; a groom held the other horse.

"I'm sorry I am late. A long day yesterday …. Long journey."

"I understand Jacob, quite understand."

Warburton's manner was impatient and there was little understanding in his voice. He had the aspect and complexion of a man who had been up for hours and had no hesitation in showing it. His eyes settled on de Vries' hat.

"I'm sorry I missed prayers," de Vries felt compelled to say. He took the horse the groom offered. The man helped him to mount. It took two attempts to get him into the saddle, which he thought was a good effort with Warburton's critical eye on him.

"I try to find time for the Lord," said Warburton unnecessarily.

"Of course."

De Vries felt disadvantaged and thought it best to say as little as possible. He did not know his employer well, and must feel his way. He was aware of the weight of the breakfast inside him. Another disadvantage. He vowed to be up early tomorrow.

"A sparkling day again," said Warburton. The two men set off at a comfortable pace, which de Vries felt to be a concession. They left the rear courtyard and stables by a road that took them around the house, allowing de Vries to see it properly for the first time. He could tell by Warburton's studied indifference that he was required to comment.

"It's a fine building! Very fine indeed! You must show me round everything."

"I shall be delighted."

A man of vanity, but whether endearing or not, de Vries reserved his judgement.

They had a journey of six miles from the Hall to the works. Warburton pointed out landmarks and features, and was a zealous guide. De Vries was able to recognise some of it from his previous visit, but Warburton's catalogue included every spinney and copse, crop and farm, making interest a task. Oxay Church brought a halt.

"An ancient building," Warburton explained. "You see the round tower. They are only found in this part of the world …."

De Vries was attracted to the church. Flint built and thatched, it was of modest proportions and recumbent among its gravestones.

"My ancestors are there."

Warburton waved an arm at the graveyard.

"I shall be there myself one day."

There was nothing for de Vries to say.

"You'll meet the parson. I don't think much of the man."

De Vries tried the minimum utterance, but his "Oh" failed to dampen.

"I don't have much time for clerics, I suppose. The Bible is good enough for me. Good enough for any man, I reckon. I don't need a man to interpret it. What do you say?"

Dangerous ground. De Vries had not considered this. His best escape was to say so.

"I have never thought of it like that, Mr. Warburton. I am a God-fearing man, I study the Book ...."

"He's a Partner in this venture, Emms is his name .... Collects things and has strange ideas.... You'll meet him."

"The church has a fine setting," said de Vries evasively "I must attend it and see this Emms."

Their route took them off rough roads into water meadows stocked with sheep and new-born lambs.

"This is where our real problems start." Warburton indicated meadow that dissolved into water. "This was all under three feet of water in January. Some of my best grazing. Every year it seems to get worse. From here to the sea."

A pair of swans were grazing at the water's edge. They stared angrily at Warburton's gesturing. Their nest lay ahead in a tangle of drowned trees.

"These were willows and alders. The fields were everything. Wheat and cole-seed, cabbages and asparagus. And cattle. Fine grazing."

"We'll get it back. It is just a question of enticing this water."

"Enticing."

"Leading it away. It cannot be forced. *'All the rivers run into the sea; yet the sea is not full: unto the place from where the rivers come, thither they return again'*. We must make their passage easy."

Warburton permitted himself a smile.

"Alleluia. That is so." They moved on, taking to an ancient raised causeway above the marsh.

"Is that the sea?" asked de Vries.

"That's the mouth of the Oxay river. Do you see the masts of ships?"

The two men raised their hands to the brims of their hats, against the sun. The flat, uninterrupted landscape wrapped around them on all sides.

"I can see smoke, and masts."

They stared into the distance where a blue haze hugged the ground. De Vries was struck again by the familiarity of the landscape, the similarity to his native Zeeland. Here, as at home, the year was shuffling forwards into spring; plants were extending tentative shoots as if to test the dependability of the longer days. Familiar gulls flocked and fed on patches of water. The self-same gulls, for all he knew, that he had disturbed in Holland. It amused him to imagine they had flown here to escape him. He re-appraised the lack of order in the landscape. In Zeeland there would have been polders and dykes, banks and paths, the product of centuries of struggle, and there would have been houses, strung out along the larger dykes, barges, cattle, wood piles, the comfort of habitation. This was virgin marsh, cold and lonely, and in his imagination, sullen from lack of attention, waiting to flood.

"*Kein sloten*," he said to himself. Warburton, hearing the words, turned to him in enquiry.

"No sluices," de Vries translated, "no control of the water."

"I expect you think us very backward," said Warburton.

"Not at all!" De Vries was quick to recognise the danger of honesty. "In Holland we have been at it so much longer. Dig or drown! All places are like this before the work is done."

Warburton nodded, visibly pleased with the answer. He nudged his horse and they rode on. As they advanced, de Vries thought he could hear the sound of labour. They rode on, keeping to a raised causeway. In quarter of an hour they could both see and hear their objective. In another quarter their horses were crunching on foreshore pebbles. De Vries was relieved. His legs ached and his backside hurt.

Their route along the foreshore led to the river mouth. The outfall was masked by islands of lurid green weed that clung to mud and stones. Oblivious to the work all around, waders flocked in the rich margins where fresh water mingled with salt. A small township had been built to the side of the river between it and the new river cut which began some quarter of a mile distant. The blue smoke they had seen rose from several large bonfires of reed and brushwood. Two wherries lay offshore and timber from these was stacked on the stony ground, together with barrels, rope, tools and canvas. An area of tussock grass had been fenced off for horses and oxen, with wagons parked nearby. A number of thatched sheds had been built in two neat rows. De Vries was unable to take in what they were for. He wanted to get down.

"I'm very impressed! You've made a good start!"

"I hope it's what we agreed," said Warburton swinging himself down from his horse. De Vries followed, stamping his feet to relieve stiffness.

"You must have a good look. Make yourself familiar with everything. Perhaps you will take all today? Then tomorrow we can sit down and talk in detail?"

"How many men have you got?"

"About fifty. Some are your fellow countrymen. The rest are slodgers."

"Slodgers?"

Again Warburton permitted himself a quick smile.

"Men from the fens. Slodgers."

They had walked over to watch a pair of oxen dragging a large flat plough. The animals dribbled and snorted.

"Oxen not horses?"

"We have horses as well. But for this work we prefer oxen," said Warburton. "They're better for ploughing, you'll see. Their weight is lower."

The plough sliced below the turf leaving it loose but unturned. A gang of men followed, cutting the turf into squares with spades and throwing it into the waiting barrows of another gang.

"Where does it go?" asked de Vries.

"It's being barrowed to the side for the flood bank."

De Vries walked to a barrow. He indicated to the man to stop and picked up a piece of turf, turned it this way and that.

"How are you using this?"

"We aren't. Not yet. We're stacking it up and waiting for you."

"Good." He cast it back into the barrow. "I will look at all the materials. They must be to my approval." He nodded to the men to continue.

De Vries had already forgotten his aches and pains. Warburton noted there was a snap of assertiveness in his voice. Men nearby had noticed it too. He saw an exchange of glances. So this was the Dutchman. And the Dutchman's hat!

"We have set out the first bit of the route with the surveyors." Warburton was keen to display his own energy, "Allowing that it is your decision that we await. We have not yet taken soil samples …"

They moved on, on foot. Warburton gathered the reins of both horses and handed them to a non-plussed labourer, strolling away. He was pleased with the gesture.

"We must build a trial section of everything," said de Vries, "We will need a section of flood bank, about four to five English feet in height. There are always problems with materials. There are never enough – that is a law of construction – and never of the right quality."

He was watching the men pushing barrows over a roadway strewn with cut reeds. Although the weather was dry the underlying damp was turning the soil to mud that oozed to the surface through them. The workmen were dressed in an assortment of clothing. The more fortunate with leather tunics and woollen hats, the less so in woollen coats with bare heads. Most wore sackcloth leggings. Local men wore wooden clogs in preference to leather boots. Feet and wheels were already sinking.

"I think we must have wagon ways for this sort of work and barrow ways for the men. You see how difficult it is already? If there is any rain they will sink. Have you used wagon ways?"

"No, but I've heard they use them in mining."

"It is simple enough. We must lay planks on the ground, parallel with each other for the width of the wheels. Four or five feet. Then we can make and run wheeled wagons. For the barrows, a single plank. We need good wood. And for planking and strutting...." De Vries talked quite loudly, making sure men could hear and would know who was in charge.

They moved on.

"Have you wood for cranes?"

"I have oak for cranes."

They were now looking down a twin avenue of red-and-white- painted poles that stretched into the nothingness of the fen.

"This is what the surveyors have established so far. I estimate that about seven tenths of this route is on land of one sort or another, the rest is in water ...."

De Vries in turn was impressed by Warburton's enthusiasm. The activity around them obviously owed much to his drive.

"You must meet the men."

The two men he indicated were the surveyors – the men in fancy breeches that Thomas Fox had seen. They were both young men and appeared to have made a point of distinguishing themselves from the rest of the workforce by cloth and cut. They wore tall crowned, broad brimmed hats with silver buckles at the hat-band, to add to their glory and long overcoats over waistcoat and breeches. The fanciness of their breeches lay in the lace frilling and knee buckles. Seeing Warburton and de Vries approaching, they bent over a brass instrument, putting on a show.

"Mr. De Vries, our surveyors," said Warburton loudly and proudly. "Mr. Friend and Mr. Parker and the machine."

De Vries shook the proffered hands. His glance at the men was perfunctory, his eyes were on the instrument. Parker clutched it lovingly.

"I've never seen one of these. What is it? Tell me how it works."

The surveyors exchanged glances and a slight smile. They would not concede their mysteries lightly.

"It's a circumferentor," said Parker, blue eyed, with blond hair sticking out all around his hat. "A wonderful machine!"

"A fine instrument," said Friend.

"A fine price," said Warburton. "All the way from London."

De Vries extended a hand to touch the gleaming brass table. Parker instinctively clutched it harder. De Vries saw the slight movement, was annoyed rather than amused.

"I think you must let me see it sometime Mr. Parker. It is necessary!"

"Of course, of course." Parker was embarrassed. "Immediately."

"Shall we walk the route?" asked de Vries, changing the subject pointedly and turning from the instrument.

"It's all set out," said Friend, indicating the avenue of red-and-white poles behind them. He waved Parker and de Vries forward, stepping back towards Warburton. Parker folded in the legs of the circumferentor and picking it up carefully, advanced down the route.

"Mr. Warburton," Friend hissed. Warburton, who hardly knew the man, looked at him in some surprise.

"Can we just slow down a bit .... We had some trouble overnight...."

Warburton stopped. Friend was a thin man with a doleful expression and bad teeth. Warburton did not take to him or his clothes.

"What trouble?"

"Our poles were pulled out. The holes stamped flat. Nearly a day's work destroyed."

"Are you sure sir? Could it have been cattle?"

Friend drew close to Warburton. His breath smelled.

"It wasn't cattle, Mr. Warburton."

Warburton fought not to move away. He held his own breath.

"Go on."

"Cattle don't lay our rods together. They were placed in the pentacle of Solomon!"

"Surely not."

Warburton found himself hissing in reply. De Vries and Parker were still advancing and were out of immediate earshot.

"I'm sure."

Friend was emphatic. He was searching in the pocket of his over-coat. He drew out a piece of paper and a pencil made from a piece of graphite wrapped in string. He showed Warburton his drawing.

"You see, a pentacle. They made four, of five poles each."

Warburton's face was like thunder.

"Who did it? Have you any idea?"

"It is a figure sir. It is a piece of geometry. I think it is a joke against us surveyors. But who would have that geometry? Not everyman."

"It's an insult to the Christian faith! It's an outrage Mr. Friend! No sort of joke, sir!"

Friend was taken aback by Warburton's fury. He had seen it as a mischievous prank.

"You've said nothing, of course?"

"Only to you, Mr. Warburton."

"Make certain you say nothing. Nothing to Mr. de Vries. Keep your eyes open. Report to me ... only."

De Vries and Parker had stopped. De Vries was looking back, curious to know what delayed them.

Warburton and Friend joined the others. Warburton ignored the enquiry in their expressions.

"What do you think of the route so far Mr. de Vries?"

De Vries enquired into the use of the instrument and launched into a technical debate with the two surveyors on the probable soil conditions, the gradient and distance from Oxay level to the sea, leaving Warburton to ponder this act of subversion. He had never expected that the enterprise would be trouble-free. Despite his dismissive way with Emms, he was alert to likely resistance. He knew from experience that trouble could fester in the fens, and erupt from nowhere like marsh gas. He decided to put a night watch on the works – armed.

Parker had set the circumferentor up for de Vries, levelling the tripod with the help of a plumb-bob. The instrument had a circular brass plate divided like a mariner's compass upon which a compass rotated on a central pin. These were under a glass cover. Two arms stuck out from this at opposite sides supporting brass sights, each with an aperture and fine wire. De Vries had bent down to sight through these and stare along the route.

"I have never seen one of these before," he said to Parker, "but I imagine you still need chains."

"I'm afraid so."

"And how do you manage in such a wet place?"

"With great difficulty, Mr. de Vries. Our chainmen often have to wade up to their waists. Or take to a boat ...."

De Vries nodded. Parker looked at Friend. The man knew his business.

"And triangulation?"

Friend pointed to the poles, understanding the question.

"You're right, sir, it is very flat. We long for a church tower or a good tree. We have to walk every inch ...."

"An important machine," said de Vries, patting it.

Ezra Dunn and Thomas Fox watched the sun glitter off the circumferentor from the damp security of the reeds.

"That instrument," said Fox, "You see them turning it and pointing it. That sets the route and men go ahead with a long iron chain and they knocks in the poles. And that fellow with the big hat, that must be the Dutchman."

"Damnation to all Dutchmen! And to their Hogen Mogens!"

Ezra spat into the mud.

*

"This Elm Farm is a nice house, but it has been empty for a long time and it is damp!" Cristeen was puffing slightly. She was wiping the inside of a window as she spoke. The wiring of the leaded lights kept catching at the fabric of the cloth and she had to stop to pull away threads. She had rolled her linen sleeves up to her elbows and tied them with strips of the cloth. Outside she could see the cart which had carried Katja, the serving girl, the cook, a manservant and their boxes and bags. She had ridden, although it had been some years since she had last done so. Katja had been offered a horse, but had refused. Katja could ride with reasonable grace but had been too embarrassed in front of strangers.

"Don't make me mama, please!" she had hissed in Dutch. "They'll stare at me."

So she had jolted half a mile in the cart, sitting on a hay filled sack and clinging to the side. She had arrived in a less than elegant condition, her stiff clothes crushed.

"It is strange. It is a wooden house. All wood and beams except the fireplace."

Katja had seen the bedroom that was to be hers. She thought it comfortable. It seemed low after the high corniced ceilings of their house in Holland, but she preferred it and liked the casement windows that were easy to open and easy to look out from. Her view was over a large pond to a row of willows, two fields with cattle and then an expanse of fen beyond.

"I like these beams and diamond panes" she said.

"They will attract cobwebs," came the response from the prosaic Cristeen.

"Cleaning will be a problem. And the floors! All boards, no tiles. And I see there are hardly any candles. We must get on with that right away."

She shot a sideways glance at Katja.

"Are you all right?" Are you homesick? Have you recovered from that cart ride? Smooth your dress again. We must have a mirror as soon as possible so we can at least see ourselves. We don't want these English people to think we are untidy!"

Katja was discomforted by her mother's abundant energy and stream of observations. She smiled to calm her.

"I am in all respects all right, mama!"

"Well, I'm sure you'll settle in. What shall we have for curtains? I have no idea where we will get fabric. I shall have to sit down with Mrs. Warburton ."

Katja stopped listening. She had not wanted to get up that morning, as she could imagine herself back in their red brick townhouse. She had even thought of Jan for security, but that had quickly gone. The servant girl was rattling about in the hearth with a brush and blacklead, swinging the swivel and pot. The manservant entered with his second armful of logs. As with the first, he made a short bow and muttered "Ma'am" to Cristeen before stacking them by the hearth. The sound of horses drew Cristeen's attention. She plucked at Katja's sleeve to draw her to the window. Richard and Sarah Warburton were approaching by the track that led up to the low wall and mounting block in front of the house. In a panic Cristeen tried to untie the strips of cloth at her elbows, failed and thrust her arms out to Katja.

"Quickly! They are all dressed up in their best, and we look terrible ..."

"It doesn't matter mama. They know we have just arrived. They must know we are working." She undid the strips.

"All the same."

Cristeen pulled down her sleeves, patted her dress, patted her hair. The Warburtons had dismounted and soon knocked on the door. The servant girl, who had heard the horses and listened to the flutter of Dutch, was ready and opened it quickly.

"Good day, Beth," said Sarah to the maid. She had paused on the doorstep, waiting for an invitation to cross.

"Come in, come in."

Cristeen's accent increased with her agitation. She beckoned them in. Richard took her hand, made a slight formal bow, advanced on Katja and did the same.

He has come to see Katja, she thought. It is only her second day in this country and already she has a suitor. I can see it in his eyes. What will Jacob say? What do we know about this man? This is not what we want.

"We have come to see what you might need," said Sarah. "Mama asked us to visit you and make a list. I see the cart is unloaded."

She smiled at the older woman, wondering if this half attractive rather pink faced person had taken in what she had said. She had spoken slowly as Mama had advised. The Dutchwoman's clothes looked too heavy for comfort and too good to work in. She looked around the room for something further to say.

"This will make a lovely room, don't you think?" She indicated the parlour. She was annoyed with Richard, who was now surveying them with a slight smile. The plan had been that he should wait outside, not simper at Katja. She had made that plain on the ride over.

*

John Sylham tried to deal with his apprehension through exercise. He decided to go for a tramp round his fields with his two dogs, Jupiter and Jove. Over his shoulder he carried his gun.

His conscious purpose was to inspect the spring crops for progress and at the same time deal with whatever pigeons came his way or any hare that presented itself. Arabella, hearing his noisy preparations, kept out of his way until the door slammed. She hoped he wouldn't be late.

The bright sun had done little for the temperature. Sylham, striding out, breathed the air in snorts. Where he and the dogs passed through the shade of a hedgerow they left puffs of white breath. Sylhams had owned this land, and much more, as he often told himself, for at least four generations. Emms had informed him once that the church records confirmed a much greater lineage but he had never bothered to ask for them. His views of Emms and the Reformed Church were Delphic, permitting considerable licence to the elements of nature. Roaring round his fields with his hat and cloak flapping and snorting off last night's wine was his favoured form of communion. Kicking at clods, he pondered the situation. The Sylham fortunes had been victims of the Civil War. John senior, his father, had been a staunch Royalist. This conviction had had nothing to do with support for the monarch and everything to do with a loathing for Puritan cant. Sylham estates had been forfeit, were still out of Sylham hands, but were being bought back when possible.

Sylham stopped to admire a field of young corn. At this time of the year it was a tender bristle on the land. Long enough to hide a hare in March, they said, and it was. Beyond he could see some of his pasture, and beyond that again, the fen. The fen was the promise. The poor and flooded land would be turned into meadow grazing. Fine silt would grow cabbage and cole. He hummed to himself, set off again, stumbling across headlands.

Finding a particularly large molehill he took delight in kicking it flat, muttering to himself "Fat Toby! Fat Toby!" The dogs investigated the remains with gusto, keen to understand the game. Toby, his brother-in-law was the impending visitor, his chief creditor and object of loathing.

The dogs suddenly took off, racing through the young corn, zig-zagging wildly. Sylham could see the hare's ears and hind legs. He took his gun in his hands, cocked it, broke into a fast walk, trying to anticipate the direction it might take. The dogs yelped in excitement, jinking but skidding on each turn. The hare doubled back on itself, running straight at Sylham, then turning abruptly dashed across his path and through a gate into the next field. Sylham hurried to the opening to take a shot but the dogs were between him and the quarry. He lowered his gun, crossing the pasture by a cow path. The dogs were already out of sight. Beyond the pasture the land was interspersed with sedge lined pools and tussocks of rush. To his surprise and annoyance, two figures were at work, one wielding a spade while the other crouched beside him. Sylham quickened his pace. His approach was soon noticed and when the two men stood up, he was confounded to find William Emms and Peter Dade. Dade had been wielding a spade, while the vicar held a garden trowel and a cloth bag. They had opened up a hole some four feet square and over two feet deep, the black earth from the excavation neatly piled to one side. Casting around for some explanation, Sylham saw that several similar excavations had already been made in various places.

"What's all this, then vicar?" Sylham had difficulty in keeping the irritation out of his voice. "Digging in my land?"

"I'm sorry John, is this your land?"

Emms looked only slightly abashed. Sylham stifled a snort. He doubted very much if Emms was ignorant of the fact. Peter Dade stared fixedly at the ground, choosing silence.

"Digging for buried treasure?"

"Digging for our greatest treasures, greatest!"

Sylham moved forward and looked in the hole.

Emms pointed with his trowel.

"Ah," said Sylham with heavy irony, "I see you have found yourself a good piece of earth. What's it for, vicar? It's too short for a grave!"

Peter Dade made a small noise and smiled at this. Emms was not impressed by such levity. An annoyed expression further soured his face.

"Look just here and tell me what you see."

He was indicating a darkened patch of earth about the size of a dinner plate. Sylham put his gun down carefully by the hedge then looked in the hole. Emms was wearing knee pads and knelt beside it. He pointed again with the trowel. Sylham noticed that the excitement was making his hand tremble.

"It looks like you've found yourself some burnt wood vicar, and there's something like a broken flower pot."

He had not meant to be derogatory, and as soon as he had spoken, he regretted it for Emms straightened up like a rising hound.

"Are you interested in the past, John? '*How much better it is to get wisdom than gold! And to get understanding rather to be chosen than silver.'* Proverbs, chapter sixteen."

"Amen. You have the better of me – I suppose I am interested in the past, but I wouldn't say I'm an educated man..."

"It has nothing to do with education and all to do with observation. Look, observe, think. See this ....."

Emms reached into his cloth bag and produced a small greenish object crusted with earth and a longer smoother object which he held out for Sylham to inspect. Sylham moved closer, not trying to take them from Emms' outstretched hand. Emms drew back slightly, trying not to flinch, for Sylham stank of sour wine. Mid-day, thought Emms, and still reeking. Sylham saw the slight recoil and understood. It was a match for his wife's breakfast greeting. He was ashamed.

"What are they?"

He drew back a suitable distance.

"The small one is some sort of brooch. It has a pin and decoration. The larger one is a spearhead. You can see from the colour that they're bronze."

"Roman." said Sylham. It was the only concept of antiquity he had.

"No!" said Emms. "Much older than Roman."

"What's that?"

"I don't know. British people. Old people. People here long before the Romans came."

"How do you know that?"

"Consider this - why would you make a spear of bronze?"

Emms offered Sylham the spearhead. He took it cautiously, first feeling the weight in his large hand, then trying to examine it.

"I wouldn't make a spear of bronze. It ain't sharp, and how would you sharpen it? It ain't sharp like steel, anyway."

Emms nodded.

"Romans used steel. I've found Roman swords and other things. They rust away. But this is older, John. You would only make it of bronze if you didn't know how to make steel.

Sylham looked hard at Emms, then back at the spearhead. He rubbed his thumb along the edge, pursed his lips, handed it back.

"Maybe. But you know John Warburton don't hold with any of this"

"John Warburton is a Ptolemy to the Christian religion," shouted Emms. Sylham was taken aback by the force of Emms' outburst. His understanding of it was sketchy but the drift was clear. He took a covert look at Emms' angry face.

"It don't do when there's differences in the parish. I say it would be better if it was all peace and …"

"Are you telling me my business!"

"If I am, vicar, I'm sorry. But I suppose I am."

The dogs provided a fortunate interruption by leaping into the trench, sniffing eagerly. Emms let out a cry and kicked, connecting with Jove.

"Out!" roared Sylham. "Smack 'em with your shovel!"

This was directed at Peter Dade. Who tried to oblige but Jupiter, with a derisory squirt of urine on the heap of diggings, was away with his companion, slobbering with glee. Peter Dade saw his opportunity to avoid potential trouble and started to move away. Sylham wasn't going to let him off so easily.

"And you, Peter Dade, what are you doing on my land. Are these all your work?"

Peter Dade stopped.

"Yes sir. I have dug them."

"Leave the lad be," said Emms. "He does the digging but I instruct him."

"But why are you digging here?" Sylham gestured in a sweep around them. "Sedge and water, reed and bog, fish and fowl…"

"The river will come through here. Just where we stand." It was Emms' turn to gesture.

"Will it?"

Sylham was mightily surprised. His grasp of the maps was slight. The precise whereabouts of the new river had always eluded him and he had been too mortified to ask.

"You must know …"

"Not the precise route," Sylham bluffed. He was not sure he wanted the new river right here.

"Well this is the spot. And what we have here is probably a burial ground. A graveyard and of our ancestors, a spot they held dear or held sacred. And we shall be driving the new river cut right through it."

"But these were pagan people, I should think …"

"They were still God's people." Emms pointed to the other excavations. "Look, John, these are graves. Pagan or not, they contain things that were buried with them. They may not have had much, but people that loved them found something to put in. Sometimes there are animal bones – food perhaps. Sometimes there is a piece of jewellery. – I have a comb, a spear, a knife, clay pots, perhaps cooking pots. These were things for the next life. A knife to go hunting, a necklace to wear, pots for a meal. They expected the next life as we expect the next life, and they were God's creatures as we are God's creatures. What's the difference between us all but education?"

Sylham was not a debating man. He looked across the watery land, overpowered by Emms' words and embarrassed by his inability to reply. He avoided Emms' eye and held his peace.

"To know the past is to know the future," Emms continued.

"How do you reckon that?" Sylham blurted, not from any desire to have an answer, but only to fill the silence. Far, far away could be heard the noise of hammers on wood and men's voices at the works.

"This is April. On the fourth of May the swifts will appear. If the weather is bad they may not appear until the ninth. No one knows where they come from – some say they sleep through the winter in the mud at the bottom of ponds. But we know they will appear. Each year. What has been, will be. *'The thing that hath been, it is that which shall be; and that which is done is that which shall be done, and there is no new thing under the sun.'* The first chapter of Ecclesiastes."

"Amen" said Peter Dade.

"As for John Warburton, he says the earth is six thousand years old!"

It was almost a howl. There's despair in the man's voice, thought Sylham, strange for a man who knows so much and has the backing of the Lord.

"Already said that I don't reckon that sort of difference, vicar, it can make it uncomfortable for the congregation …"

Emms looked sharply at Sylham – florid face, yellow hair crammed in his hat, bleary blue eyes – he had not been expecting such straight advice from this source, yet perhaps he was being unperceptive.

"It makes it uncomfortable for me, and it diminishes the word of the Lord. Belittle the messenger and you taint the message."

The two dogs had been sitting impatiently out of the reach of Peter Dade's spade. Jupiter whined with boredom and yawned loudly. Jove got up and took his turn to relieve himself on one of the piles of earth. It was all that Sylham needed.

"Must be on my way vicar, dogs are bored - got a meeting at the house with my brother-in-law. Hoped to find a pigeon or two, or a hare."

He retreated to the hedge and picked up his gun.

"Hope you're going to fill in them holes," he flung at Peter Dade.

"Yes sir."

Sylham nodded.

"And what about these things? What do you intend to do when the river arrives?"

"I shall have to call a meeting about them," said Emms, watching Sylham's face. "A meeting of the parish. That seems to me to be the proper thing."

"If you must," rejoined Sylham. He gave a sharp whistle. The dogs leapt the excavation and careered off into the meadow. This will make trouble he thought, but if it was a cemetery, what were they to do? Warburton must be told, Latimer must be told.

"We can't afford delay. The partners must debate this. It could cost us dear."

"It's my money as well as yours, John."

Sylham grunted. That was true but he reckoned that his particular problems were worse. Swinging his gun onto his shoulder, he set off. Emms watched his retreating figure for a full minute before turning to Peter Dade.

"We'd best get on with this urn."

The two men stepped into the excavation, Emms digging carefully around the exposed base of the pot with his trowel, then placing the soil on the young man's spade. Dade then piled it carefully at the side.

"He don't seem keen on finding out what we've got," he said.

"Science is a means of discovering reality and truth."

"I believe you have taught me that."

"Francis Bacon said it. And he also said that 'antiquities are history defaced or some remnants of history which have casually escaped the shipwreck of time.' And we have the support of Saint Thomas Aquinas." Working away, more and more of the pot protruded from the soil. It was obviously upside down, and broken. "He says that as God is eternal, eternity has no beginning and no end, that eternity is the movement of the heavens and goes on forever."

Crouching, eyes closed, Emms inserted the tip of his trowel under the bottom section and levered. It moved as a whole.

"I think we can lift it, Peter. Get rid of the spade and you take one side in your hands while I take the other …."

Together they eased the bottom of the pot upwards, and then to the side where they laid it down.

"Look!" Emms pointed with a thin finger. "Ash and bone. That is certainly bone!"

"But is it human?"

Emms was triumphant. He lifted out a thin, curved, unmistakeable saucer of human skull. Peter Dade crossed himself.

*

Sylham's dogs knew every scent of the route, every path through bramble and briar that a rabbit might use. Sylham followed, alert for anything that might rise or run. Browned sedge rustled in the field ditch, old growth tumbling, chased by new. As are we all, thought Sylham. The encounter with Emms had made him pensive, or if he was more honest, depressed. Money is the devil and absence of money the very hellfires. It seemed to him that he had always suffered this illness. The drainage must succeed, as he had no other way of raising capital that he had not already tried. More sheep, more wool, more cabbage, more cole, more recovered land. The unworldliness of Emms represented the trouble, yet it was hard to fault the man and his cloth for what he was doing.

He could hear his sheep in the next field and paused to listen to the majors and minors of ewes and lambs. It brought a smile to his face and he breathed in the air, straightened his back and vowed to give no ground or no edge of argument to Toby.

A pair of male mallards sprang in panic from a ditch but he made no attempt to shoot – the females would be nesting nearby. He called the dogs to heel before they could plunge into the water to search for them. Man and dogs turned into the next field, he over and the dogs under a ruinous gate. There he saw his sheep and the unmistakable shape of Clara Hare. She was watching the flight of the ducks but then saw Sylham. Over one muscled arm she dangled a large basket. Turning towards Sylham, she waited for him to approach. He saw that she had been picking dandelion flowers. Her hands were tar-black from the sap and dusted with gold from the pollen. Sylham doffed his hat. Clara was smiling. They had known each other since infancy despite the social barriers of her birth and name. Her smile devastated him, stripping him of his adulthood and taking him back to a fourteen-year-old's summer, a time as long as any year when they would meet to lie together on the river bank. There they threw pebbles at fish and plaited dried reeds to form animals and figures, hers always better than his. He had kissed her. She smelled of crushed grass, her hair of the wood smoke of the forge. She had lain on top of him to kiss him back, soft breasted, laughing at his erection, saying he was a monster and patting it through his trousers. A lost time, after the war, before care, before Arabella. He cleared his throat and spoke as formally as he could.

"Good afternoon Clara. I see that everyone is taking advantage of my land!"

Clara appeared not to understand. She shook her head.

"I've just left our vicar, digging like a mole in my nine acre meadow ..."

Clara nodded. Sylham guessed that she already knew. The two dogs had sat down beside him, suddenly obedient, regarding Clara with silent respect. Sylham was impressed by this far from normal behaviour.

"That's two pretty hares to have crossed your path today, John Sylham, but don't you worry..."

It was Sylham's turn not to understand. He noted as he always noted that this woman had a fine, mellow voice, he noted as he always noted that when she smiled she was still handsome despite her middle years. He noted she still smelled of wood smoke. He had no idea what she meant. She could see this.

"There was a hare that crossed in front of you?"

Sylham nodded.

"And I'm a Hare."

He understood and smiled.

"I shan't cross your path and I shall make it right."

Her eyes never left his. Her appearance was marred by a smear of black over her right eye. Although the weather was mild, it was far from warm, but this appeared not to bother Clara who wore a dark green dress with half sleeves, trimmed with lace at neck and elbows. It was far from new and had obviously been of good quality. Over it she had donned a smith's apron of stained and scorched leather; on her head she had tied a green scarf that framed her dark hair and had topped this with a felt hat. The apron failed to conceal her ample figure. Sylham was uncomfortable with the intimacy in her eyes and the presence of her body. He debated with himself whether he should ask her about her nocturnal wanderings, but knew she would round on him, furious at being followed. Instead, he indicated the basket of yellow dandelion flowers.

"What do you do with them?"

Reading his discomfiture, she laughed slightly, turned a shoulder towards him.

"Best of all wines!"

She held the basket aloft. Sylham did not look, stared at the ground.

"Hope you didn't mind me collecting them, only weeds, only weeds. The most potent of wines on the most potent of days, they do say, St. George's Day. But you would know that," she said slyly, "your saint, patron saint of farmers …."

Sylham had no idea it was St. George's Day. He had to be on his way and clicked his fingers at the dogs. They paid no attention, continuing to watch Clara and the raised basket.

"Do I embarrass you? You want to go?"

"I have to return to the house. I have a visit from by brother-in-law …"

Clara lowered the basket and placed it on the ground. The dogs' heads lowered in unison.

"The rich man," said Clara, "the man who gives you trouble. Kin of your wife."

Sylham was disconcerted but everyone knew her reputation for prying.

"Tell your future, John Sylham, with my friends?"

From under her apron she produced two mice which she dangled by their tails. The dogs sat upright, and shuffled, tongues out. Sylham felt himself colouring with embarrassment. She told fortunes and Lord knows what else went on besides by the light of the fire in the blacksmith's shop.

"No thank you Clara."

He nudged the dogs with his foot, but they remained transfixed by the mice. Clara laughed and clicked her fingers. The pair immediately stood up and turned to Sylham. Clara slipped the mice back with surprising tenderness for a big woman.

"One day …" she said with disarming confidence, then turning to face him she stepped closer to look into his eyes. Sylham blinked back at her, determined not to recoil. Clara for her part could smell the wine on his breath and noted the redness of his eyes. She shook her head slowly.

"What do you think you're 'a doing of John Sylham, when you knows better?" Her voice was gentle. "This new river of yours will drain out the living water from us and fish will be choking and men dying because of it. Never dig up the dead – see what pastor has found!"

Sylham could think of nothing to say. He stepped back, doffed his hat and strode away with ridiculous vigour. He forgot to inspect the lambs until well on his way, and swore at himself for his confusion, and for a job undone. How had she known about the hare? He knew what they said about her.

*

A fire had been lit in the parlour at Elm Farm to help dry the place out and to discover if the chimney smoked. It was burning well enough and the topic was now exhausted. Cristeen was finding the occasion heavy going but Katja appeared to have discovered an extension to her English vocabulary. Perhaps the heat of the fire had added to her glow, thought Cristeen drily, perhaps not. Richard was obviously enchanted with her. It was all too sudden – Cristeen had no idea if she approved or not. She could see from the watchful glances of Sarah Warburton that the girl shared her concern, although in her case it seemed to be tinged with humour. What Jacob would say if he knew of her behaviour didn't bear thinking about. She sighed. The girl had always been a nuisance, was always going to be a nuisance and no change of scene or country was going to put a stop to that. She wondered where Katja inherited it from – not her side of the family, she was sure – they were a long line of sober, respectable burghers. She suspected Jacob's grandfather. He had run away to sea at an early age and ended up in the Spice Islands with a large house filled with exotic women.

"Are you comfortable and warm? Perhaps too warm," she asked.

"It is dying down," said Richard. He picked up a poker and rolled some of the wood aside. "Perhaps Miss de Vries is too warm?"

Katja said nothing, but shook her head vigorously, disturbing locks of hair.

"What do you do in the evenings in Holland, Mrs de Vries? What entertainments?" asked Sarah. Richard was watching Katja.

"We do not have much in Harlingen." She thought of the long winter nights spent with embroidery and lace bobbins while Jacob read from the Bible or other books of instruction. "We read, we play cards on a Saturday and sometimes when Jacob has visitors we play billiards. On Sunday we attend church of course and in the afternoon we may have visitors or Jacob reads from the Bible. Katja sometimes plays the recorder."

"Mama!"

Katja blushed even more furiously.

"You must play it for us," said Richard.

Cristeen exchanged an accidental glance with Sarah. Apparently their thoughts coincided. She tried to sum up the young man before her. She hoped that she could judge him by the same criteria she would use to judge a young man back home. He was handsome in an obvious way, part of which was just his youth. Cristeen liked to imagine young men in their middle age, and in their dotage, necks thickened, bellies heavy, legs thin, features fallen. This young man had a long straight nose which would survive well, brownish hair which probably would not, grey eyes which could easily become watery and a mobile mouth which she could imagine to become wet and crumpled. She thought him rather too well dressed. There were many young men like him among the wealthy families of Harlingen, the children of Dutch prosperity, inheriting a father's business with the minimum of effort while unaccustomed to hard work or discipline. Maybe he was made of more than his appearance promised but she would have to be convinced. She guessed that he thought himself a fine catch in this small patch of Norfolk. A fine fat herring. She wished she had not mentioned the recorder.

"She hasn't brought it with her," she managed, stumbling over the strange English sounds. This immediately sounded churlish. She wondered if Richard had sensed her appraisal.

"We have a virginal," said Richard with more than a hint of triumph," a pretty instrument. Katja must try that."

Sarah contrived a sisterly dig.

"There is not the slightest similarity between a recorder and a keyboard instrument."

"I can teach her," said Richard.

"Providing Katja wants to be taught, and you can only just play …."

She smiled brightly at Cristeen. Richard flushed.

"I can play well enough."

There was anger in his voice, a flash of youthful petulance that Cristeen noted. It had no place in a gentleman of his age and standing. She had heard of this instrument but had never seen one. Rural England seemed to be more advanced that was generally known in Holland. Jacob disliked the recorder. She dreaded to think what he would make of the virginal and the proximity that teaching must involve.

"Are you a director of this canal project?" asked Cristeen, anxious to divert the subject from music. Richard was momentarily baffled by her use of the word canal.

"The drainage, the new river cut?"

Cristeen nodded.

"*Ja. Hoofdsloot*, the main channel."

"I am a director."

Cristeen nodded.

"It is such an important undertaking, I think?"

"It is of vital importance," said Richard. Not just to our family but to many other families around here. You will meet them I'm sure. Perhaps you will attend the next directors' meeting ..."

"Oh no!" she protested, "It is men's business. There is much money involved, I should think? There always is."

Cristeen was aware of an impatient look from Katja. The girl was not pleased to have the subject steered away from the greater intimacies of drawing room entertainment.

"Yes, of course ...."

The lightness of his reply told her that it was not his money, but his father's.

"And you have a direct involvement in the works?" Cristeen enquired.

The question took Richard Warburton by surprise. A look of amusement flitted briefly around Sarah's mouth and eyes, but she quickly suppressed it. Richard was too long silent.

"Well, yes."

Cristeen continued to look at him. Katja shot her mother an imploring look that Cristeen ignored.

"I understand the surveying. Setting out the route, the levels, that sort of thing – though I am learning ...."

Cristeen decided enough was enough for the moment.

"Of course. There is always much to learn."

Richard vowed to be wary of this sharp tongued, beetle-eyed Dutch doll. Like mother, like daughter they said – and yet – this peaches and cream gift was too good to refuse.

"Like lace-making," said Cristeen, injecting her lethal topic, "there is always so much to learn, so many stitches, I think you say, so many patterns, and different in England from in Holland ... Is that not so? .... So much for us to exchange ...."

Sarah's eyes sparkled with admiration.

*

Fat Toby's carriage was parked at the front of the house with two matching horses tied to the hitching post. The dark green vehicle was of an advanced design. The body was suspended by thick leather straps from carved wooden arms providing springing. Sylham, impressed despite himself, tested this by reaching out and pushing. The body rocked smoothly.

Sylham's means of transport was an unsprung wagon that might have evolved from a hay cart.

He took the dogs away from the carriage, but not before Jove had given the wheels a blessing. Feeling better, he led them to the kennels. These decrepit premises were a reminder of the contrast of fortunes between himself and his brother-in-law. There were numerous gaps in the fencing plugged with bits from the hedge – not that the dogs cared, he told himself.

Mrs. Wells, their housekeeper, was standing by the back door, ready for him.

"He's here, been here best part of half an hour. Boots off ..."

Sylham nodded, first handed her his gun then held up one foot after the other as she unlaced his boots, holding on to the door frame as she pulled them off. Mrs. Wells had been part of the household since his youth, before his wife, before fat Toby, before his father's death.

"What's he like? In a good mood?"

She made a disparaging noise, rolling her eyes.

"He's dressed up like a jar of pickled oysters. Brought you some tea and a ham."

She straightened his stock and pushed and pulled at his collar. She was short and her eyesight poor. Her attentions did little to improve matters but Sylham waited patiently. Satisfied, she produced a pair of slippers which he donned.

"Wish me luck!"

*

Arabella and her brother were in good humour when Sylham entered, but he had the instant feeling that his arrival spoiled the occasion. Toby's face betrayed scarcely concealed irritation.

"There you are John. Mrs. Wells said you'd gone out with the dogs. Shooting, she said. Get anything?"

He made no attempt to play the guest but remained propped up by the fireplace, clay pipe in hand. The room was blue with smoke – Arabella was uncomplaining when her brother smoked but when Sylham had the occasional pipe she tutted and threw open windows.

Toby Tolman was round in every part of his body rather than fat. His clothes were generally kept tightly buttoned to modify this fundamental shape, but as Sylham had remarked to Mrs. Wells, you can't disguise turnips in a sack. He was also chubby cheeked, well polished and mellow voiced, a child of Norwich, he had made his money as a draper and it showed.

"Nothing much about – that time of the year. Went to see the sheep and lambs."

"Sheep all right?"

Toby's tone was so disinterested he might as well have coughed.

"I saw wagons on the road, carrying workmen. How are the works going? To plan, I trust."

"Mmm."

"Are you staying overnight?"

Sylham thought this sounded like the polite enquiry of a conscientious host. Evidently his emphasis was wrong, for his wife scowled at him.

"Of course he's staying overnight!" she said with asperity. "And as long as he likes!"

The accident that introduced Arabella to John Sylham had occurred when her brother had been absent in the West Indies, viewing his investments in St. Kitts. Sylham had been attending to the purchase of some lost acres in Norwich and they had both by chance met at his lawyer's dinner table. He had been handsome as a young man, crackling with the vigour that he could still display. Fortune had smiled on him – theirs was a love match and Arabella had persuaded Toby that John Sylham, though a country squire in only a small way was a man of promise and ambition. This promise remained unfulfilled in her eyes and love had turned to irritation, and with childlessness, to disappointed resignation. Toby was an urban man with scant time for farmers or their rustic ways. He had not been surprised that the promise failed to mature. Neither did Sylham's wine.

"Have you come with any particular purpose?"

Sylham tried to deliver the question casually. He hoped but did not believe he had come to see the works. A feeling of doom descended as he awaited a reply. Toby took his time, laying his clay pipe in the fireplace where it immediately fell over and broke.

"John, you know I have."

"I thought you might."

"This is my sixth visit on the subject, you know, and it's painful for me as I'm sure it is for Arabella. Now matters have become pressing."

"Come to my study ..."

Sylham's house had largely been constructed in Tudor times and his study boasted a stone mullioned window. This did much to brighten the gloom of the panelled interior. His library lined one wall, spines reduced to a uniform brown by the sunlight. The centrepiece of the room was a good stone fireplace curved with a flat arch and trefoil panels. Above this hung a portrait of Sylham's father in steel corslet with the long locks and dreaming eyes of a Royalist gentleman. Toby felt he needed a stage and propped himself on the fireplace. Sylham, feeling more comfortable out of sound and sight of Arabella, opened a section of panelling to reveal a cupboard containing a number of bottles and glasses. He extracted a brandy bottle and poured a large one for himself and a smaller one for Toby. He was surprised when Toby took it without demur – he was expecting the customary comments.

"Now, this problem," he said, "I haven't got the money. You know that, and I told you that last time. Every penny is sunk in the works. You knew when I borrowed it that I couldn't pay you back until it was complete and I had a return. You agreed that."

Toby sipped the brandy.

"It wasn't agreed you wouldn't pay the interest. We had a most particular agreement on that point."

Sylham made a face, avoided Toby's accusing look.

"I can't pay the interest sir. I owe my seed merchant five hundred …"

"And your wine merchant!"

"Aye and my wine merchant, sir, and I'm damned if I think that's your business, and I owe my grocer if you want to know, and Arabella owes her dressmaker. I can only just pay the farm hands if you must know!"

Sylham was hot with bluster. Toby was right about the interest. It should be paid each quarter on Toby's seven thousand pound loan. He was in the wrong, caught fair and square and resented it. He must not lose his self-control.

"I do need the money, John, else I wouldn't be asking for it!"

Sylham drew breath, fixed Toby with what he hoped was an intimidating glare.

"There's no good keep blowing your horn sir, the fox has long gone. I can't take it from the Company, it ain't mine, you must know that. When this work is done I stand to have two thousand good acres out of it and I can let that at a pound an acre, annual, which is what I call a solid future. What's so damned pressing about this money anyway?"

His hopes of brow-beating Toby were confounded. Although he had paled, Toby seemed to grow in stature. He resented Sylham's obliqueness.

"I have investments in sugar, sir, and the reason this is so damned pressing is that they ain't doing well. You must not believe that you're the only one who has troubles, sir. The world turns outside Oxay."

To emphasize his point, he drained his brandy glass and put it down on the mantelpiece. Sylham was momentarily baffled. Having tried bluster he had exhausted his negotiation skills. He filled Toby's glass again, then his own.

"Sorry to hear about your investment," he mumbled. "What can go wrong with sugar?"

"Disease, sir. In St. Kitts. They are closing plantations. The place has turned out to be a death trap. Fever."

"Well that's a pickle then," Sylham said. He knew he could never sustain hostility for long. He felt sorry for Toby, despite his instinctive and nurtured dislike.

"An understatement, sir."

"But I can't at the moment pay."

Toby took a swig of brandy, sensing that he was winning the contest.

"As you said to me, sir, it's no use blowing that horn...."

The two men confronted each other in testy silence. Sylham nodded to himself. He saw the futility of the situation.

"Fair enough sir. So what shall I do?"

"I have thought of that."

"Have you?"

There was surprise in Sylham's voice. He had not expected it from Toby, and despite hours of thought himself had come up with nothing.

"You have a number of tenants. I would have thought it was obvious to raise their rents."

"But their rents were set on Lady Day."

"They will all benefit from the drainage. There's nothing to stop you raising them."

"They won't like it."

"Nobody likes paying more, but we need the money. You owe it to Arabella anyhow. Perhaps you could give it some thought?"

"I shall have to."

Sylham mentally ran through his tenants. The proposal would not go down well.

*

Katja crouched behind a clump of blackthorn watching the two men. The bushes were already in flower and she held her nose to prevent herself sneezing. When Richard and Sarah had left, Cristeen had announced her weariness, chased the servant girl and her brush out of the parlour and fallen asleep in a chair in front of the hearth. Katja seized the opportunity to explore the world beyond Elm Farm, putting on her clogs and a heavy coat.

Her wanderings took her towards the river. She was attracted by the sound of digging and a murmur of voices and had crept quietly to her viewpoint. The older man stood over the younger man who was in a hole. He worked carefully, stooping and changing position. She tried to understand what they were doing so carefully. She liked the look of the young man with bare arms, dark hair and eyes and a soft voice. He had taken something from the hole and passed it to the older man, then climbed out. Sensing they might be about to finish, she decided she had better beat a retreat than be caught spying. She started to walk backwards, keeping the blackthorn in the line of sight. This proved to be her undoing, because she tried to retreat too fast, caught a heel against a tussock and fell over. The movement caught Peter's eye and he looked towards her. Katja scrambled upright in confusion to see Peter wave to her. She thought he was smiling. Straightening herself out, she waved back then walked away in the best order she could manage.

"Who was that?" asked Emms, whose eyesight was useless at that distance.

"I should say it was the Dutchman's daughter," said Peter.

Emms merely grunted, examining the piece of skull. Peter Dade watched her reach the other side of the pasture and turn to look back.

Chapter 5

Jacob's first days at the works had progressed well. Working with the surveyors and four workmen they had dug the first of a series of trial pits, exposing the nature of the subsoil. In each instance he had clambered into the pit himself to poke at the visible layers, cleaning up the face of the material and measuring the depth of clay, peat, silty clay and gravel. With each of these recorded in a pocketbook he had retired to one of the timber and canvas huts specially constructed as offices. The only annoyance he suffered from this otherwise comfortable arrangement came from an elderly man with a barrel of tar who had been sent to paint the thing, both wood and canvas, to make it waterproof. De Vries was beginning to understand the local accent.

"Excuse me sir," the man had said, placing an unreliable looking ladder against the plank wall, "but I've got to go up on your roof. Be that all right wi' you?"

"It's all right," replied de Vries, "but be quick."

"I can go away," said the ancient hopefully "and come back."

"No, you get on with it. If it rains I shall be in trouble."

No you don't, thought de Vries. It was the same in Holland. He allowed himself a smile.

"Yessir, Mister de Vries."

So Jacob spent the remainder of the afternoon transcribing the excavation information onto profiles to the slop, slop of a tar brush on canvas overhead. The effect of this fascinated him as the opaque material was blacked out bit by bit.

"Night is falling!" he shouted in good humour to the ancient at one stage.

Misunderstanding him, the man shouted back:-

"'Tis only a cloud Mister de Vries, sun's along behind!"

"Thank you," he had called back, "*'The light of the righteous rejoiceth; the lamp of the wicked shall be put out!'*"

There had been no response other than the slap of brush on canvas. He was beginning to settle in. Wandering the site earlier he had encountered a number of Flemish and Dutch workmen, enquired where they came from, asked where they were staying. He had complimented Warburton on his workforce.

"They seem good men, solid and sober don't you think?"

Warburton had agreed, with the strong mental reservation that he had no idea about their sobriety. Dutchmen had a reputation for drinking. Warburton's day had largely been taken up with meetings. The first of these was with a timber merchant to price and secure the large amount of wood that was needed for planking, strutting, shoring and other purposes. He was accompanied by Edmonson and Turner. Edmonson in particular had an eye for timber and knew how much could be taken from Warburton's own land if it became essential, reminding Warburton of the merits of individual trees. The merchant had already run in deliveries by wherry – the two ships moored offshore – but bigger loads were contemplated including Baltic fir. Wherever possible cut lengths should be brought to site. Although a sawpit was being constructed, the river was too slow to use water power and all cutting would be by hand. The merchant said he knew several ship's masters, and would get competitive prices from cutters for the Baltic trade. Sealing this conversation with a handshake they next met the gangmaster, Hobson, a large fellow with a mangled nose that he poked out as though it was the badge of his profession. His appearance belied his mathematical ability. When discussing wages and rates, his mental arithmetic left the others wallowing behind with pen and paper, while he was always first and right.

"We've settled rates," said Warburton, leaning back to stretch himself from the business of paper and calculation. "Now let's talk rules."

The four men were sitting on benches, the three facing the gangmaster across a scrubbed table. They occupied part of the large covered area used as the men's canteen and wood smoke from the kitchen fire periodically blew their way.

Hobson grinned broadly. He was dressed in a leather jacket with moleskin breeches and calf length boots. These, and his hat sported showy silver buckles and his collar was of excellent lace. Altogether he exuded a precarious kind of prosperity.

"I hope these rules won't be too hard."

"My concern is for the good of the men and for the keeping of law and order," said Warburton. "How many men have you now?"

"Fifty four, not counting the cooks, and there's two on stores, and two at the smith's shop, plus two foremen, sixty."

"What sort of men? Generally."

"Don't have a 'generally'. What sort, all sorts. Men from military service, ploughmen, slodgers, Dutchmen, Scotchmen, Flemings. All sorts."

Warburton nodded.

"I ask, because, as a Christian man, I am keen to see that their spiritual needs are properly catered for. Do you understand? It is a mistake often made to cater for all else but leave a void. That void can be filled with mischief."

Hobson, whatever he had been expecting, was not expecting this. He was momentarily caught with a blank look, before his grin returned. Edmonson and Turner looked quickly at each other, looked at the table.

"Of course," he exclaimed, too heartily, "what had you in mind for these .... spiritual needs?"

"At home I hold prayers three times daily whenever possible. Obviously this cannot always be done, but I expect the men to say prayers once daily at least."

"That should be possible." Hobson did not sound at all certain.

"I hope so, Mr. Hobson. And there will be no drink on this site."

"I should think not, Mr. Warburton."

Warburton turned to point behind him at a row of beer barrels.

"Then these must be removed."

Hobson's grin had been replaced by inscrutable acquiescence.

"Yes, Mr. Warburton."

"No more beer." Warburton turned to Edmonson and then Turner.

"No more beer," said Edmonson.

"The men over there," said Hobson, seeing his chance to divert Warburton from any further severities, "you should meet them sir. They're my two foremen."

The two in question had been standing by, waiting to be summoned, neither talking to the other, ill at ease with this occasion. Warburton nodded and Hobson beckoned vigorously at them to come over, which they did, standing as though on parade. Both wore leather jerkins and coarse cloth trousers. One wore clogs, the other boots. Warburton looked at them with studied care. Hobson got to his feet and walked behind the men so that he could introduce each in turn.

"This is Maddox sir."

Maddox was dark haired and dark eyed. He was tanned to the red-brown hue of the outdoor worker.

"And this is Hellenbuch."

Hellenbuch was the fairer of the two, hair tending to red, grey eyed and scarred across one cheek with a wide red weal. It was obviously a cut. Both men looked fit and tough.

"Say good day to Mr. Warburton."

"Maddox, sir," said the first man, "Good day to you."

He spoke with a strong Lancastrian accent.

"Hellenbuch , sir, good day."

Hellenbuch's Dutch accent was as strong as Maddox's Lancastrian. Having delivered his line he stood like stone.

"Thank you very much, gentlemen," said Warburton. "I am pleased to meet you."

He raised his hands, signifying he was finished. The men turned and left.

"Able men," said Hobson, "They know how to keep men going."

Warburton was impressed by the stern appearance of the two men, it struck a chord with him. Edmonson on the other hand was uneasy, and he decided to find out more about them. He watched their departure thoughtfully.

"So that's Warburton," said Hellenbuch to Maddox when they were out of earshot. "You heard what he said. He says no beer and plenty of prayer! No good for you English!

Maddox stopped.

"Is that so? Maybe you Dutch will have to work to keep warm!"

"What is your meaning?" demanded Hellenbuch.

"Less of the old Dutch gleek!"

Maddox made swigging motions. Hellenbuch cursed and threw an arm in the air angrily; he strode off. Edmonson saw but said nothing. Hobson, noticing Edmonson's interest, caught his eye and gave him a brief insincere smile.

"Is there bad blood between the Dutchmen and the English?" asked Edmonson, watching Hobson's face.

He learned nothing, for apart from a flicker of the eyes his face was blank.

"Not so you'd notice. What there is, is good for work. Makes for competition between gangs, sir, to see who's best, or quickest...."

"Have you a list of workers?"

"I have, sir, but in my writing. You may guess it's not of the best, I'm a simple man, not schooled ...."

"Yes, yes, let me see it anyway."

Warburton was regarding Edmonson curiously, not understanding what this was about, but said nothing. Hobson felt inside his leather jacket and produced a bundle of papers from which he extracted a handwritten list, passing it to Edmonson. It was difficult to decipher Hobson's untidy script and it took Edmonson time. Warburton shifted, tapped the table with growing impatience.

"There's a lot of Dutchmen on your payroll." Edmonson pointed to names. "I make at least twenty men, though I suppose some may be Flemings. How is this, and is it wise?"

"Hellenbuch, sir, he put the word around I believe, collected men he knew. They came because they're accustomed to this sort of work ...."

"That can only be good," said Warburton with a note of irritation in his voice. He thought Edmonson was being unnecessarily pedantic. It would make de Vries' job more amenable to have his countrymen around. He must ask de Vries about the provision of Dutch services.

Edmonson was not to be put off.

"I am just concerned that there is no ill feeling. There is still some difficulty in the minds of ordinary men – hostility even – towards Holland. And this Hellenbuch, what's his background? That scar ...."

"Don't worry about that, sir, he was a military man, a soldier – it's something he picked up in the wars, wounded."

"Not against England."

"Oh no sir, against Spain!"

Edmonson looked hard at Hobson, pursed his lips and nodded. Warburton took this as his cue.

"Have you finished with Mr. Hobson? Can he get on?"

"I have – thank you for your time Mr. Hobson."

"My pleasure, gentlemen, sirs!"

Hobson doffed his hat extravagantly, making the silver buckle flash.

*

Edmonson was involved in the next meeting as well. Warburton had drawn him aside that morning to tell him of the events of the previous night and had asked him for a recommendation for the job of nightwatchman. It had been difficult to find a suitable man from the short list of locals worth considering. The criteria of integrity, honesty and stability were hard enough, but the addition of willingness and availability reduced the choice to a single individual, an aged farrier called Jessup. He was well known to both men for his involvement with their horses and had a reputation for dour patience. As a horse-doctor, he possessed a number of pistols, including some of surprising calibre. Added to this his relationship with his wife made it preferable, if pay were involved, to spend the night in the fen. Warburton had insisted the post was to be a dry one, but Jessup had his own ideas about that. It had never spoiled his work, or at least as he was fond of saying, he had never heard a horse complain. In his youth he had been a fervent supporter of Cromwell, rising to the rank of captain in the field. Although this rankled with Warburton the man had never shown him anything but respect. He was known to be a man who could handle himself despite his age.

"We want complete discretion," Warburton had told him, "the object is to find out who is responsible."

"Am I there to drive 'em away sir, or arrest them or what?"

"In the first place, to find out who it is and to stop them doing damage."

Jessup was grey haired and his blue eyes were surrounded with the white rim of arcus senilis. It gave him a permanently startled expression.

"I shall be armed, and I shall shoot if I must!"

Edmonson thought he detected a certain eagerness.

"You must only shoot if you have to. We don't want a war."

"You must only fire to defend yourself, or to scare away intruders," Warburton emphasized. "You are not to fire *at* anyone unless in self-defence, is that clear?"

"It is, Mr. Warburton."

"There is no reason to suppose there will be any more trouble."

*

De Vries felt the change and glanced outside. He realised that it had fallen quiet as the workmen departed. They had taken with them their horses and oxen and all that he could hear was gulls and the noise of an owl. The sun was dipping low and with the rise of mist from warmed earth, was bathing everything in a golden light. He rearranged the papers that he had spread out on his table, making a pile of his calculations and a pile of drawings. Warburton had called in earlier to see how work was progressing and to remind him that the de Vries family was expected to dinner.

"Time to finish, Mr. De Vries, Jacob."

Warburton sounded awkward at this familiarity, but had decided it was an appropriate moment. De Vries had appreciated it.

"Just finishing up."

"Mountains of calculations?"

"Yes. Now that I have details from the surveyors. I still lack some information ..."

"Well don't overdo it."

"I will finish shortly. When my pens and materials are all out, I like to get to a particular point. I'm sure you are the same."

De Vries gestured to the array of pottery ink pots he had brought with him, the quill pens and penknife, sand and scales. Warburton nodded.

"We have prayers at nine."

"Kind of you ...."

Now he hummed tunelessly to himself and reviewed the day's work. The information from his notebook had been transferred onto a series of cross-sections, neatly drawn in ink and labelled "Normaal profillen". Each was dimensioned to give the depth of the formed cut, the width at the bottom and at the waterline. The existing ground level was shown by a dotted line. He had used els and *voet*, not thinking in feet and inches, and would ask one of the surveyors to carry out the conversions. A description of soil conditions was neatly written on each in Dutch and English – '*Klei* – Clay, *Klei met zand en schelpen* – Clay with sand and shells, *Slappeveen* – wet peat'. He had been surprised by the amount of this, by comparison with what he knew from Zeeland. The "*hoofdoch*t" or main drain profile showed a cut three metres deep with a bottom six metres wide and sides sloping at an incline of one in two. He had pondered these dimensions for a considerable time, making and discarding calculations as they were as much a matter of judgement as of science. He had permitted himself the pleasure of inking-in the main profile in red and filling in the surrounding ground in brown and black, using different hatching for each type of soil. He knew it was embellishment for the sake of it, but enjoyed every stroke of it. He must obtain a boat and take soundings of the Oxay river to establish accurate tide levels, high and low, before finalising dimensions and levels. The key was to maintain a rapid flow which prevented silting without creating speeds that would cause erosion. He had wanted to show the water level in blue ink, but had none and had shown it instead in black, drawing little ripples on its surface.

Reluctantly he told himself he had finished for the day and stood up, closing his notebook. He sanded his drawings to make sure they were dry, shook the sand back into a jar and rolled them up. He carried a leather satchel for papers and materials that had additional straps to accommodate drawing rolls. He put everything away methodically, enjoying the neatness, the correctness of his packing arrangements, the ink pots and pens, rulers and scales. The sun was creating long blue shadows. Satisfied that everything was cleared away, he stepped outside. His horse, which was tethered nearby, was glad to see him and pricked up its ears and snorted. He mounted it, glancing round at the emergence of the infant canal from the clay and sedge.

"I can permit myself to feel a little proud!" he said aloud.

The horse knew its way, which was just as well for the rising mist had reached a man's knee height obscuring the features of the roadway. The elevation of horseback extended his view by a striking amount in this flat landscape. Although accustomed to this in Holland it always gave him pleasure. The horse's lower legs were almost lost from view and he imagined himself floating. Oxay church rose on an island from the mist, its flint tower gilded by the sun, making a hopelessly romantic image. Wallflower grew in the lime mortar, ablaze with yellow and red.

De Vries was troubled by a pang of guilt that he had not yet entered the place or made any arrangements for the spiritual welfare of his countrymen.

"I have to see to the Lord's business," he told his horse in Dutch, tying it to the churchyard gate. "I will only be a moment." The animal snorted and nodded. "So you understand Dutch? Good! We shall get on!"

The age of the place was evident through wear, or rather as de Vries saw it, through the erosion of time which resembled the erosion of tide. The steps down from the porch to the body of the church were saddle-backed with age. The grand tombstones let into the floor of the nave had lost their importance to the feet of ordinary folk. Over the centuries both names and coats of arms had been reduced to shadows in the stone. The windows were mainly of plain glass, the interior whitewashed except for traces of wall painting and a fine timber roof. De Vries thought this was a place his family could worship, where all his countrymen could worship. He must see this

Emms in action. He sat down to pray, prayed for the success of the work, for wife, daughter and dead son Jan.

His devotions were interrupted by a slight but persistent sound, a tinkling, first to one side it seemed and then to the other, as if blown by the wind. At first he tried to exclude it but it intruded and he sat back, looking around the church. He realised it was becoming louder and the source was outside. He stood up, made for the door of the porch and walked outside, curious. The tinkling continued. The direction was difficult to fix and at times the ringing seemed to come from both sides of the church, from beyond in the mist and sedge that pressed up to the churchyard walls. The horse snorted and tossed its head, ears pricked, uneasy. De Vries believed he could see movement amongst the sedge, but the sedge perpetually stirred and it could have only been the wind. One bell, answering bell, one bell, answering bell, faint and sharp, handbells like a fairground huckster. The horse started to stamp and toss his head.

"Who's there?" shouted de Vries.

There was immediate silence. For about a minute he listened to the murmur of the wind, the creaking of stems then one bell, two bells, one bell, answering bell.

"Who's there? Who's there?"

He felt chill, felt both alarmed and annoyed. Whoever it was, was hiding. It was deliberate, malicious. His shout brought silence, no reply. Incongruously a warbler in the sedge broke into loud sweet song. He listened for any stirring but there was only the sibilant rustle of the sedge.

"Is this a game, eh, that you play with me?"

He walked back to the gate, measuring his pace, unhitched the horse and mounted it, glaring showily about him. The tinkling resumed, rattling faster and faster until it rose to a shrill crescendo. De Vries banged his knees into the horse's flanks and the animal pranced off with rolling eyes. They swung into the low sun, which dazzled both horse and rider, contributing to their confusion and making the animal buck before regaining composure. De Vries thought he heard mocking laughter and urged the horse on in the most soothing Dutch he could manage. He was annoyed to find his hands were shaking. In future he would carry his Spanish pistol.

*

As a fatherless boy, William Emms had taken an interest in curious things, wondering at the diversity of nature that could be found down one stretch of cart track or in the muddy confines of a newt-infested pond. His father's death had precipitated it, as though an understanding of these small things could shut out the pain of the greater, incomprehensible world outside, the grief of his mother who had howled without dignity when the body was brought home. A minor clash, of no importance in the Civil War. Men on horses, men hunted down. William Emms had access to his father's books. When he was old enough to know what the words meant, his studies had been zoological, herbal, astronomical, geological and archaeological in that order. These distractions made him a solitary boy and latterly a solitary man and he had never married more from absence of trying than anything else. His thin looks and abstracted wanderings in the countryside compared unfavourably in the hearts of lasses, with the forceful, rude ways of country lads. As the years of promise passed and his companions of youth took themselves heartily to excesses of lust and liquor he had taken to the Church, tutoring himself to success and the Perpetual Curacy of Oxay St. Andrews. For this benefice he owed much to John Warburton for acknowledging their childhood friendship.

Now he hovered between his beloved Journal and his sermon, which should have been equally beloved, but aware that the pull of the first was winning. The remains of his supper of boiled fowl and ham lay on his desk with the end of a loaf and he moved this to a nearby shelf. Opening the leatherbound book he read his last entry to himself, mouthing certain words and nodding at his own conclusions. He picked up his quill and began to write:-

"Today uncovered an urn made of reddish brown pottery. It lies square in the path of the new cut and all the indications point to it being one of several such burials. The pot is impressed with curious designs which seem to have been made with rope or twisted leather before firing round the shoulder and lip. Most exciting of all is the impression of a THUMB and FOREFINGER where the ancient potter picked up the piece to set it out to dry. It makes me feel instantly familiar with the fellow, as though I have watched him make it, although I lack ability to flesh out the scene and circumstances."

He put down his quill to open a drawer in the desk which contained the base of the pot. Laying it on top of the desk, Emms placed his own right thumb and forefinger in two depressions upon it.

"Small hand, old chap," he said to the long dead. He tried to imagine the features of this man but nothing presented itself. He replaced it in the drawer and continued writing:-

"We have today seen into their ritual for burial. Within the urn were the remains of a person consumed by the fire of cremation but leaving such fragments including teeth and part of the skull as to make it simple to identify the remains as human. The larger part of these remains and the urn

I have locked safely in the vestry of St. Andrews against a proper re-burial. I ponder what shall be suitable for a being whose religion is unknown for I am sure that this person is truly ANCIENT and lived and died before Romans and thus before the advent of our LORD. Therein lies the dilemma. Can a Christian burial be given to one who lived and died before His Coming? Is it enough that he was God's creature? That cannot be right, for we are all God's creatures. Insofar as I am equipped for any of this, it would be better if the new river cut were diverted from this spot and disturbance of these remains avoided, except to locate them."

He stared out of his study window to the distant prospect of his church. An untalented thrush sang loudly at the top of his garden yew. The yew was hundreds of years old – a reminder of the briefness of man's span. Emms sighed, overcome with gloom. He imagined the tree overseeing the generations of his parish, seeing the first church replaced by the present, the tower extended, a side aisle added, a porch, windows changing shape with the centuries from round to lancet, from pointed to ogee. The ebb and flow of parish fortunes, the crowding of the graveyard. He returned to his desk.

"I am determined for the sake of the parish that it would be best to divert the river and leave these sites alone. I will address this matter in my sermon but I fear it will be unpopular."

*

De Vries had returned to Elm Farm much later than Cristeen had expected, leaving little time to change for dinner. To hinder things further he found he was still flustered and his fingers betrayed him. Cristeen had to deal with his buttons to prevent further delay. He decided not to tell her of his experience knowing it would alarm her for the rest of the evening. Katja added to the tension by being ready so quickly that she prowled the house, staring out of windows in the general direction of Oxay Hall. The absence of a proper mirror sent Cristeen into a late panic and more valuable time was spent in reassuring her and tugging at creases. They had boarded Warburton's coach in a flurry, causing Cristeen to remark that they would look like chickens. She thought Katja looked too excited.

Warburton's welcome was soothing. Once again the house was brightly lit and Warburton himself answered the door; evidently he had heard the carriage arrive. They were ushered in to the dining table with a minimum of delay that de Vries welcomed. It had been a long day and he had eaten nothing since the magnificent breakfast.

"We cannot keep intruding on your hospitality," he protested as Warburton pulled out chairs.

Warburton shook his head.

"A pleasure. Of course you must eat with us. It will take you days to sort yourselves out ...."

Cristeen made a small curtsy.

"You're very kind."

She nodded to Richard who had advanced on the party and smiled and inclined her head to Sarah, not knowing quite what to do. Ruth took matters in hand. She was seated at the far end of the table, back to window, and now rose, patting the chair to her right.

"You must sit with me, Mrs de Vries, Cristeen, and you, Mr. de Vries shall sit here."

He was ascribed the chair to her left. After the shuffling was over Cristeen noted that Katja faced Richard, perhaps by his design, and while Warburton occupied the other end of the table Sarah Warburton faced a portrait of an ancestor in armour with a feathered hat.

The table had been set with the best pewter, new trenchers and two fine silver candelabra, lit although it was yet a bloody dusk. The sun which had gilded the church had become a fearsome glare, crushed between the horizon and a purple cloud.

"What an evening!" declared Warburton, gesturing to the view. "This weather can't last. We shall have some very seasonal rain at any moment. This drought has greatly hurt the crops."

Everyone turned to look at the dropping sun. The movement was perceptible, measured against distant trees and the church tower.

"Not too much rain I hope," murmured de Vries. "For the works we need dry weather, three hundred and sixty-five days' drought."

Warburton laughed politely.

"You won't get that!"

The last blazing segment disappeared. Warburton took this as the signal to clap his hands, upon which a manservant entered carrying decanters of wine. He stood stiffly by the door.

"And God made two great lights," said Warburton, *"the greater light to rule the day and the lesser light to rule the night. Let us say grace."*

This solemnly performed the manservant walked round the table pouring wine, first for Cristeen, Ruth, Jacob and Richard and was about to pour for Katja when her mother intervened.

"No, my dear, I think it is wine!"

Katja blushed furiously.

"I am so sorry," said Ruth.

Jacob, alert to Katja's discomfort was quick to react.

"It is all right with water. It is all right ...."

The moment was over leaving Cristeen feeling graceless. She had noticed the quick smile exchanged between Richard and Sarah.

"I drink wine with lots of water," declared Sarah completing the rescue.

The meal gathered pace. Boiled beef was followed by roast duck and two pike garnished with butter and capers. De Vries was impressed by the size of the fish.

"There are much bigger than these, Mr. de Vries."

It was Richard who spoke. He had up to now said little. "The fens are famous for fish and eels. It is an essential part of the poor man's diet. Without it they would have too much salt in the diet."

"How is that?" asked Katja. They were the first words she had spoken.

"During winter all they would eat would be salt meat, salt cod, salt herring. They say that too much salt leads to madness, poor bones and all sorts of diseases of the blood."

"There was a time when salt was placed in coffins," said Jacob, "even by Christian people in Holland, because the devil hates salt."

"A brewer throws salt over the mash," added Warburton, "to keep the witches away."

"And you must never spill the salt," said Ruth, "or it will bring ill luck. Then you must throw a pinch over your shoulder – like this!"

She demonstrated, left hand over right shoulder, without using salt.

"You see," said Warburton, "what a thin veneer we all wear. When it rubs thin the superstitions show. We need strong faith more than salt."

"They say we have witches Mr. de Vries," said Richard, watching Katja.

Katja gazed at him.

"Witches are allowed now, in England. I think Oxay has more than its share!"

"What nonsense!" protested Ruth. "You will alarm our guests! He likes to talk in that fashion," she explained.

Richard was not to be deterred.

"That's not all. We have families who transform themselves into eels and slide into the river – eels that can never be caught ...."

"Who on earth told you that? What stories!" Ruth was embarrassed. Her head bobbed, turning from Jacob, to Richard and back again.

"Old Felix told me." There was mischief in Richard's eyes.

Katja stared at her hands, knowing this performance was for her. Her heart was thumping.

"Old Felix says he has seen them do it, they do it at will, witches and wizards and poachers and fowlers ...."

He picked an apple from a bowl, threw it from one hand to the other, catching it.

"That's why Felix can never catch them!"

Sarah laughed, and even Warburton snorted. Ruth explained to Jacob and to Cristeen.

"Felix is an old man, he is one of our gamekeepers."

"But not a very good one," Richard added, "Or maybe he's a poacher himself. Or is he a hare?"

"His name is Hare," Ruth explained, commentator on his whimsy.

"Whose sister is an ancient Hare, and she is, they all agree, a proper witch. Built like Lucifer and black as soot ...."

"That's enough," interrupted Warburton, feeling he had gone too far. "We're a godly people Jacob, whatever this young man says."

"I know that." De Vries tried an indulgent smile. "And you have a nice church."

The church tower had melted into the darkness of the night but every tinkle of glassware provided him with a reminder of his experience.

"We passed it this morning so I thought I would pay it a visit on my way from the works. Very old. A fine roof."

"My ancestors are buried there," said Warburton. "Under the floor of the aisle. You may have seen them."

"I'm afraid not. The stones are very worn ...."

"I will show you. There is even one brass. An ancestor fought in the Crusades .... I can show you where Cromwell's damned steel plated men shot holes in the ceiling, shot at the roof paintings. Then they hacked off the pew ends with their swords, Jacob, because they were carved with animals and faces and angels, in order to make it all more holy! No need to do that!"

Night had squeezed the last bloody drop of light from the horizon. The manservant was collecting plates.

"But these problems are past," said Warburton. The problem now is our parson!"

"William Emms," said Richard to Katja, "a lean man, and we know what Shakespeare has to say of lean men."

"I do not," said Katja, flustered, "I have not read Shakespeare."

"Then I must read him to you."

Warburton gave Richard a sour glance. It was evident that Warburton found this a live and troubling matter.

"Mr. Emms digs for things, Jacob. He was always a curious sort of boy."

The remains of the previous course was being replaced with currant puddings, syllabub and bowls of nuts.

"He's a partner in the Oxay Drainage, fully paid up. But now he is digging in front of the cut."

De Vries was baffled.

"I don't understand. Why is he digging?"

"Archaeology, Jacob. He collects old things, coins and old boots and broken pots and from those bits and pieces he creates his own universe and challenges the word of God."

Warburton's voice had taken on a new edge and his face was a stern mask. Where he was seated the candlelight added to his severity by casting emphatic shadows.

"But he is a pastor, a man of God." De Vries was surprised. "How can this be?"

Ruth had a sense of dread, knowing the inevitability of the topic and the inevitability of her husband's rage. It was eating at him like an incurable disease, destroying his pleasure in a hundred ways. A silence had fallen over the table, no-one inclined to break it, no-one chewing. She longed to leave, to interrupt, to install Sarah at the keys of the virginal but did not dare. Warburton drank some wine, pursued his theme.

"He does it like this – if you or I found something in the ground – ploughing or cleaning out a ditch, which I have, we would think of it as a curiosity. We would wash it, stand it on the dresser, show it to our friends, and that's an end of it. Perhaps I don't have an enquiring mind. But Emms searches for things, and searches to prove his purpose. He was always like that. I have a confession to make, Jacob, I am responsible for his advancement to this living, as we call it. We were at school together."

Jacob de Vries nodded.

"Even then he was an awkward fellow, clothes hanging off him, always muddy, always carrying something. Clever, knew the Latin names of plants. Seemed the right sort of studious man to look after Oxay. Even then he was digging and dug up some Roman axes which he showed to me – greenish things, made of bronze I should say. That seems to have been the start of it."

"No-one is eating their puddings," interjected Ruth, "or the nuts."

Food was transferred to plates, but Warburton was not to be deflected by such unsubtleties.

"He says these things are of immense age, older than the Romans, and from what I gather, he says they are older than Creation itself!"

Warburton put down his knife with a clatter and looked challengingly round the table. His audience either gazed at him or their plates. De Vries knew he was expected to respond but was fearful of too much involvement.

"How can this be?" he repeated, aware of the inadequacy of his contribution.

Richard Warburton heaved an audible sigh.

"Father believes that the Lord created the universe and everything in it four thousand four hundred years before Christ, Mr. de Vries."

"There is no doubt of it Richard!"

Warburton was angry at the patronage in Richard's tone.

"I and many others accept that timescale. It has been arrived at by scientific analysis of the Old Testament by some of the best minds .... the history of the world is all contained within six periods, Adam to Noah, Noah to Abraham, Abraham to David, David to the captivity in Babylon, the captivity to the coming of Christ, the present time from that coming, which is the sixth period now in progress and that leaves the seventh, God's chosen number seven for the time to come when the righteous ascend to Heaven. For did the Lord not create all things in six days, *'and God blessed the seventh day and sanctified it.'*"

In the silence that followed Jacob attempted to assess Warburton. He had drunk wine but there was no sign that he had drunk too much. Nonetheless he appeared to be a man obsessed who was not fully in control of himself. While Jacob's own Lutheran faith adhered strongly to the word of God, it did not extend to fixing the date of Creation nor to the six periods of the world thereafter. He felt considerable concern for his employer and for the effect this friction with a pastor might have upon the project. His feelings of concern extended to Katja. He noted Richard's close attention. Trouble there too, he told himself. The girl was too forward and too headstrong. He knew that Cristeen kept things from him because she thought it was better that way. Cristeen thought he knew nothing about the boy Lucas and their visits to the polder, but he had seen them kissing in summer twilight when she should have been in her room. He wondered, watching her fair face in the candlelight, if she was still a virgin. Katja by chance caught his eye and immediately looked away. What had she seen in his look of inquiry?

"Angels passing," said Richard.

Seeing the blank looks this produced from the de Vries family, he was obliged to explain.

"We say that when a sudden silence falls ...."

Heavy rain hit the windows, materialising from nowhere, without preliminaries or stealth. Warburton rose, went to the windows and looked out.

"Just as I said, just as I said."

The talk turned to crops, what was grown in England and what was grown in Holland. The topic preoccupied the men, allowing Ruth to relax and watch. Maintaining a pretence of listening by nodding, she turned her attention to Cristeen and Katja. Her hopes for insights into cosmopolitan sophistication were unlikely to mature, she thought, disappointed that Cristeen was as lumpen as she appeared. She watched Katja pick up an apple and attempt to peel it. She watched Richard take it from her plate, peel it and pass it back, still discussing the merits of cabbages over cole-seed. Although a pretty girl she lacked animation, having too much of her mother's stolidness. Gilded by youth, she dazzled but Ruth judged that the sun would go out of her in four or five years. She was not the one for Richard.

Later, dinner over, they had settled down to the virginal. Sarah had begun to play when the manservant tapped at the door and entered.

"Mr. Sylham, to see you sir."

"At this time of night? In the rain?"

"Yes, Mr. Warburton."

John Sylham stood in the hallway, clothes dripping.

"I got caught in that one!" he said, "Only showers."

"Come in. What brings you here?"

The two men walked to Warburton's study off the hall. Sylham loosened his clothing but made no effort to take off his riding cloak. Warburton held out his hands towards it. Sylham shook his head.

"I don't suppose I shall stop long. Oh confound it, it's dripping on your floor, I'll take it off!"

He slipped off the cloak, handed it to Warburton who handed it to the servant. There were puddles on the polished oak boards.

"I couldn't make up my mind if I should bother you or not then in the end I thought I should. I have a concern about Emms."

Warburton let out a groan.

"We were talking about him! He haunts me!"

"I came upon him this afternoon on my land. He was digging."

Warburton snorted, gritted his teeth and managed a sardonic laugh.

"Digging! The man is a mole, blind as a mole! Earthworm!"

"Didn't ask permission. Him and that young Peter Dade."

"I shall see to him! He'll be looking for employ!"

Sylham shrugged noncommittally.

"I wouldn't blame him. Emms was in charge. He says he's found a burial ground, right in my bottom pasture – where the new cut is to go. He gave me all his 'older than Roman' stuff, and Ptolemy."

Warburton stared at him.

"Ptolemy the Greek astronomer. I don't reckon as I knew what he was about, but he was talking of holding a parish meeting. So I thought I'd better let you know. We don't need delays."

Warburton began to pace around Sylham.

"What do you think he means by it? By a burial ground? What does it amount to? We must tell Latimer. Tell the other partners."

"Seems strange behaviour to me for a partner."

"But where does it take us? A meeting of the parish to do what? Is it a burial ground?"

Sylham gave a dry laugh.

"How should I know! Looked like a flowerpot to me and I told him so, and he showed me a green spearhead and some sort of pin he had, out of a cloth bag. Much older than Roman he said, you know him, he had a wild and strange look, quoting things at me ...... I'm not a well-read man ...."

"I'll have a word with Latimer. We don't want to stir things up. Don't muddy the pond."

"Can he be removed as a director?"

"Would that do any good? No. Can he be removed as our parson? Should he be removed as our parson?"

"This is all too much for me John. I'll be on my way. These are all your sort of matters. I've done my duty."

"You have."

Warburton showed Sylham to the door. He had been right about the showers. The heavy rain had stopped as abruptly as it had begun and a clear half moon made leaves and puddles sparkle. Sylham's horse, hitched by the door whinnied softly to its master.

"I've told de Vries about him. He has to know."

Sylham nodded. He had wanted to consult Warburton about rents but thought this was not the time. The manservant appeared with the cloak. He had not had time to hang it up. Sylham put it on, tugging at the wet material. He raised his hand in farewell, mounted his horse and was gone.

Warburton stared after him into the night. He could hear his daughter playing the virginal and stepped forward a few paces so that he could look back at the house and listen to the music from the upper room. The air smelled sweet. A pair of owls hooted and yelped in an adjoining field, quartering it in the moonlight. This was how it should be. Emms must not be allowed to disturb the order of things.

*

Warburton was a man who liked order and loved his land with a passion that would have surprised all but his wife and his intimates such as John Sylham. His father had instilled in him a sense of the correctness of social order, of discipline in manners, in the conduct of daily affairs, in obedience of the Lord. One night, just such a night, he had been ten and his mother Jane had been sewing by that same window in the upper room. He had been sitting beside her with sister Sarah. They had all three spent the day down by the mouth of that same Oxay river that he now sought to twin with a new, straight sibling. It had been an outing in troubled times, and although there were no reports of troops of any sort in the neighbourhood, they were accompanied by an old, armed retainer called Walter. It was doubtful if militia would have stopped a woman and children but Walter's blunderbuss was a formidable piece of reassurance. They had been rowed by Walter for a time in a small, flat boat, a duck punt that Walter knew was there. Jane asked no questions, but John saw the amusement in her eyes when the old man suggested the trip and slid the boat from concealment in the rushes. They had slid noiselessly through the secret ways of the fen, Jane at once enchanted and anxious they should not be lost.

"I knows my way back, madam," Walter would repeat calmly. They had stopped in a widened pool. The rush walls stood straight and dense around them and within this arena dragonflies danced. The old man must have known they were there for he shipped his oars and they watched, pointing out to each other the jewelled colours, the blues and turquoises, the yellow and black, the brown and red darters, the fragile demoiselles that shed their skins. John had seen and pointed out the monster pike that lay to one side of their enclosure. Dark as the water on its top, he had seen the tell-tale flickering of its side fins. Otherwise it lay like a submerged log.

"That boy of yours has the eyes of a real fenman!" Walter had declared, and John had felt real pride at such praise from old Walter. They were still sitting there when they heard the chink of horses' bridles and thump of hoofs on turf. Walter held up a hand. No one moved.

It was the sound of several horsemen, moving at a steady trot. They had sat motionless in the small craft for many minutes before Walter whispered that it sounded safe to him and paddled back the way they had come using one oar. They all knew it must have been troopers, but whose was anyone's guess. They had returned to the house surreptitiously through their own fields, Walter stopping their wagon at intervals to stand up on the stall board and listen. Warburton had never forgotten the sudden feeling of menace that hung in familiar fields. Far away they had heard shots, but men shot ducks and geese and it was not remarkable. They had clattered into Oxay Hall and slammed the thick front door.

That evening, by the window, his mother had been talking to them both quietly as she tried to before they were put to bed. She had seen the flash of moonlight on armour before she heard the horse. Her reaction was to clutch both children and watch. For trembling minutes she clung to them until fear gave way to delight.

"It's your father!"

Two men dismounted, wearing the breastplates and helmets of Parliamentary troopers, Richard Warburton and Robert Turner, his estate manager. Pandemonium followed with doors flung open, candles and lanterns lit, fires started although they were completely unnecessary. His mother was kissing his father and crying at the same time and he was being patted on the head and thumped on the back by alternate blows like some old dog.

"I can't stay. I have a troop of men. We are moving North. I can only call in. Robert said he would come with me, to see you were all well."

Robert stooped and took Jane's hand. Jane was pleased to see him. The two were inseparable. They would look after each other.

"We heard troopers this morning .... are there any more ....?"

"That would be us."

"What are you doing here?"

John saw his father's face close down at his mother's question. He looked round the room, avoided her eyes.

"We had business."

"What sort of business?"

"Army business."

Jane's heart was racing. She knew it was army business, Parliamentary business, violent business. She hated every aspect of this civil war, wanted to keep it at bay from her village, her house, her family.

"It will do you no good to know," he said, "It had to be done."

To the boy his father was as dazzling as the angel Gabriel. His short hair, gleaming cuirass, swordbelt and sword, visored helmet, shouted of a biblical image of the radiance of the Lord. The boy reached out to touch his father to see if he was real.

"Where are you going? Will I see you soon?"

The father ignored the son's request because he had no answer for it. A small act of cowardice. As the two men were about to leave his father had held his mother but her head was turned away, distraught. They thought they were out of the hearing of long ears but he had heard him say:-

"We had no choice. Emms and Hare."

Then they had stood on the grass where he now stood muttering about Prince Rupert and the Eastern Association, laughing without humour. Owls had been hooting. Moonlight flashed on the armoured backs of the men as they retreated.

*

Warburton took a deep breath of the sweet night air. He considered he had paid all his debt to William Emms. It had now to be counted as the past. Sarah still played the virginal. He heard Richard laugh. He went indoors.

*

People had walked to the big thatched barn between the showers and through the showers, bringing with them excitement and the same sweet smell of spring-into-summer rain that Warburton had been admiring – the resurrection perfume of an unfolding year. To this was added the animal smells of trousers and skirts wet at the hem, leggings splashed with mud, wet dogs, wet cloaks. The barn was a huge looming shape clad in tarred clapboard. It had been there for as long as anyone knew, perhaps as long as the church and had eased itself with the years into a posture of comfort. Doors and shutters had been flung back to admit moonlight. This fell like slabs on the floor, overwhelming the glow of candles and lanterns.

"How's it look then?"

People were still arriving, shuffling around for a perch in the cavernous interior, but Harriet Dunn's broad accent and strong voice stopped them. She attracted a small gathering around her, delighted to see Ezra Dunn with a dress stretched in front of him. Harriet held one arm of it while Bess Fox held the other so that it was stretched taut. Ezra's head stuck over the frilled collar like an Aunt Sally. His gaitered legs projected below the hem. Someone made a coarse remark provoking laughter, but behind the laughter there was whispering and concern. Men in women's clothes had a significance in the fens as the eerie and disconcerting garb of resistance, bloodshed and fire.

Ezra pulled away from the women, protesting.

"I ain't wearing that!"

Yet they knew he would, and the other men would, with masks of knitted wool or leather, as they had in ancient wars and wars just passed.

Ezra escaped to join his father on a seat made from a plank between two barrels.

"She be enjoying herself," observed Ecclesiastes, smoking a clay pipe.

"She be enjoying herself!" echoed Ezra huffily, but roared with laughter as John Lambert underwent a similar indignity. The dresses were much too small. The women would have to split the backs and patch in new material so that they hung loose and for the men to be able to run in them.

"What a vision of loveliness!" Ezra shouted at John Lambert. Lambert was undergoing a similar fitting. He waved two fingers at Ezra.

The main doors to the barn, high enough to admit a hay wain were propped ajar and guarded by Walter Clarke, who had been picked amongst other reasons, because he was an old army man and knew almost everyone. Walter was dressed in the remnants of a Roundhead uniform with a leather bandolier and a pistol stuck in his belt. The pistol was a reminder that this was not a game. He had positioned two trestles and a pole at the entrance so that each visitor must stop and duck under it. He took his job seriously, scrutinising everyone by the light of a lantern, nodding sternly, waving them on. He was now a man of many parts, fisherman, eel catcher, smuggler, pig killer, hedger and ditcher.

His fourteen year old boy posted in a hedgerow a quarter of a mile away acted as lookout.

Thomas Fox, bent as a wish-bone, shuffled up to Ecclesiastes.

"I reckon you should make a start."

Ecclesiastes heaved himself upright from a sack of grain. He had been smoking and with one move stuffed his forefinger in his clay pipe to extinguish it and thrust it in his pocket.

"A time to keep silent and a time to speak as the good Book says."

He made his way to a central table that had been set up with a lantern and chairs. He sat down, an action taking time and care and sufficient to induce a general settling and shushing. He coughed a few times to speed things along. From his central position he reckoned there were over sixty in the building, men women and children.

"Good evening friends," he began. "I know most of you and you know me. Please be seated if you can and please be quiet and speak in turn. Praise ye the Lord!"

Back came a ragged chorus. Disturbed by the noise a pair of bats flittered between the trusses, passed up and down, passed out the doorway watched by all.

"We have it all to ourselves!" said Ecclesiastes to sparse laughter. "Because of the importance of events I have invited friends from other places. Some of them you may know, some you may not. I will be asking them to stand up and make themselves known. I ask you all to take a good look at each other so that friends know friends. Day or night. As you know, the work has begun."

Ecclesiastes had a good voice when he got into his stride. It smacked of sermonising but it held their attention.

"These are serious times. What are they digging? They're digging a new river, and new dykes, draining the graffs and shutting off washlands, meddling with things that ain't theirs and they know nothing about. It all looks to start easy but that cut will drain Oxay Fen, all of Oxay Fen and what you see now as water they see as pasture. Where we now catches eel and pike and where we has plentiful fowl, they see as cabbages and cows and believe you me it will be *their* cabbages and cows, not our'n. So by this means, what was ours will be transformed by this digging into theirs. What has fed us these centuries since time began will have gone! They say we've got webbed feet. They say we've got scales on our backs. Maybe we have but we'll show 'em you can't skin an eel by the tail. We didn't ask for this and we ain't been consulted and we must put a stop to it. We have friends here from Hammett and Walder and Eriswell – stand up please gentlemen so's we all can see you!"

He paused, gestured upwards with both hands. Men stood up, looking awkward, not knowing whether to turn to Ecclesiastes or nod to the assembly. Ecclesiastes introduced them again by village. In turn they nodded, held up their hands. They had come respectably dressed for this occasion, showing Oxay that they knew how to do things in Hammett and Walder and Eriswell and Black Carr and owned a best coat and good boots and a decent pair of breeches. They sat down as nimbly as possible after each introduction.

"The purpose of this meeting," said Ecclesiastes, "is to organise ourselves and make a plan to stop the work."

This produced a silence. Neighbour looked at neighbour, some sharing a flick of the eyes, a pursing of the lips.

"How do you propose to do that?" asked a young man. His tone was challenging. "I reckon this is a serious affair, and if we reckon to stop the work, they'll reckon to bring in the Sheriff and the Sheriff's men. They ain't going to let us do a thing like that and sit on their hands."

Jack Lamb spoke his mind and he commanded respect. He was a brickmaker and charcoal burner and farm labourer, church going and tough.

"Are we planning to take them all on? The bosses and the workmen? Don't get me wrong, I want rid of the thing as much as you do, but what we start here can end with troopers and muskets."

Ezra Dunn jumped to his feet before Ecclesiastes could reply.

"We shall wear them down, Jack. We shall cost them dear, and that is what will stop it. Time is money and we have time. What they put up, we shall take down. We shall scare 'em. Tricks, Jack, and surprises. Masks and frights and all sort of devilment. They won't like being here with bogs and frogs and Captain Flood! And Masters shall have sickness in their cattle. We shall see the Mynheer off!"

"They have no right to go through burial ground. They should leave old bones to rest."

The voice was Peter Dade's. He stepped forward into the lantern light, looking pale and nervous. Another voice rang out from the recesses of the barn.

"Is that Peter Dade speaking? I thought we had Warburton for a moment!"

The insult from the dark brought a stunned silence. Dade turned in the direction of the voice. He knew who it was.

"Warburton pays me, Peter Simms, he don't own me."

He advanced further, stood alongside Ezra. Ezra avoided his eyes. They had not confronted each other since the meeting in the mud. Nothing would be said of that adventure.

"Up on the edge of Sylham's pasture, just by Carter's Graff in the fen there is a burial ground. Pastor and me were digging it. We found an old pot, and that pot contained bone and ash and a human skull."

Peter Dade delivered this news in a quiet voice. He heard the intake of breath from the gathering, saw the movements of men and women who crossed themselves.

"You mostly know Carter's Graff. It's a lonely spot, a place with a powerful mood. It belongs to the old people, that's what I say, and we have no right to put a river through it."

"If you go up there at night," said a shrivelled old man, catching the mood, "you can see the lights. Jack o' lantern on his rounds. You know what they say ...."

"I'm more concerned about how the Masters treat us," interrupted Jack Lamb. "Ecclesiastes is right. We don't exist so far as they are concerned and they steal what they want from us. It's our water and our fen and our pike and they just take it, and it's theirs. But what I say to you all is that you must ask yourself if you are ready to see this fight through. It'll likely end in blood."

"*'To everything there is a season'*," said Ecclesiastes, "*'and a time to every purpose under the sun'*."

"And a time to do something!"

No one had seen Clara arrive, but when she pushed forward a space materialised around her so that she made a sort of progress. On her head she wore a flowered bonnet, unsuitable for the evening, that framed her face and was secured under her chin with a ribbon. Over her body she wore a long smith's apron, fastened with straps that passed round naked shoulders and buckled under her armpits. From what could be seen in the moonlight, she wore a skirt, but that and the heavy apron appeared to be all. She smelled of smoke and scorching. Clara advanced on the table and standing beside Peter Dade, turned to face the body of the barn.

"Last time we met, Ezra," she said, addressing the roof of the cavernous building, "I said there were places that were best left alone. But what do we have? We have two men with frills in their breeches and a brass machine from London!"

This provoked some laughter, some nodding.

"They lay out chains and pins and stick in red-and-white poles for their brass machine, in avenues. You must have seen them, some of you. Red-and-white poles where the river is to go. And the Mynheer with the big hat strides up and down with Warburton between those poles as if it is all done! As if by putting their poles in the ground it is bound to happen. It is part of their magic!" She paused, took breath. "They make you believe. Those poles, you would think the river is bound to follow, to go where they go."

She made a charade of aiming and firing a bow and arrow, watching it fly and fall. There was absolute silence.

"But where they go takes them through the graves of the old people and I am telling you, Jack Lamb, that they must be stopped. What do you think will happen if they disturb the old people?"

"I'm a God-fearing Christian!" shouted Jack Lamb, "And I care nothing about your 'old people'."

"Then you should," said Clara quietly. "It were best for you ...."

"I care more about Sheriff's muskets."

"We shall vote on it!" cried Ecclesiastes, anxious to keep the peace. "And we should hear from our friends who have come here tonight."

"While you be voting, I be doing," declared Clara, addressing the moonlight beyond the doorway. "I'll catch the moon-drop and make my own potions!"

"We need everyone here!" Ecclesiastes appealed, but she was gone as abruptly as she had arrived.

*

The way Jessup the farrier was to tell it, he was attacked by a half-naked female water goblin, a Puck of fiendish power impervious to his bullet. He had been sitting in the hut allocated to him, savouring his brandy and listening to the sounds of the night. The door was shut. Earlier he had stood vigilantly outside the door, changing later to a position against the post, then sitting within the door in a progressive retreat from the night air and vapours. He had a belief in the malignancy of these and preferred to be tuned to the noises of the night. The construction of his hut had been hurried and the timber used was mostly scantlings, still in bark. These fitted poorly admitting the moonlight through numerous chinks. He had managed to bring the forbidden liquor in a leather bottle strapped to his chest. This had its own leather cup and he made steady use of the warming liquid.

The door opened outwards and was fitted with a simple catch. The sudden crash at it made him lurch to his feet tipping brandy over himself. His heart was pounding.

"Who's that!" he shouted in his piping voice, aware that it crackled with alarm.

He stooped cautiously, dropping the cup and feeling for his pistol. It was somewhere on the floor beside his chair. Before his fingers could locate it there was a massive series of crashes falling bang, bang, bang in quick succession. Jessup realised it was hammering and with sudden comprehension flung himself at the door. It should have burst outwards. Instead he bruised his shoulder and dropped to the floor. Outside he heard a sound that he was to describe as a sort of snuffling, half human half animal, and from his prone position looked through a knothole. There, cavorting for him in the moonlight was a grimalkin with (he said) breasts as big as turnips, brandishing an axe. Patting the floor he found the pistol and with thrashing heart discharged it wildly at the door. The explosion was deafening. When the smoke had finally cleared he saw that the pistol ball had passed right through. He looked cautiously through the bullet hole. There was nothing there. He was wholly drunk and half mad when they unnailed him in the morning. It was Hellenbuch assessing the repairs next day who nudged his foreman and motioned with his eyes to the pentacle scratched in the clay at the door. He ground it under his heel.

*

De Vries had had a hole dug. His manner with the men was brusque to the point of rudeness. Jessup's tale had been passed on by word of mouth from man to man becoming more lurid with each telling and de Vries was determined that the episode should get no furtherance. The hole was a yard square and two yards deep and he had hovered over the men while they dug it and placed a ladder in it for his inspection. He had asked Maddox to do it, without telling Edmonson and two of Maddox's men stood beside the heap of spoil, spades in hand, waiting for further directions. De Vries took off his hat and handed it to one of them.

"Give me your spade," he said tersely.

"It's very wet sir," said the man he addressed, "you had better be careful of collapse."

"I think I can manage." De Vries' tone was scathing. He was handed the spade and descended the ladder awkwardly, holding on with one hand. At the bottom his head was below ground level. The two workmen exchanged a puzzled look. The hat-bearer shrugged – it had taken them most of the day to dig it. They heard de Vries digging.

"Take the ladder out!" he called. "I can't work with it in."

The men removed it. In the poor light de Vries peered first at the walls of the hole. Taking a small knife from his pocket he scraped at the walls here and there, having just enough room to bend. He was standing in water. The men above heard him puffing and jabbing away with the spade.

Edmonson knew the hole had been dug although he had not been told. He had followed what was happening, and unable to resist any longer, suppressed a smile and walked to the edge of the hole. "All well, Mr. de Vries?"

De Vries' head shot up in surprise. The surprise was quickly mastered.

"Checking ground conditions, Mr. Edmonson."

"Very good." He made no attempt to move.

"Ladder!" called de Vries, and was soon out of the hole. He donned his hat puffing slightly.

"All well?" enquired Edmonson.

"As expected," said de Vries firmly.

Edmonson nodded and went on his way pondering this behaviour.

De Vries returned to his office, muttering to himself in Dutch;

"Peat, sand, silt, clay, more wet peat. No gravel. Peat under clay." When he reached the office he wrote it in his notebook, drawing the strata in section.

Chapter 6

"He's called a Parish Meeting!"

Walter Tyson had been told about it by his wife, who had in turn been told about it by one of her maids. He had immediately taken to horse and ridden over to Warburton. It was not like Tyson to be flustered. It was said of him rather unkindly that if a horse kicked him today he would notice it tomorrow, but this news had certainly raised his colour and the ride had brought out a sweat. Now the two men stood in Warburton's study, a small room off the hall where the Partners had met.

"Where?" asked Warburton. "Sylham said he might."

"In the church. What right has he to do this?"

"Well I suppose that since he's our vicar he can do what he pleases. Depending upon what he intends to say."

"He intends to discuss the route of the cut. That's what my wife was told."

Three days had passed since the episode of the nightwatchman – three days of peace and quiet, blessed with good weather.

"We don't want this Walter. This is a difficult situation. I don't know whether we should treat him as a Partner or a vicar."

"Either way he's making mischief."

"Are we sure? Taking the best view of things, he's doing his job."

"How can this be his job? This business about a burial ground has nothing to do with his duties, pastoral or otherwise. There's enough mischief in our water rats without the support of Emms."

"We have to decide whether we go or not. If we do, we shall have to sit quiet and listen.

Tyson grunted.

"If we don't go, we shan't know what's in store."

Warburton shifted from one foot to the other

"It must not be taken by our presence that in some way we entertain his views. We should take notes. There's other authorities that we might have to involve."

"What do you mean?"

"The Bishop."

Tyson had taken up a position with his back to the empty fireplace. He could smell the beeswax polish on the panelling of the surround. Behind him the mantel clock ticked. A portrait of Richard Warburton senior watched them from the left wall. A man in silks and lace with one hand resting on a document. Tyson's gaze rested on it and Warburton noticed it.

"I suppose it's all his doing," he said, indicating his father. "A time ago, and sometimes it seems a long time ago and sometimes only yesterday. How was it, Walter that in those times passions ran so high? For what? Here we are, king on the throne, worried about the price of corn, worried about the weather; no change. And my father wasn't a military man. Look at him."

Warburton stepped close to the portrait. The resemblance was obvious. He looked into his father's eyes, noting the flecks of paint that brought them to life.

"All a clever application of paint!" he declared.

"You've done all you need do for Emms," said Tyson robustly. "You can't spend your life atoning for others."

"He told me in this room," said Warburton, refusing to be deflected. "It was his present when I came of age. I was sworn to secrecy. He was already ill but I didn't know it. He said it would never have happened if Emms hadn't pulled out his pistol first. After that I thought back and knew I'd heard the shots. We were in a boat, me and mother. Had gone into the fen with an old fellow. He had taken us to where the big pike lay and there were all colours of dragonflies. We heard the horses and heard the shots. I had no idea what it was. Thought it was duck shooting .... He told me he had information from the Dunns. They always hated the Hares .... the Dunns watched them from the waterways and drowned places and sent to father with good intelligence. His troop cut them off. Emms was shot three times, Hare once ...."

Tyson was uncomfortable with this mood of Warburton's. He had heard bits of this before, and had also been sworn to secrecy.

"But you ain't responsible John. And Emms can't be given licence now because of it. He don't know it was your father, does he?"

Warburton shook his head.

"No. And it must be kept that way. Let's go to the meeting."

Tyson was annoyed that the confidence was becoming a burden.

*

Tyson had suggested to Warburton that they should collect Sylham. Warburton had balked at this and related the last conversation they had had about Emms.

"He's a good man," he had said, "but you know Sylham. He don't want to get involved if he can help it. More annoyed about the digging on his land ...."

The two men had stationed themselves to one side at the rear of the church. They were given a wide berth by the villagers, who bobbed and nodded as they came in, making for the front.

"See that," said Tyson, "see the distance they keep. That has a bad flavour to it. Guilty people keep their distance!"

"Come on, Walter, they're the same on a Sabbath!"

"You can see they don't want us here."

"I don't doubt that's how they want us to feel."

Emms had positioned himself in the pulpit, where he made play of reading the Book of Common Prayer while he waited. Afternoon sunlight, rich with June colour, burst through the south windows and divided the interior into bays. Dust particles danced in it, attracting the Dunn children who flailed at them with childish hands, making swirls and eddies. A subdued murmur of conversation hinted at excitement.

"I welcome everyone," said Emms in his sermon voice, "I welcome Mr. Warburton and Mr. Tyson and thank them for attending!"

He indicated the rear of the church. Most of the villagers turned to look.

"The work has begun, as you all know, to dig the new cut as part of this great enterprise. It is right that man should better himself. It is right that the land should be improved and that man should labour to celebrate the Lord. The Lord said:-

'*Let us make man in our image, after our likeness : and let them have dominion over the fish of the sea and over the fowl of the air, and over the cattle and over all the earth and over every creeping thing that creepeth over the earth*'

All these are things of husbandry, and we, in this congregation are husbandmen and our parents and their parents and grandparents before them were husbandmen. And the Lord said:-

'*Be fruitful and multiply and replenish the earth and subdue it*!'"

Emms paused for effect.

"Replenish and subdue. Care for and control. Take it from its natural state and make of it a productive material. So it is right to make what we can of our fen, our reed beds."

He paused for breath. Warburton turned to Tyson, made a puzzled face. Tyson gave a shrug. Even the Dunn children had fallen silent. They sat in a row on a pew, wide eyed, swinging their legs.

"But we have a duty to carry out our works in a way that would please our Lord. To replenish, as the Bible says. I have been told that there are many of you who oppose the work of the Oxay Drainage Partners."

"That's true!" exclaimed Ezra. He was followed by a general murmur that grew in volume, confidence feeding on confidence until there was a general uproar. Emms waited for some seconds then held up his hands for silence. The Dunn children stood up on the pew and jumped up and down. Esther, the eldest, grabbed them and sat them down.

"We don't want no drainage!" The voice of Thomas Fox carried clearly despite his age. He left his pew and walked down the aisle to the front. There, he turned around, clutching his hat.

"I reckon I must be near the oldest man in Oxay," he declared, "and Oxay don't change and don't want to change, begging your pardons Mr. Warburton and Mr. Tyson. And now we have fancy fellows, surveyors they call 'em, from I don't know where, coming with their brass instruments to cut a line through our living without as much as by your leave! No one asked us, did they?"

"No!" came the chorus.

"And we don't want it, do we?"

"No!" came the chorus.

"That's all!" said Thomas, and made his way back to his seat.

"Confound the man!" Warburton hissed to Tyson. "A poacher and an agitator."

"I have found burials," said Emms, "where the cut is to go. I am not opposed to progress. *You* must not be opposed to progress. But I say it should not go where it has been planned. That is my position!"

Warburton could take no more.

"You are a Participant, Mr. Emms!" he roared. "This is the damnedest nonsense you have ever spouted! Can I remind you of your Partnership! I tell all you people that the cut is going where it was planned to go, in land we own and fen we own. And the strongest measures will be taken against any who obstruct us or destroy our property or threaten our workmen!"

Warburton turned and left, followed by Tyson. The church door opened, slammed. A long silence followed. Ezra broke it.

"There ain't a lot more to say, vicar. We know where we stand, and we know where the Oxay Drainage Partners stand, and that's an end on it."

The villagers started to leave, turning into the aisle, avoiding looking towards Emms, who said nothing. The Dunn children pushed ahead, peeled through the opened door to the sunlight in the churchyard where they ran round and round the gravestones, gleeful to escape. Ahead of them all, Warburton and Tyson had stopped at the lich-gate.

"I'm sorry I lost my temper," said Warburton, "there in the house of the Lord. But he tries me – he is such a confounded dissembler. I can't stand a man who puts on his Pilate's voice. We've had him on peasants' rights and now because he's dug up some bits and pieces he wants to tip the cart. He gave John Sylham a lecture on what he calls history. John wants him removed. He says he's wild. Emms is taking a path to apostasy."

"Can't have it," agreed Tyson, "but what to do?"

"I'll take advice Walter, but I reckon we must inform the Bishop. My faith is simple and the Bible is my guide. Dispute it and you're on the road to perdition."

"I'll leave it with you. De Vries doesn't need to get mixed up in this."

Warburton growled affirmation.

"We'd better go." He nodded to the villagers who, finding their path through the lich-gate cut off, had formed a circle outside the church porch.

"I haven't taken you round the work," he said to Tyson. "It will be my pleasure to do so .... let me know ...."

They passed through the gate to their horses.

*

"They've gone," said Ezra, stating the obvious. "So what do we get from this?"

"Nothing much," said Harriet Dunn. "Didn't see Clara, did you? What's she up to?"

"Better off without her," said Ecclesiastes.

"She scares me!" said John Lambert. "Her and her witchcraft. She should be ducked."

His casual remark brought an awkward silence.

"Anyhow," said Thomas Fox, "we've got the vicar on our side."

"Don't know how far," said Ezra judiciously, "he only said it was in the wrong place, never said it ought to be stopped. Don't rightly know where he stands. He said it were right to make it fertile."

"Just vicar talk," said Ecclesiastes, "they can't speak like you and me, they speak all jumbled. What he said was that it was right to make what we can of our fen, and so we shall!"

"Praise the Lord!" said Fox obscurely.

"And keep your powder dry!" rejoined Ezra, completing the Roundhead adage to dry laughter from the men.

"It could come to that," said Ecclesiastes.

Emms appeared out of the church porch, blinking as the sun struck his pale face. He advanced on his parishioners. Familiarity with them as their priest immediately told him of their desperation and hostility. They avoided his eyes, stared at the ground. Fox fiddled with his hat, turning the brim round and round in his fingers.

"I'm sorry it was so short and ended like this," Emms said. "I don't like to see the village divided."

"It must be so!" said Fox with the heat of a man determined to speak his mind. "Lest you can stop it."

Emms saw the danger of replying to this.

"The Lord controls these matters," he said. "The Lord parted the waters for Moses and the Lord prepared Noah for the Flood. His will be done."

As he said it, he had no belief in his answer. The evasion was received in silence, broken eventually by Ezra.

"Aye. That's as is!"

Ezra made a wry face, nodded to Emms and started for the gate. The others followed his example in a silence that Emms understood and feared.

Chapter 7

MAY 12th OXAY HALL

TO THOMAS BATHURST ESQ.,
BATHURST'S ,
PREBEND STREET,
NORWICH.

My dear Thomas, by God's grace,

I hope this letter finds you well and in that prosperity you enjoyed when last we met.

I beg you to permit me to trespass on your good humour and experience. We have as you know entered into a considerable enterprise in these parts to win and preserve good land from the sea-water that intrudes in the fenland. To this end we have formed the Oxay Drainage whose participants will be known to you. I regret that we have encountered a duplicity of troubles which are set fair to interfere with our enterprise and at the very least lead us to incur additional costs that we can ill afford.

The first of these troubles takes the form of acts of terror on our workforce by the placing of signs and symbols on the ground and etc., and visitations by unseen wretches who hide in the sedge. You will appreciate that the fen-country is a wide and empty place, not to the liking of many of our men, who are uneasy because of the very loneliness. It seems to bring out in them all sort of fears that you would not expect in grown men. Just the other day our nightwatchman was confined in his hut by being nailed in as if he were a herring in a barrel and he has quit forthwith. I am compelled to provide an irregular shift of men to keep an eye on our endeavours at my own expense and I believe some of them to be irregular in their loyalty. I suspect many of our breedlings of involvement in this mischief and I do anticipate that things may become violent the further that our work advances.

I seek your advice in this matter and alert you to our situation. Mr. Sylham, Mr. Tyson and Mr. Latimer, my Partners, have asked that you represent them also in this respect. It may fall upon the participants to call for help from the Court and the Serjeant-at-Arms to enforce order for the continuation of our legitimate endeavours.

The second difficulty we have encountered is one on which I rely upon your tact and discretion (which I know to be of the soundest). I have formerly introduced you to our pastor, Mr. William Emms and you may have a picture of the man. He has enjoyed my preferment from a notion of our having grown up together. You know me to be a God-fearing man who holds to the Word of the Lord. I had every reason to expect the same from Mr. Emms. However, he has so far as can be seen, abandoned the Book of Genesis for some theory of his own regarding Creation. You might construe this to be an ecclesiastical matter to be dealt with by Canon law, and it may have to be so. The effect of his heresies upon the Oxay Drainage may be at the least to cause delay and at worst to stir up these same mischief makers to force a diversion of our river cut at great expense to avoid what he declares to be an ancient graveyard. (His construct of the age of this mound of soil, which is on John Sylham's land, is that it fore dates not only our Lord but Creation). He has held a Parish Meeting on the matter whose purpose appears to have been to encourage dissent and perhaps even strife.

What do you advise on both matters? The sight of the Serjeant and his Pursuivants might have a sobering effect but might equally inflame matters. As to Mr. Emms, I am minded to tackle him myself on his heretical leanings and if this does not have the desired effect, to contact the Bishop. As you know the Bishop, perhaps you can advise me how I should go about it?

My regards with this letter to your wife.
Your obedient servant and friend,
John Warburton.

Chapter 8

The spring green of trees was turning to dutiful summer drab, that colour that signals that the best is over and there will be a long wait till Autumn. A hot June start had given way to treacherous weather. It brought the first real taste of rain since work had begun. Each day had started bright enough but brassy skies produced afternoon torrents, stripping petals from dog roses and stirring up ponds. They rattled across the beds of rushes, bending them until they nodded in the water. In the evenings bruise-coloured cloud piled on bruise-coloured cloud squeezing the last light into a lemon yellow strip on the horizon.

Work was now progressing slowly, affected by the rotation of soaking and drying.

Excavated material dried like brick, the clay in particular forming an armoured crust that made spades ring and men curse. The same clay, forming ruts, dams and small ponds, refused to drain turning sections of the new river bed into quagmire.

De Vries and Edmonson met to view progress from the bank. A message had been received that Warburton and Tyson were on their way. Tyson had not visited the works before and both de Vries and Edmonson thought it ominous. Where they stood they looked down on the timber wagon ways laid on the new river bed. These ran in and out of mud ponds forcing the men who pushed them to spatter themselves up to the waist as they struggled to maintain momentum. Edmonson had tried oxen but these soon bogged in, making matters worse. The wagon ways were of pine planks and floated in the ponds, sinking and moving as each vehicle passed. The pumping action further softened the clay until the river bed, which should have been level with a gentle fall, became a switchback. De Vries was exasperated.

"Just look at that struggle. It is like working in soup. We need solid material. We need stone to compact in these mud ponds. You can see it is taking twice as long to shift materials. Where do I get more stone?"

De Vries had posed this question so often that Edmonson did not bother to reply.

"I think that is why we have this visit. What do you think?"

"I think you may be right Mr. de Vries."

The workmen normally wore clogs. Because these filled with water they took them off and laid them on the bank, upside down, to dry. Below the two men were rows of pointed Dutch clogs, rows of blunt English clogs nationally separated, but men could not work properly in bare feet. Some men had wrapped their feet in sacking.

"How do I keep to time and keep control of costs if I do not have the means at my disposal? We will need more timber, we have only two pumps."

Edmonson nodded, apparently in agreement. He had heard all this too often. It had come as a gradual change from the dry weather and optimism of the start. He was surprised that an experienced drainer should bother to complain. Didn't they have mud in Holland? It seemed to him to be a matter for slight concern in de Vries' otherwise impressive competence.

"Look, it is so wet we breed insects!" de Vries was pointing, a sardonic smile on his face, at a darting swarm of yellow and black dragonflies. They made opportune use of the mud pools, dipping at the water. The men could hear the rattle of their wings.

Looking beyond them to the other side of the cut Edmonson cast an eye over the timber pile. It was all very well for de Vries to ask for more timber. His position was ambiguous, and de Vries knew it. As works manager he wanted to push the project forward by every possible means but as a Partner he was bound to limit expenditure with similar vigour. He had organised the ship loads of Baltic pine that had arrived by cutter. It had been sawn, driven into the ground, laid down as boardwalks and wagonways, used for cranes and huts and now the log pile represented most of the anticipated timber for the job. His shrewd bargaining had provided more than the quantity allowed for and only two more cutter loads were due. There was no more to be had from Warburton's estate unless they took semi-mature trees. He thought to himself that de Vries had worked out the original quantities. So far as the stone was concerned, it might be that a Dutchman would assume it was available – Edmonson had no idea of geological conditions in Holland – however the man had made a previous trip to Warburton and it was the sort of thing that a competent man would be expected to ask. The nearest gravel pit was thirty miles away.

"Do you have much gravel in Holland?" he asked casually.

"Ja," said de Vries. "When we dig down we find gravel, but here we only have silt and clay."

Edmonson nodded, giving nothing away. It was another source of concern.

*

Tyson had ridden over to Warburton early to give the two time to talk and to take a leisurely breakfast before inspecting the works. Tyson was noted for his abrasive bluntness. He shared Warburton's beliefs and simple conviction that the words of the King James Bible was the cornerstone of all understanding, yet he coupled this with invention and innovation in his farming, trying new seed, modifying his implements. It was for this practical expertise that Warburton had asked him to visit the works. He also wanted a second opinion on his letter to Bathurst, waiting until they were well on their way from Oxay Hall before broaching the subject. He explained the letter.

"I felt obliged to seek his opinion. Do you think I'm wrong? It is a serious step to take and I take it with the greatest reluctance and caution – it is not a thing I have any experience of."

They had been moving at an ambling pace. Tyson reined in his horse, Warburton followed suit. Their horses snorted and tossed their heads, annoyed at the restraint.

"I think you have done the right thing," said Tyson, "You have, for now, merely sought advice. That 'meeting' of Emms' was the man's attempt at justification. No doubt he'd like to hold others. Do you remember at our last Partners' meeting, Emms was at pains to "take account" of things, as he put it. These people …." Tyson waved a sweeping hand at the landscape of sedge beds and water, "don't need to be told they're being taken account of, so help me, or they'll give you a list of ancestral rights that goes back to the Flood!"

Warburton swatted at small black flies that had decided they were stationary prey.

"Thunder flies," he declared, "more rain. Let's keep moving." Tyson's directness should have been balm to Warburton, but instead he was troubled by it. "You don't think it would be better to discuss the project with at least some of them?"

"No."

They moved forward, stopped to watch a heron lumber out of water and take off with a harsh cry.

"Anyway," Warburton continued, "I've got rid of that young man Dade, his abettor. Comes from a good enough family too, had Dades working for us for generations …. don't expect to employ a man who grubs around with Emms …."

They picked their way along raised green paths, dotted with puddles and lined with campion. On each side of these causeways lay flood plain meadow, half grass, half fen dotted with willow.

"You see all this …." Warburton indicated the sweep of land from the feet of his horse to the distant silver line of the sea, "by November it'll be under two feet of water .."

"I have the same ...."

"I've planted it with corn and seen them cutting it, wet to their boot-tops .... yet it's excellent soil .... I've let it go .... has a hundred swans in winter."

They could see the tops of the two cranes sticking up above a plain of sedge and stunted alder. As they drew closer they could hear the work, the sound of a multitude of spades and shovels biting at the ground, a commotion without distinct sounds, a metallic crunching. They passed into the clearance at the head of the cut where the vegetation had been stripped back and burned, leaving naked black ground. The horses kicked and whinnied, unhappy with the smell of fire and layer of ash underfoot. Tethered oxen stared at them with contempt.

"This is the first stage," Warburton explained.

Tyson was impressed. It was one thing to follow the parallel lines of the new cut on a map, it was quite another to see the size of the mess on the ground. Across the burned land ran a small river that would have blocked their path. It had been bridged in timber to provide a bridleway. Warburton stopped on the bridge, indicating the brown waters beneath.

"This is the next task – the Yule Brook – you see it runs into the river. We must cut it off with sluices so that we drain it into the new cut. You've seen it on the plans ..."

"I've seen it but I can't say it meant much on paper. Seeing is the thing. There's a lot of water."

"It backs up when the river is high, floods the meadows. We'll put a stop to that."

"You like this work, don't you John!" Warburton had almost been smiling and Tyson was amused.

"It's the future. If only we didn't have these confounded downpours .... see the colour of the water, that's all mud, all silt. Good land washing away to do harm out there!"

He gestured towards the river mouth. Beyond the cleared area the head of the cut was advancing towards them as they watched. Lines of men, working abreast in gangs, dug and lifted, dug and lifted with rhythmic movements that betrayed their skill. Each gang worked to the depth of a spade, backs turned, to be followed at a distance by the next and the next until they reached the bottom of the cut. The first rows of men flung the soil into barrows where barrow men took it away, but as the cut deepened the slope of the sides made this impossible. The material was flung into wagons on the bed of the cut and run to the cranes which lifted them onto the banks to be tipped and spread.

"It advances as we watch …."

*

As Tyson spoke, the leading gang stepped backward one pace. Each man would take six spade cuts sideways, then step back again.

Maddox, digging with his men in the leading gang, gestured at the two men on horseback who watched them from the bridge.

"Gentlemen visitors! Look lively, men! Heads down ...."

"Hey there!"

The shout came from the gang working behind them. A strong Dutch accent.

"Get a move on Maddox. You keep looking about and we'll be chopping off your toes!"

"All right, gin-swiggers, you'll have to catch us first."

The response, from a bearded man with bad teeth was accompanied by a two-fingered gesture. Maddox hissed at him.

"Not in front of our gentlemen. Keep digging!"

*

"De Vries was talking about requiring more materials," queried Tyson. He was watching Warburton's face as he spoke, but Warburton was looking in the direction of the sea making his expression difficult to read against the strong light.

"Surely this is a bit early?" he persisted. "There is a long way to go."

Warburton adjusted himself in the saddle before answering.

"In every project I have ever been involved in the cost is exceeded somewhere." He pointed to the excavation. "You see those wagon ways – they bounce up and down and pump mud everywhere. De Vries wants stone. He should put sedge rafts under them, that's the fenman's way, that's what we would do with a cart. He'll learn our ways. My man Edmonson will tell him."

"But what about cost? We need to see a bill of account ...."

Warburton urged his horse forward.

"At our next meeting. I've asked for one to be drawn up. Now let's talk to de Vries."

They could see de Vries and Edmonson in the distance, distinguishable by their large hats – the workmen wore close fitting caps or worked bareheaded. Edmonson noticed the two men and waved an arm aloft.

"Mr. Warburton," he said. "We'd better start at your office."

De Vries' office had been improved in small ways since his first day. Items of furniture had been added and it now contained three chairs, a second table and two large chests in addition to shelves and boxes. De Vries' sectional drawing of the cut had been given pride of place on the rear wall, the main profile in red ink, the surrounding ground in black and brown. Smaller drawings were pinned up around it, some with additional notes in both English and Dutch. Edmonson considered that this display showed a streak of vanity in de Vries that was equally evident in his choice of hats. While both men wore the large brimmed variety of the day, Edmonson's was a model of sobriety with a steel buckle and black band. De Vries sported a feather which Edmonson considered ostentatious and embarrassing. When Edmonson had time to reflect to himself, he admitted that closeness to de Vries had brought irritation about the man's self-confidence and arrogance. It had not, however, diminished his respect.

De Vries re-positioned the chairs and shuffled papers while Edmonson watched.

"What is Mr. Tyson like?" he asked.

Edmonson considered for a while.

"He's much respected round here for his farming. A man after your own style, Mr. de Vries, who likes machines, likes to try things. But he's a blunt man and will speak his mind. Some find him difficult."

"His machines?"

"Farming machines. Ploughs. He has a drill for sowing that cuts a furrow and sows all in one, all to his own design. He will want to see our cranes ...."

Warburton knocked on the door of the hut and he and Tyson entered. Tyson immediately held out his hand to de Vries and then to Edmonson.

"De Vries," he declared in ringing tones, "I am glad to see that you still use oxen. They have a much better centre of gravity than horses for wet work."

De Vries, nonplussed by this observation, gestured to the chairs. Both men shook their heads. Tyson moved towards the drawing of the cut.

"Your work?"

De Vries nodded.

"And your men, and the wagon ways and the cranes? All working well?"

"We have some problems with tools ...."

"How is that, Mr. de Vries?"

Tyson's tone was soft, almost off-hand but no one was deceived, least of all de Vries who became defensive.

"I do not know Mr. Tyson. It is these local people, I suppose. That is what I am told. Tools vanish, mostly at night, but in the daytime too."

De Vries crossed to one of the chests and extracted a notebook.

"Look, I have a list of tools, I have written them all down – a full account. It is costing money and it costs time. Here, you have it ...."

He waved the notebook in front of Tyson, then Warburton, and then read from it himself.

"Shovels, forty-three. Spades, twenty-eight. Picks, twelve. Barrows, nineteen, and so and so and so." He hit a page with the flat of his hand. "All gone."

Tyson turned to Warburton.

"Did you know of this John?"

"I knew there were problems. I didn't know the scale."

"It's not the men," said Edmonson. "Things disappear. At any time of day or night. I am sorry to bother you with this, but we are watched. A man lays something down, he turns around and it's gone. A rope is cut into short lengths, a bolt is missing, the wheel comes off a cart .... It's the local people, Mr. Warburton. It must be, but no one ever sees them."

"Don't you have nightwatchmen, guards?" Tyson asked. Warburton replied.

"We had a man, Jessup. The other night he was attacked and locked in his hut. He claims he was attacked by a goblin. He shot at it. Someone nailed him in."

Tyson snorted, stared at Warburton in disbelief. Warburton feeling foolish, felt obliged to explain.

"You know these people are superstitious. They may be good Christian souls on Sunday, but in the dark they're pagans. They believe in these things. I can't get another man for the job."

"There are things going on," said de Vries. He took off his large hat as he spoke. His face was serious; he was remembering his own experience at Oxay Church. "You should know that. It is affecting the men and the work ...."

"Apart from losing their tools?" Tyson made a face to the heavens. "What sort of things going on?"

"In the morning, there are signs and writings in the mud."

"Writings?" Tyson demanded.

"The names of the men. Symbols. They talk of witchcraft."

Before Tyson could explode further, Edmonson intervened.

"You should see it from their point of view Mr. Tyson. They work out here and it is a deserted place. If they stray a few hundred yards from the works, it is all water and sedge, and most of these men are townsmen. If a barn owl flies over they cross themselves. They are watched from the rushes. I know that's true, I've seen it. There are people there who watch them and move the sedge to scare them. They move around on stilts. They don't want the new river cut. And at night they put names and signs in the mud. Sticks tied to resemble gallows. Dead animals hung from branches ...."

"Does any of this matter?" pressed Tyson. "Are we going to be deterred by primitives?"

De Vries looked at Edmonson. There was a brief pause as each waited for the other.

"Some men have left," said de Vries.

"Then we need more prayer," Warburton declared. "You are describing decay, the success of wickedness and evil! We need a proper Christian cleansing!"

"We need a few armed men!" said Tyson. "That'll stop the rushes twitching!"

De Vries was concerned at the course of the meeting.

"Can we also discuss the needs of the work, gentlemen, the timber and stone. These are problems too .... we do not need any interruptions, any disputes!"

His earnestness was a rebuke to the other men.

"I'm sorry," said Warburton.

Tyson simply nodded.

De Vries gestured towards his drawing on the wall.

"Please look at this." He stood to one side of it so that he could point. "This is how the cut is being formed. These are the profiles. You will have seen it for yourselves. We clear the topsoil to the side and then we dig down, using the material to form the banks. We lay it in layers. When we have finished we have the depth of the excavation plus the height of the banks. In that way we can accommodate a river that runs above the surrounding ground level, you see ...."

De Vries pointed at the cut and banks as he spoke, indicating the levels.

"The banks must be at the correct slope, and they must be sound. They must be of the right material. Already I do not have enough clay, and so I must use wooden piles. You see, in Holland I can expect the peat to be to a depth of two to three metres and then find clay. Here the peat is much deeper. Now I want you gentlemen to come with me to the Yule Brook and see my big problem. You will see why I need materials! First I must stop the brook, then I must cut through it, then I must release it behind me. Mr. Warburton, you understand me!"

De Vries' distress put Warburton to shame. Despite his large hat and feather and his schoolmaster's manner his passion gave him dignity. Tyson softened.

"Let's see this problem Mr. de Vries. You must not mind if we seem vexed. "We must be careful over cost. It is our duty."

"It is my duty too!" said de Vries. He gestured to the door, stood back to usher them out.

*

Peter Dade watched the pike. It lay like a submerged piece of branch in the glassy water of the pool. He was part sitting, part lying on the fallen remains of an alder tree, keeping his silhouette below the skyline. The fish could have been dead but for the rippling of its pectoral fins. It would lie there until some prey passed within reach of its lunge.

Peter Dade had brought a rod with him, made from a straight length of hazel. His line was of hemp with horse-hair traces tied to a hook. He had not had the heart to put it in the water. He reviewed again and again the interview with Warburton, criticising his own speechlessness, clumsiness, silence. The deed had been done in Warburton's study, itself some sort of recognition of the generations of Dades who had served Warburtons. He had not been expecting what had happened but had not been surprised either. Warburton had been brief and to the point. No permission had been sought for digging on his land, and he did not expect that sort of thing from Peter Dade. Did he understand the trouble that Emms was making? His employ had sadly to be ended.

*

It had now become Katja's habit in the mid-afternoon to slip out of the house while Cristeen snored in her big wooden chair, surrounded by cushions. Had she stayed in and done as she was told she would have been making interminable strips of lace. To Cristeen, lace-making bobbins were a kind of Protestant rosary.

"There is always a use for lace," she would say, clicking away with them in her lap, and she had put this into practice around the house, edging and trimming.

Cristeen was now turning bobbins over bobbins with the dexterity and confidence of a lifetime's practice.

"What do you make of Richard Warburton?" she asked, head down, matter-of-fact.

"Why do you ask?" said Katja, not fooled by the performance.

"You know why I ask. He pays you a lot of attention."

Katja laid her bobbins in her lap and picked up the strip of lace she had made.

"Don't touch, don't touch!" scolded Cristeen. "Never touch unless you have to! I think he is a spoilt young man. He is too young to be a Partner. He has only been made one because he is his father's son.

"He doesn't appeal to me."

"The sea is good for your complexion!" teased Cristeen. "You could do worse than marry a rich young Englishman."

"Mother!" Katja knew she was fishing for a reaction, but could not prevent the raging flush that sprang to her face. "I have not come to England to be married off. What's wrong with a nice Dutch boy?"

"They're in Holland," said Cristeen drily, and they both laughed.

Katja's contributions to lace making had been small and not particularly well made and were a matter for reproach.

"Oh dear, I feel sleepy," said Cristeen later, as she usually did. "I'm so comfortable. I may drop off, but just you go on – you're so slow. I don't think you try." Cristeen must have known she slipped away, but slept so soundly she could not have known for how long. Katja waited until her breathing turned to snores and the bobbins fell from her fingers.

*

Katja knew she was infatuated but that made it no better. Although she knew Peter Dade by sight she had no way of knowing his name, short of asking the servant girl, which was out of the question. She remembered his wave. His dark hair and looks were a complete contrast to Lucas' blondness and pinkness. She thought him a hundred times more exciting, remembering the way that the two men had talked together, seeing the respect between them. She was determined to engineer an encounter. She had seen him pass with a fishing rod and with a cunning she had learned in the flat lands around her home she did not try to follow, but let him pass and get a good lead. She and Jan had spied on lovers that way, saying things and doing things she blushed to think about, lost in the rushes and each other. She moved carefully down the path avoiding puddles with her clogs. She must keep her stockings dry for Cristeen would surely look. She rehearsed her mother's words, her tone.

"Where have you been Katja? You have been out. I hope you have been behaving yourself?"

"Yes mama, only walking."

*

The immobility of the fish finally irritated Peter. Moving slowly he picked up his rod and took hold of the line. Drawing it through his fingers he felt for the hook. He had made it himself from a piece of metal and two pieces of white ash wood, wired together to resemble a small fish. He edged the rod out, over the water and released the hook so that it swung gently beyond the fish and with a skilful motion lowered it without a splash where it lay submerged. The pike did not move. Peter drew the lure towards it. The pike turned lazily, as if drifting with some current. Peter moved the lure nearer, to within three feet of its mouth. The fish shot forward with astonishing speed, seizing the lure. Peter had anticipated this and flung himself backwards against the alder tree, using it to rise to his feet so that he could lift the fish upwards in the water. Feeling the pull, the fish shook its head, gulping at the hook. Peter pulled.

The sound of the pike thrashing carried to Katja, who knew what it meant. She had watched Jan fishing for pike often enough, hands clasped round knees, skirt round legs, to keep out the cold by some misty polder in the dusk. He had a knack and never put anything back. Katja had soon changed from encouragement to dismay.

"No more fish, the Good Lord says enough is enough. Even the cat won't eat them!"

It was as Peter dragged the fish onto land that he saw her. With the stupidity of its kind the pike refused to let go of the lure despite being grounded and slithered around like a snake. Peter, not properly prepared for the catch, turned to find a lump of wood and saw her half concealed in rushes. He put down the rod, made a slight bow towards her. Katja's first instinct was to bob down out of sight, but the ground was muddy. Instead she returned his bow.

"I've caught a fish," said Peter awkwardly.

"Yes," said Katja. "I can see. It will get away!"

He knew who she was. He was not prepared for her blonde prettiness, when seen so close. She walked nearer, seizing her chance. Peter stooped to grasp the fish, which thrashed violently. He looked around again, wishing he had brought a piece of wood. Katja understood.

"You hold him!" she commanded, holding up the flat of her hand for him to stay where he was. Searching around the fallen alder she found a rotting branch and with quick dexterity snapped it to length beneath her right clog. She handed it to Peter who let the pike dangle in his left hand to deliver blows with his right. It hung still apart from the trembling of fins.

"A good fish," she said. "What do you call it?"

"A pike."

"Pike," she repeated. "We have them too."

Peter knew he was staring at her and noted she blushed violently. However, her eyes met his steadily.

"It is good to eat," he said needlessly.

"Yes."

She smiled slightly, mocking him, his lack of words.

"Are you the daughter of Mr. de Vries?"

"Yes. I am Katja."

"I am Peter Dade."

"Good afternoon, Peter Dade."

"Very well, I shall take this fish back ...." He held it out awkwardly. The fins still trembled.

"I have broken .... no that is not the word ... I have stopped your fishing. You must go on. I will walk away." Please, he must stop me, she begged any God that would listen.

"You don't have to walk away on my account."

He knew he had spoken too quickly. She dropped her glance.

"Very well," she said quietly.

Peter struggled to find the right approach, between forwardness and warmth.

"Thank you for your help. I wasn't ready, I should have had something like this...."

He waved the piece of wood and without thinking threw it into the water, where it made a substantial splash. They both stared in dismay at the churned water and ripples.

"Now you will catch nothing more!" said Katja.

Peter was mortified by his unintentional blunder.

"I didn't mean to do that! It just happened."

Katja smiled at him, guessing she was the cause of his confusion.

"So!" she said, and tilted her head to one side as she had practiced on Lucas. She waited for Peter to advance the conversation.

"Why have you come here? How have you come here? Do you know this place?"

"No, but I go for a walk in the afternoon when my mother is asleep. I find a path, it brings me here."

Peter nodded. "Would you like to sit down?" He indicated a fallen alder tree by waving the fish towards it. "I'll try to catch another of these if you like. You could have it ...."

"No!" she laughed. "I can see my mother's face! 'My God, what is that you've brought' and she will know I've been talking to someone!"

"Aren't you allowed to talk to people?"

"I mean she is *streng* – she would question me. 'Where have you been, what did you do?' You know the sort of thing."

Things were going better than Katja could have hoped.

"I saw you when you were digging."

"I know. You fell over."

"I waved to you," Katja protested. "What were you digging? Why are you standing in that hole?"

"Buried treasure," teased Peter.

Katja made a round-eyed face.

"Not really," he continued. "We dug up old things. Bits and pieces. I could show you ...."

"I must be back before my mother wakes up. She doesn't sleep for so very long."

Peter nodded and Katja turned to go.

"Perhaps I will see you again," she suggested so quietly, that he would not guess the importance of the question.

"That may be so," said Peter gravely. His heart was thumping. "I may fish here again. It's a good spot."

"Then I will see you!" Katja smiled and was gone, looking back once, giving the wave this time.

Peter responded in kind. "Well old friend, what do we make of that?" he said to the fish. "I shall have plenty of time on my hands. And don't she look a pretty girl!"

*

Hobson sent Middleton to the woodpile to select timber for the revetements and sluices. Because of his skill as a forester it had become his job. His particular pleasure was to collect the oxen from their paddock. A pair of the brown Lincolnshire animals had first to be selected then harnessed for work. He began by coaxing and cajoling them to a fence while pulling on their halters. There he tied them tight and dropped a double wooden yoke over their muscled necks. When this was secured with straps he hooked chains to it, joining them with a swingle-tree. The animals snorted and rolled their eyes. Middleton liked the smell of their grassy breath, both pungent and sweet. He walked them slowly from the paddock, pleased to take his time, splashing through puddles.

The logs had been stacked to form a long rectangle with successive rows at right angles to each other. The smell of pine resin and wet wood competed with the smell of the oxen. Middleton whistled to himself, walked the animals to the end of the pile and tied them to a post. He surveyed the timber, reached out to pick off blobs of resin from bark wounds, smelling it, rubbing it between his fingers. The majority of the timber was Baltic pine from Sweden, brought by boat and floated ashore. It still had the tang of the sea. He found the short ladder that he had concealed in the pile, propped it up, tried it, and climbed up. On top lay the various coils of rope, lengths of chain and poles that he had left behind on previous visits. He picked up a pole fitted with an iron shoe that he used to lever up the logs, and took in the view. It stretched from the grey horizon of the sea to the inland browns of the fen and the Yule Brook. In this flat countryside it was a view that would not be repeated except from a roof, or the church tower, or the mast of a ship. He could see Oxay Church, a cutter out to sea, a larger ship with three masts and full sail. He turned to see if Hobson was in sight, thought he saw him and waved his pole aloft in a moment of elation. At that motion he felt the logs slip and realised the danger. He danced from one to another holding the pole like a tightrope artist, running with them to stay upright, seeing in panic that they rolled faster and faster to the end of the pile, hearing them crash down. In one last frantic effort he let out a yell and tried to use the pole as a vaulter would, digging it into the pile, but it was immediately snapped between two logs and he fell astride one as it went down. The log hit the ground shaking him loose but before he could move the second log crashed onto his leg. The pain seemed to come slowly. At first he felt the impact, then the ache, then the rush of agony then he screamed and lost consciousness as another log fell on him.

His yell was heard by the diggers. Throwing down their spades, the nearest men ran to the scattered end of the pile. The oxen had panicked and broken loose, taking the post and ropes with them. Their bellowing was the only noise except for running feet. The first man on the scene stared, mouth open. His companion, showing quicker wit, shouted for more men, for help. Maddox arrived, puffing.

"He's one of my men!" he shouted. "I need eight men lifting. Get him out!"

Warburton saw Edmonson turn towards the commotion, and followed his glance. More and more men were downing their tools and heading in the same direction.

"What's up, Mr. Edmonson?"

"I can't see."

He started in the direction of the men. The others followed him arriving breathless, pushing their way through the gathered crowd to where Middleton had been laid out on a piece of canvas lined on each side by men. It had an unhappy likeness to a cortege.

"Make way!" demanded Edmonson, so that he and Warburton could see the man. Neither de Vries nor Tyson chose to come too close.

Middleton's face was corpse-like, his right leg a bloody mess of flesh and trousers. The foot was twisted at right angles. The man appeared to be unconscious. Warburton glanced at the tumbled logs. It was obvious they had slipped.

"Did they fall on him?" he asked.

"He was on the pile when it moved."

Maddox was angry. He pointed at the pile, pointed at the logs. "No wedges! I can't see any wedges, that's why it moved, no wedges!"

"He's alive?"

"As far as I can tell – his leg's smashed."

"Get straw," said Warburton, "and make a proper bed for him on a cart."

"See to it!" said Edmonson. "Get a dray horse, it'll be quicker – take a light cart."

"What are you going to do?" It was de Vries. He was looking from the injured man to Warburton in distress.

"It was Dutchmen that stacked the logs!" Maddox declared hotly, glaring at de Vries. "Didn't do it right!"

De Vries ignored him, kept his gaze on Warburton.

"He needs a surgeon!" Maddox continued.

"There's no surgeon here, Mr. Maddox," said Warburton. "None in this whole district. Take him to my house and call the midwife. We'll get her to do what she can, but he'll have to go to Lynn for speed. I don't like the look of that leg."

The cart arrived and Middleton was lifted on the canvas to be laid on the straw. He had regained consciousness and yelled as he was moved. Maddox sent one of his men for brandy.

"One of your men go with him," said Warburton. Maddox nodded. A man climbed into the cart. "Tell Mrs Warburton that I said to call the midwife and that I'll be home before long."

The cart and cargo set off, Middleton alternately groaning and yelling as it rumbled over bumps. Tyson had been hovering in the background, unable to cope with the sight of blood. He rejoined the others.

"This is not good," he said to Edmonson, "how did this happen?" He shook his head after the retreating cart.

Edmonson felt a surge of anger at the implicit criticism.

"They weren't properly wedged, Mr. Tyson. They should have blocks of wood beneath the logs. The men know that, don't they Mr. Maddox?"

"The Englishmen do," said Maddox and turned away.

"We were about to see your sluices," said Warburton. "Come on de Vries, let's look at your problems."

The four men made a judicious exit. Maddox eyed the men who had lifted Middleton onto the cart.

"Well lads, if he lives, he won't work again. That leg'll come off, for sure. This job's jinxed!"

*

De Vries pointed to the Yule Brook. They were standing on the new bank formed from excavated material from the cut. From this position the brook was below them, but still ten feet above the new river bed behind. It ran from left to right, straight across the future route of the cut and flowed like soup, loaded with the muddy washings of the fen.

"That is my next problem, and this is where I need many logs. I must drive them in – what you call piles – to form revetements on each side of the cut. And I need timber for the sluice gates and stone for the washes. And we will need a bridge."

"But surely you allowed for all this in your calculations?" Tyson snapped. The incident at the timber pile had left him in even worse humour.

"Yes, yes," protested de Vries, taking his turn to display the resentment he felt towards Tyson. "But the price of timber is very high. It has all to come by ship, and be off-loaded, and I have no local stone. How did you expect me to know that, Mr. Tyson? I use all the material I can from the excavation – it is not all the best material, but I use it to keep down the cost. I do what I can and you question my calculations! I am angry! I have this wet summer to deal with and I have these natives who steal my tools ...."

De Vries was bristling with indignation. Warburton intervened.

"No one is taking issue with your skill, Jacob, but we must keep an eye on costs."

"Yes, yes, I know."

Walter Tyson had visibly stiffened when de Vries referred to "natives". It was all right for him to call them primitives, but not this Dutchman. He thought the man's hat ridiculous, even allowing for Dutch fashion and hoped the wind would blow it off. Edmonson was rattling through facts and figures and they scrambled and slid down the wet material of the new bank to confront the brook.

"I must cut it off there." De Vries pointed to a pair of red-and-white posts driven in on either bank, near the temporary bridge. "We must drive in piles, right across, and tip in material to dam it while we build the sluice. It is there we need the logs. Big logs."

Tyson nodded, and started to question de Vries about the type of machine, and how he was going to operate it in mid-stream.

The Yule Brook sucked away at the peat layer it had found nine feet down. It had been sucking at this same layer for the last ten thousand years, moving with infinite patience. When necessary it diverted sideways in long watery coils to avoid the black roots of ancient oaks. As it moved it tidied up, filled in behind itself with silt and soil so that no one should guess where it had been.

"You know why it's called the Yule Brook?" Tyson asked de Vries.

"No."

Tyson gestured towards Warburton.

"You tell him, John."

"They say it's because it burst its banks at Yule," said Warburton. "Yule is a word for Christmas. The brook makes a great shallow lake, over to those trees in the distance, and when it freezes they hold a Godless fair on it and skate on it and light fires so that they can race and dance and whatever else at night. And they do all this on the Sabbath. The Lord is better served without it, but there's little need for an excuse for Godlessness round here!"

"Indeed," said de Vries, "or anywhere else. We'll soon have that under control. You can't skate on a polder."

Tyson caught Warburton's eye. A look passed between them.

"Soon?" asked Tyson casually.

"Soon."

De Vries was caught unawares by memories. Jan floating out from under the ice. Men tying ropes under his shoulders; Jan being dragged across the ice, his head bumping, skates screeching; Jan laid out white in their church. He shivered, realised that they had seen the involuntary movement.

"I don't like skating," he explained lamely, "it is dangerous. Lives are lost. Never trust ice."

The sun burst out from behind a cloud; hot June sun in an indigo patch. The brook sparkled and danced.

"I must leave you all," said Warburton. "That unfortunate man will soon be at my house."

De Vries nodded, pointed to the sky.

"All we need is a better summer, more of this."

"And a stop to all this thieving and superstition," said Tyson. "A bit more fear of the Lord. And a bill of account for our next Partners' meeting."

De Vries stared woodenly ahead, waiting for them to leave.

*

The arrival of Middleton on the cart had created a flutter at Oxay Hall. Beth the maid heard the banging on the door and thinking it to be one of the Warburton men had flung it open to be confronted by two mud-encrusted men. That was bad enough, but looking past them she saw the cart and what she took to be a dead man on a heap of straw. This had reduced her to helpless screaming and she had slammed the door shut again. Her cries brought Ruth Warburton and Sarah running from different parts of the house. They were beaten to the door by the man-servant Thomas who had seized a pistol that hung in the hall. He gestured to the two women to stand to one side and flung the door open to confront the men with the weapon held at arm's length before him. Alarmed, the two workmen had made a bad job of blurting out an explanation and minutes were wasted until the story was clear.

Middleton was taken to the kitchen and laid out on the table. Beth was sent to find old linen while Sarah put the two men in the pantry with a bottle of brandy. It was obvious they would be no use. Thomas rode off for the midwife.

Ruth and Sarah cut away the trouser leg from the man's mangled limb. Middleton moaned and was shivering and both felt sick as they exposed the protruding bones and mess of flesh. They had never seen anything like this. To their utmost relief the midwife arrived, followed shortly by Warburton and Edmonson. They gagged and held the unfortunate man while the midwife washed his leg.

"Mr. Warburton," she said, gesturing with her head, to draw him away. He followed her to the corner.

"Yes, Mrs Bower?"

"There's nothing I can do, sir. That leg will have to come off. Then he might have half a chance."

"What can you do now?"

"Herbs, sir, and bind him up. He needs the surgeon."

"That's twenty miles."

The midwife nodded. The two looked at each other. The midwife pulled a face.

Sarah wrote in her diary:-

"A man was brought here with a crushed leg from the works. It was a terrible sight and I felt ill. Father tried to help with Mr. Edmonson but the midwife says there is nothing can be done but take the leg off. The unfortunate man has been sent, bound up, with his leg packed with herbs, to Lynn where there is a surgeon. Even then he may not live. The two workmen were sent with him with a letter from father but they had already drunk too much. One of them was uncivil to me and stared too much at my body. I heard them saying that it was the fault of the Hogen Mogens, by which they mean the Dutch, that the man was injured. The other said there is a curse on the works and that it is witchery.

Father told mother this evening that he is becoming concerned about the progress being made by Mr. de Vries and about the cost of the works. I saw Katja this afternoon coming back late from a walk. She goes abroad quite freely when her mother is, I think, asleep. Mr. de Vries has not been asked to dine with us recently and Richard has been asking why. He has designs on Miss de Vries, I think."

*

Ezra Dunn led the fowling party followed by Ecclesiastes who carried the lantern, then the two Dunn boys and John Lambert. They were dressed in dark clothing and had smears of mud on their faces. The lantern was unlit as a half moon provided enough intermittent light for Ezra to lead the way. He parted the rushes as though swimming with palms together, arms extended and a backward sweep. Ecclesiastes and the others followed close with their arms out, maintaining the path. Ezra and Lambert carried long fowling pieces while the boys were draped with nets and ropes. It was a familiar route through the muddy creeks of the Oxay River over Sylham and Warburton land.

Ezra stopped and held up a hand. They stood still, listening. Even on this calm night they could hear the swaying of the rushes. In the middle distance, then quite near a pair of owls called to each other. Far away a fox barked.

"I thought I heard something," whispered Ezra. He moved on.

They would set up nets for ducks and collect fish and eels from the night-nets they had placed in concealed spots. At dawn the feeding birds would arrive. As dawn turned to light they would slip away. The party moved down the stretch of fen between the river and the new river cut, crossed carefully over the temporary bridge over the Yule Brook. Ezra suddenly raised his hand again. This time the gesture was urgent, and they froze. After a few seconds he beckoned them forward to stand beside him.

"There's someone there. Among the huts." He was pointing. Brief flashes of lantern light moved from left to right and back again, then finally settled in one spot. There was a long pause, then the movements were repeated. A figure was just visible, now illuminated, now between the light and the watchers. Ezra recognised it. "It's Clara," he whispered. They watched the movements of the light until Ezra motioned to them to retreat. Out of earshot he stopped. Ecclesiastes spoke, voicing everyone's thoughts.

"That woman is a witch. She's evil. Whatever she's doing, those Hares are evil." He turned to John Lambert. "Her brother drowned my cousin Joshua Dunn. Drowned him in the mud, took away his boat when the tide was rising. Joshua swam like a brick."

John Lambert was wide-eyed. He spoke with a croak in his voice, brushing his hair from his big forehead, "I know, I know – I heard she keeps mice in her pocket, turns them into other creatures – as she likes ...."

Ezra spat into the mud.

"Thirty years ago she would have been burned and I say old times were best suited for her! She'll be digging for old people. You heard her at the meeting."

"Mad," said Ecclesiastes. He crossed himself and the others followed suit. "We'll go round the other way. Right round."

*

The five hour journey from Oxay to the surgeon in King's Lynn was slow, drunken and difficult, not least for the unfortunate Middleton. The two carers had taken turns to plod in front with a lantern when the road became indistinguishable, cursing and slipping in puddles, but soon gave that up. Both climbed into the cart, stealing straw from Middleton and convincing themselves in loud voices of the skill of the horse and the brilliance of the moon. They had then fallen into a lengthy stupor to be awoken by the crashing of branches around their ears as the animal tried to graze in a field. Middleton began to babble. Overcome with remorse they poured some brandy down the man's throat, producing violent convulsions and setting him flailing as he tried to push the drink away.

They arrived outside Lynn at dawn and asked the way from a stockman with his herd who brought his dog to heel before he would reply. Finding the surgeon's house they handed John Warburton's letter to a scared pantry-girl. They were sat in the kitchen by the cook with another bottle of brandy where they immediately passed out in front of the fire.

The surgeon had been a naval man. "I'm not accustomed to the leg being there!" he protested to his assistant as they set about Middleton's thigh bone with a saw. A constable and a carpenter were holding the man flat. A piece of rolled-up leather had been inserted in his mouth. The carpenter had brought the sawdust for the floor and cord for the tourniquet.

Middleton's leg was removed neatly enough but the lack of protest dismayed the surgeon.

"Is he struggling, gentlemen?" he asked the restrainers.

"Nothing much," said the constable. Both men let go cautiously. Middleton was dead. The surgeon placed the leg where it belonged with the body, shrugged.

"Thank you gentlemen. I suppose we shall have to bury him here."

Chapter 9

Fat Toby had not just stayed for the night, he had stayed for two weeks to Sylham's anger and despair. His well nourished, well polished personage was offensive enough to Sylham, but the underlying conspiracy of the man with his sister drove him to depths of fulmination he vented on his horse, trees and any other aspect of nature in reach of a stick. He had vowed that if the man, abetted by Arabella, was impossible to dislodge quickly, he would at least take himself out of the house for part of each day. As expected Toby showed no inclination to take exercise, preferring to sprawl in a chair smoking and chatting to Arabella in a knowing way about this and that.

"I'll have a horse saddled," Sylham had tried. "We can go over to Aken Carr. It's a good gallop and I need to look at the wheat."

"I can't tell wheat from turnips!" Toby declared with what seemed to Sylham like satisfaction, "nor am I a galloping man."

Arabella had been sitting by the window, sewing. From there she was accustomed to exercise control of the whole room.

"What you need," Toby continued, "is one of these light carriages instead of thundering about on sweaty horseback. They're the thing for gentlemen. I reckon everyone will have one!"

Sylham snorted and stumped out of the room. Behind him, he heard Arabella laugh. He found Mrs Wells.

"Going out, Mrs Wells."

"Can't say I blame you. Place to be on a day like this. Pity you can't take Mr. Tolman with you!"

Sylham saw the mischief in her eyes. He managed a smile.

"I don't think he can sit a horse. I'll be back for dinner. Don't reckon Mr. Tolman is about to leave us yet, so it's three again."

"He was out yesterday. When you were out."

Sylham was very surprised. Nothing had been mentioned.

"I didn't know."

"Oh yes, and on foot. Came back in quite a state, puffing and blowing, but I reckon he was trying not to show it! He must have been walking some because he brought in half a field with him on his boots."

"That's a puzzle. Let's hope he's restless to leave!"

Mrs Wells enjoyed a conspiratorial chuckle. Sylham donned his hat and left, pondering this hopeful information. He mounted his horse and nudged into into motion, abstracted by thoughts of Toby, rent rises and the words of Clara:-

'The rich man, who gives you trouble. Kin of your wife.'

Clara wearing dark green, dusted with the pollen of dandelions. And here he was, fleeing his own home.

The horse, accustomed to being given no clear directions, chose its own route from a range of familiar journeys and headed for the ale house instead of Aken Carr. Sylham eventually noticed this and congratulated the animal on its choice, patting its neck.

"More understanding ...."

The innkeeper, Wilson, heard the horse approaching and guessed who it was by the leisurely gait. He watched as Sylham tied up the reins to the bough of an apple tree that served as the hitching rail, and opened the door to be ready for him. Wilson kept beer and wine on tap, but the substance of his business came from the supply of wines, spirits and tobacco. These "came in from the mist" as he put it. The increase in shipping due to the works had heightened prosperity. Wilson ushered Sylham into a back room he kept for visitors.

"Good to see you, good to see you!"

Sylham was comfortable in this sort of room. Bare boards, oak furniture and the smell of beer and tobacco, nothing soft about it, the antithesis of Arabella's drawing room. He was comfortable with Wilson, a taciturn man to his liking.

"Warm out," he volunteered, sitting down in an oak chair, giving an appreciative grunt. The two men were complicit in his escapes from Arabella.

"Beer to hand," said Wilson, taking a tankard and filling it from a barrel chocked up on the floor. He passed it to Sylham who immediately drank deeply. Wilson helped himself to a cautious measure for the sake of companionship.

"I meant to go over to Aken Carr to see my wheat, but somehow ...." Sylham gestured round the room with his tankard.

"Blame it on the horse!"

Wilson waited while Sylham finished his drink, took his tankard and automatically refilled it.

"I've got some nice claret in. It's travelled well. And some port that needs settling. It's in the barrel."

"It sounds good to me – I'll have some claret. Leave it in the stable where Arabella can't find it!"

"That'll be done." Wilson paused. "Did you have a visitor?"

"No. Why should I?"

Wilson made a surprised noise.

"Had a fellow staying overnight. That was two days ago. He was asking for Mr. Tolman.

"Was he now?" Sylham pulled himself up to a more alert position. "Know nothing about this. Seems Mr. Tolman has been out and about, walking, which is a surprise to me. He ain't the walking type, but Mrs Wells had to deal with his boots. What sort of a fellow was this?"

Wilson pondered. His eyebrows were bushy and almost met with the effort.

"Not what I'd call a gentleman, though I can't give you a reason for saying so, and not what I'd call a countryman either. Said he came from Norwich, but spoke like Norwich out of London. Younger than you and me and well enough dressed. Horse was a bit of a nag but I reckon it was hired. Sort of horse they give you in Norwich!"

Sylham laughed drily, sank the last of his beer. Wilson took the empty tankard.

"Did he say what his business was?"

"No. Just that he was looking for a Mr. Tolman, and that he was staying with you, or had some business with you or something. I hope it was all right to ask him?"

"Of course. Did he give his name?"

"Said it was Prentiss. Might have been, might not have been."

"There we are," said Sylham, making light of it. "Back to business. Five dozen of the claret, dozen of the port when it's clear."

"Right you are Mr. Sylham."

"And he gave no clue of his business?"

"No. But he had papers with him."

Sylham returned to his horse in thought. This, added to Mrs Wells' information on the state of Toby's boots, produced the kind of puzzle that annoyed Sylham.

'The rich man, who gives you trouble," he muttered to himself, recalling Clara's words again. "What's this all about?"

*

"I don't know how you put up with him," said Toby to his sister. "His manners ain't improved and he needs a new set of clothes or a new tailor or both."

He still reclined in an armchair. Arabella laid her work down on her sewing box, moved the table in front of her to one side and stood up to stare out of the window. Silent for a moment, she gestured towards the grounds in front of the house.

"Yes?" asked Toby, seeing the gesture.

"You might say it's the same out there. This whole house needs a new set of clothes but I can't get him to see it. He just asks me what's wrong with it as it is. Like this dress."

Arabella was wearing a sage green dress which had clearly seen better days.

"He's impossible."

"Not for me to say, but I told you so at the time. You persuaded me otherwise. You did! His prospects."

"I was in love."

Arabella's protest rang out as a cry.

"I had hopes. I thought – what did I think – I thought he had plans. He talked about this estate, his land with such enthusiasm. I thought it would translate into great things. What I thought was ambition was appreciation. He doesn't see the need for things."

"He sees the need for money and he hasn't got any, that's the problem!" said Toby.

"Nor have you," said Arabella with the remnants of loyalty.

"I would have more if he hadn't got mine!"

He heaved himself to his feet and righted his clothes, patting himself and tugging at his waistcoat. The effect was that of a pigeon arranging its feathers.

"There is a world of difference. My problems are from Mother Nature herself. You persuaded me to lend John money. I didn't anticipate it might be a one way passage. When you feed chickens, you expect the eggs! All I ask for is my interest, I ain't after the principal yet!"

Toby, agitated, had become quite pink. He pulled out a handkerchief and wiped his nose.

"Whatever he's become, he's going to have to be the gentleman over the interest Arabella, for I must have it."

He stopped, realising that Arabella was startled by his vehemence.

"I'm sorry," he said quickly, "we must play a tune together, brother and sister, what say you Arabella?"

"We shall have to make sure he raises the rents."

*

Emms was in his shirtsleeves and stooping over the remains of the skull when he was startled by the loud knocking on the door. He had laid out the various fragments on a clean tablecloth taken from Mrs Strutt's collection in a drawer downstairs, and had been fitting them together. So far the jaws and teeth had been restored and a large piece of skull lay on the cloth like a bowl. He had been working by candlelight and took one to go downstairs. It was uncommon for him to have visitors at a late hour, except where illness or death threatened, and then he generally knew of it in advance. Emms took his ministry seriously.

"Who is it?" he called, before opening the door.

"Clara Hare."

He unbolted the door, much surprised, trying to work out what could have happened. She stood on the step, dressed in a cloak of dark material that made her invisible in the night except for her face.

"Yes? What can I do?"

He held up the candle to see her face. A breeze caught it and hot wax ran over his fingers, making him wince. A faint smile ran over Clara's face.

"I'd like to come in. Can I come in?"

The question was more than a courtesy. Emms was uneasy and hesitated. While he considered himself a rational man, he was a man of God, troubled by the complexity of his position. In unguarded moments and on wakefulness he would kneel and pray for God's guidance through the difficulties of archaeology. Yet he never doubted the reality of good and evil and the age-old struggle between them. This led him to the acceptance of some force for evil and even to Satan himself and his many manifestations. So far as witchcraft was concerned he had no time for its superstition, lack of rationality, mumbo-jumbo and magic. He stood aside and indicated that Clara should come in, tipping more wax over his hand by mistake and flinching.

"I am upstairs in my study. It is lit there. I have no idea how things are downstairs. Please follow me."

He went ahead, Clara following in the pool of darkness behind him, tripping once on the steps. The study was better lit. Clara had never been there, had only been in the vicarage once before, and she tried not to stare around her. Emms lit a lamp with a taper to supplement the candles.

"I am busy," said Emms, trying not to betray his nervousness. "What can I do for you?"

"I see you have a fine thing ...."

Clara appeared to be drawn by a cord to the table with the fragments.

"You have a skull here, old bones ...."

Clara's intensity was matched by Emms as he watched her. She stretched out a hand towards the pieces. Emms instinctively drew in his breath. Clara heard and turned to him.

"All right if I touch them? Shan't do them damage ...."

Emms nodded. Clara picked up a piece of jaw, complete with teeth and examined it, moved towards the lamp to see it more clearly.

"Teeth are worn like an old horse," she observed.

"May I ask the purpose of this visit?" asked Emms, to distract Clara from further exploration.

"I have come to talk to you of common cause, pastor. I think we have common cause, in our ways, against this drainage ...."

"Clara, I am a Partner in this ...."

"Aye, as is, but I have heard and everyone knows that you have reconsidered. You told the meeting it should not go where it's planned."

"That's all I've said!"

Emms spoke more sharply than he had intended. Clara gave him an astute look.

"It were better it was abandoned altogether. It were better things were left alone. It were better old things were not disturbed, is that not so? It were better fish and fowl were left in charge of what is theirs, not summer lambs for your masters."

"All God's creatures," declared Emms defensively.

"In your books, pastor, as they should be."

"You must understand, Clara, that my faith in the Lord is absolute. Faith survives rational enquiry. Enquiry illuminates faith."

"I've heard what you said to John Sylham. Peter Dade told me. You talked about the old people, people before the Romans, who knows how old? People who made things of bronze because they didn't know how to make things of steel. Tell me that's true, pastor."

Her eyes roved round the room. She pointed at a bronze spearhead standing on its socket on a shelf.

"Things like that."

"I can't discuss these things with you."

"Why not? Do you think it wouldn't be right? Do you think I'm a witch?"

Clara picked up the lamp, making the shadows dance, and held it up to light Emms' face.

"Plenty of people in the village think I'm a witch, but they ain't got the courage to say so, in case I am and put a curse on them. What do you make of that, in this day?"

Emms was taken aback by this turn of the conversation.

"Why have you come here?"

"But do you think I'm a witch?"

"Witchcraft is held to be the doing of evil things with the help of spirits in covenant with mankind. I have no belief in the conjuring-up of spirits, any more than I believe you can discover a witch with a pricking-needle or immersing her in a river. However," he said, mustering as much severity as possible, "the very practice of arts of magic is contrary to the Christian faith."

"And these old bones," said Clara, who still held in her other hand the piece of jaw with the teeth attached, "are these Christian bones? Are they marked out in some way that we can see baptism? If they are as old as you say they are, they never, in their flesh, had Holy Communion with God."

"They will be buried in consecrated ground."

"I hope it's to their liking, pastor." She put down the lamp. "We do have common cause, we don't have to have common reasons. This digging must be stopped."

"I don't condone violence."

"But do you want the digging to stop?"

"I want it to go elsewhere. Find a new route, away from the present, to avoid these ancient things ...."

Emms reached out and took the piece of jaw from Clara. He replaced it on the table.

"I am told you have put a curse on the works."

"Who says that?"

"I hear things. And that terrible accident. And then there was Jessup the farrier, the man who was nightwatchman. Some female, he says, attacked him with an axe."

"Jessup drinks too much. He sees the world through the bottom of a glass ...."

"Take care, Clara ...."

Clara had no ready response. She took her time, nodding to herself.

"Some might say you're a magician, with your bones and bits of pot and secret diggings. Some might say it ain't fit for a pastor to be doing such things. But Clara knows it's a good thing. Clara knows, Clara knows and offers her help."

Emms was unsettled by the sincerity of her offer. He had no experience of the hand of friendship since his childhood days and had never expected it from such a source.

"Thank you," he managed, hardly knowing what he was thanking her for, aware of some difficulty with his voice. "Thank you anyway." He hoped the 'anyway' would give him scope for retreat.

Clara turned for the study door. Emms picked up the lamp to light her down the darkness of the stairs to his door. At the doorway, Clara paused.

"It is a strange thing, in the Bible," she said, "that in Exodus, Chapter twenty-two, verse eighteen, 'Thou shalt not suffer a witch to live', yet Saul visited a woman with a familiar, who brought up the spirit of Samuel for him."

"You know the scriptures?" Emms was taken aback.

"Of course I do. I know many things. Here, you're a man who knows much, and a man who knows much knows there's much to know. But you can't answer everything, even with science. Answer me this. Why do birds sing?"

She watched his face in the lamplight.

"Ahah, that's got you!"

She slipped away into the night.

Chapter 10

MAY 28TH PREBEND STREET NORWICH
TO JOHN WARBURTON ESQUIRE
OXAY HALL, OXAY

My dear John, may the Good Lord find you in health.

I have your letter of 12th instant and assure you of my good health and comfortable circumstance. It distresses me to learn of your problems both temporal and pastoral. Those acts of intimidation of which you write are an aspect which has dogged advance in many parts of our fen-land where there is an immediate and irrational resistance to any form of progress. I am in agreement with you that the sight of the Serjeant-at-Arms may be necessary. These things are best nipped in the bud. I am impressed by your cautiousness lest such a presence may inflame matters but experience has shown that failure to react is perceived as weakness and wins little respect. To this end I have alerted the Serjeant, who has ten good men at his disposal should you need them, all well equipped and armed. I have also spoken to the Sheriff who has endorsed this view, and remembering you well has sent his compliments.

So far as the second matter is concerned, it surely cannot be other than that the two matters are related. I recollect the man as lacking in certain ways in humility. It says in the Book, *"Trust in the Lord with all thine heart and lean not unto thine own understanding. In all thy ways acknowledge him, and he shall direct thy paths. Be not wise in thine own eyes; fear the Lord and depart from evil."*

What you describe is a man who has permitted himself to believe that his understanding is so prodigious that he is able to interpret the laws set by the Lord. The superstition of your fen men can readily be connected to doubts put about by such a man, for doubt in the word of the Lord leads to intrusion by the Devil.

The seriousness of this matter is evident and I have on your behalf reported it to the Bishop; a man called Lloyd who will contact you with an intention to make an enquiry into the affairs of William Emms and why he has the appearance of having fled the Faith.

Your obedient servant and friend,

Thomas Bathurst, Solicitor.
May God's good grace accompany this letter.

Chapter 11

Jacob de Vries had times in his hut when he was alone and had little to do but contemplate the plans on his wall and his reasons for coming to England. At these times he recited paragraphs from Proverbs to himself. He had been made to learn much of the book by heart by a stern schoolmaster and it suited his gloomy moods. He knew Edmonson thought him poor company at these times and kept away, but there was nothing he was able to do until his depression passed. Cristeen had said to him last night,

"Are you still glad we came, Jacob?"

She surprised him. She was sitting up in bed surrounded by clouds of linen and lace. The candlelight made moving shadows that moulded and re-moulded the contours of her face. He could see beyond the mask of years, vividly as if it were yesterday, the face of the girl he had married.

"Yes, yes!" he had replied testily, to protect himself from discovery, then, softening, kissed her lightly on the lips. "Don't I show it? Perhaps not. It was the right thing to do. There is a release. Of course there are still problems, but over here I have English problems, not Dutch problems."

In their bedroom they had a picture of Cristeen as a young woman, sitting with a tapestry on her lap, head inclined to catch the sunlight from a window. Behind her was a dark panelled wall, to one side a vase of flowers similarly bathed in the sun. They had brought it with them from Harlingen where it had occupied a similar position. It had been painted by a young man, an itinerant painter who had knocked at the door and smiled his way into the commission. They had had to admit, when he had finished that it was quite good – not of the best but quite good – and that his price was reasonable, but Jacob had had an argument with the young man over Cristeen's pose. She had been seated with her head at an attentive angle, a picture of caring concentration in her blue dress. Jacob said it was too low cut and showed too much of her bosom. He refused to pay until the artist attended to it. He had taken liberties with her clothes and with her modesty! he had shouted.

In a sulk the young man had painted in a band of lace, and all was well. Jacob had found himself looking from Cristeen to the painting, back and forward, remembering times when an itinerant painter was all they could afford, with poor quality Delft and inexpensive furniture – a much happier time before Jan's death.

His father Abram had become *burgemeester* when Jacob was sixteen. Abram had earned his money in the cloth trade and was eager that Jacob take a profession. He had set his heart on engineering, endlessly introducing the young Jacob to his friends and acquaintances engaged in Holland's struggle with the sea. Jacob would always remember the long, cold rides to distant shorelines, no different from East Anglia, to watch rows of men digging, to stand and nod politely while his father held forth and introduced him to foremen and site agents and anyone else he could find at some desolate battleground with the enemy.

"He wants to be an engineer," he would tell anyone who would listen, and Jacob's heart would sink as he knew he would be taken to stare at drains and dykes while he was immersed in statistics by men raised on them with their mother's milk.

His passage to university in Leyden had been inevitable.

"What have they taught you?" he would ask when Jacob came home. Abram smoked strong black tobacco, cut from twists that had been tied in ships' ropes. He had developed a cough because of it that would kill him.

"Mathematics," Jacob would reply, "and geometry." He could not tell him he was struggling hard in the career he had not chosen. His reply made Abram happy, and he would smile and nod at having such a clever son, and pare off another piece of the black twist with his silver handled knife.

"I like everything strong!" he would protest when his wife tried to stop him, "strong coffee, strong gin, strong religion and strong women!" and Maria had outlived him to prove it.

Abram had not taken to Cristeen. When Jacob had brought her from Leyden he had been silent for three days. She had not been his idea of a strong woman – an idea that owed much to Rubens and little to modernists like Vermeer. However he had been thrilled with his grandchildren, both of whom he had just lived to see.

"Katja will make trouble among the boys, eh? Trouble, trouble, trouble," he would say, bouncing her on his knee and exhaling tobacco smoke while Cristeen waited tensely to catch her if she was dropped.

On his death his debts had come as a surprise to Jacob, although half of Harlingen was owed money. By the time they were paid off the credit account of his life showed little profit to the family de Vries. As epitomised by Abram it had been greatly respected despite his debts but somehow the paying-off of these seemed only to reduce the family status. Jacob was employed by a firm from Groningen where his standing as an engineer and drainer rose unhurriedly. He gained a reputation for keeping things to himself, and for his choice in hats. Cristeen struggled to remain in the close-knit social milieu of Harlingen which set much more store by commerce than drainage engineers.

Katja bloomed into a pretty girl and as Abram predicted, made trouble among the boys. Jacob's work took him to increasingly desolate stretches of Friesland where the only difference between land and sea, they said, was that the sea had more lumps. Cristeen was left to deal with the wildness of the girl in these absences, and with the criticism Katja increasingly attracted. Jan took his sister's lead, doubling Cristeen's difficulties. One would dissemble for the other and the pair would be seen "running wild" as the good citizens of Harlingen put it, where no girl should be seen, out on the polder with boys.

Then Jacob would return – ("None too soon. Does he know what those children get up to?") – and order would be restored. For Katja, evening prayers were extended. She was given the task of learning whole passages of the Bible to recite them and be examined on them by Jacob the following evening.

*

On the evening of Jan's death the boy had seemed to go to bed biddably enough, but Katja had been brought to book for she had been seen lingering in the streets of Harlingen. Jacob disliked intensely these interviews with her. They had become too much a regular feature of life. He had even told Cristeen he wished she had had two sons, but she ignored the remark. "She will grow up to be a credit to you," she said firmly.

Katja stood in front of Jacob while he sat in a high-backed chair with a bible on his lap. It was unopened, to stress the fact that he was so familiar with the contents he had no need of it.

"I set you Deuteronomy, Chapter thirteen, to read. You were better doing that than wandering the streets."

"Yes father."

Katja did not bother to express either emotion or interest in her voice. Jacob fixed her with what he hoped was a stern glance.

"I will ask you some questions."

Each night it went this way. Katja complained that Jan was not exposed to this stern tuition. Jacob replied that he would, if need be. During these inquisitions Cristeen retreated into a corner with her lace or sewing.

"What must you avoid, in Chapter thirteen?"

"A dreamer of dreams."

"Why must you avoid a dreamer of dreams?"

"You must love the Lord your God with all your heart and soul and keep His commandments."

"That is correct. And what shall happen to the dreamer of dreams?"

"He shall be put to death." Katja made a face. "I don't see why he should be put to death, just because he's a dreamer."

"Because he entices you away from the true God, so you chase illusions. And what does it say about the children of Belial?"

Katja yawned. She was not tired but she had other, better plans for the evening and could see it being eaten away by the laws of the children of Israel.

"Come on!" said Jacob, sharply.

"The children of Belial tell the inhabitants of the city that they should serve other gods."

"Correct."

And on it went until Jacob was satisfied and yet he felt that for all she knew the text, she had missed the message. Katja was now giving a good performance of being three parts asleep and was allowed to leave the room.

"The girl's exhausted," Cristeen had said. "I think she learned it well enough, for someone her age."

"Well enough, but well enough is not always well enough in this world we live in." Jacob got to his feet, placed the unopened bible in the chair. "I must go to my study – I've still got work to attend to before tomorrow. Well enough won't do for me I'm afraid."

"I know," thought Cristeen. "If only it would."

The servant girl had knocked on the door about ten. Cristeen had asked her to see if he wanted a hot drink, it being so cold that the well had a crust of ice. It was the third day of a freeze and icy air seeped into the room around the window curtains. Jacob declined but rose to put more wood on the fire. Feeling the draught he took a quick look outside before he drew the curtains more tightly together. Outside he glimpsed a blazing moon and stars, brilliant in contrast to the yellow lights from houses across the polder. He nodded with satisfaction and sat down.

Nobody guessed that Katja and Jan had sneaked from their rooms, clutching their boxwood skates. Katja had spent her lingering time in Harlingen asking other children to join them, because of the moonlight and the bone dry air and the frozen polders. Her breath had come in puffs as she talked and she could point upwards to the full moon that was already high in a blue-grey sky. They had said they would, or that they might, or that they would have to ask, but in the end no one had come and Jan and Katja, tired of waiting, sped out onto the ice.

"Anyway we have it all to ourselves!" shouted Katja.

"The whole polder, the whole of Holland, the whole world!" called Jan, his skates kicking up snow dust from the ice.

Polder and fen merged into one silver glaze in the strengthening moonlight, giving no clue to the treacherous differences beneath. At first they skated round the edges, listening to the singing of the ice, but tussocks of rush interrupted the surface, and twice they fell. They moved further in to avoid them, skating round arm-in-arm, until Katja's legs began to tire and, laughing, she begged for mercy. Jan released her, to slide away to the earth wall while he, younger, faster, more agile, spun and turned, posing on one leg as he shot by in the moonlight.

"Look! Look!" he shouted, more and more daring, showing off.

"Sh!" Katja shouted, "Someone will hear us!"

"Then look!" and he pushed off in a cloud of his own breath.

It was so sudden, so unspectacular. There had been a dull crack, a hollow ping, a splash, and Jan was gone from sight. There was an interminable silence, which must in fact have been five seconds before he surfaced shouting and flailing, trying to haul himself out on ice that cracked like biscuit.

The next thing Jacob had known was Katja screaming at the door, Cristeen shouting his name in a voice crackling with panic and rushing down the stairs, coatless into the night; - Cristeen shouting she would get Pieter next door; - running until his lungs burned; - throwing himself at the ice with Katja who was somehow there with him; - men and ladders pulling him away, trying to get brandy in his mouth. Three images burned on his soul – Katja the author of it all sitting in the snow crying and clutching her skates; Jan's body brought to the house, he behind, by four men each holding the corner of a blanket, running as if there was something that could be done; Cristeen waiting in the lit doorway with his greatcoat and a hot drink for a boy already dead.

*

Jacob got to his feet, attracted by the noises of men shouting and oxen lowing. He saw them over by the collapsed wood pile. A crane had been erected and the oxen were being used to drag logs into the air, from where they could be swung into place. He could see Edmonson standing nearby. He would be checking the wedging personally.

He turned back to the wall where he had drawn the Yule Brook on his master plan following the discussion with Tyson and Warburton. Above the delineation of the brook he had drawn a three dimensional picture of the sluice as it ws to be, showing the walls, revetements, sluice gates and rushing stream complete with an angler. All the logs were shown on the drawing and numbered. The supply of wood was an obsession and he was counting them again when Edmonson appeared at the doorway.

"I thought you'd be out, counting them!" said Edmonson, in broad good humour.

"I'm sorry," said Jacob, "I'm in a dark mood. I was thinking about logs and Middleton. I suppose they are still blaming the Dutch?"

"I'm afraid so, but it'll die down."

"A death on the works – and that man Middleton – just a young fellow."

"These things happen." Edmonson was not inclined to join in Jacob's gloom.

"Do you know, I had a son, Jan. He's dead." Edmonson was taken aback.

"I'm sorry; what happened?"

"He drowned, Mr. Edmonson. It is a strange thing – when I started as an engineer it was for the sake of my father, but as time went by I became so involved with it that it was for me completely." Jacob was addressing the ground. "I don't know if you are the same, but it has become a battle with water. I don't know if this sounds deranged to you. Water is so powerful but it is so *zacht'moedig*." He paused, fishing for the English word, "meek, you say. Jan was with my daughter Katja. They were skating on deep water where they shouldn't have been. She should have stopped him, she's his elder sister, it's her job – I was working – she didn't behave well, you see and that was what happened. You can see we had to get away from it ...."

"Oh," said Edmonson, embarrassed by Jacob's unexpected candour.

"So you see, water is my battleground. Isn't it strange Mr. Edmonson that Jan should be taken by water? Is it some sort of challenge? Do you think the Good Lord is testing my faith?"

At this de Vries looked up and fixed eyes with Edmonson.

"What do you think?"

"I don't know, Mr. de Vries. It's not the sort of question I can answer."

De Vries straightened up.

"Of course not. It is a question to put into prayer. I should not have imposed on you."

"No imposition, Mr. de Vries," said Edmonson kindly. "Come out with me and count the logs." He was relieved to have a genuine reason to get Jacob moving, to break his introspective mood.

*

"Did you see them drawings, Mr. Maddox?"

The remark came from one of the gangers, a blotchy faced man with a northern accent. "Drawn in the mud with a stick or something. Nigh-on a dozen of them, I should say. They must have been done overnight."

"I saw them," growled Maddox. He wanted no talk of them, no diversions, no rumours, no delays.

"What were they then?" continued the man, determined not to be put off. To Maddox's annoyance, a group of workmen moved towards them, eager to listen.

"How do I know? Just these people. Some crazy nonsense."

"But do they mean something? I mean, are we safe?"

"You're not afraid of a few scratchings in the mud!"

"They were figures," volunteered one of the workmen. "Animals and things. A deer."

"A horse," contradicted the ganger.

"A deer," persisted the man. "It had antlers on its head. And there was a bird with outstretched wings."

He demonstrated the bird, holding his arms out from his sides at shoulder height.

"Like this."

"Are you a grown man?" demanded Maddox. "A Christian man?"

The workman shrugged.

"But what do they mean?" persisted the ganger.

"Whoever is doing this wants to put us off," said Maddox. "They've got you going, like rabbits!"

"There was one drawing of a hanged man," persisted the workman. "I saw all the drawings before Mister Edmonson stamped them in."

"I don't like it," said the ganger. "I don't reckon we're safe here."

"Get on with your work!" ordered Maddox. "We're already behind time."

*

A mystery to Sylham was like an escaped fox – something to be trailed to a conclusion wherever it led. His days were now spoiled by both Toby's continued presence and the puzzle over Prentiss, the mystery visitor. He had waited for some explanation from either Toby or Arabella, but none had been forthcoming. He found himself watching Toby, keeping an eye on his comings and goings, while at the same time fretting that he was wasting his time on such a matter and such a man. Unable to find anything unusual in Toby's movements, he decided on a return visit to Wilson at the ale house to see if there were any scrapings of information he had missed.

He had taken his dogs with him for the exercise and now the two animals sat on either side of Wilson, tongues lolling. Wilson had given them a bowl of small beer, as was his custom and the two men sat on a bench in the sun. For his part Sylham held a tankard of claret which was on its third refill. Wilson drank nothing. They had already discussed the weather, the crops and the price of wool and Wilson sensed that Sylham was on a visit for information.

"Well, have you had any more visitors? Any more fellows from Norwich?"

"No one," said Wilson.

Sylham grunted, took off his floppy hat and swatted at summer flies. The dogs snapped at the air appreciatively.

"The fellow Prentiss. You said he didn't seem like a gentleman ...."

"No."

"Why not?"

Wilson gave it some thought.

"Had an air about him. You know how you meet someone and don't like him. Can't rightly put a finger on it, but in this business you know who's going to pay their dues, and those you keep an eye on. Mind you he paid up, but he argued the bill. I don't mind that either, but it was the way he done it, as if I was trying to cheat him. Then he paid me in small coin. Gentlemen don't carry so much small coin. It was like the scrapings off the floor, something that he'd been saving. And his nails were dirty, and his clothes shone .... threadbare ...."

Sylham snorted with laughter.

"So you didn't much like him!"

"That's about the long and short of it."

"What else did he say except he was looking for Toby Tolman?"

"Nothing really. Kept himself to himself. Sat in the saloon by himself ...."

Sylham gave an impatient sigh. It was not that Wilson was uncommunicative – he obviously had little more to tell. He started to prepare to leave, downing his wine.

"However," said Wilson, "my girl makes up the rooms. She had a look at his papers – couldn't miss them."

"And?" In his excitement he automatically leaned forward to Wilson, who in perfect synchronisation swayed backwards to avoid the fumes on his breath.

"She says there were letters, which she didn't like to open, in case it was noticed – and she can't read too well anyway – and there was handbills. She says they were about sugar, if that makes sense to you?"

"It does!"

"And they were about shares, and the West Indies. Had a Norwich address, but she can't remember that."

"For the love of God man, that's what I need to hear!" Sylham jumped to his feet, stood on Jupiter's tail, who yelped. "Anything more?"

"That's all she can say – I'm sorry John, I didn't know it was important ...."

"There's some dark business here!" declared Sylham. "Something hidden that needs dragging out into the light of day, and I bet Toby's part of it!"

His glee was a surprise to Wilson, whom he clapped on the shoulder with his free hand, then, realising he was still clutching the tankard, banged that on the bench, ejecting the remaining drops and was off to his horse with the dogs after him. He struggled into the saddle of that patient animal, waved farewell to Wilson, dug in his knees and set off at a flurried gallop.

*

Arabella was sitting by the open window, tacking on a piece of lace cuff that had become detached from a dress. It was hot and although the curtains billowed slightly, it was warm air that came in. Toby reclined in an armchair, legs thrown over the arm, smoking a pipe. He knew Sylham would comment on it on his return.

"So, why have you decided to return to Norwich?" Arabella asked. She had only just learned of Toby's intentions, and Mrs Wells, hot, bothered and indisposed to help him, was organising his bags.

"Business, Arabella. I'm not a man of leisure, pleasant as that would be. Damn, it's hot! Do I have to wait for John?"

"You must make your farewells properly."

"Sister, sister!" mocked Toby. He blew several puffs of smoke in the air, wrestled with a handkerchief that was trapped in a trouser pocket and mopped at his face. Sweat beaded his brow and he was jacketless. "My concern is that I really do get my money. You really will see to that, Arabella?"

"I've told you I'll do what I can." For once Arabella was irritated.

"'What I can' don't sound too convincing. 'What I can' comes before 'there was nothing I could do'."

"I'll see he raises the rents. Are you really so desperate for money? Are you going to stay in Norwich? What's the money for?"

"Arabella, you wouldn't understand. The world of business is a complicated thing. So many questions."

"But you said you were thinking of quitting St. Kitts."

"Did I?"

"You told me that two days ago."

"Quite the remembrancer!" He climbed out of the chair awkwardly, holding his pipe aloft in one hand while trying to swing his short legs off the arm of the chair. The effort caused him to breathe heavily. He stood beside Arabella, watching her. "Dear sister," he said with heavy irony, "I shall be quitting St. Kitts if things go right. Time to cut my luck as they say, lower my sails, because, as you know, it ain't going well."

He stooped to wave his pipe under Arabella's nose. She recoiled but could not push him away without dropping her work.

"This stuff, this is the future. It grows with vigour they say and it grows in Virginia. I must get our money into tobacco, and I'm short of that deuced interest, Arabella, from your beloved husband. And that's being monstrous kind of me, because in truth I really need the capital, the pig not the squeak and I shall have to have that next.

"That wasn't what was agreed."

Arabella's annoyance showed. She didn't like him waving the pipe in her face, loathed the smell.

"I know, I know, but should the opportunity present .... Look, I've got one arm behind my back, Arabella and the opportunity does present. What's so damned exciting about this farm and draining bogs? You and John would do well to sell it all. Get that money into tobacco. Tens of thousands of acres. A fine house, servants, clothes, carriages. Just look at things here."

At this point Arabella saw Sylham approaching. She watched silently as he turned into the yard. Toby, who had not seen him, took her silence to be contemplation of his eloquence. He retreated and began walking up and down. She heard Mrs Wells' voice downstairs.

"He's up there!" she was telling Sylham, who had just pulled off his boots. "Smoking away!"

"A fine stink, I expect!"

"I should think so. He's got me packing his bags."

"He's leaving?" Sylham could not control the exultation in his voice.

Mrs Wells smiled. "He surely is!"

"Alleluia!" Sylham stumped upstairs in his stockinged feet. As soon as Arabella saw him she knew he had been drinking, but that was almost a commonplace. He had shed his coat and unbuttoned his shirt and looked red and alarming.

"There you are!" he declared unnecessarily. "I gather you're leaving, sir!"

"Toby's going back to Norwich," intervened Arabella, seeing the danger signs.

"Is he now!"

"I can speak for myself sir!" Toby hooked his right thumb in his waistcoat pocket and held his pipe in what he hoped was a magisterial clasp to his breast. He had the sense to see attack was imminent and shuffled sideways to be closer to Arabella.

"I must, sir," continued Toby, "for the sake of my business. Very grateful to you, for this stay. Very good. But business beckons. Don't it always. Arabella can look after my affairs."

"What affairs might those be?" enquired Sylham in beguiling tones.

"Come on, John, it's the matter of the money you owe me," protested Toby. "We ain't going to go into that again, are we? We've covered that ground already and if we tramp it again it will all turn to mud."

Sylham nodded, raised and dropped his shoulders. "So what business takes you back to Norwich?"

"Sugar, sir."

"So who's this fellow that's been visiting you? I hear he ain't much of a gentleman."

Toby stared at him with a brave show of incomprehension. "Don't understand sir."

"Well I should say it's easy enough to understand. The fellow called Prentiss staying at the inn."

Toby snorted, tried an affronted defence. "I don't see it's your business."

"And your meetings with him."

"That certainly ain't your business. Transactions. Transactions have to be made, whatever. You might not understand that, but that is business. You have to keep in touch – it ain't like running a farm ...."

"But when you stay in my house, you might be good enough, sir, to tell me what you're doing!" Sylham's voice had risen to a roar. Toby was flustered. In an unconscious movement he reached his right hand and put it on Arabella's shoulder for support. Sylham glared at the hand as though Toby had just festooned her with a viper. Toby removed his hand.

"Why should I sir?" he protested. Sylham ignored him and planted himself in front of Arabella. The stirring summer breeze wafted wine fumes over the proceedings.

"Devil take it Arabella, he's been coming and going from this house, my house, and meeting this fellow in the woods who might be some villain for all I know, because I ain't been introduced to him and ain't going to be so far as I can see. What's going on?"

"I don't know!" protested Arabella. "Why should anything be going on? Please stay calm, after all, Toby's leaving." She looked down. "You've got nothing on your feet!"

"Calm it is!" roared Sylham, turning from her and stumping for the door. "I call it a damned strange way of behaving." He paused at the door. "You shall have your interest sir, be sure of it!" He flung open the door to find Mrs Wells waiting there with a pair of shoes and a badly concealed smile.

Chapter 12

The meeting of the Oxay Drainage Partners had been called by Warburton and was to be held in his timbered hall as before. Tyson and Latimer had been asked by Warburton to come early and had arrived in mid-afternoon so that the three men could review matters and rehearse strategy before the others arrived. They had been studying the maps, papers, pens and accounts and these were scattered over the large table, interspersed with their pewter tankards. Warburton had provided plenty of beer. The August weather was still extremely hot and the windows were flung wide open, admitting particles of pollen and summer dust which danced in the sunlight and settled on the table. The men were in shirt sleeves and had unbuttoned their collars, pushing back their chairs for ease. They had discussed the harvest and the yield, the price of corn and the death of the "damned boy Middleton," as Tyson called him, and it was time for business. Tyson led on what was to be done.

"So the plan remains to deal with Emms first? And the accounts next?"

"The one is the reason for the other" confirmed Warburton. He had shown them Bathurst's reply which lay amongst the other papers. Latimer was smoking a long clay pipe. He sat so that his right boot was hooked over this left knee, and that boot was twitching. Latimer was troubled. He drew a circle in the air with the stem of his pipe, took a judicious puff and let the smoke trickle from the corner of his mouth.

"As a former magistrate, I can only deplore what has been going on. The Emms matter wouldn't matter so much if our common inhabitants didn't make trouble with their pagan scrawls and dressing as women and thieving and terrorising. All criminal acts. Bathurst is right, we need the Serjeant-at-Arms and a dozen troopers. That should put the fear of God into them if Emms can't be relied upon to do it!"

"Who is going to pay for this?" asked Tyson crossly. "Our financial situation has deteriorated. Perhaps Emms would like to pay!"

"Emms couldn't afford it," said Latimer. "I doubt if he can afford his investment."

"Then perhaps Emms would like to resign from the Partnership," suggested Tyson. The remark produced a silence, broken by Warburton.

"What would be the grounds for such a situation? What are the legalities?"

It was Latimer who responded.

"We can only force him out if he is guilty of an illegal act or of acts that jeopardise the enterprise."

"He *is* jeopardising the enterprise," asserted Tyson. "What else can you call it?"

"We shall put it to him," said Warburton, to the nods of the others. "Strongly."

The arrival of Sylham, smelling of beer, was rapidly followed by that of Richard Warburton, Edmonson and de Vries, who had been invited in compelling terms to present the accounts. De Vries was nervous, and after polite greetings, sat apart from the others with a pile of paper, making notes with a scratchy quill. Cristeen had been invited to accompany him and to pay a visit to Ruth. He had left her hot and flustered in the hall, patting at her dress.

"We shall be needing more money, I hear," muttered Sylham, sitting down with a lot of noise. He looked sharply towards de Vries, but although de Vries heard, he gave no sign. He knew these Englishmen would gang up on him if things got hard. Cristeen had been anxious for him and had ironed his best lawn shirt. He could smell the lavender-water she had sprinkled on it. They had discussed what he must wear. She had told him to be as severe as possible and to wear no lace or frills and he was glad he had taken her advice. All of the Partners appeared to be dressed for an execution. He scratched needlessly at the bottom of a sheet of paper, drawing a figure holding a surveyor's rod. Someone had replied to Sylham for the group of men seemed to move closer. He heard Tyson's raised voice.

"How much? Is this a time to raise rents?"

"I need the money."

Sylham's reply was defensive and in his broadest tones. He had pushed his chair back, florid as ever and angry at what must have been criticism. De Vries pretended to busy himself. This was bad news for someone who needed money as well. Sylham was spared further interrogation by the arrival of Emms. The pastor wore a tall felt hat despite the warm weather, which further emphasized his long thin stature. He took it off, laid it on the table and wished them all good day without extending a hand. The cold formality of the greeting was not lost on de Vries, who rose to his feet and made a short bow.

"Let's begin now we're all here," said Warburton brusquely. "We have much to go through." He sat down purposefully, laid both hands on the table, palms down and waited for silence. The Partners took their seats, uncertain what was required.

"We give thee thanks O Lord," Warburton began in ringing tones.

"No! No! I shall give thanks!" protested Emms. "You have no right to. It is my duty, I am pastor to this parish and to this company!"

Warburton was taken aback by his vehemence. He made a conciliatory gesture with his hands, palms up, never taking his eyes from Emms. Emms clasped his hands together, closed his eyes. The Partners exchanged glances, lowered theirs.

"Lord bless this endeavour. Lord bless those who put their labour and the fruits of their labour into it." Emms spoke with utmost clarity. "*'God is our refuge and strength, a very present help in trouble.'*"

"Amen," said Warburton. "Amen," echoed the Partners, but Emms was not finished. He had neither forgotten nor forgiven the theft of his authority at their last meeting.

"*'Except the Lord build the house, they labour in vain that build it.'*"

De Vries had a side view of Emms and from this position could see that he projected flecks of spit in the sunlight.

"Amen," said Emms. A tense silence immediately followed. The clattering sound of blackbirds broke it. They were fighting over ripe fruit. A wasp drifted in one of the windows. All heads turned to watch; it drifted out again. Warburton saw no option but to come to the point.

"I am bound to ask you William if you are happy with your position as a Partner in this matter? How can you bless what you want to impede? Are you happy with your position as our pastor?"

He would have preferred to have approached it more slowly. Emms sighed. His long face was grim.

"I feared this. There is no reason for me to be happy. Over these months I have felt your antipathy turning to hostility. You haven't listened to me."

"Don't you think that what you are doing is obstructing progress? You told John Sylham you had found a burial ground, right in the path of the cut, and you called a parish meeting with a profoundly disturbing outcome."

"That's right."

Tyson hit the table with his fist. "Praise the Lord, you'll stop the works! What for? Do you want to throw away your own money? And ours! And recover nothing!"

"But I have recovered this ...."

It became clear why Emms was wearing a coat on this hot day. From an inside pocket he produced a large bag of dark velvet closed with a red drawstring. He untied this, fingers clumsy with so much attention and gently tipped the contents onto one of the maps. The Partners leaned forward. Whatever they had been expecting from Emms' magical bag, they had not been expecting the row of pebbles and flakes of flint that Emms proceeded to arrange before them. A stunned silence fell on the room, broken by Sylham.

"It's gravel," he said in disbelief.

"Is this a game?" Tyson was angry.

"It is not gravel," said Emms with studied calm. "I ask you to look carefully. These are from the new cut, from the greatest depth. Some are scattered, some are found in groups ...."

"What are we supposed to see?" demanded Tyson. "Have we got rubies and diamonds? We'd better have!"

Emms continued with pedantic patience. "If you pick them up, if you look at them, you will see shapes, you will see they have been burned and have split in the heat, you must look ...."

He picked up stones, fragments of flint and placed them into the hands of Latimer, on his left who took them automatically, looked at them one at a time and passed them on until the fragments had made a circuit of the table and begun to return via Edmonson and de Vries.

"I ask you to put aside all prejudices and look at these with the eyes of men of this age, of scientific men. Some are beautifully made from flint. The shapes are the shapes of arrowheads, of knife blades. There are two like the heads of axes. These have been made by men. These things are thousands of years old. They must be. Many thousands."

Warburton leaned across to extract a piece of flint from the pile. He held it up so that sunlight shone through it. He replaced it, took another.

"How do you know these were made by men? It is broken stone to me."

"Chippings!" declared Sylham with a snort. "Plough shards."

"It takes a fine plough to cut an eight foot furrow," reasoned Emms sourly.

"Chippings!" Sylham waved a dismissive hand. "Gun flints!"

"There are posts," continued Emms undeflected by their scorn. "Pieces of wood, worked wood, down amongst the tree roots."

"We have roots like that also in Holland," volunteered de Vries. He was relieved that attention had been so thoroughly diverted from finance. "In our peat layers. Old forests they say."

"No," said Emms. "These are old posts in circles or sometimes in rows, like avenues."

"Fence posts!" shouted Tyson. "What's *your* theory, vicar?"

"Yes, what *does* the man of God make of this?" demanded Latimer rudely. "We're wasting all this time while you want to call a parish meeting, you want to move the cut, you want to avoid your relics, your heathen relics for all I know, your Roman remains. What for? These things are pathetic."

"Goblin stones!" announced Sylham jumping to his feet with sudden vigour. "In the year of our Lord one thousand six hundred and ninety and you want us to believe in goblin stones! They say a toad has a stone in its head, its supposed to be like a pearl, some say it's a jewel, but I've killed a few, and it's like your goblin stones, there's nothing there!"

He sat down emphatically, blew through his lips like a horse. Emms looked from one to other of the men but failed to find support. He drew tight the string of the bag and replaced it in his pocket.

"Evidently you think me some sort of madman. Your minds are closed. I remind you that *'a prudent man concealeth knowledge'*, but I had no exemplar to this day – I had better leave you to your business."

He rose to his feet, managing to epitomise contained anger. Without exception the Partners avoided his eyes. Emms replaced his tall hat, turned and withdrew. There was silence until they heard the slam of the front door.

"There you have it," said Warburton. "Item one of the agenda dealt with."

"Hardly dealt with," said Tyson.

"Well, disposed of. Now we can get on with the rest of our business. A report on the progress of the works, then the accounts. Help yourselves to beer."

The exit of Emms was an evident relief. Chairs were pushed back and beer circulated before Warburton rapped on the table.

"First, Middleton. The boy who died. Mr. Edmonson arranged for and paid for his funeral. This should properly be taken from the Partners' accounts."

"Agreed," said Latimer, to be followed by a chorus.

"However, there has been talk. Tell them Richard."

Richard Warburton had so far been silent. He had been given no choice by his father but to attend.

"They say it's the fault of the Dutchmen. The other men say they didn't bother to wedge the logs." He looked sideways at de Vries. "They say the Dutchmen are lazy and that's what killed Middleton. Or if it isn't that, it's some devil, some ...."

"Where do they say this?" demanded Tyson, who didn't approve of the boy.

Richard Warburton coloured. "About. In the ale houses. In the village."

"And on the works," interjected Edmonson in his rounded tones. "I've heard it from our surveyors. It causes bad blood."

"Is there any truth in it, what do you say Mr. de Vries?" Tyson's blunt question caused Warburton to glance at him, but de Vries took no offence.

"It is a provocation," he declared. "I have heard the same thing. The foreman Hellenbuch has told me. It is a lie against my countrymen that the English men like to put about, and so on and so on." He shrugged. "I imagine it will come to nothing."

Tyson turned to Edmonson. "What do you think?"

"It may come to something, it may not." He was too embarrassed to say anything more in front of de Vries. Since last talking to de Vries his investigations did point to the Dutchmen. Warburton moved on.

"Then we come to the progress report." He cleared his throat. "I have to say, gentlemen and fellow Partners, that we have not progressed at this stage as far as we anticipated. We have been at the work for four months now but are only up to the Yule Brook. Mr. de Vries has dammed the brook and started construction of the sluices. We had hoped to have done that in June. There are a number of reasons for the delay, which I have noted. One, the ground conditions have proved to be more difficult than expected, with more peat and silt and little or no gravel. Two, there has been a constant loss of tools, resulting in delays, and causing expense. As you know we cannot find a guard amongst our local men – and we shall come to that matter later. At present Mr. Edmonson is obliged to ride the works at night when he can, to try to prevent such thefts. Mr. Edmonson has a report to make on the matter. I can tell you that our surveyors are delayed by acts of damage almost every day. They cannot set out their poles and leave them because they are pulled out at night and moved elsewhere or thrown in the river." He paused. "Mr. Edmonson?"

Edmonson felt that although no criticism had been made, he was being held responsible for control of these nocturnal events. It made him defensive.

"You must understand it has been difficult. We have to set out the work afresh each morning, everything must be taken away at night – progress has been slowed, I can't pretend otherwise. I'm sure you gentlemen will understand that a lot of the men are superstitious. They may be godly on the Sabbath but I don't know what god they have after dark."

"This is a disgrace," said Latimer. "We must get the Serjeant-at-Armes."

"Agreed!" said Tyson. "We're all agreed."

"Take care," said Sylham. "People don't hold with troopers. It's easy to get them in, but will it be easy to get them out?"

"And thirdly," Warburton interrupted, "thirdly there has been difficult weather – I would like to complete my report .... It has been unseasonably wet this summer ...."

"I don't see that, about troopers," insisted Tyson, not to be deflected, "they would calm things down."

"I'm not so sure," said Sylham. "A cow walks into a pond, but by God you won't get it to walk out again!"

*

Richard Warburton was no longer listening. He found the whole proceedings uninteresting and watching de Vries in an abstracted way, his thoughts, never far from the subject, turned to Katja and more particularly, Dade and Katja and the mid-afternoon.

He had discovered Katja's mid-afternoon walks by chance, having ridden to Elm Farm to see her. His thin pretext – the best he could think of – was that his horse needed water. This would be true enough for he had deliberately failed to water the beast that morning. His desperation to see Katja was spurred by the increasing formality between his father and de Vries although he had pressed his mother for further invitations.

"Your father thinks it inappropriate while there are these difficulties at the works. He wishes to keep things correct. Do you like the girl?"

Richard had blustered "She's good company. We all enjoyed the dinner party."

Ruth could not help betraying her apprehension.

"I thought she was rather silent. Had little to say."

She judged the girl was stolid, like her mother. Richard always had too much of an eye for girls. She saw him flush with the quick anger he had always betrayed since a boy and turned away to hide her anxiety.

Richard had knocked at the door of Elm Farm and posed in his rehearsal position, hat in hand, smile on lips for Katja. Instead Cristeen had come to the door, blowzy with sleep and slow to understand. She tried calling for the girl, ran upstairs and returned to say she must be out walking. Richard's disappointment rapidly changed to annoyance.

"Where?" he demanded.

"I don't know where."

Cristeen looked at him plaintively, then not knowing what else to do, bobbed a curtsy and retreated inside. Richard had set off in the most likely direction, towards the fen and spotted her. He was surprised that she was out and about by herself like any country girl apart from her full dress and linen bodice. She had not heard his horse on the turf, and tying it to a tree he had followed at a distance on foot, moving with care, ashamed and excited that he was stalking her. She walked from the meadow onto a path through reeds, on without hesitation down tracks Richard did not know, where it was hot and still amongst head-high sedge and the only sound was the rattle of dragon-fly wings. He advanced with elaborate caution. The track opened out to reveal firmer ground and pools of water. The land had been colonised by willows. Dade was seated under the shade of a pollard, and he rose as Katja approached. Richard, flattening himself into the reeds, felt a pang of unexpected pain as he saw her smile and hold out her hand to him. He knew who Dade was and knew the circumstances of his dismissal. Dade gestured to Katja to sit down, which they both did, after he spread out his jacket for her. She tucked in her skirts beneath her, showing a flash of petticoats and Richard was consumed with jealousy as she turned to him, arranging her hair. Dade showed her a square basket that he had been weaving from willow. It was half-made, with the sides untidy and twiggy. He heard scraps of conversation, her voice stumbling over English sounds.

"What do you call this?"

"A basket."

"No!" She laughed. "What do you call these branches?" She had picked up a bundle of slender wands.

"Withies."

"Withies." She repeated it several times before their conversation became inaudible as he showed her how to weave. A moorhen, peering through the rushes, clucked and scolded and Richard withdrew further into the reeds, knowing the bird had seen him. Dade had been eating. He looked up, saw the bird, satisfied himself they were alone and threw a pellet of bread into the water. The bird circled uncertainly, tail flicking. Richard saw Katja put her hand on Dade's arm, pick up and throw another piece and another, until it dashed forward, seized one and fled with a great commotion. Katja leaned over and kissed Dade, arm round his neck.

Richard had retreated as quietly as he could, heart thumping, biting the back of his hand with violent jealousy. He rode home fiercely, forgetting to water his horse on his return, to the disgust of the groom, who had never liked his way with animals.

*

Richard returned to the meeting as if awakening. The Oxay Drainage Partners were listening to de Vries who droned on insistently. He had prepared a set of accounts, handwritten in duplicate and passed one to Warburton who cast an eye over them and passed them round the table. Richard took them automatically, ran an unseeing eye over them, nodded and passed them on. De Vries was complaining again that he needed more money, more resources, he explained about timber and stone and water and mud and volumes of water.

"I wonder if he knows about Katja?" he thought, jealousy racking him. "What would he do if he did? Should he be told, how and when? How to get rid of Dade without Katja knowing?"

"Are you with us?" demanded his father suddenly, his tone bleak. Richard sat up.

"Are you part of this business?"

"Of course."

"I thought we might have lost you."

Richard suffered the smiles and snorts of the Partners.

*

Overhead Ruth had flung open the casements of the sewing room where she sat with Cristeen and Sarah. Katja had protested to Cristeen that she was too young, that it was too hot, that her English and her sewing were an embarrassment and had finally been allowed to evade the engagement.

"The nearer the roof, the hotter, in this weather," Ruth said. The three women sat by the window in matching chairs. Between them they had a sewing table, long bleached by sunlight because of its position. The top had been lifted to reveal Ruth's collection of silks and wools. Ruth had guessed correctly that Cristeen would be intrigued. They had already exhausted the topics of their health and well-being, the state of the roads and the warm weather. Sarah was working on the embroidery of a collar, wishing that time could be urged on just by the wishing. Her assessment of Cristeen as dull needed no revision.

"How is Katja finding life here in Oxay?" her mother asked conversationally. "Is she settled, is she finding it easy or difficult?"

"Her English is improving daily," said Cristeen. "She reads. Mr. Emms brought us some books."

"That's good. But she must find it quite lonely."

"Oh, I think she is quite contented."

Sarah glanced up from her work, wondering how well mother knew daughter.

"She must come over to visit Sarah," Ruth said, to her dismay. "The girls are almost of an age. They can go riding and walking together."

"I'm afraid Katja does not ride very well. We are townspeople really when we are in Holland. We travel by carriage, or we walk."

"Sarah could bring her on, or they can read books together. That will help her English. Or I'm sure they can make up a party, with Richard and visit our local sights."

"That is very kind, I will discuss it with Katja. We would like that very much."

Ruth's well-meant plans were viewed with alarm by Sarah, while Cristeen felt embarrassment. It was good of Ruth to propose such an arrangement but Cristeen was in some awe of "the big house" and had felt out of place at the sunset dinner party. The occasion had made an indelible impression upon her. Richard was undoubtedly handsome but his talk of poachers and witches and the prattle about religion and remains was all nonsense to her and made her uncomfortable. He seemed too excitable. Perhaps he was spoiled. No proper young Dutch man would behave like that at the table – she supposed things might be different here in England. Jacob had said he thought Richard might be dangerous – but Jacob never liked young men. She reached out, took a handful of silks from the sewing table. She started to lay them out – peacock blue, turquoise, greens. Sarah watched the deft, practical hands that patted the silk flat then re-wound a tangled skein. She too was thinking about Richard. Her relationship with him had always been difficult. Two years her senior, he habitually treated her with patronising levity, dismissing anything she might say or ask. She had learned to ignore it and to keep her thoughts to herself and her diary. She had deep concerns over the damage that Richard could do with his interest in Katja. She wondered if Cristeen or her mother knew anything about Katja's comings and goings.

*

De Vries concluded his progress report in an orderly and unemotional fashion. He disliked the atmosphere of anxiety and criticism that prevailed. There was too much passion involved, as far as he was concerned, and events controlled by passion did not make for good business. Emms had walked out; the boy Warburton was not listening, Tyson looked flustered and angry and Sylham was drinking too much. He resented that he had been led to sacrifice his neutrality over the stupid business of the tree stumps.

"Thank you for your report, Jacob," said Warburton.

De Vries had not heard the familiar address for two months. He managed a slight smile.

"So are these troopers to come, gentlemen?" he enquired, "And who is to pay for them, and where will they stay? It is something I need to know."

"I'll billet them," replied Warburton.

"I'll take my share of the bill," said Tyson. Latimer nodded.

"I'll see to it," said Warburton.

The Partners began to take their leave, donning hats. Sylham hung back, drew close to Warburton until all had gone. Warburton looked at him expectantly.

"Not going?"

"Got something on my mind." Sylham evidently needed coaxing.

"Yes?"

"This lawyer man of yours, Bathurst, he's a good chap is he?"

Warburton was surprised. "I think so. He's always done well by me – looked after my interests – and he's a good friend."

Sylham was uncertain how to put his problem so puffed and shuffled. Warburton waited. "Is he up in matters of business?" Sylham asked.

"I should think so. Deals with commercial matters."

"Could I ask a question of him?"

"Why not, John? You contact him, I don't own him. Can I ask what sort of question?"

Sylham visibly reddened, and looked from side to side to check they were not overheard. "It has to be discreet, you see. About some business in Norwich and shares being sold. Can I rely on your absolute discretion?"

"You have it."

"My brother-in-law. He's doing the selling you see."

"Ah!" said Warburton. "I'm sure he could deal with that."

"Most grateful!" said Sylham. "Most grateful. I think I shall send him a letter."

He took his hat from a peg in the hallway, crammed it on his head and left with what Warburton thought to be a jaunty stride.

*

The chain men did the measuring with the one hundred links and sixty-six feet of the Gunter's chain. They were over-dressed for the weather and had become increasingly exhausted and foul-mouthed from dragging it through the undergrowth and carrying it over fen and water. Through the former it became entangled in briar and thorn and could only be freed by slashing and tugging. To cross the latter they had been supplied with a small boat. Not only had this to be dragged with them, but it was unstable and too small for both a man and the chain, frequently tipping both into the water.

Even when they had got the chain across it had to be stretched as taut as possible to provide some sort of accurate measurement before driving in the next pin. The chain men stopped for their mid-day "bait" as they called it, dirty, wet and sweaty and not at all happy to be in the depths of "the swamp" as they had named the fen.

Friend and Parker the surveyors had pushed on ahead, distancing themselves from the sweat and swearing of the chain men. Satisfied that they had found a level piece of turf, Friend put down the circumferentor that he had been carrying and folded out the legs. He pressed each into the ground in turn to ensure it was properly sited, then put his hat on top, hooking it on one of the sights. Parker put down the surveying poles he had been carrying under an arm. They looked about them. They were uneasy at being so far in advance of the works. Both were town bred and shared a townsman's fear of empty places. The island of turf was surrounded by tough undergrowth and collapsed alders, providing good cover.

"All right here?" asked Friend.

"I should think so," said Parker, keeping his distance from Friend's bad teeth and bad breath. Behind them lay the slashed path they had cleared with billhooks to provide a line of sight. That summer's prolonged rain had made the ground spongy underfoot while the hot weather following had produced an eruption of rank greenery. They were tired and thirsty, their hands and boots green with leaf stain and sap and they needed a rest. Parker laid down the surveying poles and patted his leather satchel.

"Time for a beer and a bite to eat?"

"Through there," said Friend, pointing ahead through a break of thorn, "there's a tree for shade, and I need a piss!"

He used his billhook to trim a passage.

"Alleluia, a clearing!"

They stepped into an open patch of ground, part bog, part island formed by the roots of alder trees and crowded in with reeds. The alders cast an inviting shade. Parker sat down in it while Friend relieved himself behind a tree trunk.

"Peaceful," he said when he had finished. He took off a bag identical to Parker's, opened it then walked to a boggy pool to wash his hands. Parker took off his large hat, laid it on the ground and from the bag produced a bottle, bread and a piece of meat wrapped in cloth. Friend held up his hand abruptly. Parker turned quickly.

"What?"

Friend made flapping movements for silence. Both men listened. There was nothing except the swaying of reeds in a slight breeze. A reed warbler broke into song nearby, churring and clicking. They listened for over a minute.

"I thought I heard something," said Friend, rejoining Parker on a nearby root. He stretched out his legs, opened his leather bag to produce his bottle, raised it to his mouthful of bad teeth and drank.

"I thought I heard rustling," he elaborated, wiping his mouth on the back of his hand. "Do you reckon we'll get this finished?"

"How do you mean?" Parker looked at him sharply.

"Partners are meeting today. Mynheer de Vries has gone to the Hall to make a report. We're behindhand."

"*We* ain't behindhand."

"Just look at this ground." Friend stood up and dug in a heel. The ground squelched and the indent began to fill with water. "It's getting wetter by the day. It's ever since that Yule Brook was dammed. Mynheer needs more drainage dykes."

"Dykes cost money."

"We'll be digging into bog."

"What do you know about drainage!" taunted Parker. A pair of ducks flew rapidly overhead. The commotion of their wings startled the men. They tensed again, looked around. From behind them in the tall reeds came the tinkle of a small bell, to be answered by another somewhere to the left, then the right, in front, behind, left, right, shrill and clear. Parker struggled to his feet, tipping over his beer. Friend crossed himself.

"Lord help us," he said. "What's that?"

To their horror an apparition began to rise from the reeds. At first all they could see was a straw hat, then a startling white face with round red spots on what must have been the cheeks, and sunken eyes. This was followed by a second hatless head, to the right.

"My God!" yelped Friend, and flung himself to the ground on his knees. He clasped his hands before him and began praying incoherently, watching with one eye. Parker had more courage.

"Hey you!" he bellowed. His voice cracked, coming out as a shrill squeak. "Damn you, who are you!" He regained control. "We know who you are. What do you want?" Whatever he had expected next, he did not expect the figures to grow. Already visible above the reeds, they now rose higher and higher, showing shoulders then waists then knees, until they towered over the men, over the reeds and stood, Parker was to say, tall as trees, waving their arms like scarecrows, impossible to see properly against the sun in the sky. He froze, mouth hanging open, trying to collect his senses. He realised that, true to the adage, he was weak at the knees.

"What do you want?"

There was a concerted ringing of bells which stopped, leaving one bell tinkling one, two, three, ten times. The figures began to shrink as slowly and noiselessly as they had grown. There was a concerted ringing to coincide with the disappearance of the hat and two white faces, then an intense silence, save for Friend who gabbled away at some nostrum he believed would save him. Parker reached out an unsteady foot and nudged him in the ribs. Friend stopped and the two men listened, frozen to the spot. Parker could hear nothing but the blood singing in his ears. He cocked his head this way and that. Friend was the first to move, leaping to his feet like a disturbed hare and running for the gap they had opened in the thicket. Parker followed in turn.

"The circumferentor's gone!" he roared. "Stolen! That was men, not ghosts!" He pointed to footprints on the grass and in the bog leading from and to the reeds. Friend's hat had been neatly placed in the centre of the turf where the instrument had stood. The surveying poles were laid out on the ground to make a child's diagram of a gallows with a dangling rope. Friend viewed this shaking and exhaling gasps of bad breath.

"There'll be hell to pay!" blurted Parker. "That thing is worth a fortune!" He kicked the poles apart to destroy the image and both men fled. From within the depths of the reed bed they heard shrill, derisive laughter.

*

John Lambert carried the instrument. He was all but unrecognisable in a woman's dress that was too tight for him and was unbuttoned at the neck and too short at the knee. This was just as well as he had to scramble into the flat bottomed punt with it, carrying his stilts. The boat contained Ecclesiastes Dunn, Walter Clarke and Clarke's fourteen-year-old son all similarly dressed. The boy had somehow whitened his face and reddened each cheek with a round spot of colour. His stilts lay beside him. Lambert wore a bonnet with straw sticking out for hair. Ecclesiastes had been making the derisive laughter and with Walter had enjoyed themselves with the hand bells. Lambert managed to extract his legs from the black water and sit down in the rocking craft. The men were grinning.

"Move, move," hissed Ecclesiastes. The boy, who sat at the rear, had a pole and propelled them silently through the reeds. The instrument glittered in the sun, reflections as bright as the sparkle off the water, dancing in their eyes. They stared at it. Lambert undid a knob, moved the brass half-circle up and down, noting the marked angles. He rotated the brass table, folded up a leg.

"What shall we do with it?" he asked. "Where shall we hide it?"

"They'll be after it," said Walter, as if this was a useful observation. "That'll spoil their meeting."

"Well what do you think?" asked Ecclesiastes. Walter, in his many occupations, had a better range of hiding places than most.

"I think it were best kept on the move," said Lambert. "Getting caught with that is a job for Jack Ketch."

This sobering thought proclaimed a silence, broken only by the swish of reeds along the hull of the boat.

"Are you saying we shouldn't have taken it?" asked Ecclesiastes. "It be too late now? Do we should take it back?"

"No!" Walter was outraged. "They follow that instrument like a tantony pig."

Ecclesiastes tucked loose straw under his hat.

"Well then?"

"Wrap it up tight, put it in an eel trap, tie it on the end of a rope and drop it in a bog, that's what you do with it. Quick!"

*

Friend and Parker tried not to draw attention to themselves. They slowed down to a quick walk as they approached the lines of diggers, but they might as well have returned stark naked. Digging men stopped, jabbed each other and nodded in their direction. The surveyors were never seen hatless or bagless, never hurrying and above all they never abandoned the circumferentor. Turner, seeing their return, advanced to meet them.

"What is it?"

He saw the men were spattered with mud and were empty-handed and guessed.

"Where's the instrument?"

"Stolen!" said Friend.

Turner's face betrayed his alarm.

"How?"

"Bells in the reeds, all around us ...."

He considered mentioning that they had stopped to eat, thought better of it. "They jumped out at us," he concocted, "we had it set up, - there were six of them, wearing masks – grabbed it ...." They had decided between them not to mention their shameful terror.

"Armed," added Parker, nodding.

"Nothing we could do," said Friend, "into the reeds and away ...."

"Where are the chain men?"

"Out there I suppose," said Friend, who had given them no thought.

Turner held up a hand for silence that was soon broken by the running footfalls of the chain men who came crashing out of the rushes. Considering their width and girth they moved with impressive speed. They saw Turner and made for him.

"What happened to you?" Turner demanded.

The three men stood gasping for air, hands on hips or slapping their chests. Eventually one of them wiped his nose with his cuff and found enough breath to speak.

"Something in the rushes. Huge! Bells. And signs. And flowers ...."

"Flowers?" Turner's face showed disbelief.

"Not flowers," corrected the second man. "Wreaths. Hazel twigs and flowers .... wreaths."

"I must tell the Partners' meeting. Now. There will be hell to pay!"

*

His arrival at the Hall coincided with a mellowing of the tone of the meeting. Good beer had been the peacemaker and the conversation was interspersed with occasional laughter. Warburton, oblivious of heat as always, sat in the fall of sunlight through the window, chair pushed back. Tyson smoked a pipe, propelling mouthfuls of smoke into the sunlight through pursed lips. Latimer lay back in his chair, tankard in hand; de Vries played with a quill pen; Richard Warburton mused while Sylham viewed the meeting with the one eye he was able to keep open. Only Edmonson retained his customary composure. The arrival of Turner was unwelcome and abrupt. He knocked once and burst through the door.

"What do you want man?" snapped Warburton.

Sylham managed to open his second eye. "We haven't finished our meeting."

"I'm truly sorry Mr. Warburton, but there's been armed robbery at the works! The circumferentor's been stolen!"

The effect was immediate. Warburton shot to his feet while Latimer sat bolt upright and Tyson dropped his clay on the table where it shattered, leaving him scrabbling at the pieces.

"Where was this?" Warburton demanded.

"This afternoon in the fen. Six men with pistols and masks. The surveyors were ambushed Mr. Warburton."

"They knew we were here!" stormed Tyson. "This is deliberate, an insult to the Partners."

"That circumferentor came from London," said Warburton, "they can have no idea what to do with it. This is a hanging matter. Who were they?"

"No one knows," said Turner. "They marched into the marsh and was dissolved up." He was beginning to enjoy his role and had noted the beer. "Mr. Friend says they just faded away ...."

"That's it!" Latimer was looking at Sylham as he spoke. "That's enough nonsense John. Time for troopers."

"By the Lord it is, Thomas, and by the Lord I hope we catch them!"

*

Peter and Katja lay side by side on their backs in the spot Peter had chosen and made their place of assignation. It was reached by a path over tussocks of grass that protruded above water level. He had flattened the reeds to form a circle within a thick stand of these and lain them to form a soft dry floor. In this hidden place it was quite still. Both wore their hats pulled over their faces to shield them from the sun but from that shade could see each other and could see the shimmer of rising heat over the reed beds. Katja had dressed the best she could without giving herself away. They listened to the creaking and cracking of the reeds in the heat. She tucked her hands under her head. Peter could not avoid looking at her breasts. She smiled at him, aware of his glance.

"There is a meeting at Oxay Hall. Both father and mama have gone there. I am free!" As he did not respond, she rolled onto her side. "Tell me where you live, Peter Dade; I don't know where you live, and what do you do now that Mr. Warburton has dismissed you?"

"I live with my mother," said Dade, "and I look after her. And for the moment I have no work."

Katja made a face. "Is that good?"

"It's good enough. I look after her, she has her chickens and her friends but not much health. And in the evenings I read to her. I can read!" he declared proudly. "The pastor lends me books."

"And I can read," said Katja, as if it was the most ordinary of accomplishments. "Mostly the bible. For instruction, father says. *'Hear ye children the instruction of a father and attend to know understanding.'*" She giggled. "Your father?"

"He's not alive. Died when I was young."

"Oh. What did he do?"

"Worked on Mr. Warburton's estate, like me. Not this Warburton, old Mr. Warburton to begin with, who died at Naseby. Our Civil War. My father was wounded at Naseby."

"Mr. Warburton should not dismiss you!"

"Mr. Warburton is not a very forgiving man."

"My father is not a very forgiving man. Perhaps it's his job. At home they think him very stern. He walks down the street, poomf, poomf, poomf in big heeled boots and people lift their hats, Mynheer this and Mynheer that. It is very formal. He says he is like Moses because he makes dry land. Mother says he is like Moses because Moses killed the frogs!"

Peter Dade laughed.

"And what else do you do in Holland?"

Katja decided not to mention Lucas and not to mention Jan. A wave of melancholy overtook her. She sat up to cover her feelings and studied Peter's tanned face and arms.

"Nothing much. It is boring. In summer we drink tea and have visitors, in winter we make lace and when it freezes we skate. Skating is very popular in Holland, but that is all there is. And of course we go to church, all dressed up, on Sunday and we say 'hello' to *mijnheer De Witt and me'vrouw De Witt and juffrouw* De Witt and go home."

"It can't be as bad as that," said Peter, half understanding.

Katja nodded, earnestly, "It is!"

"In winter we skate here," said Peter. "When the fen freezes. We wait for a good night – frost and stars – and we have a party on the ice with music and candles and a fire. I can take you! It is magical!"

Her heart turned over. She was struck by the sudden image of ice, slabs of ice and white, dead Jan trapped under these transparent coffin-lids, Jan being pulled out but there being no Jan inside him any more. Jacob telling her it was her lesson and that her punishment was never to skate again.

"Are you all right?" asked Peter, seeing her sudden pain.

"Yes, of course I am!" She sat up to cover her feelings and picked up three strands of rush which she began to plait. "My leg is going to sleep," she said, as Peter continued to look for an explanation. "Are you a good skater?"

"I have skates made of boxwood," he said evasively. She gave him a shove and a smile.

"But are you a good skater?" She could not tell him, his eyes were alight with pride. She didn't want him to know.

"I'm quite good," he said with a smile, "so they say. And on the next day, we have races, over a distance and over a mile and the winner gets a side of bacon and a barrel of beer. We can skate together!"

Instead of words, Katja completed her plait and offered it to Peter, who tucked it behind his ear.

"And I have something in return that I brought for you," he said. He fished in his pocket, sat close to her, put his right arm around her while he waved his left hand in front of her, fist closed.

"What?"

"Hold out your hand."

She did as asked and Peter placed his fist over it. She felt something fall into her palm.

"What is it?"

"Take a look."

In her palm lay a golden disc. Katja stared at it with wonder, turning it over with her forefinger.

"Is it gold?"

"I think so."

"What is it?"

"I don't know."

"It has markings like an animal but not an animal."

She held it by the edge, lifted it to flash in the sun. "Where did you get it?"

"In the ground."

"Is it an old thing?"

"I think so."

"Is it yours? Should you have it?"

"I found it."

"Where?"

"Ahah! Not telling you. In the peat, shining like that. Bright as new. Mr. Emms is not the only one. I have other things."

"Should you?"

"He has drawers full of things."

"It must belong to someone."

Peter snorted. "Someone long ago! A Roman with a hole in his pocket! So rich he didn't notice!"

Katja laughed and made as if to hand it back. "No, it's for you. A present for you."

Katja moved closer so that she could look directly into Peter Dade's eyes.

"Do you want to kiss me?"

Peter obliged but awkwardly so that Katja thought that he had not kissed many girls before. She tucked the gold disc in a pocket and took his head in cupped hands, feeling his tenseness, lying back so that she pulled him down onto propped elbows.

"Do you want to kiss me here?" Releasing his head she unbuttoned the top of her dress exposing most of her breasts. Peter drew back in alarm.

"No, I mustn't."

"Why not?"

"We mustn't."

He scrambled to his feet. Katja re-fastened the buttons, blushing, mortified.

"So!" she said, searching for some way to retrieve the moment. Even Lucas had been more competent and he was just a boy. She had got it all wrong and she realised that it pained her to see him staring into the reeds.

"I'm sorry," she said, getting to her feet and taking his arm. "I'm sorry." Peter turned and smiled in a grave but embarrassed fashion.

"I am the one who should say he's sorry."

The sun had dropped slightly so that the light was turning yellow and shadows blue. Katja fished out the disc.

"I shall keep this. It is the first present a man has ever given me!" She indicated the sun, still feeling awkward. "I think I must go before my mother returns from the Hall."

Good Lord help me, the thought kept jangling in her head, what does he think of me? Good Lord, he must think me a child!

"I'll walk with you most of the way."

*

Warburton brought the Partners' meeting to a close at about five o'clock and John Sylham immediately left. Although he had again drunk a considerable amount of beer he had managed to remember the second important thing that he had to do – get his horse attended to. The animal had a worn shoe on a hind leg that had now come loose. Clara would have a replacement. The thought cheered him up and he whistled to himself.

Oxay village straggled down lanes, straggled down the general course of the Oxay River and dispersed around a pair of greens. The smaller of these two areas of common was surrounded by muddy lanes now set in hard ruts in the summer heat. One of these tracks led to Clara's cottage, the forge and the blacksmith's pond. The forge had been constructed over the centuries from random pieces of wood and was partially supported by two lime trees. The fire and chimney, brick built, were surrounded by tools of the trade hung on hooks – tongs, hammers, pieces of shaped metal. Clara worked the bellows left-handed while holding some metal object in the glow by a pair of tongs. It was still hot although she had waited for the evening. Her hair was enclosed in a mob-cap that needed washing and she wore her smith's apron of stiff hide. She had seen Sylham approaching as she had a well-positioned view down the track, and paused to wipe away sweat from her forehead and in a surprisingly feminine gesture laid down the tongs to tuck her loose hair under the hat making a useless attempt at straightening her apron. Then she resumed working the bellows with full concentration. Sylham picked his way carefully. The horse was wary of the ruts. He tied it to a ring attached to a tree. He knew she had seen him.

"Good evening to you Clara."

Clara looked up in feigned surprise. "Good evening John Sylham."

Clara made play of selecting a hammer. She transferred the tongs from right to left hand and laid the glowing metal on an anvil where she beat it skilfully, turning it this way and that. Sylham watched, enthralled. Clara held up the object for him to see, thrusting it so close to his face that he flinched. She laughed.

"Come from the Partners' meeting?"

"How do you know .....?"

"Everyone knows about that ...."

She quenched the metal in a bucket of water and stood it to one side.

"Brought your horse then ?"

Sylham had momentarily forgotten what he was there for.

"That's right. Needs a new shoe."

"I think I can do that ...."

Without further ado Clara walked over to the horse, clucked at it, ran a hand down its flank and picked up its hoof, resting it in her lap.

"You've worn this one right through, John Sylham," she accused, "She's been walking on nails!"

Producing a pair of pincers from the apron pocket she proceeded to remove the old nails until the remains of the shoe fell on the ground. She released the horse's hoof. The horse, suddenly insecure, stood on three legs and looked round to see what had happened. Clara picked up the worn shoe.

"And now that instrument has gone ...."

"How do you know that?" Sylham was astonished. Clara merely tapped the side of her nose, leaving a soot stain.

"You've made .... a mark .... on your ...." said Sylham tentatively.

"Oh, the devil with that!" She was holding up the worn shoe beside a collection of new shoes suspended from nails and roped up in bunches. "Put your foot down girl or you'll give yourself cramp." This was addressed to the horse, which did as instructed. Sylham scratched his head, watched. Clara found a new shoe of the right size, picked it up with tongs and put it in the fire. "I know most things and I know them soon. Name of Hare!" she said with a laugh. She folded her arms across her apron to wait for the shoe to heat, moved closer to John Sylham, sniffed.

"Good beer at the Hall?"

Confused, Sylham could only blurt out a "yes".

"I hear you are reckoning to raise our rents."

Sylham had a feeling of dread. He had told her brother Felix. He supposed everyone would now know. He started to undo his jacket. It was hot enough without the blast from the forge. Clara smiled at his discomfort.

"Getting a roasting, John? Why d'you need to do it? People here can't afford it." She leaned forward and shovelled more charcoal onto the heart of the fire, gave half-a-dozen pumps on the bellows. Sparks shot up into the metal hood that projected from the brick chimney. She poked at the horseshoe.

"I reckon I need the money too," he said. "As much as most."

"For this drainage."

It was half statement, half question. Sylham made a rueful face. He avoided an answer. "I shall have to stand back a bit. I shall be cooking here!"

Clara was not going to let him off.

"You've bought into this drainage, John Sylham, and now it's costing. Why do it, I say? Your family and our family, we go back to beginnings. This drainage takes away the people's food and a belly has no ears. This cut that you are all making, it ruins the living and disturbs the dead. Don't do it."

"All very well to say Clara, but not when you owe money. I bet you never owed money in your life."

"You only owe what you borrow!" said Clara. "That Arabella of yours expects too much." Sylham stared at her, uncomprehending. "You don't need more land," she explained. "Two thousand more acres is it? And whose two thousand acres are they? It's an easy way for Mr. Warburton to call theft improvement, and you do it too to keep Arabella in fine things. Ambition rises off her like a smell on a hot day! If you had wed me John Sylham, things would have been different."

She picked up tongs and lifted the horseshoe from the fire. It was already a bright orange. She walked rapidly over to the horse and with practised skill tapped at the unshod hoof. The animal lifted its foot. She cradled it in her apron and tried out the shoe. There was a hiss of burning. An eruption of smoke and stink of hoof immediately followed. Clara talked to the animal, saying things that Sylham could neither hear properly nor understand. She dropped the hoof, not satisfied with the shoe, and slipped it back in the fire. She rejoined him where he stood.

"We both belong to this place. You've kissed me John Sylham, and liked it and don't you forget it, and wanted more!"

Sylham had no idea what to say. She was almost leaning against him, smelling slightly of sweat and greatly of burning.

"That was long ago!" he protested weakly.

"It may have been long ago to you," she replied. "Long ago as yesterday I say. Time was and time is."

She turned to shovel unneeded charcoal on the fire, but not fast enough to conceal the glitter of tears in her eyes. She pumped at the bellows making sparks fly, burning off her anger in the incandescent heart of the fire. Sylham watched her in wordless communion, staring with her into the fire that consumed thoughts of what might have been but had never been possible between a Sylham and a Hare. Firelight shone on her brown shoulders and Sylham could not help but compare their smoothness and strength with Arabella's bony white back which occasionally poked out of her long white nightdresses. She stopped working the bellows and the fire died back from white to orange to red. Flying sparks settled. They both watched it.

"The world is a sad and wonderful place for some of us," she said to the hearth. Sylham shifted uneasily, aware of his clumsiness in this sort of thing, thinking it better to stay quiet. "You are one of us, not one of them," she continued. "You don't need the land, then you don't need to raise rents, so you don't need this new river. You ain't Warburton's sort, or Tyson .... best to leave them to it." She turned abruptly. "Would you like some of Clara's beer?"

Sylham nodded. He was not sure it was a good idea, but then he thought of Arabella waiting for him, and her expression of dismay. Anyway, it would change the subject. Clara smiled and retreated to a padlocked cupboard that was more the size of a small shed. The door was ajar and she opened it to remove a large earthenware jug. At that moment her back was turned and looking past her Sylham saw tools. She closed the door again and he stared at the fire. There was no doubt that the cupboard was full of spades, mattocks, shovels and all the other things missing from the works. Clara handed him the earthenware jug.

"A girl gets thirsty at this work ...."

The jug was heavier than Sylham expected although apparently it was no more than a cup to Clara. He raised it to his lips and drank awkwardly, tipping some down his clothes. When he paused Clara took it from him and drank with practiced skill. He saw that she turned the jug to drink from the same side as him and he felt unease. She put the vessel down and returned to the fire, lifting out the shoe. Satisfied with its colour she shaped it on the anvil, turning it, hammering it, dipping it in the bucket. Sylham considered what to do. Had she meant him to see? Was it part of a plan? He was too fuddled to come to conclusions. Silence was prudent.

Clara filled her mouth with shoe-nails, arranging them to form a fan, heads out. Thus decorated she managed a coquettish smile at Sylham before picking up the horse's hoof. She hammered the nails through the shoe, from lip to hand and driven home in two deft motions. Soon finished, she released the horse, stood up and let down the top of her apron.

"Finished!" she said. Her lawn shirt was cut so low on the shoulder that it promised to slide down completely. She was very brown. "Another drink, John Sylham?" She took a drink herself and waved it towards him. Sylham shook his head.

"I had better go." He walked unsteadily around her and with fumbling hands untied his horse. She watched him, hands on hips, disappointment crumpling her face.

"Yes, you'd better go!" she shouted. "You better had, you're no use to me John Sylham! Just you remember this; old Grim says leave the old people alone. Old Grim says that Jack o' Lantern is the dancing of their souls. Old Grim says you are draining his blood!"

But Sylham was gone. He flung himself onto his horse with extravagant urgency, finding only one stirrup and making the animal whinny. He dug in his heels more than he intended, so that it broke into a half gallop, barely under control.

"Hey John Sylham!" yelled Clara, "You haven't paid!"

But Sylham didn't hear. She fished in her apron pocket and pulled out a mouse, holding it by its tail and letting it run up her arm, catching it and replacing it again and again and again. "You shouldn't be running away," she called in his direction.

*

De Vries left the Hall as early as he thought prudent, taking Cristeen with him. He rode while Cristeen made use of the offer of Warburton's carriage and coachman. The evening was balmy and bats dashed over the ears of the horses and around the seated driver. Their route took them past Oxay Church. The tower was splendidly lit by the low sun and de Vries asked the driver to stop so that Cristeen could look at it. The hedgerows hung with rose-hips, glowing like coals and swifts screamed round the roof.

De Vries was seized by a feeling of shame over the circumstances of his last visit and his confused retreat. He dismounted and walked to Cristeen.

"You go on ahead. I think I shall just call in for a moment – unless you want to join me?"

Cristeen looked at the low sun, the bats.

"No, you go in. I must be home for Katja."

The carriage moved off. De Vries had passed the building on a number of occasions since the incident of the bells but had to admit to himself that he had lacked the courage to go in. He tied up his horse and told it he would be quick, made for the porch and pushed open the studded door. He renewed his acquaintance with the stone cold, the musty smells of wood and plaster that were identical to the smells of the church back home. A pious smell, he thought to himself, the smell that lingers in a bible. He took off his hat. His eyes becoming accustomed to the half-light he moved forward to find a pew, sat down and decided he would pray for Middleton, for the future of the works; that he would ask for guidance and, he thought wryly, more materials, particularly stone. As his eyes re-focussed he became aware of a figure in the pews in front of him that seemed to be seated in prayer. He felt a pang, part alarm, part annoyance that he did not have the moment to himself. This was followed by surprise as he recognised Emms. It had not occurred to him that a priest might pray in his own church. He rose gently and was on the point of leaving when Emms turned his head and saw him.

"Mynheer de Vries! How good to see you again. The meeting has finished?"

The question was rhetorical. De Vries nodded. Emms had spoken in the tones of a man accustomed to his holy ground. There was a slight echo in the building.

"I have come here before," he said defensively. Only once, he reminded himself. It was Emms' turn to nod. He looked at de Vries expectantly.

De Vries searched for words. He had not anticipated this circumstance and wondered whether he should treat Emms as a man of God or as a disaffected Partner, who for all that was still his employer. Emms rose to his feet, towering above de Vries.

"It's a fine church," de Vries blurted out, hoping to avoid controversy of any kind. "Very old." He wondered whether to tell Emms of his last experience but decided against it.

"Would you like me to show you round?"

De Vries had been thinking of ways to make a polite but rapid departure. Trapped, he agreed with all the courtesy he could manage.

"Of course, of course, it is very kind of you if you have the time, but I must not be long, my wife is expecting me ...."

Emms made a slight bow of acknowledgement and waved de Vries down the aisle towards the altar. He stopped some way down and pointed towards the roof.

"Do you see, up there, the carved angels holding up the roof?"

De Vries could make out the figures projecting from the wall. He could see some were damaged, to the extent that wings were partly or entirely missing.

"Shot at!" said Emms. "Faces and wings shot off with muskets. Puritans, local men, and they stood here on the graves of their ancestors who carved them for the glory of God and shot them off! A fine irony Mr. de Vries, but better I suppose than shooting people."

Emms pointed to the worn gravestones underfoot, the shadows in the stone. "Superstition. Destroying other people's images. Let me show you something else." Emms set off in the opposite direction, towards the tower. "Here is our baptismal font, heads missing, a massacre of Christians! How close to the surface these things are Mr. de Vries – that's what I am trying to get the Partners to understand. People who do this believe that by hacking at stone they move closer to God's will." Emms had moved over to an adjoining wall and was running the flat of his hand over it. It was the wall on which de Vries had seen traces of painting on his previous visit. "Feel," said Emms. De Vries did as he was bid. "It's a painting," he said, "under here. The Last Judgement, what we call Doomsday. I have applied water to the surface so that the wash becomes translucent." He stepped back pointing to this section of wall and that, de Vries half looking to the spot, half watching Emms' face.

"To the left are the Blessed, to the right, the Damned, in chains, prodded by devils, heading for hellfire. In chains are a king and queen, priests, a bishop. A scroll over them reads '*Discedite, maledicti*'. Depart ye cursed! No room for shades of sin. Now come outside!"

Emms strode ahead, gaining the door of the church which he opened, beckoning to de Vries to follow. Seeing this as a way of escape, he made his way into the evening light, blinking, surprised at the brightness of the low sun outside.

"I think I must be going back ...." he demurred. "You see, my horse is tied up there. You have been very kind ...."

"This won't take a moment ...." Emms was not going to be deflected. He strode off across the grass along a path worn with use, between gravestones and the wall of the church, rounded the east end and paused beside the north wall. De Vries felt obliged to follow, noting that Emms still wore his heavy coat which he had unbuttoned, looking like a tall flapping scarecrow. He wished he had never had the fancy to stop. Emms was pointing at the base of the tower, which for most of its length was covered by lush green moss and obscured by stonecrop where the stonework plunged into the ground. A stretch of it was bare however and it was at this Emms was pointing. "Do you see?"

De Vries stooped to see the shape of a head, a single boulder crudely carved, built in to the masonry of the wall. The mouth was pouting to form a round shape, as if caught and frozen when whistling. Below the head was a foreshortened body, a part-body with vestigial conical breasts. Whatever else there was, was locked in the foundation stones of the building.

"Something very old," said Emms. "They call it 'the Boy'. A direct connection between the people here and the things I find. When they built this church they put it there or maybe it was here before the church. There is a hole for the mouth. Very deep, I have never been able to plumb it. Someone puts flowers in the mouth, and things are left – scraps of this and that. I keep a record – it didn't seem regular to me, but then I found it was, but not by our calendar. That's what we have here ..... a connection."

"Do you connect it to our trouble?"

Emms shrugged. "Things don't disappear because you paint them over, or shoot at them until you destroy them or chop off their heads, Mr. de Vries. They live on in men's minds."

De Vries was shocked at his attitude. "You will not know, that after you left the meeting, Turner came to report that the circumferentor has been stolen. There was nothing mysterious about it. Six men in masks!"

Emms' face clouded over. He turned and started to make his way back the way they had come. "If only we could have had a meeting with them all. You see how things can so easily get out of hand. This project is no good for Oxay, it divides, it will destroy. This will make terrible trouble."

De Vries felt anger at the man, but tried to reason.

"But it will provide all sorts of benefits. You are a Partner – I tell you I don't understand you Mr. Emms – you want to ruin your own investment? See your own money go to waste? How is that?"

"Are you so sure that everything you do in life is right, Mr. de Vries? Don't you come upon things that make you change your mind? Here we are, a stone's throw from great truths." Emms moved closer to de Vries, who saw that Emms had all the time been clutching a bible. The intensity of the man made him sidestep and stumble on an intruding gravestone. Emms paid no attention. De Vries recovered and followed by this only route beside the church wall, eager to escape and in this way the two retraced their steps to the porch.

"It is not enough to say you are an engineer, and therefore it is your job. I am an engineer too, but I am an engineer of men's souls. I construct a heaven using the Good Book as my tool, believing in its certain truths. What if these certain truths seem more to me like alchemy than science? Then surely the good engineer must re-adjust his position? My faith can survive the truth of Creation and if another man's can't I say his faith is the weaker!"

Emms only stopped because they had reached the porch door. He pushed it, ready to enter.

"Mr. Warburton and Mr. Latimer want soldiers in."

"Violence breeds violence."

De Vries could contain himself no longer.

"Mr. Emms, you invested in this enterprise, and now you obstruct it. You obstruct my work! Why? All these pieces you collect. They are not important. What do you want?"

"I want the cut moved, Mr. de Vries."

"But it can't be moved now! You know that is a ridiculous request! We have dug two and a half English miles! What do you think that would cost?"

"The question is, what will it cost where it is?"

"I don't understand you! You know the figures."

"There are men at Cambridge who understand."

De Vries found himself being ushered away from the porch toward the churchyard gate. "*'He that answereth a matter before he heareth it, it is folly and shame unto him'*" said Emms.

De Vries turned to him. "Mr. Emms, I came to this church to say my prayers and communicate with the Lord! I think you are a madman," he said hotly. "Good day!"

He walked purposefully to his horse, mounted it and moved off without a backward glance. The man to whom he should be able to turn had put a curse on the enterprise and, he thought, contaminated this place of worship. He now had nowhere to go.

Chapter 13

AUGUST 10TH GRANGE FARM, OXAY

TO THOMAS BATHURST ESQ.,
BATHURSTS'S,
PREBEND STREET,
NORWICH

Dear Sir,

I write to you on recommendation of our mutual friend Mr. John Warburton, with whom I have been acquainted for many years. I am also a Partner in the current venture to drain these parts.

May I be allowed to presume upon you on an unrelated matter which concerns Mr. Tobias Tolman, to whom I am related by marriage. I seldom leave the vicinity of Oxay, and have no knowledge of how things may be in Norwich, nor, I confess, any desire to visit your fair city where my lack of experience would be most evident.

I am informed that Mr. Tolman may be promoting certain investments regarding the planting of sugar in the West Indies and in particular the island of St. Kitts. This is a matter of the greatest delicacy. May I impose upon you for the confidentiality of the law in this matter, hoping that you will believe me when I say my interests are for the best and not for any form of commercial advantage or personal gain. I would be most obliged to you, and of course I shall meet all expenses if it were possible to discover the nature of any such promotion at your earliest convenience.

I am sir, your obedient servant.

JOHN SYLHAM, GENTLEMAN.

The theft of the circumferentor had had an unsettling effect because of both the brazenness of the theft and the value of the object. There was much wild speculation on this last matter but it was agreed it was worth more than a house and that there was bound to be trouble. The workmen had a fine time laughing at Friend and Parker and descriptions of them fleeing from the reeds. (No one laughed at the chain men, who were regarded with awe). What everyone agreed was that the locals needed a lesson

"About time too!" railed Maddox to his group of friends. "What these peasants need is a few rounds of musket up their arses. That'd clear them out of the reeds!"

It was nearly dark and seats had been set up all round the ale house using whatever was to hand to enjoy the good weather. The building was full inside and men lay about outside on the grass and the road verges. The Dutch kept to the Dutch and the English to the English. The men needed no excuse for refreshment after a day's digging and thirst increased with warmth. Voices were becoming louder and language more boisterous. Wilson, the landlord, had provided two lanterns which were hung from a tree outside, making manoeuvre to and from the beer barrels less troublesome. Maddox's group sat near one light, their tankards in hand and a jug on the ground.

"What makes a surveyor run?" demanded Maddox loudly in his northern tones.

"Almost anything makes a surveyor run!" declared one of his group of friends to laughter. "Mice?"

"No, I want a proper reply," protested Maddox, who had been drinking steadily, and was on his feet, weaving about.

"No idea! What makes a surveyor run?" said the same man.

"They're always in a bit of the rush!" shouted Maddox triumphantly. The men groaned and cheered.

"What makes a Dutchman run, then?" Maddox shouted. A noisy Dutch group sat nearby. Hearing his words that group fell silent.

"Can't say!" shouted Maddox' friend. "What makes a Dutchman run?"

"An English fleet!" Maddox had turned deliberately towards the Dutch group, raised his tankard in their direction. Their pipes glowed in the semi-darkness. Dutch words spilled out.

"Noisy devils," Maddox observed, "have you noticed how it sounds like coughing and spitting!" There was dismissive laughter then loud talk. From this Maddox thought he recognised one voice. "Is that you Hellenbuch?" he called. "Are you there, jackass?" he added dangerously at lower volume.

"What do you reckon will happen now?" asked one of the workmen, trying to turn round the subject.

"They'll bring in the Serjeant. That's what Turner says and men to guard the work."

There was another burst of laughter from the Dutch group. Maddox roared at the top of his voice.

"I reckon these Dutchies stole the circumferentor so's they could have a rest! What do you say to that, Hellenbuch!"

A fiddle started up somewhere, men began to sing.

"I say you should not say things like that!" said Hellenbuch who had materialised from the twilight and now stood over them. He was swaying slightly, his face glistening with perspiration in the lamplight. His scar appeared red and new.

"Oh do you, Hellenbuch!" Maddox growled. "You think we care what Dutchmen say?"

Whether or not it was his intention, Hellenbuch lurched forward one pace and kicked over the beer jug. They stared at the wave of liquid that quickly disappeared into the ground.

"An accident!" exclaimed Maddox, "Another Dutch accident, too many Dutch accidents."

"What you mean Maddox?" demanded Hellenbuch with no intention of backing off or calming matters down. Maddox lurched forward in turn until they were only a pace apart, both men snorting.

"Your Dutch accidents killed Middleton."

"What you mean we stole the circumferentor?" Hellenbuch was still struggling with the first insult. "Do you think this is a funny English joke to call us thieves?"

"You don't do anything properly and you can't work and you killed Middleton. We can take root waiting for you!"

Hellenbuch hit Maddox full in the face and he went down with a crash. Hellenbuch followed him almost immediately, felled by one of Maddox's men. The ensuing free-for-all was mainly conducted on national lines and with violent intensity. Those who were neither Dutch nor English stood at a distance to shout advice, place bets on the outcome and haul out the wounded. The appearance of Wilson with a blunderbuss brought some order. He discharged it into the air with a massive explosion and proceeded to re-load. Maddox bleeding freely from his nose, recovered his senses.

"Enough!" he roared. "Enough!" Silence was accompanied by a strange stillness. "Another day, Hellenbuch!" he bawled.

"Another day Maddox!" came the reply.

Wilson continued to load the weapon just in case and kept it in one hand until they left.

Chapter 14

Ignoring the August sun the Yule Brook and its dykes and ditches continued with the inexorable drainage of the summer rains. It was balked in numerous directions by the banks, piles and sluices of the new cut which separated it from its mother river. Seeking a reunion it pushed out in all directions along deep, soft layers of peat. These willing seams conducted it over a vast area which it proceeded to fill, moving on to half-filled bogs, oozing up in the spaces between roots and pushing beneath layers of clay deposited by an Ice Age. Here and there it found ancient, deep water courses that had been long abandoned, and replenished them beneath and behind the banks of the new cut.

Chapter 15

The troopers arrived in early September, just as the short spell of August summer gave way to further rain. Six men arrived on horseback from Norwich under the command of a Captain and a Sergeant. They were in cuirasses, helmeted, with swords at the belt and muskets at the saddle. Warburton intended that they should give an unmistakable message.

The body of men made a point of showing themselves to the village and parish, trotting up and down roads and lanes before making for Oxay Hall where Warburton had prepared a stable block for both men and horses. Clarke's son, who had followed them, reported that they had no sooner arrived than they marched and counter-marched in front of Warburton and Tyson, drilling and shouting. The villagers waited in uneasy apprehension. The following day, after morning prayers in the stables (watched by the boy who reported they prayed mightily hard), they began house-to-house searches. The process was the same each time – two men at the back door, one at each end and two men at the front with the Captain and Sergeant. There was little courtesy.

"You are?"

A hesitant answer. Name ticked off a list.

"We have come to search for the stolen circumferentor. Please stand aside."

The searches were methodical, the men unsmiling and efficient. When they spoke, it was with north country accents. They turned out chests and closets, looked up chimneys and inside bread ovens, demolished wood piles and as Felix Dunn was keen to tell, even turned over his manure heap. They found nothing. They commandeered one of John Lambert's boats and splashed around inexpertly, poking in ponds. They crawled through loft spaces and ran steel rods through thatch and hay ricks. They skewered an old crone's broody hen by mistake, trampled the eggs and were bitten by her dog but they found nothing.

In the evening they gathered in a circle to say prayers again, and as Clarke's boy reported, read the Bible, smoked pipes and played cards for pieces of straw. They did not drink.

On their arrival Clara had been exceptionally busy. The forge was kept at a bright heat that could be seen at night and there was busy hammering. The troopers surrounded the place in a show of military precision and stared. None of them seemed inclined to trespass on her territory as she stood by the forge, arms akimbo.

"You took your time getting here," she challenged before the Captain could say anything. "You know who I am."

"We know who you are, Clara Hare." He ticked off his list.

"Then get on with it."

She picked hot iron from the fire with pincers and beat at it on the anvil with a hammer. The men searched as best they could among the collection of tools, wheel rims, chain, bars, horseshoes, nails, scrap and everything else that cluttered the forge. It was soon obvious the exercise was fruitless. The Captain called them together and they left in marching order. Clara waved after them smiling. She had made horseshoes from the tools and patted them where they now hung on the wall.

"Clever Clara!" she said.

The searching continued for a week and when nothing was found the men were divided into two patrols, one for daytime and one for the hours of darkness. At the drainage works these developments provided some comfort as tool thefts stopped. Although no reconciliation had taken place between the Dutch and English workmen, both were relieved to see the comforting glint of armour and hear the noise of horses.

The night patrol had its first encounter within that week. The weather continued to be wet with heavy showers interspersed with warm drizzle blowing in from the South-West. There was a half moon. The men covered the ground on foot, each carrying a lantern. They were beginning to get their bearings amongst the network of paths and dykes that surrounded the works, keeping their movements to well-defined footways, always moving as a group and learning to watch and wait. The three men and the sergeant had seated themselves quietly under the shelter of a tree. Rain dripped from their helmets and they wore capes over their armour. They had a view over the works to their right while to their left lay a stretch of bog and water. The men sat quietly, tapping each other if they wanted to attract attention, whispering if words were needed. The sergeant was the first to notice the dancing blue lights on the water. They flickered and ran across the surface, dying and leaping. He nudged the others. They all turned to watch, fascinated.

"Ignis Fatuus," said the sergeant, who had seen it before, "Will-o'-tho-wisp." One of the men crossed himself. "Wild fire."

"What is it?" asked another.

"No one knows," said the sergeant.

"They say it lures you to your death," volunteered the third. "The rain don't put them out ...."

They watched the silent display, faces illumined by the flames. The silence seemed to grow in intensity. No one moved. The flames ran towards them then abruptly retreated and went out.

"That was a wonder," said the sergeant. "By the Lord, that was a wonder! It's gone!"

"They say it's the souls of wandering spirits ...." said the third man.

The sergeant snorted with derision and was about to deliver a withering reply when they were pelted with a hail of stones that crashed into the tree overhead, hit them on helmets, cuirass and shoulders, hit one man in the face, bringing him down unconscious, hit them on arms and legs, and abruptly stopped. From somewhere within the reeds they could hear the rhythmic splosh of oars as a boat pulled away, a derisive laugh, the thin sound of a flute playing some sort of jaunty tune.

"His helmet off, lads," said the sergeant as they recovered their fallen man. He was furious. "Next time we'll show them!" He patted his pistol. "Praise the Lord!"

"Amen!" replied the men unbuckling the helmet.

*

"The Good Lord knows what I cannot know, but this may be one of the last entries I make in my Journal in this place," wrote Emms. *"Perhaps I should be suffering from doubts, but I am not. Tomorrow I am to be interviewed by His Grace, Bishop Lloyd, of whom I confess I know next to nothing. He has come with two priests and they all lodge at Oxay Hall. What a place our village has become with soldiers and grand men, when what we need are scholars. I feel sure that the Bishop will dismiss me, unfrock me, but my faith is strong. It can survive the truth of Creation where other men's cannot."*

Squally rain battered on the window. The remains of yet another cold supper of boiled fowl cluttered his desk. He paused from his writing to open a desk drawer and take out his recent acquisition of flints, laying these in a neat row in front of the fowl carcase. He picked them up in turn in his right hand, running his thumb over the edges in the manner of testing a knife. Selecting the largest, leaf-shaped example he picked it up to saw at the chicken remains. In a short time he had severed the breast bone down one side. He nodded to himself, gave the flint a clean with a handkerchief and put them all back in the drawer. He picked up his quill.

"If I am correct that the ground is a layer-cake, we have Romans at three feet within the silt, then our own ancient people before them at some four or five and these simple tools at nine or ten feet, three times as old as the Romans. Mr. de Vries says I am a madman. He almost surprised me today. I note in this Journal that I have buried the urn and its contents in the graveyard, having made careful drawings of all parts of it and the fragments of bone. *Hic Iacet* who knows who, but a resident of this place, now six paces from the third aisle buttress on the South side. *Requiescat in Pace.* Now I must prepare myself for tomorrow's events, for I am on trial for my beliefs.

He scattered sand on the last lines, blew them about the page and closed the book.

*

Bishop Lloyd was a small round man with a sense of his own importance. He disliked travelling, preferring the comforts of Norwich to the uncertainties of the parishes. He had made sure the journey from Norwich was broken overnight and had arrived at Oxay Hall in time for dinner on the second day. The Bishop's coach had made a slow progress through the countryside. Bishop Lloyd believed in being seen. He had never met Warburton, but was relieved to see that Oxay Manor lived up to his expectations as a lodging. Warburton's letter, as Justice of the Peace, via Bathurst had provided details of Emms but given no clue as to the author. He was pleased to find Warburton appeared to be a sound man of the church, and a man of undoubted substance, as Bathurst had described him.

Warburton had made sure that everything possible was done to cater for Lloyd's creature comforts, although he had been slightly annoyed to find that he was expected to provide for a curate, a further two priests who were to act as witnesses, a secretary to write it all down, a clerk whose duties were undefined and two coachmen-cum-porters. The latter had been consigned to the kitchen for their supper while the others sat rather awkwardly at Warburton's table.

Lloyd, at Warburton's request, had said an elaborate grace from his position at Warburton's right hand, and then set about eating with the sort of gusto that Ruth, watching him, thought more suited to some ill-fed curate.

She caught Sarah's eye. Sarah smiled and both women were obliged to study their plates. Warburton, who had not found the grace to his liking, being too Catholic for his taste, reminded himself he did not have to like the man who had come to do a job. Richard sat to his left, uncommunicative.

"Now tell me what it is about Emms?" Lloyd obviously had no objection to speaking with his mouth full. "I have your complaint of course by way of Tom Bathurst. I beg you to flesh out the bones a bit. What sort of man is he? His father knew your father I believe? Normally I would think that a good foundation for continuing harmony."

Lloyd paused in a moment of indecision between a further slice of mutton or a roast partridge, whose crisp, upturned breast positively begged for the prongs of his fork. He opted for the partridge, skewered the bird, transferred it to his plate and split it deftly in two. The two priests, who sat with the curate, secretary and clerk, had no choice between partridge and mutton in the remote country they occupied. Sarah watched them watching Lloyd, and was sorry for them. She signalled to the manservant, who stooped to her.

"More wine for the gentlemen, I think ...."

Warburton had had time to collect his thoughts. "Things were sometimes complicated, your Grace, by the war. The relationship did not survive, like so many."

"Ah yes. Your father was one of the Parliamentary persuasion, the Eastern Association, if I'm right, but Emms was not. Sad times. But there is nothing to be gained by dwelling on it. What's done is done."

He attacked the second half of the partridge, having reduced the first to fragments. Warburton wondered what else Lloyd knew or had been told by Bathurst. Bathurst's father had been his father's confidant.

"However," said Lloyd, "you have certainly done the right thing by the man. His Perpetual Curacy is in your patronage, and I have the licence. I understand you may feel sorry for him, being brought up alongside each other, but there is another in this matter." He paused, to find that all were looking at him in incomprehension. "The Good Lord, of course! His duty is to his Master, who is a jealous God as it says in Chapter twenty of Exodus. From what you have told me, Mr. Emms in another, less tolerant age, would have attracted a cry of heresy, no less!"

"I don't know that it's as serious as that." Warburton felt obliged to make protest at the seriousness of the charge, which alarmed him despite everything.

"But he undermines everything. You have the erosion of the authority of the Church, you have a pastor who, far from reinforcing that, sets fire to the tar barrel so to speak, by promoting notions that undermine your drainage works and in so doing, undermines his own patron."

"I had not thought of it in those terms."

"Ah well, you have not the training, sir, and why should you have, to see the politic of it. This undermining of your works is support for these superstitious peasants who are ever ready to slip back into ungodliness. Take that with his denial of Creation and we have an unholy stew!" Perhaps prompted by the word, Lloyd looked around the table for more to eat.

"It is only my intention to have him removed from office, not to have him executed!" Warburton protested, trying to inject some levity into the situation. Richard, who had so far kept himself to himself, passed a salver, on which rested a pike, to Lloyd. Prelate and pike regarded each other. Ruth watched with annoyance. She had hoped it would be left untouched, guaranteeing something cold for the following day. Lloyd had no inhibitions and cut himself a section of the flesh.

"Fish!" he declared, "Such a fine thing for a delicate digestion! I cannot go to bed on a heavy stomach!"

"Indeed not!" said Ruth.

*

The long table in Warburton's Hall had been laid crosswise so that it faced a solitary chair and table where Emms was to sit. Lloyd saw no reason to vary this arrangement, even when Warburton pointed out that it was intimidating.

"A man of God is accustomed to tribulation," was his unsympathetic reply. He had passed a terrible night, rolling this way and that with indigestion and saw no reason to make life easy for anyone. Latimer and Tyson had been requested to join the panel and sat one at each end of the table. John Sylham had not been asked. Warburton, knowing him well, judged he would only refuse and the refusal would embarrass him. Warburton, as squire, sat next to Lloyd, the two priests sat on each side. The curate, secretary and clerk had been given a separate table on which they had deposited paper, inkwells and quills. There was shuffling and coughing. It was a colourless, overcast day and candles had been lit to supplement the inadequate daylight. Lloyd wore ecclesiastical garb as did the priests. Due to his small size, Lloyd looked like a baby rolled up in a shawl. The effect was emphasized by his small pink hands which stuck out and rested on the table.

"Mr. Bathurst is a persuasive man," said Lloyd, more to pass the time than anything else. "Well respected in Norwich and a benefactor to the

Church as I'm sure you know. We owe him much. The Church always has empty pockets ...."

He looked meaningfully at Warburton, then at Tyson and Latimer, who returned his glance expressionlessly. A silence fell. Heads turned to stare up into the roof of the Hall or to watch smoke rising from the candles. The silence was relieved by the sound of Emms' horse on the gravel, followed by the front door opening and closing, then the sound of footsteps on boards, leading up to the door. Warburton thought it sounded like a man being led to execution, as indeed it was, and was sorry for William Emms despite himself. Emms entered, dressed in a long dark cloak, hat in one hand and a Bible and some sort of package in the other. He took in the layout of the room, walked up to the table and made a short bow towards the seated man. Warburton had been struggling to his feet but Lloyd stilled him with flaps of a hand, indicating he should stay seated.

"Good morning your Grace, gentlemen," said Emms in a firm voice that he had been practising.

"Please sit down Mr. Emms," said Warburton. Emms took his seat, laid his Bible and his package on the table, folded his hands in front of him.

"Before we start these proceedings, let us say the Lord's Prayer together," said Lloyd. *"Our Father which art in Heaven Hallowed be thy name ...."*

They intoned the words together. Warburton, watching Emms covertly, thought that Emms appeared calm. He had told Lloyd that he must make the running as he was out of his depth in this sort of matter. Lloyd took this with satisfaction. He had no intention of playing second fiddle, but needed Warburton's support and evidence.

"*.... for ever and ever. Amen.*"

Lloyd addressed Emms.

"Mr. Emms, I wish you good day. I believe you know Mr. Tyson, Mr. Latimer and Mr. Warburton of course. The other gentlemen are here to perform the duties of scribes to ensure that a proper record is kept of the proceedings."

Emms nodded.

"I believe you know why I am here, but I shall put it in plain language. I am here as your Bishop to examine the beliefs that you have expressed to these gentlemen – and others in your flock, concerning a number of matters. Serious concerns have been expressed to me concerning the propriety of your ministry. Namely, that you have permitted yourself to interpret the Holy Book, conceiving and proposing a blasphemous chronology for mankind, denying the six periods that mark the dealings of

God with men and denying that our earth was created according to the wisdom of great men and the very facts of the Bible in the year four thousand and four before Christ."

Lloyd paused for breath and for dramatic effect and to allow the scribes to catch up. The sound of their quills seemed unnaturally loud. Lloyd looked long at Emms, looked to Warburton and back to Emms.

"It says in Isaiah '*Woe unto him that striveth with his maker*! *Let the potsherd strive with the potsherds of the earth. Shall the clay say to him that fashioneth it, what makest thou?*' But you have asked that very question, and I am told, have constructed a chronology from pieces of wood and stone dug from the ground. Things without lineage or record, which you prefer to the Holy Book. Is that not so Mr. Warburton?"

"You produced bits of stone and pot," said Warburton, who was not finding this easy. "You brought them to the Partners' meeting. You said they were knife blades and arrow heads and were thousands of years old."

"I did," said Emms firmly. "And they must be. They come from a considerable depth. By my calculations they must be over six thousand years before Christ."

The silence this brought was broken only by Latimer sighing loudly and Tyson drumming on the table with his fingertips.

"Well now I have heard it for myself!" said Lloyd. "Are you in full possession of your faculties? Do you realise the implication of such a heresy?"

"I did not set out to have any conclusions, your Grace," said Emms, sitting very upright, back pressed into the chairback, knees and feet together, emphasizing his gauntness. He appeared neither shaken nor dismayed. "I asked and will continue to ask all the questions that the Good Lord has given me the enquiring mind and apparatus of reason to ask. If this is seen as blasphemy or heresy, then I am sorry, for it is not intended to be."

"It seems very like that to me!" Lloyd burst out with anger. His indigestion was eating at him.

"Can I ask you to consider this. These are the facts with which I wrestled – they are there for anyone to see for themselves. At first if you are digging, there are the things of yesterday. A boot buckle, a link of chain, a nail. Iron. Then further down, perhaps a coin with some strange head and writing – Roman. Then bronze. A piece of metal with a clasp. These."

Emms produced the bundle that he had till now been balancing on his knees. It was some sort of material tied round with a leather thong which he unknotted. Rolling the bundle open he revealed the two heavy green axe heads he had shown to de Vries. He stood them upright on the haft end, and waited.

"What are we supposed to make of these?" said Tyson irritably. He thought Emms was being allowed to say too much and too much of it was claptrap.

"These are older than Roman, from what I can see. Let me show you!" Emms rose to his feet, an action he appeared to do in stages because of his long frame, and before anyone could voice protest had laid them in front of Lloyd. "Bronze!" he declared, waving a hand over them. "Bronze before Roman, below Roman! Don't you see? Well below Roman. In our type of fenny ground, common things left on the surface, such as a billhook or a spade will soon be covered up by the annual decay of reeds. Who hasn't lost something this way? I have tried to measure this by cutting vertically so that the layers of decay can be seen, but it is difficult to separate one layer from another and my excavations have all filled with water. What I can tell you is that at a great depth, perhaps twelve feet, there is no more peat. The soil turns to gravel."

"What has that to do with these?" demanded Lloyd. "I must ask you to come to some point. You heard what I said at the beginning." He eased his stomach by sitting back in his chair and pushing against the table with his small hands. What he needed, he thought, was a medicinal brandy. His stomach gurgled. "Come along man!" he urged, to disguise the noise.

"It is evident that some inches of compacted material accumulate in a hundred years. What we have is a clock. A great clock in the ground, or if you prefer, a chronicle!"

"But all it is, is earth!" protested Tyson.

"You cannot deny the facts." Emms addressed Tyson directly. "You cannot deny the things in the ground. The layers of material. The time it has taken to accumulate."

Tyson stared at him woodenly. Any fenland farmer knew dykes must be cleared annually or be quickly lost, that marshland rose, drowning trees. Emms could see from Tyson's face that he had got him. Tyson resorted to bluster.

"This is just claptrap dressed up as science!"

"Where does this take us?" demanded the suffering Lloyd. "What is the point?"

"The point is ....," said Emms, returning to his bundle and selecting a handful of his flints, which he laid on the table in front of Lloyd ".... these were made by men who lived before the Romans, and before the men who made these bronze axes, thousands of years ago."

"How many thousand?" demanded Lloyd.

"Many thousands," replied Emms evasively.

"Answer the question." Lloyd was becoming pink with irritation.

"I don't yet know."

"One thousand, ten thousand, or are you going to say a hundred thousand!" He turned to Tyson, throwing his hands in the air. Tyson snorted.

"Bits of stone," said Warburton. "Pure fancy they were made by men." He saw a way of making things easier for Emms. Emms refused to take it.

"You must look at them!" He propelled the flints around the table-top with a long forefinger. "These are arrowheads, sharp as any steel. Just look at the workmanship!"

"Who are you saying were the workmen?" demanded Tyson. "Workmanship .... workmen. Who made them?"

"Our ancestors made them."

This remark brought an instant and ominous silence, watched by the scribes until broken by Tyson's outburst.

"You're not suggesting these things were made by an Englishman?"

"I am. Long ago."

"I suppose you think Englishmen ran about half naked like Red Indians, with these things." Tyson was furious. "This is not only preposterous, it's, it's ...." He searched for the right words. "It's sedition!"

Latimer had remained silent throughout. He tried to restore some reason and order.

"What are you saying, Mr. Emms? Are you saying that our ancestors were incapable of working metal? Where does it say in the Bible that men were incapable of working metal? How did Noah make his ark? Not with these! An ark three stories high. Not with these! It's beyond reason, man."

"And all that is now, comes from Noah," added Lloyd.

"And are men supposed to have forgotten?" demanded Warburton.

"Englishmen!" added Tyson. "At that! I've heard enough!"

"But these things are real!" protested Emms. "I only ask that they are looked at with the apparatus of reason the Good Lord gave men!"

Warburton felt it was time to return to the effect of Emms' theories upon the workings of the parish.

"The Bishop is more able to judge the propriety or otherwise of your views on biblical matters. As far as our drainage works are concerned, your activities encourage dissent amongst the commoners of this parish! They don't know or care about your apparatus of reason, but they do know you are opposed to the route of our works. In that, you are allied to those whose aim is to wreck the enterprise! To me, this is the practical outcome, and I think I speak for the Partners!"

"It is not my choice. I have not allied myself to them. If they come to me, it is not my fault and surely nothing to criticise!"

Tyson snorted, still angry. "It's all very well to dress it up, Mr. Emms, but you are a well-read man, you know what you are doing."

Latimer intervened, waving a hand at Emms' flints. "Leaving these aside, it seems to me that the job of a parish priest is to look after his parish and to direct his parishioners through the word of the Lord and the teachings of Christ, whatever the man within. Who cares, Mr. Emms, if the priest knows for a certainty which horse is going to win on the Flat in Newmarket, or speaks Hindu or jumps dykes, his job is to minister, minister to his flock, feed their spiritual needs. And if I can pursue this metaphor, Mr. Emms, the food for this purpose is already prepared in the Good Book and he is to serve it, not indulge his fancies as some sort of 'apparatus of reason'!"

Lloyd nodded appreciatively. His stomach was full of acid and he had made up his mind on the matter of Emms. It was now a question of going through the motions at respectable length, then lying down. A brandy might help.

"It does seem to me that you have confused your duty with your personal inclinations. There seems no doubt about it. Is there anything you can say to persuade us that we are wrong? That our serious concerns are misplaced?"

Emms had sat quite still throughout, and now there was a protracted silence, broken only by Tyson's sighs and irritated puffing, and by Emms, still standing, gathering his flints.

Warburton had so far said little out of a sudden feeling of remorse over what he had set in motion, but Emms' silence was more than he could bear.

"William, our families have known each other for generations, we have known each other all our lives. Defend yourself for God's sake!"

Emms looked at Warburton, held his gaze. "What good is defence? You tell me? Did my father try to defend himself, John? *'Whatsoever thy hand findeth to do, do it with thy might; for there is no work, no device, nor knowledge nor wisdom in the grave whither thou goest.'* I wish you all good day gentlemen, by which I mean farewell. I will remove myself. That is what you want. Nemesis. Another Emms gone."

Emms replaced his flints in the bundle, rolled it up and left with as much dignity as he had entered. They watched until the door closed.

"Does that mean he's gone?" asked Tyson. "I didn't follow that."

"Oh yes," said Warburton stiffly.

"I didn't understand that bit about his father." Tyson persisted.

"I believe that concludes matters," said the Bishop. "I'll get out the necessary letter to Emms and the Parish. Do you agree, gentlemen?" Latimer and Tyson both nodded. "Have you a brandy for my stomach, Warburton?"

"That was swift," said Tyson in a tone devoid of sympathy. "A good thing done. Outrageous! Unbelievable! Should have been rid of him sooner!"

*

A week had passed since the brawl and a review was called for. De Vries and Edmonson stood at the table in his hut, contemplating a map which had been weighed down with a stone at each end to stop it curling. The map showed the whole length of the new cut with progress marked on it by weekly cross-hatching and dates. Edmonson had his forefinger on the latest entry. Both men looked grim.

"We are still slowing down," he said, "Look at it. Each week a little less. Compare it with eight weeks ago. And this is accurate. I just can't seem to get the work out of them – you know why."

"This is *onzinnig*, absurd. Have you done everything you can?"

Edmonson was touchy. "Of course I have. I've interviewed Hobson and Maddox and Hellenbuch and they all give me the same story, all's well, no hard feelings, no problems, but things have happened. Yesterday there was a flood behind Maddox's men. A dyke was breached and flooded the Dutchmen's work. No one knows how, but I don't believe it was an accident. I had to bring up pumps, and there were Maddox's foremen grinning. This morning we had a wagon collapse off the wall onto Maddox's work. A section of bank slipped. It's too easy to make these things happen."

"Are we losing tools?"

"We've stopped losing tools since the troopers arrived."

"That's something." De Vries indicated positions on the map. "We are almost out of timber again because of piling here .... and here and we have poor quality ground in these areas ...." He made circular motions, pointing with a quill. "I pray to the Lord each night Mr. Edmonson that we get better ground, but we don't, and the Partners won't pay to bring in stone."

"You can see their point of view. We would need so much. Think of the expense ...."

De Vries grunted. "I don't like the stuff we have to use."

"Neither do I, Mr. de Vries, it's full of water. We're capping it with clay – that seems to do the job ...."

"This weather is intolerable."

*

John Sylham had not been asked to attend the Bishop's examination of Emms and was relieved, making no enquiries about where it was or when or who was going. Arabella who, like most of the people in Oxay, knew all about it, was both ashamed and annoyed, seeing it as a further mark of lack of respect for her husband. With nothing to do that afternoon, Sylham had finally worked up the courage to talk to Arabella. The acrimony surrounding Toby's leaving had further soured their relations. Sylham now slept in a separate bedroom and saw little chance of resuming marital relations in the near future. Arabella had guessed something was up as he was not the sort of man to linger in the house on afternoons, whatever the weather. She waited with growing impatience in the drawing room, hearing his voice downstairs as he delayed, talking to Mrs Wells. Not for the first time she wished she could get rid of Mrs Wells. Apart from fussing round John, she made excuses for everything about him and her attitude to Toby had been close to impudence. Naturally he was devoted to her, she thought and sniffed. She had positioned herself at a small table writing an unnecessary letter to an unloved aunt and taking as long as possible on this dreary afternoon to give him all the time he usually needed.

"I don't like to go up there on a day like this," Sylham was telling Mrs Wells. "This is the sort of day for a hanging."

"Go on with you. What's all the mystery about?" Her face was alight with excitement. Sylham had told no one about his letter to Bathurst, but had of necessity put Mrs Wells on the alert to intercept a reply – a commission she accepted with glee. "I hope it isn't about anything troublesome?" she had tried, disingenuously.

Sylham had been forced to laugh. "I shall tell you nothing!" Now he hesitated in his own hallway while she made a pretence of dusting.

"Mrs Sylham has been waiting for some time already ...."

"I'll tell you what it is, Mrs Wells." Sylham suddenly confessed. "I don't rightly want to go on with the drainage works, and I shall be in trouble ...."

Mrs Wells rolled her eyes. John Sylham took a deep breath and entered the room too abruptly. Arabella, turning her head and putting down her quill, was immediately struck by his tidiness of dress – no sign of mud about him, she thought. Having negotiated the door with such determination, he appeared to have run out of impetus and stood there, looking to left and right.

"Yes?" she enquired.

He advanced two paces like a badly rehearsed actor taking his position on the stage.

"Arabella, do I have to go through with this damned drainage?"

She was dressed in pale lilac silk. This, with her pale skin and powdered hair, gave her an insubstantial appearance that he could not help contrasting with Clara's brown solidity – and, he thought, her shoulderblades stick out like wings on a plucked chicken.

"I should think you do," replied Arabella. "What do you mean?"

The reason for the visitation was now clear, and she tried to control rising irritation. He had skirted round this topic before and had got her answer.

"I don't want to put the rents up. If I didn't owe your brother money, I shouldn't have to. That's one end of things. If I wasn't up to my crupper in this project I could've paid him back."

Arabella avoided eye contact and there was silence, each waiting for the other to speak. She despised the helplessness in his words. When nothing further was forthcoming she stood up to face him.

"They won't give you your money back, that's certain. You must know that." She saw from his face that he did not know, had never thought of it. "It's a ridiculous idea," she continued. "You have a contract with the Partners. It's not your money any more – some of it is spent already. You can't just pull out because you feel like it!" She knew she should feel pity at the misery that flooded his weathered face but instead felt nothing but disappointment followed rapidly by pity for herself and this childless marriage she was trapped in. "The only way you'll get any money back is if the whole thing collapses," she said, cruelly. "And don't expect me to beg Toby to let you off. I won't be put in that position. I'm tired of making your apologies. Do you know why you weren't asked to the Bishop's Enquiry?" she pursued.

"No. Why?"

"You weren't asked to the Bishop's Enquiry because you would have had nothing useful to say!" She burst into tears.

"Haven't I?" yelled Sylham. "So I'm summed up, am I, by my loving wife, and that is it? Nothing useful to say!"

He turned on his heel and stamped out. Mrs Wells heard the doors slamming behind him, upstairs, downstairs, front door and nodded to herself.

*

The men on the site knew what had happened between the Bishop and Emms but it made no difference. Few of them had been to the church, relying on Edmonson's brief and effective morning prayers for their salvation.

An artificial peace had descended. Bristow and Edmonson watched closely for any signs of wrecking or violence. It had been made clear that jobs and wages were at stake. A surly reluctance had replaced the earlier competition between teams, leading Edmonson to fear the men were biding their time.

The news of the attack on the soldiers had led to derision about their capabilities and courage. Edmonson confessed to de Vries that it was not a happy situation but there was nothing he could do about it. The men dug on, on a day when sunlight was interspersed with showers and the great, full arcs of rainbows that put the activities of the men in place, making them stop to look into the sky in silence, to note the dozens of butterflies, the flowering camomile that sprouted from spoil heaps, the cow-parsley as high as a man.

The English gang were in the lead in four rows followed by Hellenbuch's men in the same formation. Maddox's men cleared the topsoil and dug the silt and peat to four spade depths. The Dutch men did the same taking the cut down to some five to six feet. Next, more of Maddox's men dug out the bottom to the level set by the surveyors, throwing material into wagons. It was filthy work, the bottom of the cut full of water, the wagon wheels partly awash. Perched on each side of the cut a gang of men with pumps spent hours trying to keep the bottom clear of water. Leather hoses lay in the mud, gurgling and spluttering. Maddox's men worked in clogs, but with bare legs, trousers tied up as far as possible or with the legs cut away. The water drained slowly away behind them, following the fall of the new bed, but at the same time was replaced by water running in from the head of the works. The bed of the cut was criss-crossed with temporary trenches in an attempt to control conditions and these were spanned by planks to provide barrow-ways to the wagons.

The prevailing colour was black, the dull dark black of excavated peat and the water that ran out of the peat, the black of men's clothes, of the planks, of the tools they worked with. In this strange monochrome world in the cut only the faces of the men provided contrast. Up the embankment was the coloured world, the rainbow lights, the flowers.

The man who made the cut let out a yell and threw down his spade, dancing back so frantically that he fell over. His workmates, assuming he had chopped his toe with his spade, gave a cheer. The man lay where he had fallen and pointed with an outstretched arm and finger, waving at the dark earth at something of lighter colour. The nearest workman reached out his spade and poked at it tentatively, revealing a brownish shape. He turned it over to reveal a human hand, peat-stained but unmistakable. From the staggered bank of earth behind it projected a wrist. The men gathered to look. Some crossed themselves.

"Call Mr. Maddox," said the ganger. "That's a hand and there's more in there!"

Maddox arrived in a short space of time and sent a man for Hobson. Hobson sent a man for Edmonson and Edmonson brought de Vries. Before long work had almost ceased and a crowd had gathered in the cut and on the banks to stare at the amber coloured hand. Edmonson urged the men to stand back.

"It is certainly part of a body," he said to de Vries, "and there's more in there."

"There's more in there, Mr. Edmonson," repeated the ganger, as if this solved some problem and they continued to stare.

"Give me your spade," said Edmonson, and taking one from a workman, poked gently around the protruding wrist bone. The soil fell away to reveal more arm and something larger that might have been leather or material. "I'll get Mr. Warburton and Mr. Latimer. Put a guard on this."

By the time Warburton and Latimer got to the site, de Vries had had canvas erected to form a tent over the object and the men not immediately affected had been persuaded to return to their work positions, although they were doing very little. Latimer, as a former magistrate was assumed to know what to do and found himself put in charge.

"I need two men, Mr. Maddox, with skill and respect. We must clear the soil from the remains. With respect, Mr. Maddox."

"Use small tools," said Warburton. "We must preserve evidence. This is a suspicious death. It must be murder."

"There's no sign of disturbance of the earth Mr. Warburton," Maddox volunteered. "It must have been here some time." He still sported the shadow of a black eye and a cut at the corner of his mouth.

"We'll judge that, Mr. Maddox," snapped Latimer.

The word "murder" had been picked up by the workmen within earshot. It was passed on immediately from man to man, even from Englishman to Dutchman. "*Vermoord!*" Men stopped digging all over the site to wait. In the ensuing hush, two larks could be heard singing.

Within the tent the chosen workmen cleared soil armed with a trowel and a small spade. Edmonson had told them to excavate well back, to clear a rectangle then begin to dig down. The hand had been laid to one side on a piece of canvas. Little was said as the men dug and scraped away. The profile of a body gradually emerged from the peat, a life-size amber cameo, lying on its side, knees drawn up and arms stuck out. The body wore the remains of clothing – some sort of cloak with a hood, shoes on the feet. The watchers could see that the skin had shrunk onto the bones of arms and legs. A shrunken face was partly visible under a leather hood, teeth exposed, gums gone. There was no smell of decay, rather a musty, sweet smell like turned humus. The workmen faltered, stopped, unsure what to do next. Everyone looked to Latimer.

"We must get the body out," he said. "It must be examined."

Warburton, noticing the hush that had fallen over the works, turned to de Vries.

"Do you think the men are working out there, or do you think they are watching? This is no excuse for idleness." Irritation crackled in his voice. De Vries turned to Edmonson.

"Can you see to it Mr. Edmonson?" Edmonson nodded and left with Maddox. Tyson was not feeling well. He had said nothing so far. The sight of the hand had turned his stomach and now the sight of the body made him feel sick. "Are you going to lift it?" he asked.

"We must," said Latimer. "We need planks." Tyson excused himself, and walked outside where the air smelled salty and fresh. Edmonson was speaking to a group of workmen, Maddox at his side. They seemed to listen, but no one moved. Maddox spoke to the men, still no one moved. Heads were shaken. Maddox turned to Edmonson with a shrug, held his hands aloft in a gesture of defeat. They moved to the next group of men.

Inside the tent the workmen had manoeuvred a plank underneath the body, and prepared to lift it. To their surprise it had little weight and it came up with a jerk and a sucking noise.

"Another plank!" said Warburton, and the remains were properly held. Latimer and Warburton stooped over them for a closer look. Latimer had few qualms, and taking the trowel from a workman, poked about at the hood and head.

"There is a ligature round the neck," he said, "there's no doubt that this is murder. Can we take it to your house John? You're nearest."

"To one of my barns. The Coroner must be informed."

Latimer nodded. "There must be an inquest."

"This is just what we need," said Warburton. "Who is this? There's no one missing so far as I know. How long has it been here?"

Edmonson and Maddox appeared inside the tent. "Mr. de Vries," said Edmonson, "the men won't work."

"Damnation!" shouted Warburton. "Why won't they work?"

"The men are saying you've dug up the devil or a witch."

"Saying what? Is this a Christian country or not Mr. Edmonson? What have you got to say, Maddox?"

Maddox was uncharacteristically nervous. He brushed at his cut mouth with a forefinger. No one had ever heard Warburton swear.

"It's the colour of the body, sir, and the colour of the clothes .... it's already gone round the men that it's dark, ... leather, sir, and black ...."

"Preposterous!" exclaimed Warburton. "What shall we do, Thomas? Shall we show the body? Let them see for themselves?"

"I don't think that would be a good idea," said Latimer.

"Not a good idea," came the voice of Tyson, who was still outside, clutching a handkerchief to his face.

*

The inquest was held in the presence of the body on a warm Thursday two days later. A coffin had been made for it, shorter and wider than usual as it could not be straightened or re-arranged without dismemberment. The Coroner, Sutton presided. A former soldier with a no-nonsense approach, he had a trooper stood at each side of the door of the barn to provide formality and stood a timepiece on the table that formed his desk. He had also brought a gavel which he had no hesitation in using. Seats in the barn were occupied by Warburton and the other Partners, de Vries, Maddox, the midwife Martha Bower, Hobson, Edmonson and the two workmen who had extracted the body. A jury of twelve had been formed. So far as serving on the jury was concerned the villagers could be divided into the curious and the reluctant. Edmonson, who had been given the thankless task of rounding up the twelve required had tried to strike a balance between the two. Some, like Clara, had flatly refused to serve. The jury sat at a long trestle table to one side, Walter Clarke, Ezra and Ecclesiastes Dunn, Peter Simms, Peter Dade, Jack Lamb, Felix Hare, Thomas Fox, Robert Turner, John Lambert and two tenant farmers.

The Coroner had stated he would start at eleven and kept an eye on his clock. At eleven precisely he rapped on the table with his gavel. The light in the outbuilding was not particularly good and he had asked for the door to be left open, which also provided ventilation. As he had remarked to Warburton, it was always a warm day when there was a body to be dealt with. Ruth Warburton had arranged for curtains to be draped on the wall behind the Coroner to conceal the rough plaster wall. The Coroner rapped again to quell the talking and coughing.

"This is a rather unusual proceedings. I am the Coroner, and I appear before you by Statute of Edward the First to enquire, when a man is slain, if any know the person slain, or if he is a stranger, to enquire if any know when he was slain, and if any person is said to be guilty of his murder; then I have the authority to go to that person's house and make such enquiry as may be fit. I shall be asking persons to give evidence and that evidence must be given under oath, sworn on the Holy Bible. I will begin with the evidence of the two men, Martin Mansell and Robert Page, who uncovered the body."

From the notes of Coroner Sutton
Evidence of Martin Mansell

"I was working along the bottom of the cut, digging alongside Mr. Page. Mr. Page is my ganger. The man next to me let out a yell and fell over and we all thought he had chopped his toe, because that's what happens when a man chops his toe, then we saw this hand in the muck. It was a sort of brown colour like it had been cooked or pickled. It was me who turned it over. Mr. Page said to call Mr. Maddox, so we did, then a lot more people came including Mr. Edmonson, then Mr. Warburton. Mr. Warburton said to clear the muck away carefully, so we did, me and Robert Page, and as we cleared it away we saw it were a sort of human body but all bent up and flattened like it had been squashed under a big weight and it was all this sort of leather colour and wearing some sort of leather clothes. It had a horrible expression on its face!"

"Had you ever seen this man before?"

"No."

Evidence of Robert Page

"I helped Martin dig it out and it was horrible and it had its teeth sticking out and it made me feel sick ...."

"Thank you Mr. Page, but would you just be so good as to corroborate what Mr. Mansell has told us."

"You what?"

"Will you just confirm that you agree with what Mr. Mansell has said."

"I understand .... I agree."

Evidence of Martha Bower, Midwife

"Mr. Warburton asked me to lay out the body sir. I know Mr. Warburton well." (Here the witness curtsied to Mr. Warburton) I do the laying-out for the village sir, and for most of the other villages round here and I have been doing it for nigh on thirty-five years.

"I expect you have dealt with many ... differing circumstances of death?"

"Oh yes sir, all sorts, mostly peaceful, but I've had my share of violence sir, and putting together, being busy during the war as a girl, and since then, sir, this being a fishing and shooting and farming place. Accidents do happen ...."

"Quite, Mrs Bower. Would you tell us the sex of the deceased."

"It were a man sir. His organ was still there."

"Quite. And his age? Have you any idea?"

"I couldn't say. Perhaps a medical man could ...."

"But from your experience?"

"He was a grown man. In his middle years I would say, but all so shrivelled up his bones were sticking out like a bag of tools. I tried to straighten him out a bit but I was afraid of doing damage, sir. He was ready to snap."

"So you would say he was a male, of middle years?"

"Certainly sir."

"And anything else?"

"He had worn teeth, and bad teeth and long hair. Other than that .... about five foot six .... Maybe ...."

"Thank you Mrs Bower."

"And his hands were in a bad condition and there was this piece of rope round his neck, pulled really tight, dug right into the skin ...."

"Thank you Mrs Bower. Mr. Latimer will give evidence on that ...."

"Thank you sir."

Evidence of Mr. Jacob de Vries

"I was called to the place after the hand had been found. Mr. Edmonson investigated the find and it became evident that there was more to uncover, and that this was a *lijk*."

"A what, Mr. de Vries?"

"A dead body. I had a tent erected to cover the remains and get them out of sight."

"You have no reason to believe that this could be one of your workmen?"

"No sir. I have much experience of digging in the ground, and it is my opinion that the body has been there for some time. The dark appearance of the skin is what you would expect from staining from *veen* –

peat. This body is not of a man connected with the drainage works, so far as I know, but Mr. Maddox will know better than me for the English workmen and Mr. Hellenbuch for my countrymen. I would not know if a workman had gone missing. I do not know all their faces."

"Of course not, Mr. de Vries. If you think the body has been there some time, can you estimate how long?"

"That is difficult to say. It could have been there for twenty or thirty years."

"In that state of preservation?"

"It seems possible. Trees, things, are sometimes found preserved. It is the nature of the peat."

"Looking at it the other way, Mr. de Vries, how recently could the body have been buried, in your opinion?"

"Not recently. It is much stained and shrunk. Please remember I am no expert in this sort of thing, I am an engineer I am not a doctor."

Summary of the evidence of Mr. Maddox

None of his men is missing. Those who have quit are accounted for. There was no sign of recent disturbance of the ground above the body. Maybe the corpse is a foreigner.

Summary of the evidence of Mr. Hellenbuch

No Dutchman is missing. Dutchmen don't strangle people with pieces of rope.

Evidence of John Warburton, Esquire

"I was called to the scene by Mr. Edmonson and when I got there I saw a canvas tent had been erected. I arrived with Mr. Latimer, both of us having ridden there in the company of Mr. Edmonson. Inside the tent were a number of people who were waiting for us. A severed hand was lying on the ground and there were obviously further remains in the ground. I agree with Mr. Maddox that there were no signs that the earth around the body or above the body had been recently disturbed. Mr. Latimer instructed that two men should carefully uncover the remains. They did this using a trowel and a small spade. The body was as you see it, hunched up and compressed, all skin and bone, as if all the flesh had decomposed."

"How do you account for that, Mr. Warburton?"

"I can't. There was no particular smell of decay, only a smell of the earth. The body was wearing the pieces of leather clothing that are still on it. We had planks brought and placed under the remains so that they could be lifted without further damage. The body seemed to me to be in a fragile state."

"That was a shrewd and pertinent move Mr. Warburton and I compliment you on your foresight."

"Thank you. We then had a closer look at the body and Mr. Latimer noticed that there was a ligature round the neck and that there was no doubt that this individual was a victim of murder. We both looked at the ligature."

"And no one has reported to you the disappearance of any local person?"

"No."

"Would it be reported to you? I have to ask you this for the record, Mr. Warburton."

"If any local person were missing or had fallen foul of a crime, I would expect to be informed. If it were not a person from these parts, that would be different."

"Of course."

Evidence of Thomas Latimer, Esquire

(Mr. Latimer was formerly a magistrate in these parts and I have encountered him before).

"I attended the works as Mr. Warburton has described, and we had the body removed on planks. It seemed to me to be important to preserve evidence for a future occasion such as this."

"Thank you Mr. Latimer. Your experience in these things has undoubtedly helped. Can you throw any more light on the condition of the body when it was discovered, and its state of preservation?"

"The body was in a contorted position and appeared as it might have been if dried or cured. The flesh has largely shrunk."

"What in your opinion was the cause of death?"

"I have no doubt that it was the ligature around the neck. It appears to be a length of cord of some sort, tied very tight. I conclude the unfortunate fellow was murdered. He could not have done it himself and it would be a most improbable accident."

"Mr. Warburton has already told us that he is unaware of any local person having disappeared ...."

"I have nothing to add to that. This person must have been a stranger."

"Or has been in the ground some time?"

"Or has been in the ground some time."

"I am looking for some help, Mr. Latimer, from a man with your experience. It seems this unfortunate was a stranger. He may have met his death here, or may not, but was buried in this fen. It seems clear that the cause of death was strangulation with this ligature, by persons unknown. What is not clear is when this could have occurred."

"It is no more clear to me Mr. Sutton. The best I can say is that it must have been some time ago."

"Then that may have to satisfy the jury. Could it have occurred during the war?"

"It could, but even then I believe I would have known of it."

Robert Turner, wearing his best silver buttons, had been appointed chairman of the jury. They were considering their verdict, and had been left alone in the barn. Ezra Dunn and Peter Simms, bored with discussion, stood by the squat coffin.

"Can we have a look?" asked Ezra.

Turner shrugged. "I suppose so."

"I think it's right we should!" declared Ezra. Some gathered round – John Lambert, Walter Clarke, Peter Dade, Felix Hare. The lid was loose and Ezra lifted it, held it vertical. Some men crossed themselves.

"Just look at that!" said Walter in broadest tones. They stared. The body was creamy white, covered with a short fur of mould.

"Just smell it!" said Peter Simms, clutching his nose.

"Put the lid down!" said Turner.

"You'd better tell the Crowner that his body needs burying!" said Walter Clarke. "He's gone off!"

Coroner Sutton's notes recorded the verdict of his jury in more formal language than had been given.

"Oxay. Death of male of middle years. Cause of death, strangulation by ligature. Murder by person or persons unknown. Identity of victim unknown. Date of crime unable to be established, possible victim of the late war."

*

"It is unusual," Sutton said to Latimer and Warburton. The jury had mostly departed, the two troopers were standing by, waiting to be dismissed. "I think we may as well close the records on this one. I see no point in further investigation." He looked quizzically at Latimer.

"Agreed," that man replied. Warburton nodded.

"I'll get to horse then. Seal the coffin. I'll have it collected in the next few days."

"What will you do with it?" asked Warburton.

"A lime pit, I think. We have one outside Norwich for cases like this. Sooner the better."

"Very good," said Latimer. Felix Hare had been lingering nearby. He heard all they said and left. "Perhaps we can get the men back to work, God willing."

"We *must*," said Warburton.

Out of their hearing Ezra turned to Ecclesiastes. "What do you reckon?" Ecclesiastes made a face. "Reckon? I reckon that there is something strange. That ain't no Civil War soldier, for where's his uniform and he ain't got no boots. That's some sort of moon-calf. I don't like it."

*

The quietness of the fen was intense. Katja took her customary route down the lane to the meadow. From there she would enter the world of tall reeds and shimmering heat. Last night's moon, like a forgotten lamp, hung white in the sky, ready-lit for the next occasion. She was in no hurry, having made no appointment with Peter for the afternoon because of the Inquest. She had stopped to stare at a mass of striped caterpillars on the leaves of ragwort when she caught sight of Richard from the corner of her eye. He was some distance behind her, on foot, and appeared to be ducking into the hedgerow as though following her and hiding. This annoyed and flustered her. Her purpose was a solitary romantic visit to the secret spot. That would have to be abandoned and Richard led elsewhere. She had no option but to continue straight down the path or turn back on herself. Katja decided on the former and giving no sign she had seen him, quickened her pace to see if he really was following.

The path became more and more overgrown. Unmanaged hedges on both sides began to meet overhead, cutting out sunlight. She now had to pick her way between shoots of rose-briar, but refused to look back. Fat pigeons shot up, disturbing her. She picked her way past the white stained elders where they had been gorging on unripe berries. She was becoming alarmed that the path might run out. The path was now heavily pitted by the hoofs of horses or cattle and had dried hard so that she stumbled and stubbed her toes in her clogs. When she saw that a branch had fallen across the path ahead, she realised she had to give up. She stopped and turned, surprised to find she was panting and saw no sign of Richard. She began to retrace her steps, cautiously at first, then faster, wondering if he had gone off somewhere else and that the idea he was following was just a fancy.

He stepped into the path from the side, not far ahead. Katja's immediate thought was that he was dressed in a ridiculous way for an afternoon walk. She was uncertain what to do or say and nervous at being alone with a man dressed in knee breeches, long stockings, silver buckles, and a waistcoat on a warm afternoon – not normal walking clothes. She looked down, contrasting this with her workaday dress and clogs. She decided to keep moving, try to pass saying as little as possible.

"So here you are, Katja de Vries," said Richard moving so as to block her path. "One of your walks?"

"Yes," she answered, "I can go no further .... you see the branches .... I must go back." She gave him only the quickest glance and made to walk around him, but instead of stepping aside he spread his arms sideways, obstructing her.

"I know where you go," he said pointedly. "You've passed it. The path across the meadow."

Katja's heart leapt. She continued to stare at her clogs. He reached out and put a forefinger under her chin, trying to raise her head. She shook her head indignantly. Richard laughed humourlessly. "I know what you get up to with Peter Dade, I've seen you ...."

"I get up to nothing with Peter Dade!" Katja blazed.

"What would your father say?" He had bent his head down towards her and was grinning unkindly in her face. She realised this was no game. "He's no good for you," Richard was insisting, "just a peasant with no job. Did you know that? So come and walk with me."

"I want to go back." It was all she could think of to say, trying to keep her fear out of her voice. Richard's response was to crook his left arm for her to take, shifting sideways to point in the direction of return. She realised that to escape she had no option but to take it. She put her right hand as lightly as possible on the offered arm, whereupon Richard grabbed it tight, pulling her close to him so that she was held in a lock with her right hip jammed against his left. He started to half march, half drag her up the path.

"Why do you do this!" she protested, "you're hurting me."

His reply was to seize her by the collar of her dress, pull her towards him and kiss her while she pushed at him with the palms of her hands.

"I don't think the girl is enjoying that, Master Warburton."

The voice came from directly behind Richard. He released Katja and turned to see Clara, in her apron, hands on hips.

"Mind your own business!"

"I've made it my business." She advanced towards him. "What would your father have to say about this? I should say she just wanted to walk by herself. What would you say, Master Warburton?"

"Witch!" Richard shouted at her, shoving past without a further glance at Katja. "All witches should be burned!" He set off at a ready pace up the path.

"And I wish you good day too, Mr. Warburton, and my regards to your father!" Clara called after him. "Come with me," she said to Katja. "I'll walk with you to the top of the path. You should look to yourself Miss de Vries, with Mr. Richard Warburton. I saw him following you, from the forge. Danger comes in bright colours with that one." She waved Katja on. Katja stammered her thanks. "Don't you worry girl," said Clara. "I'll say nothing. But be warned – be careful. I tell you, when he was just a boy, he beat his horse until it bled, for throwing him. And you just throwed him."

*

Later that day, Emms, Clara and Felix picked their way towards Oxay Hall by the light of the August moon. Felix carried a dark-lantern but had only occasional use for it. He knew his way and they followed footpaths, paths familiar to him and paths smelling of fox that clung close to hedges. At times they edged through scrub or manoeuvred through woodland. Emms was dressed in black as usual, as was Felix. Clara had taken the unusual step of covering her head with a shawl. Felix and Clara stopped, as they had done often, to allow Emms to draw level. He was far from sure-footed in the half-light and his height was a disadvantage.

"Are you sure we're still going the right way?" he asked.

"I'm sure," said Felix. "It's not far now."

*

Felix had set things off. He had told Clara what he had overheard and Clara had broken the news to Emms. He had been taken aback to find her on his doorstep again, but had asked her in.

"I saw you, pastor, I watched you in the churchyard burying your bones. Your bones you dug up in Sylham's meadow – the grave. I thought you ought to know." She had explained about the lime pit. "Can't have old people put in a lime pit, pastor. My old people, your old people. They should never have dug him up. Bad things will come of it. The man must be properly buried. My friends say so."

"Your friends?" Emms had asked. He was horrified at the news and fearful of Clara.

"My mice." Emms had stared at her blankly. "You put them in a cart hoop and ask them the questions," she continued "and put the answers round the side at five points and they will tell you. You whisper in their ears, 'Come on Gabriel, I am your Daniel, explain to me,' and they will go to the answer straight."

"It is a sin to use the Good Book for magic!" Emms had protested. "Witchcraft!" His tone of disapproval failed. It was qualified too much by interest.

"That's a word you should never use," said Clara. "That's a word that could still kill me. Anyway," she said with sudden acuity, "you shouldn't talk to me of magic while you collect your bones and stones and say the world is older than the Bible; you have your Urim and Thrummim and you shouldn't talk to me of magic, pastor."

Emms had gone out early next day. His housekeeper, Mrs. Strutt was avoiding him, as ever. She had left a note on the sideboard which told him that she could not continue with her duties and that he would find two cold chops under the cover. She had never warmed to him nor he to her; she had been frightened by his collection and refused to clean his study. Her departure although half-expected was nonetheless dispiriting. He had taken the chops with him and had talked to himself while he heeled the spade, stopping from time to time to take a bite of bread and a bite of meat.

The spot he had selected was between two dense yews and to the rear of the churchyard, a gloomy place rejected for burial and hidden from the road; no one would see it in advance. Although his work would have dismayed his sexton, he had after an hour managed to dig out a grave some two feet deep.

*

Clara led the way along the edge of a field of stubble, her skirts swishing through the stalks. They passed through a gap in the hedgerow and across a meadow, disturbing sleeping cows, who shook their ears and snorted. The outlines of Oxay Hall were now visible against the starry sky. Clara held up her hand and touched her ear. They listened to the night sounds of a fox, owls hunting, the scuttling of a rabbit or hedgehog.

"No geese," she whispered, "anything but geese!" They advanced cautiously, avoiding molehills and tussocks until they reached nettles and outbuilding walls. Clara indicated she would go ahead and rounded the corner of a building. From there she beckoned to them to join her. Stabbing with a finger she pointed at a lit barn. Felix recognised it from the inquest.

"In there," he confirmed, "on the left hand side. It'll be light to carry."

"Wait," said Clara, and was gone. Despite her size and strength she moved noiselessly. Emms and Felix, hearts thumping, could hear the noise of horses, stamping and moving. A dog barked somewhere nearby, but not in alarm. Clara re-emerged from the darkness.

"There are two soldiers," she whispered, "asleep in the stalls, there!" She jabbed a finger at the next door barn. "Keep watch, pastor, for I reckon us Hares are the ones for the job." She beckoned to Felix and they slid into the darkness to appear as dark shapes momentarily lit in the dull light from the barn. They emerged shortly, bent, carrying the squat coffin between them on their shoulders. Emms held his breath uselessly, until he had to gasp for air. He had lost sight of them and started when they emerged suddenly, making no more noise than a rat in straw. All three rounded the corner and re-traced their steps, Clara and Felix breaking into a swift walk that Emms had difficulty in following. They passed through the meadow and back into the cornfield before Clara, at the front of the coffin, stopped. Felix and Emms gasped for air, making white clouds of breath in the starlight. Clara appeared unaffected. They put the coffin down.

"Where are we taking him, pastor?"

"You know where, Clara. The father shall sleep with his sons."

"In the old place," said Clara, "the graveyard is the old place, pastor, old before the church was new. I know it."

They carried the coffin back the way they had come by footpaths and tracks and through the gate to the churchyard, where they stopped to allow Emms to lead the way. He took them past the church, treading carefully past gravestones until they reached the yews which he pushed aside for them to reveal his work.

"You've been busy, pastor," said Felix.

"We must do things right!" Emms declared. "*'For the living know they shall die : but the dead know not any thing, neither have they any more a reward; for the memory of them is forgotten'*".

Clara and Felix looked at each other, uneasy at this outburst. "Lower him in!" Emms continued, picking up a spade. Before they could move, the yews behind them were violently parted, revealing two men.

"Stand still!" one bellowed in a north-country voice. "We've got you!"

Felix and Clara were gone. The two men lunged forward in pursuit but fell over the unseen mound of earth that Emms had earlier excavated. Unable to find his footing, one of the men grabbed Emms' ankle and pulled him down, half in and half out of the grave. The second man seized hold of Emms' coat.

"What about them!" said the first man pointing in the direction that Felix and Clara had taken.

"We'll never catch them." He turned to Emms, pulled him up by his clothes.

"You're under arrest. We followed you. Do you think we're stupid!"

"You are defilers!" yelled Emms, "Take your hands off! *'The righteous shall never be removed : but the wicked shall not inhabit the earth!'*"

"Tie his wrists," said the second man. "He's mad."

"*'Upon the wicked he shall rain snares, fire and brimstone, and an horrible tempest : this shall be the portion of their cup!'*"

"Get him out of here," said the second man, twisting Emms' arm up behind his back. "Walk!"

*

It was only four days after the inquest and John Warburton was less than pleased that Ruth had invited the de Vries family to dinner. He felt it was inappropriate at the present time.

"Things are not going well at the works. The men won't go back, and we're still waiting for the new parson – it's not a good time."

"On the contrary," Ruth had said, "it's a very good time. Life must go on and it's hard for his wife and the girl. These upsets are nothing to do with them and they are friendless in a foreign country. It is a very good time!" She forbore to mention that in part it was due to Richard's persistence that it was taking place, but suspected he must know. Her efforts to arrange another visit for Katja had failed since the last, as Cristeen seemed unable to conclude any proper plans for afternoons. She had been pleased when dinner was accepted.

It was a warm evening with a huge, low moon, the air full of moths. Ruth had sent their coach, wishing she could have made the journey herself to enjoy the night air. At Elm Farm the women were not ready when the coach arrived. Katja, for reasons that Cristeen could not fathom, had been apathetic when Ruth's note was received.

"Do we have to go, mama?"

"Yes we do. You like Sarah, you like the big house and Richard will be there. You know that Mrs Warburton is a very nice woman. Besides, your father really has to go ...."

Katja made a face and said nothing and Cristeen became annoyed.

"You should really have taken up the invitation to go riding. I think it was not very polite not to. It is a good thing to learn. You are not very experienced at handling a horse. What is the matter with you?"

Now the problem was Katja's appearance. Cristeen was hair-perfect, with every linen surface of her dress crackling with starch. Katja on the other hand seemed lazy, unable to give proper attention to detail, and as Cristeen told her, her falling bands were a disgrace and had to be re-ironed.

Jacob had changed some time ago and was pacing about outside by the coach, becoming increasingly impatient.

"The ladies will be coming soon," he said to the coachman, aware he had already said this.

"Very good sir."

"It is a fine evening."

"It certainly is, sir."

He had said that as well. Upstairs Cristeen had tutted and tugged at Katja's dress, undoing and re-fastening buttons.

"Why aren't you trying properly? I can feel you aren't trying properly. It is like trying to put clothes on a sack of turnips. Tuck in your collar properly!"

She fastened a brooch at Katja's breast, straightened out the falling bands.

"That will have to do. We must go or be late."

The journey to the Hall should have been idyllic, with evening scents blowing in the open windows. Jacob was unaware of the tensions between mother and daughter, being wrapped up in his own concerns. He did not notice that Cristeen made attempts at lively conversation while Katja stared out of the window. He was worrying about the cut, worrying that the men were refusing to work where the body was found, worrying as usual about materials. The men had taken to calling the place the Devil's Dyke and were demanding a man of the Church to bless it. He worried about the slow progress and rising water levels. He worried how long it would be before the sluices could be opened. He worried about autumn and winter weather, which all seemed to be the same in this confounded year.

"Lord knows I sometimes wish I had never taken this on," he said aloud, waving at the scenery. They were passing fenland criss-crossed with shimmering water-filled graffs. Cristeen looked at him sharply.

"I hope you are not going to spoil the evening."

De Vries snorted. "I shall try not to! We have some good weather at last! Praise be!" Cristeen ignored his irony.

"I just hope that you men are not going to talk business all evening. We shall not let you, shall we Katja?"

Katja detached herself from the window sufficiently to say "No mama."

Lamps had been lit all over the Hall although they were not yet needed. Ruth Warburton was at the door to greet them, watching as de Vries handed down Cristeen then Katja.

"What an evening!" she exclaimed, taking both of them by the arm.

Ruth's seating plan ensured Katja was next to Richard. She had placed herself at one end of the table with Cristeen on her left and Richard on her right. Sarah sat beside Cristeen and Katja beside Richard with John facing Jacob at the other end. She enjoyed the compliments of de Vries and the effusions from Cristeen but noted immediately that Katja's glance was downcast when Richard bade her 'good evening' and stared at her.

Warburton said grace.

"My text is from Ecclesiastes; - *'There is nothing better for a man than he should eat and drink and that he should make his soul enjoy good in labour.'* We thank thee Lord for giving us food for both body and soul, and for these friends to share it with. Amen."

"It's some time since we all sat down at the table together," said Ruth. "I remember we had such a red sunset. I don't think we shall get one tonight."

"I remember the pike," said de Vries politely, "*de snoek*" he said for the benefit of Cristeen. "They were such big fish."

The manservant moved round them as before pouring wine. A glance passed between Cristeen and Katja. Cristeen said nothing and Katja's glass was filled as she stared at her plate.

"We shall be having a new pastor, before long," said Warburton. "He's a young man, from Hertfordshire. It will be good to have new blood. It will be good to return to a more normal situation where the Church knows its purpose."

"I don't know what Mr. de Vries must think of all this," said Ruth. The manservant had gone and now re-appeared with a brace of roast pheasant and a haunch of venison. Cristeen noticed that Richard had his wine glass re-filled. He had said nothing so far.

"You should be assured, Mrs Warburton, that your difficulties with Mr. Emms are not so exceptional or that we do not have such things in Holland," said de Vries. "In Hallum we had a pastor who smuggled French brandy and hid it in the church and when he ran out of space he buried the barrels in graves. He was discovered because there was flooding and the barrels popped out!"

There was laughter from Ruth and Cristeen.

Katja stared at the meat on her trencher. John Warburton had been carving generous slices and the dense reddish substance oozed some blood. She had never seen venison before and assumed the meat was uncooked. Another torture, she thought. Richard was cutting his up and staring at her. She concentrated on reducing the slices to small cubes. Sarah, seeing and understanding her predicament, tried to help.

"Do you like venison?" she asked Katja. Katja looked blank, not recognising the word. She realised she was beginning to blush.

"*Hert*," said de Vries, "deer meat."

Understanding, Katja nodded. "I have not tried it before." She speared a piece, put it in her mouth, chewed it without tasting and swallowed. "Good," she said.

Sarah flashed her an amused look, for which she was profoundly grateful.

Warburton, seeing in de Vries a fellow male drawn reluctantly into this dinner, launched into a discussion of recent events.

"Well, the thefts have almost stopped," he said, "but the troopers haven't seen hide nor hair of my circumferentor. The surveyors are back to poles and ranging rods."

De Vries nodded.

"It is slower but they do the job ...." He did not like to tell Warburton they were still being pulled out. "We must get that section dug, then we can release the sluices. There is a lot of water ...."

"I know, I know. John Sylham was complaining, Tyson was complaining. They have had to move cattle and Tyson has lost a field of cabbages. I've put out a letter to all the Partners on the financial matter requesting their further investment ...."

"That's good, that's good."

Ruth was watching Richard. His behaviour puzzled her. He had hardly said a word since he had arrived, and nothing at the table.

"Richard, you're quiet this evening," she prompted.

"It's my natural way when I've nothing to say mama." She was shocked by his churlishness. Cristeen tactfully cut at her food.

"I thought that while the weather lasts and before winter closes in you could all take the carriage to see the Ouse at King's Lynn, then go to the town. You could take Katja to see the South Gates and St. Margaret's church."

"That would make a nice trip," said Sarah, coming to her mother's aid.

"I don't know if Katja would be interested in old town walls," said Richard.

Ruth turned to Katja for a response.

"I think I might," said Katja, wondering where this was leading. At the far end of the table Warburton and de Vries were enjoying the wine. Warburton was declaring that Emms was an Ishmael.

"You know what an Ishmael is, Jacob?"

"I know my scriptures!" de Vries responded.

"So what have they done with Ishmael?"

"They've locked him up in Norwich while they decide. He may be fined, they may keep him in for a time but in the end they'll let him out. I shall see they do."

"Did I tell you I met him in the church? I told him he was obstructing the work, he told me the cut must be moved. Now he is moved! He could not see it coming. The man is *gek*! Mad!"

"You should come over so that we can go for that ride we talked about," said Sarah. The two men were deep in conversation about materials and money, despite assurances there would be no such talk.

"You should," said Cristeen, "you know that you are not very sure on a horse. It would be a good thing."

"I think Katja prefers walking," said Richard. He put his knife and fork down to add emphasis.

"Oh, walking," said Ruth, "do you?" Katja's stomach turned over.

"I do take a walk sometimes. It is good."

"Katja walks in the fen," said Richard. Cristeen looked hard at her daughter.

"Do you?"

"I do sometimes mama when you are asleep." Cristeen managed an unconvincing laugh.

"Well, you know, sometimes in the afternoon if it is warm and I have been busy.." She was watching Katja. Sarah had a feeling of ill omen, but had no idea how to intervene. Richard was avoiding her eyes, concentrating on Katja.

"Is it safe to go out alone?" she asked, as much to Ruth as Katja. Ruth floundered.

"I don't know .... a girl does not usually go out alone ...."

"But Katja is not alone!" said Richard as if defending her. "She has Peter Dade as an escort. Although he is only a peasant. You know, the boy that father dismissed."

Cristeen stared at her daughter aghast, looked sharply down the table at Jacob. The two men appeared to be absorbed in their own affairs. Ruth, sensing catastrophe, changed the subject.

"When we have had dinner we will have some music. Sarah will play for us." She noted that Cristeen had gone whiter than Katja. "Now tell me what you have done in the house, Cristeen. I hear you have made all sorts of improvements." Richard's jealousy was unforgivable. She would find a time to apologise to Cristeen, but knew the damage was done.

The remainder of the evening passed without incident with Richard entertaining with talk as though nothing had happened while Sarah played and sang with a gaiety she did not feel. Warburton and de Vries enjoyed such a convivial time they drowned her out with their clapping. Ruth and Cristeen were politely appreciative and avoided the intimacy of each other's eyes.

Cristeen took Katja by the arm as they took their seats in the carriage. Jacob was still at the doorstep saying his goodbyes.

"I don't know what I shall say to your father. How could you!"

"Must you tell him?"

"This must stop. How could you, when I was asleep!"

"Don't tell father."

"It must stop. Now! I must think about whether to tell your father. I have never been so embarrassed!"

Katja burst into tears. Jacob, entering the coach was dismayed.

"What is all this? Why? You were very quiet all evening?"

"Oh she is just tired," said Cristeen. "Women get tired you know." To her relief Jacob pressed her no further and to her even greater relief snored most of the way home. The two women clutched each other in mutual misery.

*

Sarah stared at the diary page for a long time before writing. When she began, she wrote slowly with long pauses for thought:-

"We had a dinner party today for the family de Vries, but I cannot say I enjoyed it. Mother, and I think Mrs de Vries anticipated a warm reunion between Richard and Miss Katja de Vries. Miss de Vries arrived in an ungracious mood that was more than matched by the ill-nature of Richard. I hold myself to blame that neither mother nor Mrs de Vries were aware of the habits of Miss de Vries for she walks abroad quite freely in the afternoons. Perhaps that is the way in Holland. It has transpired through the indiscretion of Richard that she has had the company of Peter Dade on these sojourns, who is no more than a farm boy and from a very middling family and has no job. I suspect the motives of Richard in releasing such information, which is a terrible thing to say of a brother."

She stared at it and re-read it. Having finished she tore it out, folded it and tore it into strips, tucking them into a drawer for later disposal. On a new sheet she wrote.

"A dinner party this evening for the family de Vries."

She blotted it with sand and shut the book.

*

Earlier the same day Oxay Grange had seen the convergence of an array of transport, none of it elegant, all of it agricultural, which had brought Sylam's tenants. In addition, several had walked, taking advantage of the weather and the opportunity to exchange opinions in advance. The meeting was in Sylham's parlour – a large enough room, heavily beamed, with a huge open fireplace. It was crowded and hot. The windows had been thrown open and late-comers leaned on the cill from the outside, half out, half in. Sylham had tried to provide some formality by sitting behind a table, back to the fireplace. All other furniture had been cleared. Dressed in his best suit he was sweaty and uncomfortable.

"Is everyone here now?" he called. "I need to have a bit of order!" A hush eventually fell. "You all know why I've called this meeting. I thought it best to put it to you in person; I'm not a man that likes to do things by letter, as you know and I don't doubt that you've heard the rumours. Well I'm afraid they're true, I must raise your rents this Michaelmas, when rent day comes, and that's the long and short of it."

There was a leaden silence.

"I've waited as long as I can."

"That's not the best of news," said an elderly man, "I can't pay no more."

"He can't pay no more, Mr. Sylham," repeated his son beside him. "It ain't that long since you raised them last time. We ain't suddenly got rich since then. Least ways I ain't!"

"Nor me!" came the chorus.

"They do say it's the cost of all this work," said Ezra Dunn. The Dunns, the Hares and John Lambert were all Sylham tenants. Clara Hare was in a far corner, which she had to herself, watching with folded arms. "I've heard the other gentlemen are set on raising the rents as well. I've heard there's more money to be raised ...."

"The Partners' business is the Partners' business," said Sylham, crustily.

"Begging your pardon," said Lambert, "but I reckon it's ours as well if we have to pay for it." There was foot stamping, a few claps of applause. Sylham wanted to tell them how much he needed the money, how he needed to pay Fat Toby, but had the wit to hold his tongue. Arabella, back turned, in a voice as withering as a north wind, had told him to say as little as possible and get on with it like a man.

"We don't want this new river, Mr. Sylham," said the elderly man. "We want it to go away. We want the Dutchie to go away, and all his Hogen Mogens and all the drunken fellows and those soldiers so we can get on with our lives!"

Sylham stood up to give himself more presence. It was beginning to get out of control. Clara, unseen till then in the corner, chose her moment.

"Vicar's gone. Soldiers have come. Fields is flooded, Yule Brook's biding her time. Mynheer's dyke is builded wrong, John Sylham and she's in the wrong place. They took our man away and put him in a lime pit – he didn't get his *nunc □imities*. It's all to the bad, and you know that John Sylham, you know that. This draining has to stop. You know it really. We know you do."

This time Clara seemed to speak for them all. Whether they understood her or not didn't matter. Her speech seeped into their common blood and beginnings and the words were as good as understanding. There was a rumble of approval. Sylham was silent, uncertain what to do. Clara resolved matters. "Happen we'll just leave you to think it over," she said and left, to be followed by others until the few prepared to debate things found themselves deserted and left as well. Soon Sylham was alone.

"That wasn't much of a success," he told himself aloud. Wandering to the window he watched the departure of the various carts, horses and pedestrians. Clara's words seemed to echo round the room. "Vicar's gone. Mynheer's dyke is builded wrong and she's in the wrong place." From the point of view of raising the rents the meeting had been a complete failure. He considered the dismissal of Emms. That was not his way of doing things. The man was an irritation, but he was Oxay, through and through. Things were changing. All to the bad, Clara said. Soldiers, dykes, bodies, troubles, money, meetings. He sighed. Any moment now Arabella would be at the door to beard him, demand how he got on, what the rents were set at.

The knock on the door was obviously not Arabella. He crossed over and opened it, expecting to see one of his tenants. Instead it was Mrs Wells, aglow and triumphant.

"I stopped the man before ever he got to the door!" she proclaimed, waving an envelope under his nose and darting into the room. She motioned to him to close the door, which he did. "Mrs Sylham never saw a thing!"

"I'm not conducting a conspiracy against Mrs Sylham!" protested Sylham, suppressing feelings of guilt and disloyalty.

"Of course not!" said Mrs Wells, handing him the letter. "Nor Mr. Toby!" She gave a wicked laugh.

"Sh!" said Sylham. "You'd better go."

Mrs Wells gave him a conspiratorial nod, a curtsy, which she never did, and was gone, closing the door with exaggerated care. Sylham opened the envelope and extracted the letter.

AUGUST 28TH 1690

TO JOHN SYLHAM ESQUIRE
GRANGE FARM
OXAY

Dear Sir,

I thank you for your letter of 10th instant and commend my greetings to our mutual friend Mr. John Warburton.

It is no presumption on your part to seek our advice on the matter of the promotion you describe. Bathurst's is a firm of both commercial experience and discretion. We have been happy to follow your instructions, our usual terms to apply, as will be sent separate at some convenient time.

Our enquiry in this matter has uncovered that handbills have been circulated concerning the Fortuna Plantation, which it is asserted is an enterprise of great value yielding considerable profits, the which are to be assured by purchasing shares in the said plantation on the island of St. Kitts. There have been a number of public meetings for the promotion of these shares. Mr. Tobias Tolman has featured at these meetings and is described on said handbills as proprieter of the Fortuna Plantation. The plantation is projected as producing great quantities of fine sugar which will be grown, boiled and transported to this country, although why the proprieter should wish to share such good fortune escapes me.

The island is promoted as being of near arcadian clime, much suited for ladies of tender disposition with the prospect of fine residences and congenial living. I am much concerned that recent intelligence reaching me regarding the wars with the French bring news that they have laid waste that island and that the plantations are in ruins, and may even now be in the hands of our enemy. If this intelligence be true, then it were best Mr. Tolman be acquainted with it as otherwise his promotion may be naught but a cruel deception. I await your instructions as to what now to do and enclose for your attention one of said handbills.

I am, your obedient servant,

THOMAS BATHURST. SOLICITOR.

Sylham read the letter again from the beginning, then folded it carefully and placed it in a pocket inside his jacket.

"Has to be a trip to Norwich," he said. "Has to be."

Chapter 16

The Yule Brook now found old waterways, filled in ponds, field drains and ditches, places where a tree had once stood and slipped quietly in. It found rabbit burrows and drove out the rabbits, drowned moles and followed worms, chasing them higher and higher until they had to swim for dry land. Geese circling over their diminishing grazing came down at dusk to gobble them up. Eels flourished and meadows were alive with nocturnal slitherings in the grass. Wilson of the ale house noticed that the joints between the flagstones in his cellar were dark with damp.

Chapter 17

Frosts had begun. The debris of autumn was frozen into the ice of puddles; sedge was pinioned by it in the marsh; the leaves of dock and arum curled, turned black and died.

The men had crunched to work, swathed in heavy clothes and white breath. It was the kind of weather when spades had to be abandoned for mattocks. They worked and waited for the signal that the new pastor had arrived.

Edmonson and de Vries had had their morning review of the work, and in this case, the arrangements. Both had dressed in their best to convey some sense of occasion, Edmonson in sober, workaday clothes, de Vries in one of his hats. They viewed the plan on the wall. On it were drawn two clear sections of the cut, the Northern section connected to the sea, the Southern shown heading inland, its projected course in broken lines. Between the two lay one hundred yards of ground, cross-hatched and marked "UNTOUCHED". De Vries pointed to the Southern section.

"Have you seen it this morning?"

"Yes. I've paid a visit."

"It's full of water."

"This morning it's full of ice."

"It is becoming critical to get this out!" He rapped with a knuckle at the untouched land on the map.

"I think we are almost past critical," replied Edmonson. "The excavations fill up immediately. We now have four more sluices, not including the Yule Brook, all stopped up with nowhere to go. That dam must go!"

"Let's hope this pastor does the job. We'll be digging from boats if he doesn't."

*

Warburton and Tyson shared the carriage with the new parson, Bullen. Bullen was a contrast to Emms, a fresh faced young man exuding enthusiasm and vigour, a man who was never without a bible clasped in his right hand. He had not yet had time to acquaint himself with his parish and stared out of the window with some wonder at the huge panorama of fields and fen, impressed by the size and emptiness, wondering if there were any people. He was wrapped in a large coat with turned up collar but even then the cold was seeping in to his bones. He wondered if he had made the right move.

"Does no one live here?" he asked.

Warburton exchanged a glance with Tyson. "No," he replied, "but that don't make it uninhabited, Mr. Bullen. What you see is one of the Lord's larders. Over there, for instance –" He directed Bullen, with a hand on his shoulder, pointing with the other, "you see that whiteness ...."

Bullen peered as directed. "Yes, I see whiteness ...."

"That's geese. Thousands of geese. They come here in winter. You will have goose, Mr. Bullen, I'll see to it."

"Where do they come from?"

"No one knows; they come in from the sea, from Denmark they say or from Russia. And the water is full of fish and eels."

"Almost an Eden, Mr. Warburton, but where are the people?"

"They're out there."

"You make it sound as if they're invisible!"

"You come from Hertfordshire I believe," said Tyson.

"Yes, Mr. Tyson, a fine county."

"Mmm," said Tyson. An easy sort of place, Hertfordshire! You will find things different here."

Bullen was hurt by the snub and returned to the window, rehearsing in his mind the service he would hold. He had brought consecrated water from

Oxay Church and hoped it was safe on the back of the coach. He read his bible, partly to avoid Tyson.

Edmonson summoned the workmen by firing off a rocket which left a blue-grey trail in the cold air. The men had to walk the mile-and-a-half to the site while a further two carriages had been laid on to transport the Partners and Bullen from the huts. The men were being paid to attend. Now the Partners were assembled in a huddle, flapping their arms and rubbing hands together to restore circulation. From the section of undug ground the view over the fen only ended where it was lost in a distant wintry haze that was the colour of lead.

"There you are, Mr. Bullen," said Edmonson, trying to make the man feel at home, "a view that stretches from ear to ear, so to speak. In that direction Lincoln, and in that Cambridge and in that ....", he pointed Northwards, "the North Sea."

"Where the wind is coming from," said Bullen.

De Vries had supplied him with a table on which Bullen had stretched a cloth. On it stood the bible. His consecrated water stood in a bottle on the ground. A short distance in front, the men were gathering in two masses, English and Dutch, to hear the pastor. Hellenbuch and Maddox had been asked to stand in front with the Partners holding spades, and did so looking awkward. The troopers, their Captain and Sergeant stood to attention, four on each side, in full uniform with muskets, their cuirasses and helmets catching the sunlight. Warburton thought it lent a satisfactory formality but Sylham was uneasy and said so.

"Do we need the soldiers?"

"Don't you think it gives a sense of security? It makes a point."

"Surely it does!" confirmed Tyson.

"I don't hold with the military," said Sylham. "They attract trouble."

Warburton detached himself from the group of Partners and stood in front of the table.

"Hats off!" he said loudly. "I have asked the Reverend Bullen to conduct this service as a memorial to the body discovered here and as a memorial to Mr. Middleton, and I have asked the Reverend Bullen to bless this place." He retreated to allow Bullen to take his place.

"We will begin with the Lord's Prayer," said Bullen.

The watchers had gathered early in the sedge, wrapped in clothing and old sacks, taking up invisible positions that would bring them within earshot.

"What do you make of this Bullen?" John Lambert whispered to Ezra.

"Just a boy."

"Warburton must think him good enough."

"Good enough for what?"

They heard the rumble of the voices, said the Lord's Prayer under their breaths, and in whispers added their own uncomplimentary and unChristian wishes for the departure of de Vries and all concerned.

"I never thought we'd see soldiers out here, like that," said Ecclesiastes, gesturing.

Bullen had got into his stride. He had advanced several paces and undone his coat to adopt a vigorous form of delivery that involved holding his bible in the air. The men stood with bowed heads, staring at their clogs. "'*Whatsoever thy hand findeth to do'*" he proclaimed, "'*do it with thy might; for there is no work, nor device, nor knowledge, nor wisdom in the grave whither thou goest.'*" As they got colder and colder they began to shift their balance from foot to foot, then to move their shoulders and exchange glances. They had long since lost the relevance of Bullen's text. So had Latimer. He had a cold and his impatience was evident in his cough. Tyson, chilled to the marrow, eventually took charge. In one of Bullen's pauses for breath he muttered to him.

"The men are freezing Mr. Bullen. Freezing. We're all freezing."

Bullen heard, looked to Warburton and saw his fixed expression.

"I now bless this ground!" he declared loudly, forsaking his previous text. Warburton had shown him the abandoned face of the work in which the body had been discovered. Bullen returned to the table, laid down his bible and picked up the consecrated water. With the Partners he walked the few yards to the appropriate spot and shook the bottle. Nothing came out. Tipping it further, he shook again without success. Edmonson saw the problem.

"It's frozen, Mr. Bullen. From standing on the ground."

Bullen held up the bottle. A plug of ice had formed in the neck. As they stared at it impotently a hoot of derisive laughter rang out from the cover of the sedge where Clara had been concealed. Warburton's face was thunderous. He called to the Captain.

"Send your men after that!"

The Captain gestured and the troopers, stiff with cold, started on unwilling legs in the direction of the noise. They carried their muskets at the ready.

"No!" Bullen protested, but he was ignored.

The workmen had watched these proceedings with amazement at first, but now it was in danger of turning to ridicule. Warburton rounded on Hellenbuch and Maddox.

"Dig! Move forward, in front and dig! One turn will do."

They did as they were told.

"Work here starts tomorrow!" he announced in a loud voice.

"You heard that. Work here starts tomorrow!" Edmonson echoed.

"That was a pity Mr. Bullen," said Latimer unkindly.

"Who was that laughing?" demanded Bullen. "What are the soldiers to do?"

"Any of them," said Warburton. "You see what we have come to!"

Sylham knew who it was and said nothing.

*

In the sedge the villagers melted away by the paths they had come, leaving the soldiers to crash about and plunge in iced pools. One of them, in front of the others with his musket held high, saw a retreating figure.

"Stop!" he yelled. When the figure continued to run, he raised the musket to his shoulder, released the safety catch and fired. The crash of the shot stopped the departing workmen and froze conversation between the Partners. All eyes turned towards the fen, where a puff of smoke rose lazily, then was whipped away by the wind. Tyson looked at Warburton with an expression of satisfaction. Sylham, who had said nothing so far, stepped up to Tyson.

"It don't do to end a prayer meeting with musketry, Walter. It don't do at all."

He shook his head and walked away.

*

All precautions had been taken. It got dark early at this time of the year and the barn had been blacked out as much as possible with sacking, straw and old material. The two Lambert boys and Clarke's son had been posted around the building at some distance to give early warning of strangers. Clarke himself manned the door, pistol in belt. The door was kept closed and admission was obtained by knocking and undergoing scrutiny with Clarke's lantern. A central table had been set up again and the meeting was well attended. Word of the day's events had spread rapidly and the mood was sober, people acknowledging each other quietly, without noisy salutation. Ecclesiastes already sat on the plank by the table. He nursed a fowling piece. Ezra stood in front of the table waiting for his audience to settle down. No one smoked. Tobacco smoke can be smelled for a quarter of a mile on a still cold night.

Ezra rapped on the table with his knuckles. His face was grim. Silence fell quickly.

"This is a serious time," he said, "and it's difficult to know where to start. I reckon you all heard the shot if you didn't see it?" He paused. There was a rumble of assent. "They took a pot at John Lambert –" He tried a tight smile, - "which I reckon was stupid, because there ain't much eating on him!"

This achieved slight noises of appreciation. "So now we've to be shot at by Mr. Warburton's soldiers, which we don't like. In fact I could say we take exception to it. And why did they shoot? Because we was there. That's all. Not because of anything we done. And now they need more money for this cut, because it's all costing more than they thought, they've raised our rents to pay for it!"

"I ain't going to pay!" shouted Thomas Fox, his old croaky voice breaking with excitement.

"So what do we do?" Ezra asked. "They're going to rob us of our living and charge us for it!"

"We know what to do," said Walker Clarke from the doorway. "We need to get on with it. Time to burn down their huts. It's the only way."

This appeared to be the popular view.

"We ain't got them running yet," said Lambert. "Slowing them down is one thing, but we have got to stop them."

"We're on our way again," said Jack Lamb. "When we last met I said it would end in muskets. Do we know what we're doing? The way we're going, someone's going to be killed. You said we could wear them down, Ezra, with devilment and the like, but all we've done is delay it. We must ask ourselves if we're ready to see this through. I wasn't last time, but I am now. I don't like it, but I'll do it. I just want everyone to know what they're in for."

Jack Lamb had moved forward as he spoke and when he finished there was silence. He looked around the barn at the half-lit faces.

"John? Thomas? Peter? Walter? Ezra says it is a serious time. I'm telling you it don't get more serious than this." He moved towards his left in order to stare into that corner of the barn.

"I see you there, Clara Hare, what do you make to all this? Whatever we start, it has to go on to the finish."

Clara, who had been half in shadow moved forward into the yellow light of a lantern. She wore her flowered bonnet but was otherwise dressed in dark material from head to toe.

"I've come prepared," she said, "dark for darkness. It's not just the shooting and not just the rent, they put our old father in a lime pit to eat away what the earth left. Nothing but bad will come of disturbing the dead."

"When last you talked about 'old people', I thought you were mad," said Lamb, "but now I have to say that maybe you have a point. They have no right to dig up a Christian soul and put him in a lime pit like a dog. I tell you Clara I agree, they must leave the dead alone."

"Alleluia!" shouted Ecclesiastes. "*'The righteous shall never be removed : but the wicked shall not inhabit the earth'*. Don't you think it's a sign that the body was there, and that the vicar's water froze and that they missed you, John Lambert?"

"Could be," said Lambert, who stood near the front, "but it could ha' been because I was running like hell, no thanks to Clara!" There was laughter. Peter Dade had been leaning against a wall, he straightened himself and spoke.

"Mr. Emms wanted to stop it, and I reckon that Mr. Emms is as good a man of the cloth as we could wish for, whatever they say. Carter's Graff was his piece of holy ground, he said, and that it was burial ground afore we ever had a churchyard. Mr. Emms buried that skull we dug up and did it proper in the churchyard, a Christian burial. They don't want that sort of thing so that's the man they've taken away! Everything they do, they shove us aside so's they will get their beautiful drained land and summer pastures!"

He had been listened to with respect and when he stopped there was a reflective silence, broken eventually by Bess Fox.

"So what do you reckon Peter?"

"I reckon we have to stop them, whatever it takes."

"Does anyone say otherwise?" asked Ezra. There was no answer. "Then we had best get dressed and get on with the job. It's a good night for it."

*

Bess Fox had collected twigs and the wild witches' broom that grows on the branches of the silver birch. With twine and ribbons she had bound and modelled these into human forms with a trunk, head, arms and legs using elder twigs – elder, beloved of witches, never cut elder after dark – for the bone structure. Harriet Dunn made clay figures from diggings from the old marl pit behind their house, giving each a wide open gash of a mouth and sloes for eyes. When she had finished she took spears of elder from Bess Fox and stuck them through the bodies. Rebecca Clarke packed the manikins in baskets. The men were engaged elsewhere, in charge of nooses, gallows, dead animals and arson. They had collected together their firearms and powder as their fire raising would be certain to bring the troopers. These were mainly fowling pieces and pistols, although Walter Clarke had produced a flintlock. Clara had gone off on her own. No one asked where, or what she would do; she had said she would join them later, a message received with mixed feelings. The men dressed as females in an assortment of ill-fitting clothing and had masks and hats stuffed with straw. There was a sombre mood and there was little joking about their outfits. They had decided to take a single dark-lantern for emergencies and for fire. Otherwise they would move in the semi-darkness. The night was clear, with a frost and a sickle of waxing moon. This, with blazing starlight would provide plenty of light.

*

Warburton had invited Tyson, Latimer and de Vries back to the Hall to have an opportunity to meet the new vicar. Sylham had not been included because of his critical remark and what Warburton considered his desertion at the end of the ceremony. Although wives had been asked none had come and Ruth and Cristeen found themselves alone with Sarah, who appeared under protest. She had already been introduced to Bullen too emphatically by her father and had taken an immediate dislike to him which she tried not to show. They had dined and Bullen had been given a hard-backed chair to sit amongst the ladies. Tyson, Richard and Latimer sat facing him while Warburton warmed his seat at the fire.

"Well at least you have seen our difficulties at first hand," said Warburton, "I don't like saying this of a man of the cloth, but things deteriorated badly under Emms, and in the end I believe he was deranged. A great embarrassment for us all."

"It appears so," said Bullen with the sanctimonious tone that was annoying Sarah. This is going to be so boring, she thought to herself. Bullen was already glancing towards her more than she liked, trying a grimace which he appeared to think was a smile. She avoided eye contact.

"What we need," said Tyson, "is a proper return to Christian values. We need a few good sermons from you, Mr. Bullen. Teach these people! '*The Lord giveth wisdom : out of his mouth cometh knowledge and understanding.*'"

"Amen," said Bullen and Warburton together. "I shall certainly do my best," Bullen continued. "And I shall invite your countrymen, Mr. de Vries. We must look to the welfare of everyone. Do they have your permission to attend?"

"I do not run my countrymen," replied de Vries somewhat stiffly, "but our Reformed Church has no difficulties with your Church."

"Mr. Bullen is a sound man on the Creation," Warburton announced. "perhaps you would read for us now from the Book and say a prayer for us all? ...."

"Certainly," said Bullen, "and say a few words."

*

At Elm Farm Katja leaned out of the parlour window oblivious of the icy air. Alarmed at first by Peter's rap on the window, she now held his head in her hands and stared at nose length into his eyes.

"What are you doing here!"

"I know your parents are out."

"But what are you doing here?"

"Why haven't you come to our place? I've waited for you. Three times."

"I couldn't tell you. Mama knows we've been meeting. I am forbidden to go out, and forbidden to see you!"

"How does she know?"

"Richard Warburton told her. He knows, he must have seen us!" The look in his eyes stopped her. She tugged at his head, shaking him to and fro. "No, you mustn't mind, it doesn't matter. It's *niet be'langrijk*!"

"I'll deal with Richard Warburton."

"*Nee, nee, nee*! Mama will get over it and she hasn't told papa. See, I kiss you!"

She did so until Peter gently eased away.

"I must go," he said, "I have people to meet."

"What sort of people? More important than me?"

"No, but I have to meet them. It's freezing, you had better get in."

"Look, I can get out of this window!" Katja started to clamber out but Peter held her shoulders. She struggled half-heartedly and stopped. "But I *can* get out of this window!"

"Katja I have to go. I just wanted to know what was wrong .... how do we contact each other? I can't come to this window ...."

"Can you write?"

"Of course I can read and write," said Peter proudly.

"Then leave me messages over there!" She pointed to the dark line of the front hedge. "I'll put something – a jug in there."

"But where can I meet you?" asked Peter.

"I'm going to the church with mama. On Sunday afternoon. I've never been there. Mama thinks I need *bedaren* – you know, like a ship on a flat sea!" She laughed.

"Calming."

"And she'll pray for hours. I might just be able to see you. But she must not see you."

Peter nodded.

"Now get inside. You'll hear and see things tonight, but I've never been here, do you understand?" Katja stared at him, excited.

"No, I don't. Tell me. What do you mean?"

Peter kissed her and pushed her gently back to close the casement. He waved and was gone.

*

After the episode of the stones the troopers preferred to have a roof over them. Temporary cover had been erected for the horses and oxen to protect them from the cold and keep their fodder dry. This protection took the form of makeshift huts that were moved forward with the works. The patrol had soon established a billet in one and were sitting in the hay. From this position they had a view of the huts and stones. A ground frost had fallen, providing reflected light. They could see the breath of the oxen lying nearby, asleep and occasionally snorting.

"Cold and getting colder," hissed the sergeant. His men merely nodded. They were wrapped in heavy coats, collars turned up, but still the chill was getting through. There didn't seem any point in speaking. They had half-an-hour in this comfortable spot before moving on and would make the most of it.

The women knew where the men would be, how long they would be there, the pattern of their patrols; - Lambert's older boy had watched them for a week. They were dressed in black and wore black woollen masks and went about their business in silence, visible only as darkness against starlight. Bess Fox tied her twig figures to trees and to the uprights of the cranes, binding them on with strips of cloth dipped in chicken's blood. Harriet and Rebecca found sites for their figures in wagons, barrows, on a wood pile sitting them down by bending the moist clay. When secure, Harriet produced a knife and cut their throats almost through, tilting the clay heads back to stare at the stars. Rebecca shivered as she stood back watching.

The men moved amongst the huts at the opposite end of the works. They brought with them their gallows from which hung two dead crows, and a noose from which suspended a dead cat. Each carried a tied bundle of straw, tar and turpentine. They split the bundles and stuffed straw under the canteen, store huts, the huts of de Vries and Edmonson, the huts of the sawyers and carpenters, the rope store and the wood pile, anointing each pile with turpentine and tar. Peter Dade and Ezra Dunn lit brands from the dark-lantern and ran from one to the other, setting the huts on fire. The effect was immediate; towers of flame shot skywards followed by the hot burn of tar with its clouds of smoke.

The troopers saw the flames immediately and scrambled to their feet grabbing their firelocks. The sergeant shouted at them to come on and they set off at a run in the direction of the flames. These had already begun to consume the wooden buildings. As they drew near the sergeant held up his hand and indicated they should get down. They lowered themselves into a frozen ditch, the ice crackling and singing beneath them, watching for movement. Clarke's older boy was trying to set a fire at the far end of the wood pile when they saw him. He shouldn't have been there but he felt the men hadn't given him a big enough job of work.

"It's women!" hissed one of the soldiers. "Look at the skirts!"

"He's running too fast!" said the sergeant. "That's a man. And what if it is a woman?"

Clarke's boy poured turpentine over the logs and looked around for something for a brand. He went back to the carpenter's store for a switch of straw, and shielding his eyes from the heat lit it to carry it back.

The sergeant himself fired at him. All the men had loaded muskets, but he had pointed at himself with his finger. The shot narrowly missed. Clarke's boy froze at the explosion, then realising what it was, dived round the wood pile. The shot had crashed into the logs. Ezra, Walter, John Lambert, Jack Lamb and Peter Dade were already clear of the huts, staring in awe and admiration at their handiwork from the safety of the rushes.

"By God it's soldiers!" shouted Walter. "They're shooting at my boy!" He crashed forward carrying his flintlock, reached the wood pile beside his boy Will.

"I'm all right!" said Will. Walter snorted, took aim in the general direction of the shot, and fired. Instantly three shots were returned. The other men joined Walter behind the wood pile.

"Have this!" shouted Ezra and emptied his fowling piece in the direction of the soldiers. He and Walter re-loaded. While they were in shadow, the position of the soldiers was partially lit by flame.

"They move in fours," said Lambert.

"They'll have heard that at the Hall," said Ezra. "The rest will be on their way. Let's get out of here."

"Not for just a minute!" hissed Walter Clarke, the old army man. He had re-loaded and now took careful aim. No one liked to stop him. "I snatched that last shot;" he said, "this one's for trying to shoot Will!"

He fired, smoke and powder flying everywhere. A return volley thudded into the timber. Ezra looked at John Lambert, they turned to Jack Lamb. All three raised their weapons, tucked themselves amongst the logs and fired. Peter alone was unarmed.

"Now we go," said Walter, patting Will on the back. One of the huts began to collapse, adding more fuel to its own fire. The night sky was filled with sparks.

"We can be seen," said Peter Dade. Ezra agreed.

"Wait a bit."

*

Clara, forswearing a mask, stood behind the soldiers on a tussock path through the sedge. The frost had made it firm and she had been able to follow their progress. She was wrapped in a shawl that was gathered round her waist with a leather belt. She had held her hands over her ears during the shooting and now produced a tinder box from inside her shawl. Thumbing the wheel she watched the sparks on the tinder, blowing gently until a flame was born and transferring the infant fire to a handful of dry reeds. When this ignited she stuffed it into the sedge in front of her. The wind was behind her, blowing towards the soldiers in the ditch. The sedge caught fire instantly, flames dashing through the seed heads to be followed more lazily by the white heat of the stems. The furious crackling alerted the sergeant, who spun round to see an advancing wall of flame.

"Out of here!" he shouted, "run for it!" They started to move, crouching. One of his men grabbed his coat, shouted.

"It's Howard, he's been hit!"

The sergeant struggled past his men, aware of the heat of the fire. The soldier had been hit in the left of his face and his shoulder, unknown to the others. He stooped down to the man.

"Can you hear me?" The man replied with mumbles and a groan. "Pick him up, and hurry!"

Half carrying and half dragging the wounded man they moved in a crouch to a position of safety from the fire where they stopped to look in the direction of the wood pile. They saw the unsettling sight of six female figures, complete with hats, doubled up and running fast from right to left.

"Fire!" shouted Willetts, the sergeant. He was still holding Howard's arms and couldn't move. The two men looked at him, looked at the figures and hesitated.

"Fire!" he roared.

"It might be women, sergeant!"

"It's not godammed women! It's men!"

He dropped the unfortunate man's arms, shouldered his firelock and fired, but it was too late; seeing no one he fired uselessly into the shadows.

*

Skeins of geese were honking overhead in the first light as de Vries kicked the glowing stump of timber back into the ash-pit that had been his hut. He had to stand six strides away, the heat was still uncomfortable. He could identify the position of one of his tables by the shape of some ash and the unconsumed foot of one leg. Part of a chest survived where a piece of wall had fallen on it. A pottery jug had somehow survived intact. There was nothing else.

"All my plans! My drawings! My pens, my inks, my records! All of that work!"

De Vries was distraught and waved his hands about. His breath hung in puffs in the cold air. He and the Partners had made several tours already and made yet another as dawn became daylight. Each time things appeared worse. Most of the huts had been consumed. The oxen had escaped, simply dragging out their tethering posts. The sedge fire had cut a desolate black swathe across the fen until it extinguished itself in a frozen mere. The frozen ground that should have been crisp and white was trampled and muddied and spattered with smuts. Behind them a gang of workmen were still throwing buckets of water over one end of the wood pile. There was nowhere to sit down, nowhere for the workmen to eat, and smoke still trickled from the remains. The whole place stank of extinguished wood.

De Vries and the Partners had all arrived in the night, alarmed by the shots and fires. Now they were cold, hungry and angry. A bright frosty morning did nothing to gladden things as it revealed more and more detail of the destruction.

"I'm sure you can reproduce them," said Warburton sharply to de Vries. His sympathy was wearing thin at this third performance of de Vries' lamentations. He had picked de Vries up on his way to the fires, and been furious that the man had put on a hat that immediately fell off when riding and was so important to its owner that Warburton had to wait for it to be recovered. He was getting tired of the man's perpetual complaining about wood and stone and everything else. In truth, he told himself, he was becoming tired of Mr. de Vries.

"But these people are criminals! Are you going to let them get away with it?"

De Vries turned angrily to face Warburton, but all Warburton could focus on was the hat. He felt a dangerous surge of anger and struggled to find something diplomatic to say. Tyson was never similarly burdened.

"What do you think we've been doing? I suppose it'd all be done better in Holland!"

Latimer intervened. "This is a time for us all to pull together, gentlemen. We must not let this slow us down!"

"Sir!"

Mason, the Captain of the troopers approached them, came to a halt and saluted. Like the Partners he had been up all night, having galloped to the site with the off-duty troopers as soon as they heard gunfire. In his hand he was carrying a piece of folded, sealed paper.

"How's your man?" asked Warburton.

"He's well enough, sir. Your midwife, Mrs ...."

"Bower."

"Mrs Bower has cleaned him up and bound him. He'll have a scar on his face and he had shot in his shoulder – some sort of duck shot I should say – but he was lucky. I'm sorry we couldn't get them for you sir."

"Any identification?"

"No sir. It's all in this report." He handed the folded paper to Warburton. "All the men could see dressed up men, wearing masks and women's dresses. We could've got them – we were doing all right till someone lit that fire behind us." His anger produced a tremor in his voice.

"It's an old tactic, Captain," said Latimer. "They've used it for hundreds of years."

"Begging your pardon Mr. Latimer, but it was new to us."

"Did you see who lit it?" asked Warburton.

"No sir. Not a sight."

"We need more troops!" Tyson exclaimed. "You hadn't enough to surround them!"

"No sir."

"I'll write to the Sheriff," said Warburton. "Will you be reporting to him?"

"I will send him the same report as you, Mr. Warburton. It is my intention to get these rioters! Be assured." He saluted again and turned away.

Sylham had been standing slightly apart from the others. He had been partly forgiven for his previous observations on soldiers, but a coolness still existed. He had picked up the remains of a burnt spade – a piece of black handle in a blade, and held it out before him.

"You won't like me for saying it," he began, "but more soldiers cost more money and you need things like this if the work is to go on." He flung down the remains of the spade. "Perhaps we should have listened a bit to Emms." Tyson let out a disgusted snort. "No, wait a bit," Sylham continued, "perhaps if we had talked to the villagers a bit more, this might not have happened. Instead of bringing in soldiers. I've said it before – soldiers are trouble."

"I'm not listening to this!" Tyson exploded. "Are you on their side?"

"Now Walter, stay calm," said Latimer, but Sylham walked away. "This is not a time to fall out. For a start we need money. With Emms out of it, what do we do? That's the thing to think about."

"More Partners?" asked Warburton. "We shall have to think about it." He privately realised Latimer was right. He would have to trouble Bathurst again. "I'll talk John round. He has some strange ideas. He'll be all right. He's one of us when it comes down to it." He pointed. "There's Edmonson."

Edmonson arrived by horse. He had inspected the working end of the cut and he was unsmiling.

"They won't work," he said without ceremony. He carried a bag. "The place is littered with things." He took from the bag one of the clay figures and showed it to them. "This, and these ...." – he showed them one of the twig figures, "and signs on the ground. A dead crow."

"Superstitious rubbish!" shouted Tyson, struggling to control himself. "Do we live in a Christian country? Why won't they work?" He seemed to be boiling he was surrounded by so much vapour.

"I've met with Maddox and Hellenbuch. They say the men are afraid," said Edmonson.

"Do you believe them?"

Edmonson shrugged. "I don't know. Apparently the men say they ain't paid to be shot at."

"They haven't been shot at! It's all a damnable excuse for more pay!" Tyson was turning red with anger. "There's your man!" he declared pointing at Bullen. The pastor had just arrived and was tying his horse to a blackened fence post. They watched him approach, picking his way with care round ash and debris.

"Good morning gentlemen!" No one answered. "This is a terrible thing. I came as soon as I heard. I must have slept through it." The Partners exchanged scathing glances at this announcement.

"What we need Mr. Bullen," said Warburton bluntly, "is some good sermons from you." Further flights of geese passed overhead, calling. "Those damned birds are mocking us!" he declared. They could hear the steady swish of their wings, could see them begin to circle in the distance. A few flakes of snow began to descend lazily.

"I do not like snow!" said de Vries. "I am going home now and will start drawing!"

"I'll start ordering," said Edmonson. "I've made a list. Is that in order, Mr. Warburton?"

"Of course. Good man," said Warburton mechanically, wondering how much this was going to cost. "This is only a set-back. We must make this clear."

*

Captain Mason had obtained a replacement for his injured man. He had divided his small troop in two, one half under himself, the other under his sergeant, Willetts. With these two troops he was determined to search the village instead of simply patrolling the works. His anger at the ambush and fire daily increased with the frustration of turning out house after house to discover nothing. Mutual suspicion had soon blossomed into open hostility and searches became an excuse for harassment. Not a single gun was found, despite turning over hay and muck-heaps, fishing down wells, poking into thatch, demolishing wood-piles and generally ransacking buildings.

"We know you did it!" was the cry, and one by one the villagers were made to stand outside, against a wall or against a tree, covered by a trooper with a musket trained on them while the search went on. Men, women and children.

Ezra was providing some entertainment for Willetts. He had been stood with Harriet and Esther in front of a cart. Harriet had an arm round Esther's waist. Ezra was plainly furious. The armed trooper was aiming at him.

"I reckon you're a bit of a wild one," opined the sergeant. Within the house they could hear the third man dragging furniture about.

"You ain't got any right to do this!"

"Is that so? And you would know that, would you? You and your friends who think it's all right to shoot at us? And burn the place down. So where's your gun?"

"I ain't got a gun."

"Ain't got a gun!" mimicked Willetts. "Are you trying to tell me, you mudlark, that you don't have a roast duck now and then? I seem to remember that these fens are famous for a nice roasted bird!"

"We trap 'em."

Within the house was a resounding crash. Ezra started forward. The trooper's finger caressed the trigger. The third soldier appeared in the doorway clutching a bundle of cotton and woollen garments.

"Women's clothes, sergeant! In a chest!"

"That's my clothes!" protested Harriet. "You put them back!"

"In a chest ...." Willetts advanced on his man, took a garment and shook it out to reveal a very plain dress, far from new. He held it up by the neck as if it was evidence. "A woman's dress!" he declaimed. "In a chest. Hidden from view. Now what were those rioters dressed in?" he asked of the trooper with the musket.

"Women's clothes, sergeant," that man replied.

"These are my clothes," insisted Harriet. "I keep them in my chest!" She hesitated to step forward, eyeing the armed man.

"Not *his* clothes," said Willetts, gesturing towards Ezra, "but *your* clothes!"

"*My* clothes."

"Sure you ain't been out wearing them?" demanded Willetts, stepping over towards Ezra. "Seems it's a habit here, wearing women's clothes ...."

The armed trooper sniggered. Willetts flung the dress in the direction of Harriet, who caught it.

"Look at the size of it," said Ezra, with sudden inspiration. "How could I get in that?"

This was so patently obvious that even Willetts had to admit it. He nodded, pulled a face he imagined to be judicial. "And there was a woman there. I saw her. Lit the fire. Some sort of a witch."

"Don't know what you're talking about," said Ezra.

"Nobody knows what we're talking about. That's for sure. Whatever happened here, nobody did it, nobody saw anything, nobody has a gun .... who is this nobody? I'm told you have a witch in the village."

"There ain't no witches any more!" said Ezra.

"Clara," blurted out Esther, who until then had said nothing. Harriet clutched her close.

"There's a name!" crowed Willetts. "That's children for you. The innocent ones tell the truth!" He snapped his fingers and motioned for the men to leave. Once mounted, he turned back to Ezra. "Don't you think we won't be back!"

Harriet clutched Esther tightly. Esther let out a wail. "I shouldn't have said that, should I!"

"It don't matter Esther, it really don't matter. There ain't no witches any more."

"She didn't mean harm," said Ezra. "Anyhow, she's only a Hare, when all's said and done."

"I'm afraid to see what's happened to our house," said Harriet, changing the subject, "and I don't want this dress no more! Not now!" She flung it down on the ground and made for the door.

*

It was the sort of day in the fens that only a duck-hunter could enjoy. A lowering grey sky pressed down in an attempt to merge with rising mist. Between the two a narrow band of luminous grey represented daylight. In this half-light Clara made her way to where she knew the head of the works lay. She had no interest in the destruction at the scene of the fire. An idea had been forming in her mind about the sluices. Now she picked her way across hoar-frosted meadow, over ice-glazed stiles and between stands of rattling reeds. In the distance she could hear voices, spades, the squeak of wheels. She moved cautiously for she must not be discovered. Her path was blocked by a dyke and there were trees about her she did not recognise. She moved to the left to follow the dyke to a crossing, uneasy at the bad visibility. Walking perhaps a hundred yards she stopped to regain her bearings.

Not far off, in the wrong direction she heard the snort of a horse, and only just having made that out, heard the drum of hoofs. She stood stock still, looking in to the band of mist before her, her back to the dyke. At first there was a darkening of the mist, the increasing beat of hoofs, but the noise seemed to turn, veer away from her, lessen, recede. Clara was uncertain what to do. She started to retreat along the bank of the dyke, only to hear the drumming increase. She stood her ground, straining her eyes into the mist. From the low swirl, three horsemen materialised, the bodies and heads of the horses above the mist, the legs lost. She recognised the troopers astride them. They slowed down and walked their animals forward. The men were bare-headed, their hair lank with moisture. They positioned their animals in a rough half-circle so that Clara was trapped between them and the water. The hot animals snorted, adding to the rising mist. Steam rose from their bodies, and Clara was aware of the smell of horses and leather. She saw that the man in charge, the sergeant, had a twig doll tied to the pommel of his saddle. Yellow ribbons that had been its hair stuck to the horse's hide. She waited, but the men watched her silently, waiting for some instruction. Clara took a quick look behind her. The dyke was covered with an insubstantial skin of ice, no thicker than a glaze. She noted the pistols and muskets the men carried in holsters, the scabbards at their sides. She avoided meeting their eyes, folded her arms on her chest, drawing in the cloak she was wearing.

"What do you want?" she demanded.

"Are you Clara Hare?" It was the sergeant, Willetts.

"What if I am? Why are three men stopping a woman going about her business?"

"What's your business Clara Hare?"

"My business is none of your business!"

"Perhaps you've been playing with fire. Or making little bundles of twigs, like my friend here." He pointed at the doll with a jabbing finger. "That would be our business, what do you say?"

"I say clear off and leave me alone!"

"I expect you do, but that ain't a polite way to talk to His Majesty's troopers. About our lawful business. Some say that you're a witch, Clara. What do you say to that?"

Clara was not surprised. It was an accusation she had been expecting. "Who said that?"

"Don't matter who said it. Does matter if it's true. Now once upon a time there was a way of sorting the matter out. But I expect you know that."

Clara feared for what was coming, prepared herself to jump into the dyke, out of reach.

"I'm told Master Hopkins made a good harvest in these parts," said Willetts, turning to address his men. "Before the 'enlightenment' as now they call it. You know, lads, that there was incontro-something or other proofs that you'd snared a witch. Pricking was good. You see, you find the devil's mark on a witch, and when you prick it, with something nice and sharp, she don't feel no pain, and you draw no blood. Or on the other hand, they used to swear by finding the third teat, because lads, every woman has two, but a witch has another one! Aye, another one for suckling her familiar. And, you know what, lads, they keep that teat in the most secret places! Ain't that so Clara?" Willetts nudged his horse with his knees, urging it to go forward. The animal, no more than four feet from Clara, refused to move, rolling its eyes.

"Forward lads!" urged Willetts to his men. "If you duck a witch, the water won't have 'em because they deny baptism!"

Clara made no movement. The troopers followed Willetts' lead, digging knees into the flanks of their animals. The horses reared rather than go forward, collided with each other, turned to retreat, whinnying.

"She's spooked the horses!" shouted Willetts, jumping down. "Damn you, I'll do it myself!" He ran at Clara, intending to push her into the water, but before he could, Clara turned and jumped in, shattering the thin ice and swimming for the other side. The men watched as she pulled herself out, floundering at first to get clear of mud and rushes. She quickly pulled herself upright, gathered her soaking dress together and, carrying the skirt of it before her, strode into the mist without a backward glance. One of the troopers, uneasy, patted his horse, muttered to Willetts.

"Reckon we should get out of here, sarge. We might get into trouble if Captain hears of this."

"She floated!" said Willetts. "You can't drown a witch. We done nothing wrong." Nonetheless he returned to his horse and mounted the animal. "You see what she done to our horses!"

"Yes, sergeant." The trooper pulled the collar of his jacket up and shivered.

"Lily-livered lot!" exclaimed Willetts, and turned back into the mist. The glaze of ice was already re-forming over the dyke. Wisps of mist repaired the breaches made by men.

*

Clara's anger helped her at first to ignore the cold as she continued on her way to the sluices. She concealed herself in a brake of elder, chasing out the pigeons that were eating the remaining berries. Bodily strong and fit, she talked herself softly into silence, "Hush there, you should hush. Clara don't feel cold, Clara don't feel cold," until her teeth stopped chattering. In front, no more than a hundred yards away, she could see the men at work. They had constructed a pile-driver from one stout log suspended from a tripod of others. This was winched up with a windlass and allowed to fall with a thump that made the unstable ground shiver. They were driving log piles across the bed of Yule Brook, to cut it off and build a sluice.

"No you shan't," said Clara, breaking her silence. The ground shivered again as the log fell and the mist seemed to tremble, the sound to throb in her head, to shake the bones within her flesh. "You try to stop Yule Brook, you might as well try to turn the tide. Clara knows what to do." The log fell again and again, the heartbeat of a giant. She retreated from concealment, slapping herself for warmth as soon as it was safe to do so, mulling over her plans. "Yule Brook helps us, Clara will help Yule Brook." The monstrous heartbeat carried from the mist, following her homewards.

*

Among the Partners, a period of ostensible calm followed the fire and shooting. A time for reflection for some, for restrained anger for Warburton, Latimer and Tyson, for recovery for de Vries. For Sylham it was a time spent screwing his courage to the sticking point for the business in Norwich.

Warburton, in an attempt to reconcile the Partners, had called to see him. He brought news that Sylham did not want to hear. "We've been obliged to increase the men's pay. There was no other way to get them going. The work has to go on. Winter's closing in."

They had met in Sylham's hall. The carpet was bare, the walls needed painting, and Warburton wore the clothes of a wealthy man.

"All right for you!" thought Sylham. Warburton had arrived on a wealthy man's horse with a wealthy man's saddle. Even Warburton's hedgerows were kept like a wealthy man's hedgerows – cut in season, ditches cleared. Annoyance made him reply too sharply. "It's easy to give in quick if you have the money. When you don't, you argue longer."

Warburton had remained reasonable. "They've been shot at, they've been plagued by these witch dolls, the works have been set on fire. They started to leave .... what do you expect?"

Sylham was not to be pacified. "So now we're paying for soldiers as well. It's a bottomless pit, not drainage!"

He resolved to deal with Toby. His announcement to Arabella that he was going to Norwich took her by surprise. Her attempts to find out why met with a reason she suspected. Sylham had laboured hard at the unaccustomed exercise of invention and the best he could come up with was a visit to his land agent – one of the few men he knew in Norwich.

"I must sort out the matter of the boundaries," he explained. "There are parcels of land between me and Warburton that have never been properly defined. He was here about that. We must do it before we divide up the new land. Has to be done, fire or no fire."

Arabella was suspicious but could prove nothing. She merely nodded. "Will you be paying your respects to Toby?"

"Shouldn't think so," said Sylham, reddening. He was a poor liar and knew it. "I shouldn't think I'll have the time. And Norwich is damned expensive. I shall be quick as I can."

"Where will you stay?"

"The Angel." He considered this a master stroke. A lifetime before, when they were both young, they had stayed at the Angel so that Arabella could visit the tradesmen of Norwich. She had bought materials – for curtains, clothes, upholstery – things to soften the wood and stone of a farmhouse, things to grace a table when they entertained. To his horror a look of pain crossed Arabella's face.

"That will be nice for you," she said.

"Is there anything you need?" he volunteered, stabbed with remorse over their lost love. Once upon a time Arabella would have given him a list and he would have proudly handed it to the haberdasher, cutler, chandler, draper, grocer.

"I shouldn't think so," she said.

Mrs Wells guessed what he was about and exuded conspiratorial comradeship that annoyed Sylham, despite their normal closeness. The hurt in Arabella's face was difficult to forget. "How long will you be away sir?" she asked disingenuously in front of Arabella.

"Just two nights, Mrs Wells. One on the journey, one before setting back.

"What if you are delayed sir?"

Sylham could see Mrs Wells had one eye on Arabella. "I shan't be delayed."

"I was thinking of linen, sir."

"Thank you Mrs Wells."

"Business is business. Must have you looking your best."

"I'm sure I shall be all right Mrs Wells."

"Must be spruce for your meeting!" Here she had sufficiently turned from Arabella to give him a wink, which he repaid with a glower. Mrs Wells laid out his belongings in neat rows, watched by Arabella. Sylham repaid her impertinence by cramming them unfolded into his saddle-bags, topping the lot with a bottle of brandy.

He started very early, in the half-dark following a cold night, under clear skies where the moon refused to hide, but hung there until the sun came up. It was the sort of weather Sylham enjoyed and he made good progress on steadily improving roads through Swaffham and on to East Dereham. There, in morning light, he drank a third of his bottle of brandy in the warming sun. Whether it was the brandy or the clear blue sky, his feeling of guilt over Arabella was being replaced by thorough ill-will towards Toby. He lunched among fellow travellers at a wayside inn, the horse was fed and watered and by seven in the evening he arrived, saddle-sore, at the Angel. In the courtyard he slid off his horse and shouted at the boy to bring his saddle-bags.

"Stopping long?" asked the landlord, a not particularly courteous man, with little respect for red-faced country farmers dressed in fashionless clothes – and smelling of brandy.

"Not if I can help it," replied Sylham, more than a match for him. "Two nights is all I need." His eye was caught by the clutter of bills pinned and pasted to the panelling of the entrance. Age was determined by state of decay and among the newer postings, Sylham had recognised Toby's from the one sent by Bathurst. This one had a newborn look and Sylham, grinding his thumb into the red lettering of the heading, was able to produce a smear of ink.

NOTICE TO INVESTORS

FORTUNA PLANTATION, ST. KITTS.

An opportunity is available for INVESTMENT in ONE of the PRIME SUGAR PLANTATIONS which are now among the MOST IMPORTANT and VALUABLE ASSETS of their MAJESTIES' dominions.

Situate in ST. KITTS, a veritable EDEN of the ANTILLES whose climate has been compared to that of the Azores, SHARES are now being OFFERED FOR PURCHASE BY THE DISCERNING INVESTOR at No 22 MAGDALEN STREET, NORWICH daily at ELEVEN of the CLOCK where full PARTICULARS and etc. can be obtained from the PROPRIETOR.

TOBIAS TOLMAN ESQ.

PROP. FORTUNA PLANTATION.

The landlord had been watching Sylham's face as he read the bills. Sylham's lips had been moving with the effort, rounding off with 'Fortuna Plantation' as though spitting out pips. "Interested, sir? Mean anything to you?"

"Interested." He tried to keep the reply non-committal, but evidently failed. "New, is it?"

"Yes. I'm told there is quite an excitement about it in Norwich."

Sylham was aware the man was studying him. "What's for supper? No, don't bother, I'll have the ordinary." Sylham was wary of city ways. He asked the inquisitive man the way to Magdalen Street, declining a guide for the morrow and considered whether he would call on Bathurst first. The ominous, remembered words "our usual terms will apply", brought him to his senses. He would proceed on his own.

Next morning, fortified by a solid breakfast brought to him in the dining room by a solid girl, he felt up to the task and even looked forward to it. He primed his determination with a further reading of the handbill before straightening his stock, adjusting his hat and stepping from the Angel into the crisp air. He took the directions given by the landlord (confirmed by the solid girl) but these were useless. The help given by passers-by proved contradictory and by the time he found Magdalen Street he had worked himself up into an angry sweat that could be added to his ill-will. Number 22 was a handsome enough half-timbered building. According to a handwritten sign tacked to the door, Fortuna Plantation had taken an office on the second floor. Nurturing his bad humour, he clumped up well-worn stairs to the top, where he was surprised to find the door open in front of him and a considerable number of people in a large room which occupied the whole of the upper floor. The air was blue with tobacco smoke, but through it he could see Toby standing central to a long table surrounded by men. The table was strewn with papers with which all seemed engaged and he took the opportunity to move quietly forward. Toby waved a hand over the papers. He was wearing a stiff collar that bit into his neck, reminding Sylham of a trussed roll of beef. His jacket was so tight he had difficulty with the gesture. Sylham moved nearer, standing behind a large man to listen.

"What you see are the maps of Fortuna Plantation, all numbered and properly drawn up to a survey. As you will see, not all boundaries are defined. That means, gentlemen, that for you who are fortunate enough to invest in such a piece, you may extend the holding as you will."

It was evident from his delivery that he had made this speech a number of times. As he delivered it he rotated from left to right and back again to include all his audience. Due to his collar his head seemed fused to his body. He was sweating.

"A team under proper supervision can cut back a hundred yards in a day – clear it. Virgin territory for the taking."

"What about labour?" asked a voice.

"Indentured, sir. All the labour you need, organised by agents and run by masters. We have agents in England, Scotland and Ireland, and in St. Kitts. And of course there are slaves, as many as necessary."

Another voice. "How do we ship the sugar?"

"We have, sir, a procession of ships lining up to take cargo. You must believe me sir that sugar is like gold itself."

Sylham could wait no longer. "What about the French?" he boomed in the voice he used to drive cattle from the secret spaces of the fens. Startled faces turned towards him. Toby recognised both voice and man and a look of shock crossed his face. He contrived a sickly mockery of a smile, but betrayed himself by clutching the table with his small hands.

"John Sylham," he announced to the spectators. "My brother-in-law, gentlemen, come to take up the offer I hope." He tried humour. "He'll pay the same as the rest of you! Good to have you with us. I hope you're well!"

"I asked, what about the French? I'm told the French have taken the island and that the plantations are ruined."

Toby pushed round the table to confront Sylham. He had turned from pink to white and there was a tremor in his voice. "Your jokes, your jokes!

They don't go down well, brother John. You'll have people believing you!" Total silence had fallen. The spectators turned as if to surround the two men. "Forget your debts, John," Toby blurted. "Go on. That's what it's about. We can resolve our business."

"Gentlemen," said Sylham, ignoring him, nodding to left and right, "I advise you to take time and await better intelligence. I'm not at liberty to name my source, but assure you it is a man of the best standing. What harm can it do to wait?"

"This man is a creditor!" squawked Toby, his voice giving way. "He's trying to ruin me. Pay no attention! The rogue can't pay me back!"

Where money is concerned trust is fragile and already there was a movement towards the door. Toby made the mistake of pushing through the retreating backs to stand in front of the door with outstretched arms.

"This is the opportunity of a lifetime!" He tried to bar the way.

"Then it can wait a day or two!" growled the beefy man who had stood in front of Sylham. "Out of the way sir!" He pushed Toby aside where he tried to shake a hand, catch an eye here, extract a promise there, while his audience drained away.

Sylham stood silent, waiting. When the last footsteps had echoed down the stairs, Toby rounded on him with fury.

"Damn you sir!" Spittle flew from his mouth. "Do you know what you've done? Not just me sir, but your wife, sir! She stands to lose half and I stand to lose half. You are a witless fool, John Sylham. My sister is married to a witless fool!" He clapped his hands on each side of his head as though shutting out torment and began to walk round in a circle in the centre of the empty room.

"I wish you good day sir," said Sylham. "And trouble you not to bother me again – I'll find your interest somehow." He felt pity for the man in spite of everything. "I shall say nothing to Arabella."

*

Arabella was curious, even suspicious, about the trip to Norwich. Sylham had returned three days ago and since then he had been in good humour but treating her with distance. Full details of the losses in the fire had been prepared by Edmonson and circulated to the Partners, making grim reading. Arabella pressed Sylham on his share whenever the opportunity arose. Where, she asked, was he going to find the money for new tools and huts, let alone pay off Toby, if he did not raise the rents. Realistically. He had managed Mrs Wells by offending her when she assumed complicity.

"How did you get on with your business sir?" she had asked slyly, accosting him in the hall. "Did it go as you expected?"

"It went well enough, Mrs Wells."

"Yes sir ....?" She waited expectantly.

Sylham gave her what he hoped was a stern look. "That's all, Mrs Wells."

She tried the direct approach. "I thought you might have seen Mr. Toby while you were in Norwich."

"Is that so?" Sylham could not manage a direct lie. "My land agent is in Norwich."

"That's what Mrs Sylham said." Mrs Wells was annoyed. "I thought somehow that you had other business."

"You keep to your business, Mrs Wells and I'll keep to mine." Sylham fled this barrage of questions, taking his dogs and hip-flask, needing to think. He might not hear from Toby for some time, if ever, but if the work was to proceed he had to find capital.

He had convinced himself he thought better in the open. The truth was that he found diversions in the open that prevented thought. Winter had begun to nip at the heels of autumn. Most leaves had fallen except the rustling skeletons of beech and strangling ivy. He clicked his fingers for Jove and Jupiter to trot beside him, crossing a field of his sheep. A flock of crows rose unexpectedly from where they had been foraging among the animals. Ignoring his shouts, the dogs were off, chasing hopelessly among the panicked sheep. He stood watching until they gave up and loped back to him, tongues out and dribbling.

"Heel, heel you devils!" he shouted in a mixture of irritation and affection. They were approaching the point where grass gave way to sedge and water – where Dade and Emms had been digging. Their excavations showed as black earth. "Graves," thought Sylham. He vowed to employ Dade if he could ever find the money. As for Emms, he had liked the man.

From where he stood, he could see the church tower and automatically took a route towards it. Unable by temperament to talk to the living, he found comfort among the dead Sylhams who lay in the grass. That was another matter, he thought, that had long impressed Arabella – that the Warburtons were in the church, while the Sylhams were in the graveyard. She had even gone so far as to say she hoped he would be buried inside. And her. "Sylhams will always want to be outside," he had responded robustly. "When we die, we want the air!"

He strode purposefully across the fields to the churchyard gate and opened it, allowing the dogs to bound in ahead of him in search of rabbits. From the gate he turned left towards the church, climbing the path up this island of the dead to a position where he could see beyond the far side and over the vast expanse of reeds that crowded in. Here he could sit on a grey leaning stone inscribed "Geo. Sylham Esq. 1592". He patted the stone, made himself comfortable, took a swig from his hip flask and contemplated his surroundings. He found it reassuring that most of the stones around him had lost their identities to the passage of time and the work of weather and lichens, leaving them now as blank as they had been from the quarry. Thereafter many had toppled, worn through by frost and rain and finally had broken. It was a place to dwell on the futility of all man's endeavours.

His dogs came galloping past him without stopping, making him turn and see Clara. She was already close, having a disarming ability to move quietly. She was dressed in ordinary day clothes instead of her working apron and carried a bunch of greenery. She continued to look at him when the dogs sat down in front of her. She made no effort to speak. A chill breeze ruffled her skirts.

"Well, shall I speak first?" blurted out Sylham. "I thought I was alone."

"I knew you were here."

"How did you know?"

"Crows told me. They saw you crossing the field."

"You saw them rising!" scoffed Sylham.

"As you wish. Anyway, I saw you taking your ease on old George."

Sylham patted the gravestone. "I sometimes come up here for a think."

"Best place for it."

"What brings you here? I didn't have you down for a churchgoing girl."

Clara laughed. "I don't come to go inside. I come to talk to the Boy. He gets lonely if no one comes to see him."

Sylham was nonplussed.

Clara advanced on him, followed by Sylham's dogs and hooked her free arm in his, pulling him to his feet. "You come with me, John Sylham. Happen he'll be pleased to see you. He don't often have two visitors."

"Have you dressed up like this just to visit the Boy?" asked Sylham in wonder. She was steering him between gravestones, making for the church tower.

"Got to be properly dressed for the Boy!" They stopped and Clara stooped. She brushed aside some fallen leaves to reveal the protruding head, pouting mouth and torso. The dogs immediately dived in to see what she was doing and as suddenly turned and fled when they saw it. Clara laughed and took from the mouth some scraps of dead plants which she put in a pocket. "Dogs got a fright!" She laid down the bunch of greenery that she had been carrying, placing each individual sprig beside the other on the ground. "Do you just feel in there," she said to Sylham, indicating the mouth.

Sylham demurred. "Why, what's in there?"

"Scared of little old Boy, John Sylham?"

"No."

"Go along then!"

Sylham moved forward, knelt down awkwardly and extended his hand towards the mouth. The lips shone as though polished. He cautiously extended his forefinger and put it inside the mouth, felt around, withdrew it. "Water. Wet."

"They say there was once a spring here. Boy was the mouth of it, on this island, before ever they built this church. They built this church on top of Boy so that they could have the lifeblood of the spring for Christ, but they didn't dare pull out Boy, or build on top of Boy, so they built the church like this, so Boy can see out. Forever."

Sylham was kneeling close to Clara, so close that she brushed against him. The breeze stirred her hair. "Clara, you smell of smoke!" he accused. "Smoke and fire. The smoke of rushes."

She laughed, and Sylham's heart turned over.

"So a blacksmith smells of smoke! A shepherd smells of sheep and a baker smells of bread!" She began to place her offerings in the mouth of Boy. "Elder. The Cross was made of elder, they say, and Judas hanged himself on an elder. You can cure your warts by rubbing them with elder, John Sylham. Ivy, for everlasting life. Ash, tree of the universe. Igdrasil, which drops honey and binds together all things. Apple. Apples of Iduna that the gods eat to renew their youth. To travel over the rainbow bridge to Asgar." She patted her handiwork and stood up, followed by Sylham.

"Are you a witch, Clara?" he asked.

"Are you going to help me?" asked Clara evasively.

"I don't know Clara, I don't know what you mean. I never know what you mean ...."

"It's no good shooting at soldiers, they'll only send more and people will be killed. It's no use trying to light fires to stop water. It has to be done differently and Clara knows the way." She picked up her skirts to leave. "I'm going this way, and you'll go that," she said. "Look, your dogs have got a rabbit, clever things!"

Sylham turned to where she had pointed behind him. The animals were leaping around a hole beneath a yew. Sylham only glanced, turned back too quickly for Clara to disguise her wipe at her eyes.

"You've caught me with water-gall eyes!" she protested. "That's a sharp wind from the north!"

Sylham could only watch her dumbly.

"You're a good man, John Sylham," she said and before he realised what was happening she had kissed him on the lips and walked away.

He stared after her, astounded, wondering whether to chase after her or call after her, but in his indecision did neither. "What do I do?" he demanded of Jove and Jupiter, who had come walloping back and sat side-by-side, tongues hanging out. "Damn you both, what do I do?"

Clara, rounding the east end of the church called back, her words almost lost in the wind. "Shall need your help," and was gone.

Chapter 18

DECEMBER 2nd OXAY HALL

TO THOMAS BATHURST ESQUIRE
BATHURST'S
PREBEND STREET
NORWICH

My dear Thomas, by God's Grace,

I thank you for your information that you believe that Wm. Emms can be released without much damage despite his actions. There is no point in locking up a hound that does not do its job, though I fear in the case of four feet it would be despatched while two feet go free! His father and mine were of opposite persuasion in the late war and I have done what I can, but that is now at an end. We now have a young man called Bullen, who has yet to prove his worth.

I hesitate to take further advantage of your experience and good humour, but we have had another episode with our slodgers, as we call the rustics, where they have set fire to huts, tools and etc., contained within them and shots have been exchanged. The situation is become like that at Sandtoft, of which I believe you have heard, in '86. I propose therefore to Petition the Sheriff for further troops and establishment of good order before these miscreants get into their heads to make more trouble for us by doing likewise. On this matter I seek your expert advice.

Finally, in a similar vein of hesitation, but also as our trusted lawyer, I now seek your advice on the position of Wm. Emms (I am uncertain whether or not he is still Rev. Wm. Emms) as a former Partner in our enterprise. I suppose we may have to pay back the unexpended portion of his investment, as we have dispensed with him. Can you advise me what entitlement he has when drawing up the articles to formalise the new Partnership? I have no desire to penalise him now he is gone.

We shall be seeking new investment in consequence of the above matters and in that regard may advertise in your city if we cannot find interest here.

As you may imagine, we will meet all charges in respect of your advice on these issues. Ruth begs me to send with this letter all regards to your wife, trusting in her continued good health and hoping they shall both meet before too long in Norwich.

Your obedient servant and friend,

John Warburton.

"I think you should draw up an account on these matters to date," said Bathurst to his secretary. "Things seem lively in Oxay."

Chapter 19

Cristeen had thought that Katja would be difficult about their Sunday expedition to Oxay church, but to her pleasant surprise the girl had agreed with every sign of pleasure.

"It's a good idea. I need to get out, it will make a good afternoon walk."

Cristeen had shot an enquiring glance at her but could read nothing from her face.

Jacob was not coming. He was in the parlour, in front of a fire and had asked not to be disturbed. He was immersed, as was his practice since the fire, in a large leather bound portfolio which folded out flat to allow him to draw. In this he was re-creating the lost plans and profiles of the cut, improving, adding notes and descriptions, bringing them up-to-date.

The women dressed in their best, in case they met anyone, and, as Cristeen insisted, they must for the House of the Lord. It was sunny but very cold with puffy clouds running before a freezing East wind. Overnight icicles still hung on eaves and hedgerows, refusing to melt. The remains of a powdery snowfall clung to the windward of trees. They put on heavy coats and bonnets and set out, leaving shallow footprints.

"This place is really quite beautiful in the snow," said Cristeen, "but not as beautiful as back home."

"I think it is more beautiful," said Katja. Their breaths made white puffs. "There are more trees and back home everything is so straight, while here it wanders all over the place. And I prefer the church."

"And you prefer the boys," said Cristeen dryly. "We know about that!"

"Mama," protested Katja feeling herself flushing. The subject had been avoided since the dinner at Warburton's.

"You are going to tell me about it one day. Not now."

Katja felt a stab of guilt over what she had arranged, but she soon subdued it.

Cristeen had knelt towards the front of the church, Katja some rows behind. It was bitterly cold inside and Katja made little attempt to remember her prayers. She watched her mother and listened. Cristeen always prayed under her breath and she could hear the whispering. Timing was essential. She knew precisely how long it would take for her to complete her devotions and knew she had ten minutes. She left quietly, walking backwards up the aisle. Cristeen did not notice.

Outside she was blinded by the sunlight bouncing off the snow and stood blinking under cover of the porch until she was able to focus. In the time she had been inside, the sun had gathered strength and droplets were beginning to slide down the icicles on the eaves. She listened to the soft dropping in the dense winter silence, waiting for some signal. A small avalanche slipped off the porch tiles, making her jump. Nearby, a pair of blackbirds foraged amongst leaves under the shelter of a tree. A clumsy pigeon took off from the yews, starting a powdery cascade. From behind the yews, Peter appeared.

"We don't have much time ...." she said. Peter kissed her. His lips and face were icy.

"Can you come out tonight?"

Katja stared at him.

"Why?"

"The fen is frozen - thick enough to skate. You said you liked skating. The village is going. I can get you skates. Show me your feet!"

"Wait," said Katja. "You speak too fast. I don't understand."

"Come skating tonight. I'll bring skates. There will be music and a fire and roast meat and mulled beer ...."

"I don't know ...." said Katja doubtfully. She shot an anxious glance in the direction of the church door. "Mother's in there. I'm scared."

"I know. Just show me your feet!"

Katja put her right hand on Peter's shoulder to balance herself, plucked up her skirt with her left and extended a foot in a clog. Peter smiled.

"Take that off. I can't tell anything from that log of wood!"

She grasped him firmly and shook her foot. The clog dropped onto the flags of the porch with a resounding clack, revealing her stockinged foot.

"Hold the porch."

While she changed her grip, Peter stooped to pluck a length of dry grass that poked through the snow. While she clutched the masonry he measured her foot against the grass and snapped off the excess, putting the grass in his pocket. "That should do!" He picked up her clog and while she wobbled on one foot, inserted the other in it and placed it on the ground. He stood up and she embraced him.

"I must go back in!" she said desperately. "Mama will finish soon. Go!"

"I'll show you something first."

"No!" protested Katja, but Peter had taken a firm grip of her hand and led her from the porch over crunching snow to the tower.

"Lean against it," he urged, "quickly." He leaned his back against it and pulled her to a position beside him so that they both were against the wall. Behind them, unseen in the ground, the Boy stared expressionlessly into the scuttling sky, Clara's offerings in his mouth like cold breath. "Press yourself flat and look up! Press! Head back! What do you see?"

Katja was flustered by his urgency, but did as she was told. "I can't see anything. Sky. Clouds. I must get back!"

"Yes you can. Don't look at the tower. Look up at the clouds. Concentrate. We're still, the clouds are still, concentrate!"

She tipped back her head and suddenly, without a sound, the tower lurched vertiginously, toppled over her. She pushed herself off the wall with a cry. Her heart was pounding. Peter caught her, laughing.

"What was that?" She turned back, scared, to look at the tower and the sky. "It moved and I feel sick!"

"It's just a trick, it's the clouds that move. All children play it. They say you'll remember me forever now."

"Will I?"

"That's what they say. It's magic."

From somewhere on the other side of the church they heard a faint cry of 'Katja'. It was Cristeen's voice.

"Will you come tonight?" asked Peter. Katja swallowed, feeling unsteady.

"I'll try, I'll try."

Peter kissed her lightly and was gone, stepping back into the yews. Katja rounded the tower to see Cristeen's back as she stared about her.

"Mama!" she comforted, "I'm here."

"Where were you?"

"Here, looking at gravestones. I left you at your prayers. It was cold sitting still."

"Let's get back," said Cristeen, "it will be colder still when the sun drops. We're going to have a red sky."

She felt annoyed that Katja had taken so little time praying when she had so much to tell the Lord.

*

The fen froze over every year up to the salt water mark and froze enough for skating almost every other. Walter Clarke's eldest boy had been given the job of testing the ice. He had gone out just before dark, first testing the shore edges by jumping on them and listening to the ice 'talk', as they said. Satisfied with that he walked out and drilled holes with a wood auger that squeaked and crunched until it dropped slack into water. He measured the depth of these holes on the tool with the cut of a file. Next he tried the seaward edges – the direction of the samphire and sea-aster where the water could be salt and the ice thin. The measurements were then shown to Ecclesiastes who knew best and had to make the decision. Ecclesiastes had been satisfied.

Word spread rapidly to people who had anticipated the right answer and were already prepared. Skates of all sorts, some elm, some yew or box, were polished and treated with beeswax and goose grease. New leather was inserted for old in straps and bindings. Walter provided barrels, some empty as seats and some full from who-knows-where. Lambert's sons carted wood for fires to be lit on the shore and Clara, to some surprise appeared with a dozen torches made from strips of sacking wound round poles and dipped in pitch. As near as was possible there would be a truce between Hares and Dunns. Clara knew it, and this was her offering. Ezra and Lambert with other villagers carted beer from the alehouse. Fox and two friends from Eriswell set themselves up on sacks of straw to play the fiddle, bagpipes and a flute. By nine in the evening more than sixty villagers had gathered. The fires were lit and Clara's torches, stuck in barrels of sand were dragged out onto the ice and placed in positions to warn of reeds, trees, or the limit of safety where salt water flooded in on the tides. Workmen attracted by the commotion soon joined the occasion, standing apart from the villagers, drinking and smoking and watching the show. In the firelight and star brightness men, women and children flew in pursuit of grace and speed. Men whose lives had been spent at the pace of a carthorse raised one leg after the other in mechanical grace and kicked themselves to reckless excesses, snorting breath. Children, out of control, screamed and slid and fell over, pursued by their mothers. Peter Dade and Clarke's son were appointed child minders and skimmed in and out amongst them, picking them up and herding them towards the shore until they escaped again. Peter was pleased to have the task – he could keep an eye open for Katja. Fox and his friends from Eriswell were joined by two more men with fiddles from Hammett and began to play. At first they played slowly. It was a game everyone knew, they would play faster and faster as the evening progressed. The slow music was an opportunity for display, for young men to show off and old men to mock them in voices tinged with envy as they tapped their toes to the music. Younger women were coaxed onto the ice in a flurry of protestations that no one took seriously for it was the only opportunity in the year to fall into a young man's arms in full public view – and to do it over and over again. Older women took a matronly turn round the ice together, arm in arm, nursed the injured or saw to the roasting and cooking for later in the night. They were roasting a hog, and if the hog was rather skinny, no one was going to complain.

The fires were visible for miles around. Warburton saw the sparks then the glow from his study window and felt a surge of anger. He knew what they were and where and stormed in to Ruth.

"Do you see the fires!" He pulled a curtain and pointed in their direction, into the night.

"The fen is frozen," said Ruth, dismayed at his agitation. "It's their skating, only skating …."

"These confounded people! On the Sabbath! The impudence of it, the lighting of fires …. lighting fires! Shall I send the troopers?"

"No, whatever you do, don't do that!" She took his arm, pulled him away from the window and sat him down. It took a good deal to unsettle him, but he was certainly agitated now.

Sarah, elbow on the window ledge of her room, had also seen the fires and was filled with a yearning to be there. She opened the casement, admitting a blast of chill air, and leaned forward. In the night-silence she could just make out the sound of fiddles. For a while she listened, saddened by the moonlight, then withdrew, closing the window. She picked up her quill and began to write in her diary:

"The villagers are playing music by the ice and the moon is up in a clear sky. The fen has frozen and they will dance and hold races. It would be a fine pleasure to be part of it ...."

She thought of finding Richard and asking him to take her, but could not face her father's anger.

*

The same fires confirmed to Tyson and Latimer that these godless commoners had abandoned their veneer of Christianity and were going about their heathen rites. Tyson stood outside. From there he too could hear the music and laughter in the still night air. He snorted to himself, retreated indoors and checked shutters to make sure he had done all he could to shut out noise. Sylham on the other hand had come down to watch as he did every year. In slender youth he had been a dashing skater, one of the best, but years and marriage had put paid to that. As usual he had asked Arabella if she would come with him, to watch, to see how the village enjoyed itself and as usual she had refused saying it was ridiculous, that it was no place for a gentleman, that it was suitable only for children. Now he had taken up a position by himself, apart from the villagers. In other circumstances he would have joined them. Jack Lamb saw him and pointed.

"Sylham. Watching," he said to Ezra, nodding to where he stood. "That's the place for him. Outside, looking in."

"He's all right, is Sylham."

"Have you paid your rent yet?"

"No I haven't, and I ain't going to."

"Wonder what he'll do."

*

Winter darkness had fallen early and Katja had spent hours worrying how and when to get out of the house undetected. Her restlessness had communicated to Cristeen, who was at her beloved lace-making in front of a fire, her bobbins clicking.

"You are fidgety, Katja."

"I'm tired mama." She tried a small yawn, delicately stifled, hoping it would become infectious. Her parents never sat up late except when Jacob was working and he didn't work on the Sabbath. Now he had his Bible propped up on his knees and had been reading, making judicious noises and nodding. He lowered the book but did not close it.

When we were at home, I used to ask you to read and memorise the words of the Bible. They are the essential foundation of our lives. We haven't been doing that since we are in England. A sin in itself, I think."

"You have been so busy," said Cristeen. "No sin. You haven't had time." Click, click went the bobbins, even as she talked.

"I should have found time," said Jacob. "It is a poor excuse not to. Do you remember Deuteronomy Thirteen, Katja? It was always a favourite text."

"Yes, papa." She knew he would read it.

Jacob thumbed through the pages, found his place and began to read:-

"*Certain men, the children of Belial, are gone out from among you and have withdrawn the inhabitants of their city saying, Let us go and serve other gods which you have not known Then shalt thou inquire and make search, and ask diligently; and behold if it be truth and the thing certain that such abomination is wrought among you; thou shalt surely smite the inhabitants of that city with the edge of the sword destroying it utterly, and all that is therein, and the cattle thereof, with the edge of the sword.*"

"We had that, I regret to say, with Mr. Emms. Do you know, he told me the drainage was no good for Oxay, and that this Good Book seemed more to him like alchemy than science!"

"A shocking thing in a pastor!" declared Cristeen, but she was falling asleep.

"And these villagers are out there with their fires," Jacob continued. "This new pastor seems a good man. Perhaps he can bring them back to the fold."

"Perhaps they think *we* are the abomination," said Katja. "They do not want us."

"What nonsense." Jacob was irritated and dismissive. "What do these village people know of anything? It's the same here as Holland."

Cristeen's lace bobbins had finally slipped from her hands and lay on her lap. Her head tilted to one side and she began to breathe deeply. Jacob exchanged a glance with Katja, touched Cristeen's arm.

"Time for bed, mother."

Katja excused herself and went up before them. Now she lay fully clothed in her bed waiting. After a short time she heard her parents clump upstairs, Jacob calling out "Good night". Three times she rose to look out into the night from her window, staring at the glow of the fires and the sparkling starlight. Finally, satisfied with the amount of elapsed time she opened her door and crept to theirs where she could hear her mother's steady breathing and Jacob's snores. She moved down the stairs, took her coat and left by the parlour casement, swinging her legs out and pushing it to behind her. She was alarmed by the noise of her heart and the clumsiness of her fingers. In the night air she could hear distant music and laughter and set off for the fen.

By the time she had reached the fires, Peter had passed over control of the children and had begun to skate to the quickening music. He was joined by Ezra Dunn and Lambert's boy, all three with hands behind their backs and the forward stoop of a speed skater, the three local experts pursued round and round by the men from the villages. He saw that Katja had arrived and kicked past her with a brief smile, faster and faster, skates pushing out and out in a quickening rhythm until she could hardly see him in the distance, then picked him out as he flashed past Clara's torches, the others following. She knew it was for her as he crouched lower and lower, gone then suddenly appearing, hurtling head-on towards her from the dark. He stopped with a turn in a spray of ice.

"How was that?"

Ezra and Lambert's boy shot past them on their way round again.

"That was fast!"

"We can do it together, I've got your skates."

They half walked, half skated to one of the barrels. Peter sat her down and offered her a pair of skates.

"I can only stay for an hour," Katja announced. "I must get back."

Peter ignored her.

"Your size." He held up a skate. "I measured them. See, I've even got my piece of grass!" He pulled the piece of knotted grass from his pocket, held it against a skate, threw it away. Peter helped her to put on the skates, tying the lashings around her ankles.

"Our skates are longer and flatter," she said.

"Skates are skates. Let's see you use them."

Taking her arm they wobbled to the ice and set off, Katja immediately finding her feet and skating ahead of watchful Peter. Like him, she clasped her hands behind her back and stooped as he had, feet splayed, gathering speed until he was obliged to make a real effort to catch her up.

"You can use them!"

"We skate well in Holland!"

Harriet Dunn nudged Rebecca Clarke and the two women stopped basting a spit of ducks to watch as Peter and Katja shot past.

"It's the girl de Vries," said Harriet, "Isn't she the pretty one to be out on her own. And that Peter Dade! Wonder what the Mynheer would say, bet he doesn't know."

"Peter Dade has an impudence," said Rebecca in admiration, "look at them go!" She poured fat on the fire by mistake and men cheered as flames shot up spectacularly. They snatched off the ducks to applause.

Peter and Katja, separated from everything and everyone in their world of speed, now together, now apart raced round and round the torchlit circuit.

"This is the fastest man can travel!" shouted Peter, showing off, arms akimbo.

"The fastest woman can travel!" Katja called back. "Ever! Here or in Holland!"

Clara was replacing torches. She walked carefully round the edge of the fen where ice transmuted to earth, a lit torch in one hand and a wicker basket of new torches in the other. She had been uncomfortable amongst the music and bonfires and her self-appointed task took her to a safely unsocial distance. She moved from barrel to barrel, lighting a new torch, taking out the near-spent one and beating it on the ground to kill it. Here, in the further reaches from the sparks and laughter, it smelled of salt water and sea-asters, and it was here in an alder carr she glimpsed Richard Warburton concealed in the darkness, beyond the reach of firelight but not beyond the reach of the moon.

Richard had not had Katja's difficulties but nonetheless had had to leave the Hall secretly, taking his skates when everyone had gone to bed. He had for some time been watching the spinning figures with bitter jealousy. Katja's blonde hair was easy to follow as it caught the torchlight and as they skated the circuit, flashing past him, he heard snatches of conversation and hated Peter Dade. He hated Peter Dade's arm round her waist, his speed, his confidence.

Clara, alarmed by what she had glimpsed in his face, extinguished the torch she was carrying in the snow and drew back behind reeds.

*

A heavy shawl of loneliness hung over Sarah, making sleep impossible. Twice she had opened the casement to lean out and listen to the increasing tempo of the fiddlers. She made up her mind to visit the skating. She changed quickly and put on a heavy coat against the cold. With great care she left her room and tiptoed to Richard's. With the caution of a burglar she turned the handle and slipped inside. His bed was empty, the bed clothes thrown back. She retreated as quietly as she had come, dumbfounded.

"I must go back soon," said Katja, skidding to a halt. "If father ever found out!" I would be in so much trouble!" For the first time she had remembered Jan and the thought of it and of her heedless excitement made her feel physically sick. She paused, gathering herself, staring at the ice. It seemed suddenly hostile. She fought back the images accumulating in her mind. "I must go back."

"A bit longer ...." His entreaty pierced her. "One more round," said Peter and they skated round slowly, arms around each other's waists, until Peter guided them both in to solid ground where they scrambled off the ice. "I'll walk with you."

"No. You might be seen, I'll go on my own."

She stooped and began to undo her skates. Peter helped her, found her boots, waited while she tied them. As she finished and stood up, they kissed until she pulled away.

"Send me a note," she said, and was gone, scurrying into the darkness.

Peter Dade returned to the ice lost in thought and took off for a solo turn round the circuit. Some of the torches had been replaced, but where Clara had stopped, they were guttering or spent. The villagers generally had tired of skating and had begun to gather by the fires to eat, drink, sing and keep warm. The musicians, who were by no means sober, had worked themselves into a fine frenzy and some of the villagers tried with hilarity to keep pace, dancing on firm ground. The ice became deserted and smoke began to drift across it like a low mist. From his place of concealment, Richard watched Peter Dade approach. Clara, watching them both, saw Richard step out behind the skating figure.

"Peasant! Ploughjack!"

Peter turned to an abrupt halt, his skates screeching on the ice. Richard was not finished. "That girl is too good for you, slodger. Who do you think you are?"

"Have you been spying on me?" replied Dade evenly. "Peeping Tom!" But Dade was not going to exchange further words. He had seen Richard had no skates on. He turned his back on him and pushed off to complete his round. Richard, who was still carrying these essentials, roared with fury and set out across the ice, taking three steps before falling. He beat impotently at the ice with a fist. Clara carefully beat a retreat. She wanted no contact with Richard Warburton. She regretted her job was incomplete as the flickering torches were dying in their barrels. It would bring skating to an end.

Peter was disconcerted by Richard's performance, but not dismayed. Richard Warburton already had a reputation in the village for idleness and womanising. He wondered how long he had been watching them, then his thoughts turned to the matter of a next meeting with Katja. He adopted the crouch of a speed-skater, arms swinging, humming to himself, passing the fires and speeding again into the dark reaches of the ice. Richard fell in behind him without Peter noticing at first. A good skater, he could keep pace with Peter and drew alongside. Peter turned, startled, without breaking his pace and Richard Warburton lunged at his face with a fist. Peter ducked and the blow missed, leaving Richard floundering. For a moment it looked as if Peter might punch back, but old taboos forbade him to strike a blow at gentry. He skated away from Richard before he could regain his balance and made for the darkness beyond the torch barrels. Richard recovered and followed at speed, still able to see movement against the starlit ice. Rage fired him to reckless effort and he gained on the moving figure quickly. The hiss of their skates fell into unison, although Peter twisted to left and right, trying to shake him off.

"You can't do it!" Richard shouted at him. "I'm faster, Dade!"

With a final effort he kicked out at Peter's rearmost foot, bringing him crashing down on the ice, limbs sprawled. Richard shot past and turned, puffing, to make his next attack. Peter, winded, struggled to collect himself. He had got up on one knee when there was the hard, hollow twang of snapping ice. Peter tried to straighten his leg, push himself upright, but instead of his body rising, his leg went down with another crack, all support failed and he was up to his waist in water. Somehow he flung a leg up onto the ice and grabbed uselessly at the surface, but the ice snapped, turned over, and he plunged back, kicking.

Richard Warburton froze, watched, then took a cautious step backwards, tried his weight on his rear foot. There was a dull click. He took another step backwards and the ice moaned. Another and another until there was no sound except his panting. In front of him, in what seemed like a distant performance Peter Dade appeared to grip the edge of the ice again, push himself onto it, but again it snapped and down he went with a hard sharp cry like a gull. Warburton listened but there was nothing but the clattering of ice fragments, bobbing against each other in the water. Over towards the shore he could just hear the voices, laughter and music. His teeth began to chatter.

"Are you there?" he tried, not daring to approach and unable to grasp the finality of it. He waited, muttering to himself, eyes fixed on the spot.

"God in Heaven, God my father, God in Heaven," he tried a little louder and listened again for any sound from the dead silence. When there was nothing he took a step backwards then another, with increasing speed on solid ice, then began to skate, slowly at first, gathering speed outside the torches in the secrecy of darkness until he reached the shore far from the fires and eyes of people. With clumsy hands he took off his skates and ran and walked back to Oxay Hall, a fugitive, by hedgerows and trees, where he hid his skates in an outbuilding and crawled like a thief through a window to lie shaking in bed. No one had seen a thing.

*

Warming himself by the fire, Ezra asked where Peter had gone. John Lambert said he had seen him with the de Vries girl. Ezra said the de Vries girl had gone home some time ago and he had seen Peter after that, but now he had disappeared. They looked at each other, Ezra shrugged and they laughed at their imaginings. Harriet Dunn said men only thought of one thing and she and Rebecca Clarke roared with laughter.

Peter Dade's mother was too old to go to the skating and slept through the night. His absence in the morning alarmed her and meant the fire wasn't lit. Dressing herself in a bad temper she struggled over to tell Harriet Dunn. Harriet raised the alarm.

By nine in the morning the men were out in parties, and singly, looking for him with an increasing sense of foreboding.

"It ain't like Peter to go missing. Not leaving his mother," declared Ecclesiastes, giving voice to the obvious in the minds of everyone. Low morning sunlight sparkled on the hoar frost that clung to trees, making a scene of beauty. Every rush had been brushed with white and grass crunched underfoot.

"Been a cold night for any poor beggar out in it," said John Lambert. He poked at a frozen puddle with his boot, cracking the skin of ice. "We'd best hurry."

It was Ezra who thought to patrol the far edges of the ice where brackish water began. He was on skates, covering the ice methodically. He had dealt with things like this before and knew the importance of diligence. He saw the far-off break in the ice and approached cautiously as far as he dared. New ice had frozen the area and within it were small floes and a dark shape. He crossed himself and skated away.

Jack Lambert held the long rope while Ezra and Walter, sitting in a flat bottomed punt, propelled it over the ice with inverted oars. The boat slid easily, the men knew the technique. They soon dropped onto the new ice, which broke around them. Ezra at the stern reached over and took hold of

Peter Dade's jacket in both hands. He pulled the body half on to the punt which sagged downwards with the weight. Water drained into the punt. Ezra shouted and Jack Lambert, rope over one shoulder and round his waist, leaned and walked backwards. The punt slid steadily onto unbroken ice. Jack pulled them all the way back to shore. The three men stared down at the stiff white-faced body. Ezra bent down to shake ice from its hair, but it held fast. He brushed uselessly at Peter's clothes which were hard and brittle. Both skates were still strapped fast to his feet.

"Who's going to tell his mother?" he asked.

"She's at your house Ezra," said Lambert. Ezra nodded silently. They lifted the body between them and laid it in the punt.

"She's going to take this real sore," said Ezra.

*

Sarah wrote in her diary:

"This morning there has been a terrible accident discovered and the whole village is in mourning. Last night the villagers had their skating on the ice, which they do whenever the occasion permits. Father is very opposed to it, but I confess I had a mind to attend with Richard, only to find he may have gone solitary and not told me, which I did not anticipate. I am glad I did not attend, for now they have found the drowned body of Peter Dade who had fallen through the ice where it was of insufficient strength. Everyone is shocked. He lived alone with his mother who has collapsed and is looked after by Harriet Dunn. This Peter Dade was dismissed from father's employ some months ago for his interference in the progress of the drainage work and his complicity in this with Mr. Emms who was our vicar. I am much afraid that this news will be taken ill by Miss de Vries who seems to have formed an attachment to him. So many events have recently clouded life in Oxay and although this appears to be an unhappy accident, others appear to arise out of this drainage project. They say in the village that nothing but bad will come of it. Well, we have had too much of it already.

However, mother appears to be determined that life shall go on. On another matter, she continues to find excuses to introduce the new vicar to my company although he is not to my liking."

*

Peter Dade's funeral took place on a cold cloudy day with a scurrying wind that stripped remaining leaves from trees, bowled them between the gravestones and shook the churchyard yews. Oxay Church was full, as duty demanded – Dade names were scattered throughout the graveyard. It was compulsory for the Partners and wives to attend, and for the family de Vries. There was a clear divide, for while the gentry arrived late and had seated themselves at the back of the church, the villagers, whose business this really was, had arrived early. They made a sombre group in the first eight rows, a solid wall of turned black backs dividing the church between their grief and the polite sorrow of bystanders.

At the front, Harriet Dunn sat beside Dade's mother, a small figure swathed in black, with Ezra and Ecclesiastes on each side of the women. The coffin stood in the aisle on trestles. Candles had been placed at each end of it, but did little to augment the sombre light from old, narrow windows. Clara and Felix had come and sat in the eighth pew, slightly apart from others.

Family de Vries had come with the Warburtons in their carriage, but to Katja's relief there had not been room enough for Richard. He had quickly made that an excuse to ride on his own. Katja had travelled between her parents, speaking to no one and Warburton had contented himself with remarks about the countryside. There was a continuing distance between the two men that prevented anything else and the two women had stared out of the windows to avoid an exchange of glances.

Now Cristeen watched Katja. The girl had howled inconsolably when Jacob had brought the news. Cristeen had had to sit with her for the best part of a night, caught between agony and anger, keeping Jacob at bay, brushing aside his questions and his Bible. Now she was so white her skin was pellucid and she had dabbed some of her mother's colour on her cheeks in round patches that only drew attention. She refused to look at anyone, stared miserably at her prayer book and counted to herself to obliterate time and thought until she reached one hundred and started again.

Bullen, in good voice, talked about the man he had never known in the confidential way of vicars who rely upon gleanings. His congregation listened to these intrusions on the man they had known and wondered that he dared to impose on Dade these attributes and motives he never had. No essence emerged. Ezra, watching the man's expressions and gestures, thought he might as well have been talking about an Eskimo as the man in the coffin.

De Vries was also watching Katja. He had been dumbfounded by the violence of her grief and was suspicious of Cristeen's explanation.

"Of course she's upset!" Cristeen had protested, "She liked the boy."

"How did she know him?" Jacob had demanded. "You say she liked him. How did she meet him? I know nothing of any of this, I don't know the boy!"

"Jacob, it was nothing," Cristeen insisted, hoping the Good Lord would see she was saving Jacob from his own rage. "He was someone she talked to – we can't lock her up, she's a girl not a nun!"

"Perhaps that's what she should be! Young Warburton pays her too much attention. I still don't understand it."

Cristeen bridled. "Have some feelings – how would you feel, at her age, if someone you knew, of your age, suddenly died."

She had paused momentarily before the word 'died'. It gave her away, as she had intended to say 'drowned' but the word was too much for her and she had choked back tears that had threatened to overwhelm her. Jacob had clutched her awkwardly in realisation, asking nothing more.

But now Bullen had reached Peter Dade's death and said the word "drowned", the word that she had never spoken or summoned to mind since that awful night, the word suppressed and thrust into the wounded recesses of her mind.

"Peter Dade is drowned," said Bullen, repeating it in Dutch, perhaps for the benefit of Dutch workmen attending, or family de Vries, or showing that he knew a few words and would include them in future sermons. "*Verdronken,*" he said, and Cristeen began to cry. She cried for Peter Dade and Jan, who were one and the same in her mind, cried because at last she could do so in a foreign place for some other mother's boy, could let out the anguish she had brought with her. She reached out and took Katja's hand and both wept in their own ways for Peter Dade. Katja could not and would not tell anyone of her love for dead Peter. She loved him with the ferocity of youth that has no expression save madness. Further along the pew, Richard, ashen cheeked with bloodless lips, watched the women and felt sick in his belly – a sickness that rose to his throat so that he swallowed again and again and again but felt no better, trying to swallow fear.

"*Come unto me all ye that labour and are heavy laden, and I will give you rest,*" said Bullen.

Jacob, near to tears himself realised that a dead weight had gone, that they could share grief with these people, that there was no test of faith in this place or at this time. He reached out to join hands with Cristeen and Katja.

"Jan's death was not unique. You see," he whispered to Cristeen in Dutch, "cry for Jan!" She nodded, seeing some ease in the pain she knew to look for in his eyes.

"We shall now say the prayer that Jesus taught us ..." said Bullen.

The congregation said the Lord's Prayer. Katja, moving her lips but saying nothing, wanted to see dead Peter, as other villagers had who had packed him into the wooden box, but knew she couldn't, and there he was, close but out of reach, beyond reach that had held her close such a short time ago. "Thy kingdom come," they said around her, "Thy will be done."

Burial. A smell of crushed grass, new earth and damp. The villagers arranged around the grave to form a stockade of black-clothed backs that again excluded the gentry and all others, staring down at the lowered box. Katja could see nothing of the private space within the fortress. Bullen's words were a mutter. Ezra and Ecclesiastes held Dade's mother up by the elbows, there were movements, stooping, a rattle of earth. On the far side standing well back, Katja could see Richard Warburton's pale face but avoided his eyes. She knew that Cristeen was watching her and pressed her chin tight to her chest, pulled her cloak tightly over her head. The dark circle broke up, dissolved, revealing the grave. She felt a hand on her hand and looked up, surprised to find Sarah beside her, taking her arm. She allowed herself to be led away to one side. Jacob had taken Cristeen's arm and together they were making across the churchyard for the gates and lane beyond which was blocked by a confusion of horses, carts and carriages. Sarah waited for some moments.

"Katja, I am so sorry," she whispered to the tearful girl. "You can, you must come to me. I know ...." she stressed the word. "I know what he meant to you." She took Katja to the gate and handed her to her parents.

*

In the confusion of leave-taking that followed, the Partners gathered in one corner of the graveyard while Richard, without a word, took off on his horse. It was the first time they had all met since the angry exchanges after the fire. They exchanged greetings, stood around awkwardly in the way of people at a funeral, avoiding the subject of death, getting cold.

"How are things now?" asked Warburton of de Vries.

"Still slow. We have to get the sluices finished."

"How many men are back?"

"Only about half."

Warburton's face showed his irritation.

"Why's that?"

De Vries shrugged, looked to Edmonson and made an open handed gesture towards him. Edmonson sighed.

"It's the usual. Some have quit the county. They say they don't need this work. Hostility, superstition, winter work ...."

"What about these troops?" demanded Tyson.

"I've written to the Sheriff," said Warburton. "I expect a reply daily.

"What about money?" asked Latimer.

"That is a question," said Sylham, hovering at the back.

"Can we raise a bank loan?" asked Latimer, ignoring him.

"Do you think we look good security!" retorted Warburton irately, beating his hands together. "Fire, shooting, bodies .... All these confounded people against us!" He pointed at the dispersing villagers with an outstretched arm. Unfortunately for him, Ezra at that moment looked back and saw the gesture. He stopped and turned. Ecclesiastes then stopped and turned followed by Dade's mother. Warburton slowly dropped his arm but not before his gesture had been seen by Lambert and old Thomas Fox who nudged Harriet Dunn on one side and Clara on the other. Half the village, stopped, turned and stared, the two groups looking at each other across the stone strewn space of the churchyard. Ezra broke the silence.

"Good day to you, Mr. Warburton," he called.

Warburton, for once discomfited, could only stare.

"*'Then shall the dust return to the earth as it was; and the spirit shall return to God who gave it.'* Ecclesiastes, Mr. Warburton, Chapter 12, Verse 7."

Warburton nodded, unable to think of any suitable reply. Ezra took Dade's mother by the elbow again and with Ecclesiastes they walked away with dignified slowness. Their move became a general one and the churchyard began to clear.

"So now we have piety from them!" growled Tyson, "What was that all about? This Dade?"

By chance de Vries caught Warburton's eye and understanding passed between them.

"I think our problems are far from over," said de Vries. "I think it continues, *'Vanity of vanities saith the preacher; all is vanity'*."

"We have nothing to do with this Dade's death!" protested Tyson. "Was that fellow blaming us? Get the captain to bring him in!"

"No."

It was Sylham. They stared at him but he felt an odd detachment from the aims and ambitions of these people who sat at the back of the church.

"We're becoming tyrants to our own people!"

There was silence as Tyson, Latimer and Warburton looked at each other. The others were still, waiting for some sort of explosion. Warburton knew this was neither the time nor the place.

"I think we should re-join our wives," said Warburton.

Sarah and Clara, as two unattached women, had sufficient bond to pass the time of day at the forge or on the few occasions Clara thought it right to attend a church service. Other than that, they knew of each other more than knowing each other. As there was a general movement away from the church, Clara held back. The villagers were the first to go, leaving on foot. The collection of horses and carriages were nothing to do with them.

"You go now," she told Felix. "I've business."

Felix shrugged and moved on. Clara steeled herself for what she had to do, here. There was unlikely to be any other chance to approach Sarah on her own without a visit to the Hall. The women, waiting for their menfolk, were passing platitudes amongst themselves, agreeing that Bullen had done well with the service, nodding, searching for those things that people say when there is nothing to say. They had paused at the lich-gate and Sarah, bored with this, had allowed herself to be politely detached and was reading nearby gravestones for distraction. Clara made for her apprehensively.

"Miss Warburton?"

Sarah looked up, smiled. Clara wore a black shawl over her head and shoulders which framed her brown face. Without the distraction of her working clothes, Sarah thought, she is a handsome woman. "Miss Hare?"

"Can I have a word with you. Please!"

The request surprised Sarah, but there was anxiety in Clara's eyes that made her nod and move a little further from the others.

"I don't know how to put this to you, but I have something I must tell you concerning your brother."

"Oh." Sarah moved yet further away until they were out of earshot. She glanced back to the lich-gate only to catch Ruth's eye. Ruth gave a small wave, keeping in contact. Sarah called to her. "Shall not be long!" She looked enquiringly at Clara.

"This is not easy for me, Miss Warburton, but it was now or call at the Hall. I must get straight to the point, for it is a burden. I have told no one and will tell no one but you. Look you, you must know or have guessed that Mr. Richard has had his eyes on Miss de Vries. What you do not know is that it has been my duty to rescue her from his attentions some months ago." Clara stopped, looked anxiously into Sarah's face, trying to read how this was received.

Sarah, lest Clara should be after some monetary objective, was sharp. "What do you want from me?"

"I understand your caution. People *are* cautious with Clara, but I want nothing, Miss Warburton. Save for you to know that the night Peter Dade drowned, he and Mr. Richard were calling each other names on the ice. Fire and sparks between them, real fire and sparks. I left so's I shouldn't be seen, but as it happened, Mr. Richard was like to be the last living soul to see Peter Dade."

Sarah stared into Clara's face, perhaps trying to read some comfort there, but Clara was immobile, offering nothing more. With sickening clarity she recalled Richard's absence on the night. She was afraid to ask more, but Clara was the only source she had. "Were Mr. Richard and Peter Dade both ...." she searched for a neutral word, "attached to Miss de Vries?" She recalled the last dinner party, Katja's habit of walks.

"She was meeting Peter Dade of her own accord. I don't know if her father knew of it. Peter Dade was a fine young man."

"But Richard?"

"She wasn't meeting him of her own accord, but I think he found out her ways and where she went."

Sarah reached out to Clara, putting a hand on her arm. "Thank you very much. Thank you *very* much." Cold horror hit her as a blow in the stomach.

"Are you all right, Miss Warburton?" Clara could feel that Sarah was steadying herself.

"I'll be all right." She glanced round again towards the lich-gate. Ruth, who had been waiting to catch her eye, beckoned impatiently.

"Coming mama!" she called quickly, releasing Clara. "Promise me you'll say nothing. I will talk to Richard."

"You have Clara's word."

"What was that all about?" asked Ruth as Sarah joined her. "That was Clara Hare the blacksmith, wasn't it?"

"We were just passing the time of day, mama. She was reminding me that our horses should be seen to."

Ruth shot a quick glance at Sarah's face, but could find nothing at odds with this explanation.

"Into the carriage, ladies," said Warburton. "This cold is beginning to get to my bones."

Sarah shivered.

Chapter 20

The Yule Brook had lifted peat beds that had lain undisturbed since their formation, floating the iron-hard roots of old trees. It found the furrows and ditches of ancient field systems where early men had cleared trees and planted spelt and emmer wheat. It found the furrows between strip lynchets and used them as ditches, stretching further and further into dry land. It surrounded and swamped the shallow island where the surveyors had stopped to eat and the circumferentor had been stolen. Alder trees, accustomed to inundations, gave up the struggle and fell.

Ezra noted the rising water, marking it by notches, first on the exposed root of a willow, then higher as the root joined the trunk, then on the trunk itself.

In Warburton's water meadows, had he inspected them, he would have seen small fish swimming in his ditches.

When it found the dam across its path, it was at first baffled. Trying to find a path around this human obstruction, it was thwarted on each side by timberings and revetments driven deep, beyond its reach. It had never before encountered a tree it could not shift. Yule Brook paused behind this work to consider the situation, leaning hard against the logs, tar and canvas. It would build up its strength while it waited.

Chapter 21

December continued to surprise, producing a thaw and mild weather interspersed with light frosts and rain. John Sylham was sitting up late by his fire wondering whether another log was necessary. Arabella had already gone to bed and he was enjoying yet another of several tankards of beer. In the end he prised himself to his feet and flung on a piece of oak. He was about to sit down again when he thought he saw movement outside. Sylham's curtains were seldom pulled.

Seeing nothing out of the window despite a fine moon, he went through to the rear of the house, through the pantry and the dairy with its sour smells and quietly opened the back door. From there he heard one of his horses whinnying. He stepped quietly into the yard. As his eyes adjusted he made out a figure moving in front of his stables. Advancing cautiously he could see that it was Clara dressed in black. Two of his working horses, a grey and a chestnut, had their heads over a stable door and were watching her with pricked ears. They had been fitted with their collars which usually hung on the wall. As he watched she leaned towards each one in turn, breathing in their nostrils, as was her way, murmuring something he could not catch. The animals made no noise.

"I know you're there," she said quietly without turning. Sylham moved forward.

"What have we, what have we ....?" he said.

"I've come to borrow your horses, John. I need them for a spot of work. This is your help."

"Have you indeed! And what do you want them for?"

There was sufficient moonlight to see she was carrying rope halters. She leaned against the door, one hand on a horse's muzzle.

"I think you know."

She leaned forward and kissed him full on the lips, tasting the beer on his breath. Sylham, astonished, stood stock still.

"That's your payment, that's for now."

She opened the door to the stable, not bothering to close it behind her, and while he watched slipped a halter over each of the animals' heads in turn. She gathered the ropes and walked them quietly out behind her into the yard. She shut the stable door, one handed. Sylham had neither moved nor said a word.

"Has to be or they'll go on and on and on. You go inside John Sylham, because you hasn't seen Clara, do you understand? Clara is invisible!"

She pulled a black shawl over her head. The strangeness of the circumstance and the drink made him slow and confused.

"I'll take care of things for all of us."

"What things? What are you talking about?"

"Better you don't know. You go inside. What you hear, you don't hear."

Sylham nodded as though in agreement. He had no idea what she was talking about, but intended to find out. "Look after my horses, won't you?"

"I would never harm a horse. It's best you go indoors."

He turned for the house. Clara flicked the halters and set off with the horses following her like good children.

Choosing her route with care she led them across Sylham's meadows where the only sounds were the soft thud of their hooves and blowing of their breathing. She knew where troopers would be and had planned how to avoid them. She slowed her pace as they drew nearer to the cut. The horses at first trod in wet mud, then in water-logged ground. She let them take their time, humming quietly to herself. The cut appeared as an endless void in the foreground, black, with undrained water glittering in its depths. She stopped to listen, hearing only night sounds and trickling water. She led the animals amongst the debris of construction and new huts until they reached a pile covered with tarpaulin. Lifting this she pulled out coils of rope which she knew to be there. Unhindered by the semi-darkness she attached lengths of rope to the horses' collars in place of traces, and cutting and coiling these, hung them over the hames. This accomplished she set off again leading the animals along the squelching floor of the cut, making for the intersection of the Yule Brook and de Vries' half-built sluice. Here she led the horses up a path on the embankment, clucking and coaxing, until they were on original ground beside the dam of pile-driven logs. This had been built some hundred feet from the cut to hold back the Brook until the sluices were complete. Behind the logs men had lowered three layers of tarred canvas that had flattened into the logs with the pressure, sealing every gap. Behind the tarred canvas was a buffer of dumped earth. The water in the Brook stood ten feet above the bottom of the cut. Raking shores braced the logs against this pressure, their feet buried in the floor of the cut. Clara unravelled the ropes from each horse and laid them on the ground. The animals nodded their heads silently. She threw the ropes one by one over the nearest shores with the ease borne of her strength and scrambling down the embankment retrieved the rope ends, throwing the slack back up before returning to knot them. She still hummed to herself despite her efforts as she inspected her knots and ropes, pulling and testing. Finally she attached the ropes to the links on the hames.

Satisfied she took the horses' halters and led them away until the ropes rose from the ground as the animals leaned into their work.

Sylham had followed her through the night, trying to be quiet, but in his efforts to keep up, crashing and stumbling, but guessing her route. He concealed himself on the far side of the cut, watching her actions. The grey was most visible in the half-light and he could see Clara's face and bare arms. She stood between the two horses and smacked them on the rump, urging them on. He heard them snort and half heard, half saw the thump of their hoofs as they strained to get this weight moving. After a moment Clara moved round to their heads, taking the halters and Sylham watched her back them up, letting the ropes fall slack. All the time she talked to them, patted their necks then returned to her previous position to deliver a sharp slap and urgent words that Sylham heard but could not understand. The animals lurched forward. At first he heard the ropes creak with the strain, then he heard the groan of complaint from the first shore followed by a sharp crack. Clara was up to the horses' ears, speaking, urging, patting their necks. They leaned into their job again. There was a series of dull cracks and thuds and the horses stumbled forward to the sound of rushing water, followed by a roar and the ring of log striking log as half the dam toppled over in one piece. An astonishing wall of water and logs shot towards the sluices and consumed them, then shot towards the far bank where he was concealed, thudding into it like a solid mass before breaking and turning in a torrent of foam to hurtle down the cut. Sylham saw Clara grab at one of the horses' collars but she was not quick enough and the shore logs, swept away in the torrent dragged first one and then the other horse sideways until they fell kicking in the mud. Clara threw herself at the grey's head and somehow managed to release it. The animal struggled to its feet and galloped off. He saw her repeat the task with the chestnut which had managed to lurch to its knees and was being dragged relentlessly to the water's edge. The animal faced the torrent and was unable either to back up or find any grip. It shook its head and whinnied, arched its back and tried to stand, only to be dragged flat again. Clara cut the rope attached to the log and the animal reared back, fell down, then dashed off out of sight. Clara paused to wonder at the scale of destruction

The revetments of the sluice had been undermined by the scouring torrent and had collapsed completely. The pent-up waters then began a swift demolition of the exposed embankment. As she watched, it slid bit by bit in huge sections into the cut, a moment visible then dissolved. The sheer force of the water from the Brook had eaten into the opposite embankment, finding the earth and peat layers that had worried de Vries lying soft beneath unbound soil. It sucked at these, extracted the soft matter and brought the rest down, swept it away in seconds. Yule Brook had stored two square miles of water in Oxay Fen and now it rushed in to celebrate the new route to the sea. Fast and boisterous, it refused to be confined. It pushed and shoved until sections of embankment began to sag and slide throughout the length of the cut.

Sylham moved forward to a position opposite to Clara on his side of the cut. There was no way to cross without leaving her to go upstream. He could see the danger and waved but she did not appear to notice so he waved again, shouting and gesturing uselessly against the roar of water. She saw him and waved back, making no effort to leave, then held both arms up to the sky and appeared to execute a dance. Sylham believed he could see she was smiling.

The rushing sound of water woke people all over Oxay. It sounded like waves beating on the shore in an Easterly gale and people got up to listen to it, guessing something had gone wrong. Lambert's boy was first to the cut and back with a breathless tale which he was soon spreading from door to door. Ezra and Harriet were at the scene early with Ecclesiastes, Thomas Fox and Lambert, staring with awe at the destruction. As Ezra observed, water was on the move everywhere, all heading one way. The grey light of dawn was beginning to extinguish stars as they struggled to the junction of the Yule Brook with the flooded mess of the cut. They were on the same side as Clara, who was in trouble, watched by a small anxious crowd. She was isolated now on a small island formed by a section of revetment that still survived. Felix was hopping about, shouting uselessly for someone to help her. Ezra asked what had happened.

"She wouldn't run for it!" said Walter Clarke. "We tried to get her away but she wouldn't come and then the earth fell away and there she is!"

"You can swim!" Felix shouted at Ezra. "You could make it! We can tie a rope to you!"

Ezra looked directly at Felix, which he had not done for as long as he could remember.

"Have you taken leave of your senses Felix? I won't save a Hare. You go, find out how you like swimming."

"I can't swim, I can't swim!" he yelled exuding blobs of spit.

John Lambert had made a length of rope and was trying to throw it across but each time it dropped in the flood and was swept away.

"We need a light line!" he shouted in despair. "Has anyone got a line?"

He tried and failed again. Three horses rode up, bringing Latimer and John and Richard Warburton, all with lanterns. They were closely followed by de Vries, Tyson, Edmonson and Bullen, similarly equipped. All dismounted to stare at the scene, holding their lanterns this way and that, trying to construct a picture.

"The dam has gone!" Warburton roared at de Vries. "The whole thing! It's taken the sluice with it!"

"What about that woman!" shouted de Vries, pointing. "Who is she?"

"It's that damned blacksmith!" Warburton roared above the noise of the water. "I'll bet she has something to do with this!"

"We can't let her drown!" shouted Lambert to Ezra. "Even who she is, we can't let her drown. She ain't her brother! It's right to try. We must."

"We can't let her drown, Mr. Warburton," shouted Ezra.

"We can't do anything from here," said Warburton. "Hold the lanterns up!"

They watched as Lambert tried once, twice, three more times to throw the rope to Clara. While they watched, her island lost another piece to the swirling water.

"There's Sylham!" yelled Ezra, cupping his hands to try to make himself heard above the roar of the water. "On the other side .... look!"

"What's he going to do?" demanded Lambert. "He can't do that!"

Sylham had made up his mind. He was a good swimmer, had learned to swim in Oxay River in long distant summers, with Clara. He had images of her, skinny in a wet underdress. "I'll be in trouble now!" – diving off the bank to swim to the other side to laugh at him. He had learned to swim to reach her, puffing and doggy-paddling, drinking Oxay River water, pulling himself onto the bank to dry out alongside her in the summer sun and talk about what they wanted to be.

He pulled off his boots and his coat and waved to Clara to tell her he was coming.

From what the onlookers could see on their side of the flood, Clara appeared to be shouting "No!" and banging her knees with both hands in frustration that she could not make herself heard. They watched as

Sylham walked barefooted down the sliding bank, waved to her and struck out into the water. He managed two powerful strokes forward, but in that time had been swept yards sideways. The current on this side was kindly, sweeping him into eddies, turning him around and pushing him into a mud bank that grounded him downstream. They watched him, moving so slowly, haul himself further out of the mud on his belly, digging into it with his hands to achieve some purchase until he could seize tussocks of grass and drag himself out. Where he was, there was nothing he could do but watch.

Ezra looked at Lambert, looked at the flood. More of Clara's island slid quietly into the brown water. Clara was holding on to a piece of timber, quite still, waiting for some decision.

"It seems I'm the centre of attention," said Ezra. "Fit me up. You'll have to go up-stream, pay out plenty of slack and play me. I might drift over. You're the fisherman Walter. I ain't going to be able to swim far in that. Nor for long neither!"

Clarke and Lambert fitted him up with rope around his chest and under his armpits. Six men took the rope and moved upstream. Ezra slithered down the remains of the bank and threw himself as far forward as possible, flailing. For a moment he made progress then the water foamed over his head and he disappeared. The men pulled and he re-appeared swept into the side by the flow. They pulled him out, choking where Harriet slapped him on the back making him gag and bring up water.

"I'll try again," he said, struggling for the bank.

"Thank you," said Felix. "I never thought I should say that to 'ee, but thank you, thank you!"

"Can't let her drown," growled Ezra.

"Let me try!" said Bullen. He had been standing behind them, so far unnoticed, and was stripping down to his trousers. "I'm a good swimmer. Rope me up!"

"It's no job for a pastor!" said Lambert, looking him up and down. "Can you swim?"

"Damn it man, we don't just save souls!"

Bullen reached down and seized the rope, took it from around Ezra's shoulders and slipped into it himself.

"Get into your positions!" Bullen shouted.

The men moved back to their footholds, kicking in the mud with their heels, as they would for a tug-of-war, spitting on their hands. Ezra scrambled upright and added his weight to the rope. Edmonson joined them then Warburton, de Vries and Tyson. Bullen slipped and slithered down the bank as Ezra had done. Lambert shouted:-

"Give him slack!"

They moved forward until Lambert was satisfied and Bullen jumped, as Ezra had jumped, into the heaving green-brown water to disappear under the flow. At that moment, Clara's island disappeared. Lambert, distracted, never saw it go. Walter, who had his eyes on it, said it was like a duck diving – straight down, not a sound, with Clara atop of it, then nothing there but a couple of logs that tipped over so slowly and followed.

"Get him out!" bellowed Ezra and they hauled out Bullen and dumped him gasping to the side, shouting to Harriet and the others to look after him. "Follow the flow!"

They ran as best they could trying to keep up with the logs, along the wrecked banks and through new mud traps and pools but within seconds it was useless and the logs were swept out of sight. Warburton and the other horsemen set off at a gallop in the half-light for the mouth of the cut, their horses stumbling and splashing in and out of water, trying to avoid the indistinct line of the old river bank and the deep mud holes around it.

Sylham, on the other side, could not believe that Clara had gone. Recovering from his efforts, he had been shouting encouragement, yelling uselessly that help was coming, that she was to hold on. In that moment before she disappeared, he was certain that she stretched out her arms to him and smiled, and with that smile, vanished. He shouted and cursed impotently at the river, ran for some distance downstream, then turned to run back up with no idea of what he was doing, except that he must cross over to those on the other side. Stabbed with a pain he had never felt for anyone or anything, he groaned like a wounded man as he ran, until he was too exhausted to run any more and collapsed on a willow stump to let the tears run down his cheeks.

*

"This is hopeless!" shouted Latimer, puffing already. "I'm too old for this!"

"Just keep going!" Warburton shouted back rudely. "There's a chance she'll be washed up, on the bank or out to sea. Split up – we'll cover more ground."

Warburton intended to drop the less able. They went their separate ways, mostly on horse, sometimes dismounting to inspect dark shapes that turned out to be shadows. Dawn light extinguished the stars and made their task easier. A raw north wind welcomed them at the shore-line, flicking up the waves. Oxay River was tipping itself gleefully into the sea, complete with a cargo of debris. A carpet of cream foam blew about where fresh water met salt, obscuring everything. Noisy terns danced and screamed above it, picking out food.

"Miserable place," said Warburton. He and Edmonson urged their horses into the sea and trotted up and down, the animals kicking up the spume. Tyson, Latimer, de Vries and Richard Warburton arrived and they spread out, churning up and down. After half an hour they had found two dead oxen, logs, rope, barrels, canvas, tools – every form of wreckage – but no Clara.

"We will need a boat," said Edmonson. It was evident everyone was tiring and he was determined to continue. "I'll organise it."

"I think we should face facts," said Richard Warburton irritably. "She can't have survived."

"I agree," said Tyson, tired, bad-tempered and hungry.

"I'll organise a boat anyway," said Edmonson.

"Well I'm going back!" announced Richard, turning his horse.

"We'll go on," said Warburton.

De Vries' eye had been caught by a scoured trough of material to one side. "I want to look at the ground, Mr. Warburton."

"As you like." Warburton was ungracious, disinterested. "Catch us up." He nudged his horse forward.

De Vries jumped down to stand on firmly packed yellow gravel exposed below the peat. He jumped on it, then tried to dig his heel in it. Finding it unyielding, he gave a wry laugh and opened the saddle-bag of his horse. From this he took a trowel and scraped and dug at the hard-packed material, transferring into a small leather bag. Satisfied he had enough, he put the trowel and bag back in the saddle-bag and re-mounted his horse. He urged his horse on to re-join the others.

The troopers turned up, were ordered from their horses, and, townsmen through and through, tramped up and down uselessly in a row, falling over and shouting. By ten, Warburton, Edmonson and de Vries had combed the entire estuary. In the hard uncompromising light of a watery sun, they shaded their eyes with their hands from the glitter and tried to assess the damage. They found two wagons, half-buried, full of tools, part of the crane, more dead oxen (one poor beast had died in its tether). They found Sylham's haltered horses on the edge of a salt marsh, filthy, shivering, but otherwise unharmed. Edmonson collected them and tied them by a rope to his saddle.

*

Bullen had recovered sufficiently to set out on his own, thanks to the efforts of Harriet Dunn. He was still half wet, having been given a coat by the villagers, but no one had offered their trousers. In this condition, riding was uncomfortable and slow. After a few minutes he dismounted and led the horse behind him. He followed what had been the path of the new cut.

He was attracted by clumps of reed caught up in something and went to investigate, heart thumping in case it should be Clara. To his relief he found the reeds were snagged on roots – at least that was his first impression, until he noticed timber posts with the marks of working. He kicked the reeds away from one clump, then another and another and realised he was looking at several circles of timber, sticking from the mud. Just visible, between the posts beside him, he could see woven branches. Scuffing around with his feet, he found a piece of flint of a curious shape, and a piece of wood, partially buried. He was examining these when he heard horses approaching. He had just time to put these in the pocket of his coat before the horsemen rode up.

"Wondered where you might be, Bullen," said Warburton. "That was a brave thing you did. You might have got her."

Bullen, confused by praise, blushed, pointed to the posts. "I've found a curiosity here ...."

"What curiosity?" Warburton's eyes roved over the exposed posts.

"These posts ...." Bullen stumbled on. "They appear to be placed in circles and there's some sort of wall ...."

Warburton cut him off short. "Damn it man, don't you start! What we need here is some strong religion, not fancies and curiosities and damned women blacksmiths!" He turned his horse and rode off angrily. De Vries followed. Edmonson made a sympathetic face at Bullen before joining them.

*

De Vries urged his horse alongside Warburton. They were heading back now, and he was keen to provide good news. "Mr. Warburton, the ground .... I have something." He was fishing in his saddle-bag as he talked. "Let me show you ...." He stopped and Warburton, giving him a resigned look, stopped as well. De Vries held out his hand towards Warburton, who could not see what it contained. "Take this .... see .... it is what we have been looking for all the time, but it is much deeper than we could believe. It is good stuff." He waved his closed hand again. Warburton stretched out his in turn to feel de Vries let into it a handful of gravel bound with coarse sticky sand. He looked at it, looked at de Vries, saw the earnestness in the Dutchman's face and felt ashamed of the mistrust that had been his immediate reaction.

"Yes, it looks good stuff," he repeated tonelessly. "As you say."

Clutching it in one hand he turned his horse, the others following suit, making their way back towards the Yule Brook. They were intercepted by a calling figure who waved them down. It was Turner, covered in mud and in an obvious state of excitement.

"We found the circumferentor, Mr. Warburton! It was exposed in a drain when the water left!"

The surveyor Parker appeared, cradling the instrument to his chest like a baby. He had evidently been cleaning it for the brasswork was bright. Parker was grinning broadly. It jarred Warburton to cruelty. He let out a bitter laugh.

"We shan't need that again, Mr. Turner. Looks to be in one piece! I wonder if they'll take it back!"

Moving to the water's edge he threw in de Vries' handful of hoggin, watching it splash yellow in the muddy water, dusted his hands and took his reins. De Vries, understanding, caught his eye and said nothing.

Sylham had fought his way to a point up-river where he could cross. He made for the site of the dam, where he was greeted with warmth by the villagers, but he brushed them aside. "Have you seen Clara?"

"I'm afraid not," ventured John Lambert.

No one wanted to add the obvious in front of either him or Felix who, grey and subdued, sat in a heap on a box.

"But you must have!" Sylham shouted, pushing people aside to make for the river bank. They watched and waited as he trudged up and down like a madman. Watched and waited until he exhausted himself with the futility of it all and sat down by them on a log. Harriet Dunn took the opportunity to throw a horse-blanket round his shoulders, which he pulled tight. Silence fell as they waited for the horsemen to return, except for the troopers. They had lit a fire and by contrast, stood around it laughing and joking. Ecclesiastes nudged Ezra, rolled his eyes in their direction and wrote an obscenity in the mud with a stick. Ezra smiled bleakly and wiped it out with his foot. Walter Clarke shouted that he could see the horses.

As they drew nearer, Sylham got to his feet, abandoning the blanket, but Warburton, in front, was shaking his head as he approached.

"No John, nothing. Not a thing. Sorry, Hare." Felix nodded.

Edmonson dismounted and took the haltered horses to Sylham, more from compassion than any other reason, seeing the misery on the man's face and knowing Sylham from youth. "They were by the shore," he explained. "Calm enough. They've come to no harm!"

Sylham ran a hand over them, brushing at the mud on their flanks, stooping to feel their hocks and fetlocks. He was hiding his tearful eyes. "They're well enough," he managed to say.

Tyson, never tactful, came to the point that had been eating at him. "How did that woman get your horses? Didn't you hear?"

Sylham straightened up and eyed Tyson with distaste. "I didn't hear."

Edmonson rescued him from further criticism. "She'll have stolen them, Mr. Tyson. She always had a way with horses, they doted on her. A good thing for a blacksmith ...."

"A witch!" said Tyson. "*'Thou shalt not suffer a witch to live'*. Exodus."

"Exodus Twenty-two, eighteen. There is nothing more for us to do here gentlemen. I suggest we take ourselves home and prepare for the meeting. Mr. Edmonson, carry on the search to noon. Mr. de Vries, we need you at the meeting," said Warburton.

"I shall not be continuing with this enterprise," said Sylham. "I have finished with it."

"I think we may all be finished with it," said Warburton. "The Partners must meet."

Chapter 22

Sarah had been racked with uncertainty how to approach Richard. She must not accuse him, she knew – the best approach would be to ask him what had occurred. She lay at night rehearsing her words, only to find them disintegrating in the cold light of morning. Her uncertainty might have defeated her resolve except for the death of Clara, which was now all but find them disintegrating in the cold light of morning. Her uncertainty might have defeated her resolve except for the death of Clara, which was now all but certain. A promise had been made in exchange for Clara's silence. For that alone, she knew she had no option but to question her brother.

However, a second reason soon presented itself. Richard had withdrawn almost entirely from their company at the house and spent his time on horseback with no explanation or apology. Warburton senior was too occupied with salvaging what he could from the flood to care one way or the other about his son. In truth, he was tired of his exhibition of indolence and glad he was out of the way. This left the two women alone in the house for much of the daytime. The visit from Cristeen caught them in the kitchen with the cook, planning the supplies for Christmas. The three women retired to the drawing-room, Ruth in particular feeling ashamed of her clothes. Cristeen was in contrast dressed in her most formal, gloved and swishing with stiff silk. She had applied make-up inexpertly to her cheeks and wore a cape around her shoulders. The effect was severe.

"We are so pleased to see you, Mrs de Vries," declared Ruth. "We apologise for our condition."

"I apologise for calling without warning," said Cristeen. "These are not good manners, but I have chosen a time when Jacob is out. It is best."

Ruth exchanged a glance with Sarah. "Yes?"

"This is a very hard thing for me to say, Madam."

"Yes?"

Cristeen swallowed visibly, soldiered on. "It concerns Mr. Richard. He has been visiting Katja in the afternoons. Three times. And Katja is much distressed, *radeloos* we say, over the death of that young man Dade and these visits upset her so that she runs upstairs and hides and will not come down, and cries. I have told Mr. Richard that she does not want to see him and that he is not welcome, but he has told me to mind my own business, he has come to cheer her up. I'm sorry Mrs Warburton, but I am afraid that Jacob may come home, and then there would be trouble."

"Thank you, Mrs de Vries," said Ruth. "You are right to bring it to our attention. It must stop. Please sit down and join us in some refreshment."

But Cristeen would not be delayed. She had walked all the way over and would walk all the way back.

"I shall speak to him," said Ruth, watching her squat retreating figure, "when I get a chance."

And so shall I, thought Sarah.

The opportunity presented itself that evening. Richard blew in with a flurry of snow and cold from the December dark, flung his hat, crop and gloves onto a chair in the corner and stumped upstairs in snowy boots. Sarah had been waiting for him in her room since Cristeen left. Her heart thumped wildly and she decided to act before her courage collapsed. She ran silently along the corridor in stockinged feet and without knocking, turned the handle and rushed in. This gave her the advantage of startling Richard, who turned abruptly, saw who it was and tutted with irritation. Petulant, she thought. She had meant to approach things carefully, but annoyance at his reaction made her rashly outspoken.

"What happened on the night of the skating, Richard? You must tell me. You were seen arguing with Peter Dade. You may have been the last person to see him alive!"

"What is this all about?" Richard bought time, unbuttoning and taking off his coat. "You burst in here – I'm cold, I'm wet, I'm trying to change." He laid his coat on his bed, started to unbutton his waistcoat with infuriating composure. Sarah looked behind her and seeing the door was still open, closed it purposefully. Richard watched this action with an assumed smile. It gave her the impetus she needed.

"Smile if you wish, but I will still ask you, were you the last person to see Peter Dade alive?"

"Is this some sort of inquisition? Peter Dade's dead, who cares? I may have been, I don't know."

"You were seen."

"Who was I seen by?"

"I'm not at leave to say."

The half-truth had its effect. Richard gave her a cold stare that had little of the brother in it.

"You were seen and heard, arguing over the Dutch girl Katja, the Katja that you have been going to see, although she won't see you. What are we to make of all that?"

"Who is we?"

Sarah shrugged.

"Where is all this going?" he demanded. "You had better get out." He moved to the door, opened it and motioned to her and to the corridor. "Out."

"If you have done something wrong," Sarah persisted, seeing something in his eyes that might have been fear but was certainly some form of weakness, "you must tell us. How did Peter Dade drown? Was it something you did?"

Richard's reply was to take her by the shoulder and push her out of the door, slamming it. Sarah stood outside, shaking. He suddenly opened the door and thrust his face into hers, eyes to eyes.

"If you say anything like this in front of father, I shall quit this house, do you understand? Leave this place. I'm tired of Oxay anyway and this Dutch girl and this mud, and of you! Everything!" He closed the door in her face.

*

The Partners' Meeting was never going to be other than a sombre occasion. They met, as they had in the heady days of the beginning, in Warburton's timbered hall, sitting round the massive trestle table. The log fire had been lit, but did nothing to lift the gloom. It had been made with damp wood and hissed rather than crackled, despite much poking. Whereas they had been seven, they were now five, but Warburton had set out seven chairs as a reminder. Of Richard Warburton there was no sign. He had taken off on his horse in the morning, although he knew perfectly well what was going on.

Warburton wanted it all over as quickly as possible. Sitting at the head of the table, he tapped it with his ink pot. "Gentlemen, our business is straightforward and melancholy and I daresay we would all like to get it over with."

He held aloft a roll of parchment. "I have here the Articles of Agreement that we have all signed. I have engrossed these, as I believe we all agree, for the dissolution of the Partnership. I ask you each to sign in the place indicated, bringing this affair to an end. As discussed, I have taken the liberty of paying-off the workmen and I have dismissed the troopers."

"A good thing," growled Sylham. "No more money needed, I hope."

"No more money. There is a small residue in our funds which would have gone to the completion of the works. That will be divided among the Partners."

"What about de Vries?" asked Tyson.

"Mr. de Vries is fully aware of what we are about today, and has been paid to date. He takes ship shortly."

Warburton passed the papers to Latimer, who signed and passed them to Tyson.

"There's a space here for Richard Warburton," said Tyson. "He ain't here. What about him?"

"He has made his position clear and I shall sign for him," said Warburton. "He wants no further part in it."

"Never wanted it in the first place if you ask me," remarked Tyson sourly. "What about Emms?"

"Bathurst will contact Emms."

The papers passed from Tyson to Edmonson to Sylham. Sylham signed, and stood up. "That's an end of it," he said. "Now things can go back to what they were, and I think that a good thing too! Shan't have to raise my rents!"

A frosty silence greeted this. For Sylham it was nothing short of an oration. "I'll be on my way."

They watched him leave. No one moved. When he had gone there was obvious relief.

"There is no sign of Clara Hare," said Warburton, following a line of his thoughts. "I doubt there ever will be. Lost in the fen. One body in, one body out."

Chapter 23

Sarah moved the candle nearer and wrote 'CATASTROPHE' in capital letters at the top of a new page, then underlined the word. Beneath she wrote:-

"It is not too big a word to describe recent events. I feel at last that I can commit them to these pages. Before, I felt they were too large to be reduced to mere words.

Father's project is in ruins and human life has been lost. Hard on the heels of the drowning of the boy Peter Dade, we have had the loss of Clara Hare our blacksmith (who is said to be proficient in 'black arts'). She has been the perpetrator of the ruin, taking by stealth Mr. Sylham's horses in the night with which she tore down the new dam, destroying both it and herself. The Yule Brook, having been long stopped-up and very full, swept all away doing much damage. Her body has not been found and is believed buried in deep mud. Many hundred acres of land have been consigned to the sea or flooded. A meeting of the Partners was held last afternoon at which it was decided the project should be abandoned. There is great gloom affecting Mr. Tyson and Mr. Latimer, and father is grim and sighs a lot and will not come to the table. However, the abandonment of the project may have the effect of bringing to an end the unpleasant upheavals that have beset the neighbourhood.

Mr. de Vries has nothing more to do and can expect no further remuneration and he and his family return to Holland. I must say that the removal of Miss de Vries can only be for the best. There has been an ill effect upon Richard which I cannot bring myself to confide in these pages, but which may in time be easier to manage. I love him as a brother but cannot excuse him my suspicions. He has now announced his intention to seek betterment abroad, which is for the best, and is talking of the Colonies. Father has not opposed this and indeed seems in favour. Richard's humour has not been suited to our simple life.

I have this evening read the whole previous year of this diary from a time prior to this scheme of drainage and I cannot say that it seems to have brought much benefit to anyone.

Mama said this evening that Oxay can get on well without these foreigners and that without them, we may be permitted to settle down to a more ordered life.

Mr. Bullen, whom I feel was in danger of being treated unfairly, has proved himself by his actions to be a man of valour and we look to have a respected pastor. Mama has invited him to visit."

*

"Mr. de Vries! I wish I could welcome you on board in better circumstances!"

De Vries had just stepped down from the carriage and turned in surprise, recognising the voice. A bitter wind tugged at his hat.

"Captain Burgess! What are you doing here?"

He held his hat on with one hand and shook Burgess' hand with the other. Cristeen and Katja climbed down onto the wharf in a flurry of skirts and linen. Cristeen managed a small curtsy, her hair flying, while Katja managed a pale '*hallo*'.

"I have never been away," said Burgess. I've been bringing most of your timber from Sweden. A good job while it lasted. Mr. Warburton arranged for me to pick you up. Come on board, it's too blustery here. Thomas, can you get the boxes ...."

Warburton had sent his manservant with the cart and the two men began to off-load the luggage from the back of the coach onto the wharf. Burgess guided his passengers onto the boat.

"You know your way around," he said, "the cabin is the same. We'll be off as soon as your boxes are aboard .... catch the tide. It's a brisk day, we'll make good time."

"You haven't changed!" said de Vries.

Later, running before the wind in short choppy seas, de Vries joined Burgess on deck and they sheltered in the lee of the deckhouse like two old friends while Burgess pointed out the sand bars and shallows marked by white water. There was little to be seen of the shore through the spindrift.

"Not a good day to see the sights Mr. de Vries, but I guess you're glad to see the back of it. What a waste. There is no accounting for the backwardness of people. I suppose it is the isolation of the place and the lack of education. You said as much when you was going the other way. It stuck in my mind – you said it wasn't a Christian sort of life – reckon you were right. Engelse Dyckage!"

"It brings your work to an end, Captain."

"I did well enough out of it. To tell you the truth, I'll be happy to be on shorter runs. It's long and cold up to Sweden for timber. Gin and wool for me!"

Burgess was surprised that de Vries appeared to take things so calmly, and disappointed not to have provoked more of an explanation.

"You must feel, after all your work and engineering," he probed, "that everything you have done has gone to nothing."

De Vries looked into the haze with unseeing eyes, taking time to consider before replying. It would have surprised Burgess to know his main feeling at this moment was a lightening of the heart.

"I came to do many things Mr. Burgess," he replied, "and some of them have been well done."

"What will you do when you get home?"

"Go back to work of course, Mr. Burgess."

"They never found the body of the woman?" Burgess was fishing for his pipe, but remembered de Vries' attitude to tobacco and stopped.

"No, they never did. Some sort of witch who has rejoined her ancestors."

"Best be out on the sea, I say! The deep dark fens! I told you they were full of strange people."

"There were certainly some strange things. It is a place, I think, where the past is too near the present – where the two can easily be confused. Anyway, the ignorant will always stand in the way of progress. But I have my Bible Mr. Burgess – that is what is needed in that sort of place – I have it here!"

To his horror, de Vries dipped in his coat and produced a leather bound Bible, opening it and flipping through pages until he found a place. Burgess had no option but to stay where he was and listen, and so the two sat sheltering from the spray that rattled on the sails and deck while de Vries, voice raised to fight the wind, read to him of the Flood.

"'*Make thee an ark of gopher wood : rooms shalt thou make in the ark, and shalt pitch it within and without with pitch ....*'"

*

Katja was lying on one of the cabin beds, Cristeen on the other. Both women stared at the timbers of the ceiling listening to the slap and chatter of waves on the hull.

"Are you looking forward to being home?" asked Cristeen for something to say. The girl had been silent since they had boarded.

"No."

"But it will be good to be back in our own house, won't it? To be back in a town with pavements and have dry feet. I got to like Elm Farm but I prefer a town house. A brick house is easier to keep clean." She paused, Katja still said nothing. "It will be Spring soon. We shall have to think of new things for us to do for the new year .... I shall make new clothes for you ...." Again there was no response. With some irritation in her voice, Cristeen tried again. "You know, Katja you will look back on this trip and you will think of all the interesting things you saw and did in England. You will get over the other things – I know how hurt you are now, but you will get over them for your own sake and you must get over them for your father's sake. You have your whole life ahead of you. You will see, believe me."

Katja sat up.

"Mama I think I'm a little sick – do you mind if I go on deck? I can't stand it down here."

Cristeen looked at Katja. The girl was white faced.

"I'll come with you."

"No, I want to go on my own."

"It'll be cold!"

"I have my shawl. I want to go on my own! It will do me good."

Cristeen sat up to inspect the girl, reached out and straightened her hair, a gesture of tenderness she had not exchanged with her daughter for a year.

"You do look pale. Take care."

Katja rose, wrapped herself up and climbed the short stair to let herself out on deck. She shut the door firmly behind her and looked about. She could see her father and Burgess to the rear by the deckhouse but they appeared not to notice so she moved forward and sat on a hatch beside the mast. Fishing in her clothing she pulled out a draw-string purse and took from it Peter's golden disc like an animal but not an animal. With this in her hand she stood up and leant back against the mast as Peter had shown her, pressing her back into it until she could feel the living movement of the ship trembling against her. She tilted her head back, looked up where mast and cloud merged and clasped her hands behind her around the smooth wood concentrating until it reeled over her, falling like a tree, but not falling. She lurched away from it, heart thumping. Peter was there and would be, in every church tower and sky and '*stadhuis*' in Holland. She felt a hand on her shoulder.

"Are you all right?" her father was asking anxiously. "Are you seasick?"

"I'm all right papa. I only stumbled."

De Vries gave her a searching look, in which she saw he knew more than he was saying.

"Don't say," she begged.

"You had better keep to the cabin. We will be home in a couple of days and things will be back to normal."

*

William Emms lit a second candle and stood it on one of the piles of books that were perched on the edge of his desk. The room was small, the desk was small and when he pushed back his chair it hit his bed, but it was the only lodging he could afford. Emms had received a letter and written a letter. The former, from Bullen, was totally unexpected and he had pinned it flat on his table using two bronze palstaffs and the sole of a Roman boot. Bullen had written:-

"Dear Emms,

We have not met but I am sensible of the circumstances of your going. I do not know if this is a proper act or if I could be censured for it, but I could not let this particular matter pass without communicating with you.

We have had a cataclysmic flood which has devastated the works of drainage being undertaken. The agency of this destruction was the woman Clara Hare, who by some accounts was a witch, although it is not thought proper in these days of enlightenment to use such a term. With horses appropriated from Mr. Sylham she tore down the great dam that had been constructed across the river, releasing much water. The flood so caused inundated both farm land and fen. In the act, the woman became a victim and every able soul was obliged to search for her, although she has not been found.

In this search I by chance encountered an unusual sight. There were exposed by the scouring action of the water, some five or six circles of wooden posts, clearly placed in such regular positions by the agency of man, for the posts had been wrot. They were at a depth below ground level which indicates they were of some antiquity. Investigating these in some haste – for we were still searching for the woman – I found the enclosed which I send to you, for I have been instructed (I wish I could say kindly) in your interest by Mr. Warburton. It is a curious piece of work which I apprehend to be flint, and with it was trapped in the mud 'in loco' a piece of wood through which it appeared to be inserted. You may imagine my interest as it is not within my knowledge that the inhabitants of these parts were accustomed to use such tools, however backward. There might have been more to tell after further investigation, but Mr. Warburton ordered the posts to be pulled out or sawn off and burned, and had men cover the entire area with earth. I did not like to protest too much as he is my patron. However, I determined that this curious object should be yours and I have made a note of the location in which it was found. My interest has been sufficiently engaged that I will remain alert to any further opportunities that present themselves for scientific study, science being the balm to be applied to superstition. If I may be so bold, dear sir, I will keep you appraised.

I am your obedient servant.

Wm. Bullen. Reverend. Oxay"

*

Emms had assembled the fragments of wooden shaft sent to him by Bullen, and had cut a replica from a piece hacked from a hedgerow. He inserted the flint in it and began to tie it in place with a piece of cord, round and round then cross-lacing it, pulling it tight. He cut off the loose ends and made several strikes at the air. Satisfied, he laid it on his table and pulled out the letter he had written to re-read it, muttering the words to himself.

"To Sir Robery Southwell, President. The Royal Society of London for Improving Natural Knowledge. Arundel House, London.

Most Honourable Sir,

I hope you will forgive my temerity in writing to you, when I know by common account you have so many matters to take up your time. I am late of a chaplaincy in Norfolk where my studies have led me to produce a pamphlet which I have entitled 'A Treatise on the Artefacts of the Fens with an Examination of their Age and Provenance'. The title itself, I hope, makes the contents clear and in it I advance a new light upon the Calendar of Antiquity through excavation and the logical examination of both the placing of objects and the sophistication of their manufacture. I have concluded that a greater age must be given to many artefacts than is consistent with dating them by the method adopted by those who hold the dating of the Bible to be a Fixed Point. I have been obstructed in my work as you may imagine for there are always those whose ignorance leads them to stand in the way of progress. I offer my Treatise for the examination of your Members and would be honoured to present it in London if you should wish."

He powdered his letter with a flourish and realised he was content.

*

Yule Brook chuckled and bubbled as it made for the sea over beds of gravel as old as an ice age. It wandered, almost thoughtfully, over fields it had not visited this thousand years, testing the going for soft spots.

Under the church tower the Boy, like a squashed frog under all that weight, dribbled clear water, its mouth re-connected to an ancient spring. Clara's twigs prospered, putting out fragile roots.

"Wherefore let us intreat our ancient Water-Nurses

To shew their Power so great as t'help to drain their purses

And send good old Captain Flood to lead us out to Battle,

Then Two-penny Jack, with Scales on his Back, will drive out all the cattle

This Noble Captain yet was never known to fail us;

But did the conquest get of all that did assail us;

His furious Rage none could assuage; but to the Worlds great Wonder

He tears down Banks and breaks their Cranks and Whirligigs assunder."*

From *The Powte's Complaint*

* Whirligigs, i.e. wind pumps

Other fiction titles from Arena Books –

The Girl From East Berlin

a docu-drama of the East-West divide

by James Furnell

Few novels appear on such a grand scale as this. What begins as an inauspicious chance meeting in an East Berlin art shop leads to an adventure exploring the many social and psychological aspects characterising the division of a great European capital. It is an encyclopaedia of the soul of a city; unlikely again to be described so comprehensively or in such depth.

ISBN 978-0-9543161-7-4 **£18.99 / US$ 32.99**

Two Days in July

a docu-drama of Claus von Stauffenberg's attempt to kill Hitler

by Stig Dalager

This gripping book, by one of Denmark's leading writers, presents the story of Claus von Stauffenberg's assassination and coup attempt against Hitler on 20th July 1944 with perhaps greater clarity and psychological insight than any straight factual account could succeed in conveying.

ISBN 978-1-906791-12-4 **£14.99 / US$ 23.99**

The Ubiquitous Man

travel beyond the brink

by Christopher Orland

A mesmerising high-tech thriller speculating on the field of commercial teleportation. The year is 2104 and the teleportation of people from one continent to another has become an expensive and controversial reality. Hotshot salesman Guy Rennix of UK firm *Tempus Biotronics* is offered a business trip from London to New York, travelling via the ultimate mode of transport with unexpected consequences.

ISBN 978-1-906791-15-5 **£14.99 / US$ 23.99**

Printed in the United Kingdom
by Lightning Source UK Ltd.
133445UK00001BC/166-210/P